HER WICKED SCOT

THE HIGHLAND WARRIOR CHRONICLES
BOOK FOUR

CHRISTINA PHILLIPS

PHOENIX 18 PUBLISHING

Edited by Amanda Ashby
Cover Art by Kim Killion Publishing
05/26

ISBN: 978-0-6451584-8-9

This book is dedicated to Cathleen Ross, who recently discovered she is a descendant of Kenneth MacAlpin, and is still my friend! The ancient gods and goddesses work in the most mysterious of ways, that's for sure!

CHAPTER 1

THE KINGDOM OF FOTLA, PICTLAND.
WINTER 843

*T*he northern wind was bitter, and snow blinded the path ahead as Ewan MacKinnon and his eleven compatriots approached the Pictish royal stronghold of Fotlaeviot. It had been scarcely two weeks since they had left the kingdom to return to their king at Dunadd in Dal Riada, and as the ancient stone walls of the stronghold came into view through the blizzard, an unnatural vise gripped his chest.

He hadn't expected to be ordered to return to the kingdom. He'd wanted a respite from duty, to spend time in his own stronghold after nine months imposing his king's will in Pictland. But MacAlpin was determined to stake his claim in Pictland, which meant none of his warriors were free to decide their own fates.

Ross Macintosh, fellow warrior, and longtime friend, appeared by his side. "What ails you, man? It's not like you to trail behind. Aren't you looking forward to the undoubted hospitality we'll receive from the royal house of Fotla?"

There was a grim note in Ross' voice, despite his attempt at humor. Doubtless he, also, was tired of the interminable diplomatic missions they had undertaken this past year. But a warrior never disobeyed his king.

Even if his king could not be trusted.

He crushed the treacherous thought before it consumed him. There was no evidence to support his dark suspicions against his liege, MacAlpin, and he would never voice them. Not even to Ross, whom he trusted with his life.

"I doubt the Fotla king will welcome us. Our presence merely underscores how little confidence MacAlpin places in the Picts ability to ensure justice is served."

The last time they'd been in Fotla, an attempt had been made on the life of MacAlpin's eldest son. Although Constantine lived, with no apparent ill-effects from the arrow, the would-be assassin was still free.

Both MacAlpin and MacAllister were convinced the assassin was a spy from Northumbria. After many years of relative peace, the southern barbarians were once again eyeing their borders with Dal Riada and Pictland. In the spring, they had attempted an incursion which had been swiftly repelled.

Ewan wasn't alone in thinking it was an exercise to test the strength of the new alliance between Scot and Pict. He could well believe the Northumbrians wanted to destabilize that alliance.

What he didn't want to believe was that the Picts were in league with them. Yet his king suspected treachery. Their mission was to uncover the truth. And exact justice.

Ross drew closer and nodded towards MacAllister, who was leading the group, his back rigid despite the long hours in the saddle. "MacAllister's presence concerns me. I can't help but suspect there is another reason we've been ordered back to Fotla. Why else would MacAlpin have his most trusted adviser accompany us?"

Aye, that detail bothered him, too. MacAllister was the king's man to the very marrow of his bones and experience this last year had shown Ewan that MacAllister's true intentions were rarely transparent.

Ewan slowed his horse as a dozen Pict warriors emerged from the swirling white, clearly intending to accompany them to the stronghold.

There was but one answer. "I'm certain that we shall soon find out."

~

IT SEEMED they were not expected to make camp and endure the frigid elements. Instead, after a brief and distinctly chilly reception from the Fotla king's advisers, they were shown to two bedchambers in the east wing. Even sharing with five other warriors, it was immeasurably preferable to a tent in this foul weather.

Stuart MacGregor grinned as he slung his pack to the floor. "We have been allocated the chamber of delights."

"Chamber of delights?" Ewan didn't bother trying to hide the mockery in his voice. "There'll be no illicit affairs undertaken with noblewomen in here, MacGregor."

MacGregor shrugged good-naturedly. "Maybe not. But I was referring to our last stay in Fotla. Two beautiful Pictish ladies entertained me in this very chamber. It was an open secret that this was their preferred rendezvous. You can't tell us you knew nothing about it."

A couple of the other warriors laughed, and the talk turned bawdy. Ewan swung away and paced the floor to peer through the narrow window. The truth was, he had arranged no illicit assignation with a lady while in Fotla. Not that any of the men would believe him, even if he admitted to such a thing.

Which he never would.

Rourke MacConall came to his side, folded his arms, and

glowered across the chamber. The familiar sight of Rourke's unamused expression lightened Ewan's mood and he laughed.

"The time at sea has not improved your humor," he said, and Rourke slung him a sardonic glance.

"My time away hasn't improved MacGregor's love for gossip, either."

Ewan agreed, but he had no wish to discuss MacGregor's faults. "Our king keeps you busy. You deserve a respite after a year from Dal Riada." God's blood, what was wrong with him? He had to learn to curb his tongue, but his unremitting distrust of MacAlpin was corroding his good sense.

Rourke cast another glance around the chamber before focusing on Ewan. "MacAlpin was adamant I accompany you to Fotla. I'm sure my father would have preferred me to stay behind."

Ewan grunted in response. There wasn't much else he could say. Rourke's sire was MacAllister, and they had never seen eye to eye. MacAllister had never looked kindly on Rourke's wild rebelliousness in his youth, as though it might reflect badly on his status with the king.

Although Ewan's own father had once been a part of the king's inner circle, unlike Rourke, he'd never had to endure the icy wrath of his sire for his misdeeds. Yet their fathers' close friendship wasn't the reason Ewan considered Rourke one of his closest confidants.

It was because their mothers had been dear friends and he and Rourke had grown up together. Even after his mother died, Rourke's had always welcomed him.

Familiar guilt ate through him, burning like acid. It didn't appear to matter how many years passed. Her death, and the reason for it, would haunt him until the end of time.

With brutal resolve borne of long practice, he thrust the memories back into the darkest corners of his mind. There, they would fester forever, but dwelling on things that couldn't be changed did no good at all.

He inhaled a deep breath. The chamber was too crowded. He'd spent long hours in the saddle, and even though the weather was frigid, he needed to clear his head. Stretch his legs.

He grasped Rourke's shoulder in farewell, before marching from the chamber.

~

BRIANA, Princess Euphemia of Fotla, was chilled to the bone and caked in snow. Her mamma would be furious. She glanced at her ladies, as they emerged from the stables, but despite their wind-reddened cheeks and similar state of disarray as herself, their eyes sparkled, and smiles were brighter than they had been for many days.

Her mamma's anger would be worth the last hour's freedom of riding in the nearby glen. It had been glorious until the weather had suddenly turned, catching her unawares, and they had made a swift return to the palace through a raging blizzard.

It was a little disconcerting. Usually, she was so attuned to the changes in the weather but this time there had been no ethereal warning from the great goddess to beware. She didn't want to think it but could not help herself. Had her beloved goddess Bride truly deserted her?

"My lady," her dear friend, Nairne, said. "Should we have servants bring a canopy to protect you as we return to the palace?"

It was only a short walk to the palace. But Briana knew what Lady Nairne really meant. "I fear the queen will not be appeased by such a concession." She sighed. It did not matter how much they had all enjoyed their carefree ride. It had been remiss of her to subject her ladies to the frigid winter elements. "Please forgive me for insisting we should take advantage of the break in the weather. I should have known it wouldn't last."

"Oh goddess." Lady Gavina said. "We have been confined within the palace walls for so long, my lady. It was delightful to feel the cold wind on my face once again. And we were in no danger, with our warriors to protect us."

Briana glanced at the two men who had accompanied them, who were standing in the snow a stone's throw away and speaking to a third warrior, who had emerged from the other stables across the way. Unaccountably, unease slithered through her, even though she had known each man for years and trusted them with her life.

One of them swung away and marched over to her, where she and her ladies remained in the doorway of the stables.

"Is anything amiss?" she asked him.

"My lady." He gave a swift bow of his head, a glower etched into his face. "The Scots have arrived."

She sucked in a sharp breath as her ladies exclaimed with excitement. That explained her disquiet, although their arrival wasn't unexpected. Mere days ago, a messenger from MacAlpin had arrived at the palace and informed them a contingent of warriors from Dal Riada was on the way.

The slight could not be plainer. The Scots didn't trust the Picts to ensure justice was served in the matter concerning Constantine, MacAlpin's son.

"I see. Are they in the great hall?"

She hoped not. Neither she nor her ladies would wish the Scots to witness their disheveled state. It did not quite make sense, but she felt it put them at a disadvantage.

"They were taken to the two chambers in the east wing, my lady."

"Very well." She glanced at her ladies. "Doubtless the queen will summon us shortly. We must make haste and make ourselves presentable." With luck, her mamma would be so preoccupied with the Scots arrival that she'd overlook Briana's transgression of riding in inclement weather.

They stepped out from the shelter of the stables and hurried across the snowy courtyard as her ladies tried to guess who might have returned to Fotla.

"Do you think it likely the same warriors who came here last month will be among them?" Nairne said.

"It would make sense," Gavina replied. "Since they are already familiar with the area where Constantine was attacked."

"I'm certain that even if their upstart king has sent new warriors, they will be as pleasing as their compatriots were," Lady Eara said.

"Indeed, it appears the Scots are incapable of being anything less than captivating, when they wish to bedazzle us," Nairne remarked.

Briana didn't join in the banter although she couldn't help but agree with her friends' opinions on the Scots. But no matter how engaging the foreign warriors were, it didn't blind any of them to the truth.

In the spring, under the guise of forming an alliance against the ever-present threat of the Northumbrians in the south and the Vikings in the north, the Scots had despicably betrayed the Picts. A bloodied massacre in the Scots' royal stronghold of Dunadd had eradicated Pictish lines of inheritance for Fortriu, the Supreme Kingdom of Pictland, and enabled MacAlpin to claim blood rights to the throne.

Scots might be charming, and political necessity decreed Picts had no choice but to make the most of the current situation, but none of the Scots could be trusted with more than a meaningless flirtation.

One of the guards threw open the doors to the palace and she stepped over the threshold, distractedly flapping her cloak to dislodge the stubborn shards of ice that clung to the wool.

Beneath her hood, her wet hair stuck to her face, her gown was damp, and her fingers were numb. The sooner she—

"My lady." The masculine voice, with its bone-melting Gaelic accent, stopped her dead in her tracks and her heart slammed against her ribs in frantic denial. No. It couldn't be. Of all the Scots' warriors who might have witnessed her bedraggled state, why did it have to be Ewan MacKinnon?

Since sinking through the sodden, straw-covered floor was not an option, she stiffened her spine and slowly raised her head. He stood not a spear's length from her, looking utterly resplendent in his foreign plaid and thick deerskin jacket, and his piercing blue eyes stole whatever remained of her spinning senses.

Goddess, help her. From the moment he had first arrived in Fotla over a month ago, her wits had fled whenever she was in his company. It was infuriating, quite disgraceful, and if she didn't speak soon her ladies might suspect something was amiss.

And so would MacKinnon.

She inclined her head but feared her windswept condition made a mockery of the regal gesture. "You have returned to us, MacKinnon."

It was a dreadful greeting, in so many ways she didn't even want to think about it. She was well versed in the rules of etiquette and political interplay. Why had her usual proficiency in such arts deserted her now?

Because they always do when confronted by this foreign warrior.

"Aye," MacKinnon said. "We appreciate your king's hospitality, my lady."

It had been a great debate between her parents. Her mamma had wanted the Scots to make camp beyond the safety of the ramparts. Briana couldn't help wishing her mother had won that argument, since then this excruciating encounter would not be taking place.

She offered him a brittle smile. "My king is gracious, indeed."

Unforgivably, his gaze roved over her, as if he had just noticed her sorry state and heat seared her. This conversation was most unseemly, and no one would fault her if she simply bade him good day and continued on her way.

Except it appeared her feet had frozen to the floor.

"Were you caught in the blizzard?" He sounded doubtful as though ladies of his acquaintance would never do such a fool-hardy thing. And although she had regrets about exposing her ladies to the rough storm, it was not MacKinnon's place to condemn her.

"Horses need exercising, whatever the weather." Which was true enough, but the royal horses were ensured of adequate exercise, whether she personally rode her mare or not. Irked that MacKinnon clearly believed she was in the wrong, she added, "It would be bleak indeed if we were confined to the palace for almost half a year simply to avoid the possibility of being caught in a snowstorm."

What was she *saying*? She might not agree with her mother in some matters, but she would never voice those frustrations with anyone other than, perhaps, her trusted ladies. Yet here she was, sharing one of her secret vexations of living once more under her mamma's authority to Ewan MacKinnon, of all people.

Why did he gaze at her as if he found her remark a source of fascination? It was most disconcerting.

"That's true," he conceded, and he gave a fleeting smile that caused her stomach to churn in nervous disarray. He had never smiled at her the last time he'd been in Fotla. But then, they had barely spoken. In fact, this was the longest conversation they had ever shared. Although good manners required she smile in return, it was beyond her, and he stiffened before taking a half step back. "Forgive me. I shall detain you no longer, my lady."

And now he was dismissing her. How galling. It was not his place to end this encounter but as she appeared incapable of diplomacy when in his presence, she could scarcely blame him.

She remained ramrod straight while he bade her ladies good day and only when the great doors thudded shut behind her, did she exhale a long breath.

How dearly she had hoped MacKinnon would not be in the Scots' contingent when they returned to Fotla. But he was, and there was nothing she could do about it.

"Do you think the Scots will be invited to the feast this eve?" Lady Gavina asked Lady Nairne, as they made their way across the great hall. The last time the Scots had been in Fotla they had attended feasts and flirted outrageously with all the ladies. The queen had given her tacit approval for illicit assignations. Far better to keep one's enemy close, and discover their secrets, than not.

"It would be most agreeable if they are." Nairne threw back her hood and sighed dramatically. "If only Prince Constantine were among them, but I fear he will never return to Fotla."

Briana forcibly pulled her tangled thoughts from MacKinnon. If she didn't join in the conversation, her ladies would think something was wrong. "One can scarcely blame him," she said as they reached the stairs. "Besides, don't forget why the Scots are here, Nairne. And it's not to enjoy our company."

"Indeed, my lady. But they enliven the evenings, do they not? Surely, there will be time for entertainment when they are not hunting the elusive assassin."

"I do hope so." There was a dreamy note in Gavina's voice as they emerged from the stairwell and walked along the corridor. "I long to dance with the incomparable Ewan MacKinnon."

Briana entered her antechamber. *Don't react.* She could not bear it if any of her ladies guessed how even the mention of his name could discompose her so.

"Oh." Nairne flapped her hand in Gavina's direction. "You should take care, Gavina. Remember, it was Ewan MacKinnon who quite broke my dear sister Lilas' heart in the spring. She was inconsolable."

"That was Ewan?" Disappointment threaded through the question. "I did not realize. I had forgotten the name of the warrior."

"Indeed," Nairne said. "I believe he bedded half the ladies at Ce-eviot without a care for poor Lilas' feelings."

"Didn't Lady Lilas say she overheard Ross MacIntosh telling MacKinnon he should forget about a lady from his past?" Eara tapped her chin with her forefinger. "What was her name? No one from Ce-eviot that I can recall."

"Moreen." Gavina gave a great sigh. "MacIntosh called her a witch. Doubtless, she is a mysterious lady from his past who quite stole his heart away."

During the summer, Nairne had received a letter from her sister, who was one of the Queen of Ce's ladies. Unfortunately, she had fallen utterly for a visiting Scots warrior who did not return her affection.

Nairne had been devastated on her sister's behalf, and distressed that, due to the upheavals in Pictland, she could not visit Lilas to offer her support.

Briana had sympathized. But when she'd discovered the foreign warrior, whose piercing blue gaze had stolen her breath and rendered her a witless mute, was the same one who had so callously used Lilas, shame had burned through her.

To be sure, she had never intended anything more than a fleeting flirtation with the visiting Scot, in the same way she flirted with his countrymen. He was the enemy of her people and could never be trusted. But that was irrelevant because, somehow, Ewan had managed to truly intrigue her. Regardless of his heritage, how could she find such a man so enchanting? Had she learned nothing from her short-lived, disastrous, marriage?

Ruthlessly, she pushed the slithering memories back into the darkest corners of her mind. She had succumbed once to base lust and the hollow charms of a handsome warrior. But she was no longer a young girl with stars in her eyes that blinded her to reality.

The Scots were here for one reason only. They were not, after all, welcomed guests. Merely an unpleasant reminder of how their upstart king wished to exert his power across Pictland.

And as for MacKinnon, she would protect herself in the only way she knew how.

By keeping him at a frost-tinged distance.

CHAPTER 2

Thankfully, Briana and her ladies had time to dry their hair and change their gowns before she was summoned to the king's inner sanctum. Her ladies accompanied her, and she wrapped her shawl around her shoulders to protect from the chill of the passageway. As they passed through the great hall, Rohan, the faithful noble who had proved his loyalty to her during her marriage, bowed his head.

"The savages are ensconced in the east wing, my lady," he murmured, as she paused before him. "Our king is too generous."

It wasn't often he told her something she already knew, but she kept that to herself. When it came to her escaping the palace during the winter, Rohan appeared to be in the same mind as the queen, and she had no wish to enlighten him of her illicit ride in the snow if he was unaware.

"I imagine MacAlpin would be displeased if his warriors froze to death in our fields."

Rohan's lips twitched with amusement. "Yet we can scarcely be blamed for the winter weather."

"I'm sure their king would try to, nevertheless."

"I suspect you're right." He smiled at her ladies, before

returning his attention to her. "I shall not keep you. Rest assured, I shall endeavor to discover all I can of the savages' plans."

She inclined her head and continued through the hall towards her father's chambers, but Rohan's words lingered in her mind. What did he mean? The Scots were here to ensure the Picts were doing all they could to find Constantine's attacker. What whispers had Rohan heard?

And why hadn't her beloved goddess blessed her with any insight? It had been weeks since she had felt Bride's divine touch.

Intangible unease coiled around her heart, a phantom fist that made it hard to draw breath. An insidious denial flickered, vague yet implacable.

Has it truly been weeks? Or was there something lurking in the shadowy fissures of her mind that she simply could not quite recall?

Gavina sighed deeply, pulling her sharply back to the present. "My lord Rohan is so dashing, yet he never indulges in more than fleeting flirtation."

"Alas," Nairne said, "I have heard he prefers the company of tavern wenches."

While her ladies whispered of Rohan's delightful attributes, Briana hid a smile. To be sure, he was handsome, but more than that he had stood by her side in the scandalous aftermath of her marriage, despite his blood connection to her husband. And then he had forsaken his familial ties and transferred his fealty to her, to ensure her continued safety.

Her smile faded and she smothered a sigh as Drest, a high-ranking warrior and close confidant of her brother, Artair, opened the door to her father's antechamber. Her ladies remained there, with her mother's entourage, and she entered the inner sanctum alone.

"Briana." Her father strode across the chamber and took her into his arms. She breathed in deep, and his familiar scent of woodsmoke soothed her soul. How she had missed him, when

MacAlpin had held him hostage in Dal Riada after the massacre in the spring. Deep in her heart she had feared she might never see him again, but she wouldn't be grateful to the upstart king. He had only released her beloved father and Artair last month, so he could discover the whereabouts of her dearest cousin, Mae.

After a long moment, her father released her. "You are aware the Scots have arrived."

"Another insult to our honor." Her mother came to stand beside the king. "We are more than capable of investigating this matter ourselves."

"The trail was cold before the Scots left Fotla earlier this month. But the upstart will be satisfied with nothing less than a blood sacrifice to avenge the attack on his son."

A dark suspicion unfurled, and she attempted to smother it. Surely, she had misunderstood her father's words. "You believe they will find a culprit, regardless of his guilt?"

But that wasn't what she meant, although she could certainly believe the Scots capable of it. Her real worry was that her father might sanction such an act, to appease the foreign king and ensure the Scots left Fotla as soon as possible.

And much as she wanted that same outcome, she didn't want it at the expense of such deception. If there were assassins loose in Fotla, they needed to hunt them down. Who knew which side they might be on?

"I would put nothing past MacAlpin. Yet I cannot deny, had you or one of your brothers or sisters been attacked in such a manner, I would not rest until the offender had been found."

She squeezed his hand, glad they were alone, save for her mother. There had always been a special bond between them, but such intimacy would be unthinkable had the royal advisers been present.

"The scheming MacAllister accompanies them." Disdain dripped from her mother's voice. "We must be vigilant. He sees too much."

It was MacAllister who had uncovered Mae's disguise a month ago. But if her own mamma had not betrayed their trust, the Scot would never have been able to prove his suspicion.

The injustice burned deep, and she could not help responding. "Then we must be sure not to disclose anything to him."

Her mother gave a tight smile, that didn't reach her eyes, but said nothing. There was nothing to say that could redeem her actions.

Oblivious, her father kissed her hand. "I must ask you, Briana. As a chosen one of our forebears' goddess, has Bride come to you lately? I confess, these last nine months, I fear the ancient ones have forsaken us."

Dread gripped her, a suffocating terror that crushed her chest and threatened to close her throat. Bride had not returned since the night of the sacred Blood Moon, when she had whispered in her ear to find Mae and bring her back to Fotla-eviot.

She'd tried not to worry about it. Tried to smother the threads of trepidation that wound through her heart but now the unvarnished possibility would not be thrust aside.

Was Bride's absence because Briana had misunderstood her beloved goddess' message? Was this Bride's punishment, banishment from her presence, for allowing Mae to be captured by their ruthless enemies?

She couldn't share her fears with him, without implicating her mother. And while it was conceivable the king had known of the plan to sacrifice Mae to placate the Scots' king, it was equally possible he was not aware of the details.

It was one thing for her to silently rage against her mother. But the royal house of Fotla could not afford any cracks to show in its facade. The kingdoms of Pictland had been splintered enough, since MacAlpin had claimed the Supreme Kingdom of Fortriu for his own, and it was imperative that, to the outside world at least, Fotla remained united.

For the stark truth was, they needed this alliance to survive.

Needed the strength in numbers the Scots could provide if either the Vikings or Northumbrians decided on a full-scale invasion.

She knew this. They all did. It was why they had to protect this alliance, despite its dreadful cost, so they could defend their land and people against even worse enemies.

She drew in a steadying breath. It would do no good for her father to guess the depth of her distress. After all, there was nothing he could do about it. He was not a chosen one of Bride.

"The goddess has not blessed me with a vision. But I am certain when the time is right, she will show the way."

Once again, a ripple of unease slithered along her spine, as though she was missing something of great import that shimmered just beyond her grasp.

But what?

The king sighed heavily. "I understand, daughter. But I had to ask."

He turned to the queen, and she inclined her head before she spoke. "Much as it irks, we have decided to welcome the savages and invite them to a feast this eve. The sole purpose of this is to encourage their warriors to spill secrets they would keep close during the light of day."

"Very well." Her voice was calm, for which she was grateful. She certainly didn't wish her parents to guess how the thought of seeing MacKinnon at the feast discomposed her so.

"Let it be known to your ladies their devotion to the continued security of Pictland is greatly appreciated."

"Briana." The king's voice was grim. "We do not wish you to imperil your integrity. But your status is such that it might persuade an unwary confidence."

Goddess. She hadn't expected this. Last time, her mamma had expressly forbidden her from indulging in such political intrigues. Not that she'd had any intention of doing so, but her mother hadn't known that.

"You wish me to seduce a high ranking Scot?" She could

scarcely believe her father was asking such a thing of her, but she needed to be sure. Yet even if he was, this was not something she could do.

Even for the sake of Pictland.

Unbidden, Ewan MacKinnon's face swam through her mind and treacherous heat bloomed. His dark fascination was a poisoned thorn and although, despite how she tried to deny it, he was the only man she could imagine in her bed, it was that very reason why he was the last man she could ever welcome into her arms.

"What? No." The king sounded shocked. As though such strategies had never been undertaken before. "We are speaking of flirtation, Briana. Flattering the enemy into a state of complacency where they might become incautious in their boasting. The wine will run freely and doubtless too, so will their tongues."

Hastily, she pushed the shameless images from her mind. Such liberties would never happen. Certainly, not with MacKinnon.

"I understand." Thankfully, her turmoil did not show in her voice. "Although I believe the only one who might possess such information is MacAllister himself, and I doubt anything will induce him to give up his king's secrets."

"I fear you could be right," the king said. "But it appears his son, MacConall, is among the men this time. If anyone knows something, it is likely to be him. The bond of blood is strong."

"As a gesture of goodwill, we propose to allow the Scots to sit with our nobles." The queen drew in a sharp breath, clearly displeased by the notion. "However, if you do not wish to debase yourself in such a manner, you will sit with us, as usual."

"I know my duty." Her voice was cool. "I shall stomach the Scots presence and attempt to discover all I can."

~

PHANTOM BUTTERFLIES COLLIDED within her breast as Briana and her ladies made their way to the great hall. Ewan MacKinnon had returned, but she was not required to converse with him. Which was just as well, since she had already proved that her ability to engage him in conversation was as abysmal now as it had been last month.

It was too infuriating that she could not stop thinking of him. She had made a vow, long before the death of her husband more than a year ago, to never allow another man to addle her good sense. Once was more than enough.

Yet it didn't matter how many harsh talks she gave herself. From the first moment she had caught sight of MacKinnon the cursed man had dazzled her, as though she were a naïve four-teen-year-old maid instead of a widow who knew all too well how meaningless such shallow passion was.

As she had told her mother, her duty was clear. MacConall was the one she needed to charm and while she doubted any man who shared MacAllister's blood was susceptible to such strate-gies, she could but try. She just hoped MacKinnon was not seated anywhere near her.

The table she had been allocated loomed before her. The Scots were already standing at designated intervals before the benches, waiting for the arrival of the royal family and nobles. At the head of the table was her chair, a silent proclamation of her status that her mamma had insisted upon.

And standing to the right of the chair, facing her as she approached, stood Ewan MacKinnon.

Panic thudded through her breast. Goddess, no. It was bad enough he had returned to Fotla. But what cruel twist of fate had placed him right beside her for this eve?

Her ladies whispered behind her and with a start she realized she had halted. It seemed every eye in the hall was upon her, judging her, even though, surely, she had only faltered for merely an instant.

Refusing to glance around the hall to confirm her certainty, she tilted her head and proceeded to stand before the chair. The noblewomen of the court, in their vibrant gowns and precious jewels, took their places and they all dutifully waited while the king and queen entered the hall and sat at the high table on the dais.

It was her cue to sit, and everyone else followed suit. Ramrod straight, she fixed a serene expression on her face and hoped no one could see how tightly she gripped her fingers beneath the table. As the senior royal at the table—as the *only* royal—she was obliged to start the conversation. To put everyone at ease and allow general discourse to proceed.

Her mouth dried. Her heart hammered. The tense silence screamed in her ears, compounded by how the murmur from neighboring tables was becoming progressively louder.

MacKinnon dominated her vision, even though she remained gazing straight ahead. Yet from the corner of her eye, his expansive chest and muscular biceps taunted her with blatant provocation. Thankfully, he was too big for her to catch sight of his face, unless she turned to him. Which, obviously, she needed to, unless she intended everyone to endure the feast in an excruciating silence.

She caught sight of Lady Gavina who looked both thrilled and tortured as she sat mutely beside MacKinnon. Like a spell unravelling, ice-cold clarity drenched her overheated paralysis.

It was not Ewan she needed to speak to. It was MacAllister's son. How had she forgotten so basic an instruction? This was what happened when reckless emotions ruled one's head.

As servants brought out the first platters, she turned to the man by her side. With Ewan no longer encompassing her vision, how easy it was to loosen her foolish tongue. "Welcome to the Kingdom of Fotla."

Now all she needed to do was avoid looking at Ewan for the rest of the night, and all would be well.

CHAPTER 3

*S*top looking at her.

Ewan shifted on the hard bench, but his damn cock throbbed, and it was impossible to get comfortable. And despite his frustrated brain's harsh command, he wasn't looking at Briana. Except it didn't appear to matter where he trained his gaze, all he could see was her coolly beautiful face as she'd swept her icy green eyes over him as though he wasn't even there.

Goddamn it. From the moment he'd first met her last month he had been unable to get her out of his head. They had barely spoken the last time he'd been stationed in Fotla, but the princess had made her disdain for him clear. Even earlier today, her displeasure at his presumption of greeting her in the great hall had been palpable.

What he couldn't understand was why it irked him.

With a monumental effort, he smiled at the young noble-woman by his side. It wasn't usually this hard to focus on a lady who was clearly an expert in the arts of flirtation. Hell, it wasn't hard at *all*.

Until he'd met Briana.

"Are you quite well, MacKinnon?" There was a curious note in the noblewoman's voice, and he hauled his disconcerting worries back into line. Goddamn it, he had no clue what they'd been talking about. What the devil was wrong with him?

"Forgive me, Lady Gavina. I lost myself in the beauty of your eyes." Her eyes were pretty enough, but they were not a hypnotic green, like Briana's.

God help him...

She laughed, clearly forgiving him for his lapse, and he managed to keep his mind on the conversation so he could answer her without disgracing himself further.

It didn't stop him from noting how Briana appeared entranced with Rourke. And Rourke, the bastard, was lapping it up.

He downed a long gulp of wine. Would this feast never end? Yet when it did, Briana would leave.

Aye. He was losing his lust-crazed mind.

MacAllister appeared and bowed to Briana before giving Rourke a message. Rourke's face tightened in obvious irritation, but he didn't respond. Instead, he stood, offered apologies to the princess, and kissed her hand before leaving the hall. MacAllister, interestingly, returned to his seat.

"Alas," breathed Lady Gavina. "I fear you must attend to our princess, MacKinnon. It is most irregular for my lady to be deserted in such a manner."

Against his better judgment he turned to Briana and caught her startled gaze. Instantly, she looked away, focusing on her platter, her profile emanating a regal air that was anything but welcoming.

Shit. They weren't here to insult their hosts. What the hell had MacAllister been thinking? Nothing could be so urgent as to order Rourke from the hall, but if there had been an emergency, why hadn't he summoned the entire contingent?

Yet his duty was plain. It was inconceivable that he continued to ignore the princess, now Rourke had gone.

"Forgive me," he said to the noblewoman. It seemed he had done nothing but ask her to overlook transgressions this eve. Before he could continue, she smiled, and patted his arm.

"It is quite all right," she whispered. "Perhaps we shall dance later, and you may make amends."

Another time, the possibility of furthering their acquaintance would have fired his blood. Tonight, the prospect left him cold. He drew in a measured breath, as though he were about to meet the Norse on a battlefield, and turned to the princess.

Her gown was a deep shade of forest green, with long sleeves intricately embroidered with golden wolves. The gowns of Pict ladies were utterly unlike those of Scots noblewomen, but even in Pictland he'd never seen anything quite like this before.

Wolves were, after all, the symbol of a warrior.

Yet he couldn't deny it. Despite her fragile air, the motif of the fierce predator somehow suited her.

"My lady," he said.

She shot him a hostile glance. "MacKinnon." Her voice was as chilled as her eyes.

Certainly, he understood why she would distrust Scots, yet her animosity didn't extend to the other warriors who had accompanied him. But there was no getting out of this.

"If I might be so bold, my lady, you are looking quite splendid this eve." As the compliment left his mouth, it took all his considerable willpower not to wince. Why did pretty words fall so easily from his lips when he flirted with other ladies, yet sounded so insincere when he directed them to Briana?

"Now I am not battered by the winter elements?"

In truth, he thought she'd looked delightful with her hair escaping its confines, her face glowing from the icy weather, and with snow sprinkled over her cloak. More approachable.

How wrong could he have been? He suspected she might throw the contents of her goblet in his face if he shared such tactless revelations. "Invigorated was the word that came to mind."

She raised her eyebrows. "Invigorated?" She responded in her entrancingly accented Gaelic. "That is a noble observation, indeed. But I must insist you return your attention to Lady Gavina. There is no need to flirt with me, simply because Rourke MacConall has been called away."

He should have known she would be under no illusions as to why he'd finally acknowledged her. Conversely, it made him want to reassure her that wasn't the reason at all.

Unfortunately, he was certain she would never believe him.

"My honor would never allow a lady to be left without the benefit of a sparring partner while enjoying a feast."

"I can assure you, I have no need of... a sparring partner." Was that the faintest hint of a smile he detected? "What strange ideas you Scots possess, to be sure."

"Are we Scots so very different to Picts in this matter?"

Her gaze caught his, and the unexpected warmth in her eyes speared a bolt of hot lust through his groin. By some miracle, he managed to keep the primitive groan of need locked in his throat.

"I'm not certain you would truly wish to hear my opinions of Scots, MacKinnon."

"On the contrary. I'm intrigued."

"And yet etiquette demands I do not insult our esteemed guests."

His grin faded as he recalled why she had such a low opinion of his people. Not only because MacAlpin had annexed the Supreme Kingdom of Fortriu. But because, until recently, her own father and brother had been held hostage in Dal Riada.

He should steer the conversation into safer waters. Under no circumstances should he allude to his king's actions. And yet it was a losing battle. It was wrong, he knew it. But he would not hold his tongue if a few words might clear the air between them.

He refused to consider why he wished for such a thing.

"It's gracious of your king to receive us as honored guests. We're under no illusion, my lady. The matter of the assassin must be resolved, but no one is happy about the circumstances that led us here."

Her eyes widened. Had he been too indiscreet? Yet surely it was worth it, if it showed her, even in a small measure, that not all Scots betrayed their allies for gain.

I have no proof MacAlpin betrayed the Picts in Dunadd. And yet the suspicion gnawed deep, a constant barb of unease that had only magnified during the last nine months.

"My king is honorable, indeed." Briana glanced at the dais. "And I'm grateful for his return. But his freedom was gained at the expense of Lady Mae."

There were many things he should say to rebut her accusation. But she wouldn't believe any of them. And he had no desire to ruin this tentative truce between them by defending the indefensible.

Stop. He had to purge these speculations from his mind. They were nothing short of treasonous and he had no wish to lose his head for something that could never be confirmed.

"If my word means anything, I believe Lady Mae is happy. Braeson worships the ground she walks upon." Shit. He pulled himself up. "I mean, Lord Finn." It was hard to reconcile that the commoner Finn Braeson he'd grown up with had now been acknowledge as MacAlpin's son. "The prince will do anything to ensure her happiness."

Finn had told him Mae was the only woman for him. And although the last time they'd spoken, the man looked like hell, it was obvious to anyone with eyes in their head that he adored his bride.

Briana toyed with her knife before glancing at him. "You are a close confidant of the prince?"

For a tangled moment, he imagined she spoke of Constantine before common sense kicked in. "We are warriors. And aye, he is a good friend, also."

"Yet you cannot deny the way he deceived us all regarding his heritage does not bode well for their future."

He frowned. Was Briana's antagonism towards him all due to the fact she believed he had been complicit in the deception surrounding Finn? Yet that didn't make sense. The deception, ordered by MacAlpin, had only come to light at the end of their stay, and the princess had made it plain she found Ewan's presence objectionable from the day they had arrived.

"My lady, I'm not betraying any confidences when I tell you Finn wasn't acknowledged by the king until we came to Fotla. Indeed, I had no idea of his elevated status until Lady Mae's identity was uncovered."

She was silent, as though contemplating his words. Another course was set upon the table, and a servant refilled his goblet. But he didn't take another swallow of the wine. He was too entranced by the delicate profile of Briana's face.

Bewitched...

Aye, he could believe it. Despite how his people were taught to despise the old, pagan, ways.

Finally, she caught his gaze once again. Gold flecks highlighted the emerald of her eyes, a detail he hadn't noticed before. But then, they had never conversed for longer than a few painful moments before tonight.

"It seems your king is more devious than I imagined. And I assure you, that knowledge shocks me."

She had just insulted the honor of his king, yet he had to battle the urge to grin at the way she raised her eyebrows at him, as though daring him to refute her remark.

"Kings will always use any means to achieve their ends. But he will never harm Lady Mae. Finn will protect her with his life."

"I hope he does. She deserves nothing less for the way she was hunted across our land like a sacred white deer."

He sighed. "Scot or Pict, it makes no difference. We are all at the mercy of our kings."

"Perhaps." She glanced at the dais and her face softened. He could not have torn his gaze from her had MacAlpin himself commanded it. "Yet not all kings are alike."

He didn't agree. But if she wished to harbor that fantasy about her own father, who was he to shatter it?

~

DESPITE HER BEST INTENTIONS, Briana couldn't stop from looking once more at the Scot by her side. His rich saffron shirt did nothing to conceal the magnificence of his biceps, and it seemed the only purpose of the plaid slung over his shoulder was to enhance the warrior strength of his chest. With less reluctance than she liked, her glance traveled up and caught his intense blue gaze.

Ah, goddess. The blue of his eyes had haunted her dreams since the day they'd met. It was most vexing, but not nearly as disconcerting as to admit that her dreams had fallen far short of the reality.

Unbidden, an image flooded her mind of Ewan wrapping her in his strong arms and crushing her against that breathtaking chest. The air around her thickened, making it hard to breathe, and prickles of heat danced over her flesh, as dampness bloomed between her thighs.

Mortified, she pressed her knees together, even though it did little to suppress her body's treacherous urges. But this was why she needed to avoid him. She could not fall prey to base lust, the way she had when she'd been a naïve maid.

Yet, until the feast ended, she had no choice but to suffer his presence.

Brutally, she gathered her scattered wits. Much as she shamefully enjoyed gazing into Ewan's eyes, she had to remember her duty.

It was most unlikely, but maybe he could help shed some light on any subterfuge MacAllister and his king planned in Fotla. He had, after all, surprisingly eased her mind about Mae.

"It's a pity," she said, affecting nonchalance and pretending an interest in the food on her platter, "Rourke MacConall was called away. Are you well acquainted with him, also?"

"Rourke?" There was a thread of confusion in Ewan's voice and alas, she couldn't blame him. She wasn't usually so clumsy when it came to changing the subject. She hoped he did not question her on it. "I know him well, my lady. We were like brothers when we were young."

She forgot about the dangers of looking at him, until their gazes meshed, and her mouth dried. *Focus.* Perhaps there was something of import to learn, after all, if Ewan had once looked upon MacAllister as a father.

"You grew up together?"

"More or less. Alongside Ross MacIntosh and Connor MacKenzie. The four of us were going to change the world."

He gave a mocking smile, and she was entranced by the flash of dimple in his cheek. How had she not noticed that before? Although, until this eve, she had never given him reason to smile at her in such a manner.

And then his words penetrated. Connor MacKenzie. And the small flicker of warmth in her breast sputtered and died.

"MacKenzie." There was a chill in her voice that she couldn't help. "The Scot who coerced my dear cousin Lady Aila into marriage."

Ewan's smile vanished and she ignored the small stab of regret that pierced her heart. She could not afford to forget who the enemy was, yet how easy it was to do so, when MacKinnon held the power to dazzle her with such ease.

"To my knowledge, the Princess of Ce and MacKenzie are well suited. Connor places Lady Aila's happiness above everything."

Did Ewan think her a fool? Political marriages were about

one thing only. And it had nothing to do with the happiness of the bride involved. "Are all Scots such attentive husbands? How fortunate their wives must be."

"The same question could be asked of Pict husbands."

Irked, she picked up her goblet and took a long swallow. It was most unseemly for any unrelated man to be so blunt. The fact that the man was a Scot, and Ewan MacKinnon in particular, was infuriating.

Just because he was right was beside the point. And her vexation at his response most certainly had nothing to do with the humiliating shortcomings she'd endured from her own noble born husband.

"My lady." Ewan's husky voice was a sinful caress against her skin. She gripped the stem of her goblet before she dropped the cursed thing. It was not her imagination. The Scot was leaning across the table, so close, his warm breath dusted her cheek.

How... how *dare* he?

But she could not even turn her head, never mind tell him to remember his place.

"I did not mean to offend you."

He was apologizing. As he should. So why did her heart pound as though he were whispering scandalous bedchamber secrets in her ear?

She inclined her head, before he guessed how dreadfully he affected her. "I'm not offended. Merely concerned for the well-being of my cousin."

Aila was her second cousin, but all the royal houses of Pictland were connected by blood and marriage. And although she had been but ten years old at the time, she well recalled attending Aila's first wedding, when she had married a prince of Fidach, one of the northern kingdoms in Pictland.

It had been a rare thing, indeed. A love match. The romantic notion had fixed in her head, and she had been determined that nothing less than a love match would do for her, also.

What a foolish child she had been. She had adored her charming, flirtatious husband blindly, but while he had liked her well enough, and not been especially unkind, it hadn't stopped him from bedding other women. And worse, fathering children on them. The betrayal and the one-sided love had slowly destroyed her.

"I understand how it looks." Ewan pulled back, and she hitched in a ragged breath. She focused with fierce concentration on her goblet, but it was no use. She could no sooner deny the magnetic allure of looking at him once again as she could deny the ancient, mystical power of the moon.

"Do you?" Instead of the cool tone she strived for, the words were husky. Inviting. She desperately hoped he hadn't noticed.

"As a political strategy, it makes good sense to strengthen our position against the Norse—and the Northumbrians— by inter-marriage between Scot and Pict. But those who engineer the alliances don't have to live with them."

Entranced by his frankness, she could not tear her gaze from his. "Arranged marriages between the royal houses has always been the way in Pictland. It is not the strategy that stings, Ewan. It's the unscrupulous tactics of your king."

"I cannot speak for my king, my lady." There was a stiff note in his voice. Had she offended him? It hadn't occurred to her she might, but it should have. More than that, what was she thinking to speak so candidly?

It was one thing to confide in Mae, and her trusted ladies. But she couldn't afford to share her thoughts with this warrior when every word might later be repeated to his despicable king.

The tables were cleared, and when she rose from her chair, her ladies flocked around her as the hall was readied for the night's entertainment. But instead of retreating with the rest of the Scots, Ewan remained by her side.

It was most distracting.

And then Drest appeared and stood silently behind her, his

arms folded, and his usual dark scowl on his face. Doubtless, her brother had requested he keep her in his sights this night and annoyance flashed through her at his presumption.

If she needed additional bodyguards now the Scots were back in Fotla-eviot, that was something her father would discuss with her. It was not Artair's place, and she would tell him so at the earliest opportunity.

"It is good to see you again, MacKinnon," Lady Nairne said, without a hint of what she really thought of him for breaking her sister's heart. "Pray tell, is Lord Constantine fully recovered from his injury?"

Briana kept a serene smile on her face, but inside she silently groaned. It didn't matter what she thought of the Dal Riadan prince. Or that whenever she was in Ewan's presence her good sense left her. It was inexcusable that she had forgotten to ask after Constantine's health.

"He is, my lady. There should be no lasting ill-effects from the arrow."

"That is good news, indeed." Nairne inclined her head. "We are all anxious that the assassin is hunted down as swiftly as possible."

Ross MacIntosh joined Ewan and after he had kissed her hand in greeting, he proceeded to charm her ladies, the way he had a month ago.

How odd his pretty words and hard, warrior body did not affect her in the least.

If only she was so immune to Ewan MacKinnon.

CHAPTER 4

*M*ute, Ewan eyed Ross as he effortlessly engaged with the Pictish ladies. They laughed and flirted and fluttered their eyelashes, clearly enjoying the lighthearted banter. Before they had come to Fotla, before the massacre at Dunadd, he'd had no problem doing the same with the noblewomen in the Kingdom of Ce. Hell, it was an agreeable pastime he'd enjoyed since he'd been old enough to notice the fairer sex.

And Pictish noblewomen didn't have the same constraints imposed upon them as Scotswomen, who would never indulge in illicit affairs so openly. It had added an intriguing element to an already pleasurable interaction.

He cast a swift glance at the silent princess by his side. She appeared absorbed by Ross and how could he blame her? Instead of charming her during the feast, he'd bombarded her with political talk. A most unsuitable subject to discuss with any lady, never mind a princess.

No wonder she had shot him down with a well-placed barb against the tactics of his king.

Although it was likely just as well the feast had ended when it did. Otherwise, he might have lost whatever remained of his senses and agreed with her.

For a fleeting moment, he caught the eye of the brute of a Pict who stood guard over Briana, and the ice in the other man's black glare sent a chill down his spine. Clearly, this warrior didn't care if every Scot in the hall knew how much he despised them.

Stuart MacGregor and several other Scots strolled over as the music began. He knew enough of royal protocol to understand that until Briana took to the floor, none of her ladies would, either. Since it appeared Ross, as the senior officer, had set his sights on Lady Nairne, he knew his duty. He inhaled a deep breath and turned to the princess.

"My lady, may I have the honor?" He held out his hand. It would be torture to dance with her, but maybe he'd be able to redeem himself by entertaining her with light, inconsequential conversation. If nothing else, it would prove he could converse with her as well as he could with any other woman. And with luck, it would break this unholy bewitchment she held for him.

Alarm flashed across her face, instantly smothered, but it was enough. It was clear the very idea of holding his hand repelled her.

"I thank you," she said, sounding almost regretful. "But I am quite fatigued. Would you be agreeable to keeping me company while my ladies dance?"

"Of course." He gave a half bow. He generally prided himself on understanding women to a certain degree, but he could not work out Briana at all. If she found his presence so distasteful, why had she just asked him to keep her company?

Ross tossed him a glance he couldn't fathom and didn't want to. A combination of curiosity and mockery. He would doubtless hear his friend's thoughts on the matter later.

A strained silence spun between them. It appeared Briana was fascinated by the dancing. If Ross had asked her for the honor, would she have given him the same excuse?

The notion that her answer would undoubtedly have been different unaccountably rattled him. As did the illogical obsession to pull her into his arms and dance with her, regardless.

Except dancing wasn't what he had in mind. The need to feel her luscious body pressed against his was a dark obsession he needed to cull. If only he knew how.

Ruthlessly, he shoved his licentious thoughts to the back of his mind. "My lady, would you care for some wine?"

She turned to him, and in the glow from the multitude of candles that lit the hall, her auburn hair shimmered like a molten sunrise.

Instead of complimenting her upon the phenomenon, as he would without a second thought had she been any other woman, the alluring vision locked his throat. Only when she gave a soft gasp did he manage to tear his mesmerized gaze away.

"My lady." A male voice interrupted their torturous cocoon, and he glowered at the Pict who offered Briana a goblet of wine. "I trust all is well?"

"Quite well, thank you, my lord." She gave the man a smile and took the goblet, before proceeding to introduce him to Rohan, a relation of her late husband. It did nothing to improve his mood.

He returned the man's stiff bow with one of his own. He recognized Rohan from when he'd been in Fotla before, but they had never spoken. But he recalled the way the Pict had always seemed to be furtively watching Briana from the shadows of the stronghold.

"It must be hard," Rohan said, "to be sent from your land in the midst of winter, MacKinnon, to track a murderous traitor in a foreign kingdom. We Picts are capable of meting out appropriate justice ourselves."

Although he thought the same thing, coming from Rohan the statement raised his hackles.

"We are here to assist, not interfere." That was diplomatic.

Not strictly true. He was damn sure MacAllister would interfere if it suited his, and their king's, purposes.

"I fear the would-be assassin is long gone by now," Briana said, and Ewan bit back a curse. There he went again. Talking of politics in front of her. Even if Rohan had been the one to broach the subject.

"I believe you are correct." Rohan gave him a calculating glance before returning his attention to the princess. "The Scots have had a wasted journey."

"Even if he's gone, we might find evidence of who he is," Ewan said. Although his king suspected the Northumbrians were behind the attack, and he and his fellow warriors were sworn to secrecy, he was averse to allowing the Pict the last word in the matter. Besides, MacAlpin merely suspected the Northumbrians. He had no solid proof. "For all we know it could be a Norse spy, sent to destabilize the Scot/Pict alliance. Which means the royal family of Fotla may yet be in his sights."

"That is my concern, also." There was a hushed note in her voice, as though the fact they agreed about something was remarkable. Hell, he was taken aback himself. Especially given the topic. "Although we've heard no reports of Vikings this far south, our northern kingdoms are in dire peril."

"The Vikings encroach from every direction." For the first time, Rohan's smirk had been replaced with a grim expression. "It pains me to admit, but the Scot could be right."

"All the more reason we work together on this." Ewan gave the other man an insincere smile. No Pict warrior extended the hand of friendship to a Scot, and he understood why. But there was something more about Rohan's bearing that caused his senses to prickle as though he was preparing to go into battle.

"I agree." Rohan returned an equally false smile in his direction. "Which is why I'll be accompanying your contingent in the morning."

Of course he would. Ewan managed to keep his opinion of the

Pict from showing on his face. "Good. If we're lucky, the weather will ease."

He wasn't counting on it, though. Between the blizzards and storms that had rampaged during the last week, this quest was scarcely more than a farce. But it was a farce that needed to yield results.

"It will clear by the morn."

Briana sounded so quietly confident, he frowned at her, uncertain he grasped her meaning. "My lady?"

Her beautiful green eyes ensnared him, and fire burned through his veins, thickening his cock with unbridled need.

There was only one way to cure this affliction. Unfortunately, it was the one thing that would never happen between them.

Christ, he had to focus. What had she just said?

"The air?" He repeated, feeling foolish.

"Indeed," she responded, as though his question hadn't been out of place at all. Thank God. Even though he still had no idea what she was speaking of. "I've always been attuned to the winter elements. My grand-aunt Brilicie, the dowager Queen of Ce, links it to the mighty goddess, Cailleach, who reigned supreme on the night of my birth."

He was still none the wiser. Although since she spoke of pagan things, that was no great surprise. Despite how his own grandmother followed the ancient ways, he had been brought up in the church of Christ. "I do not know of this mighty goddess of yours."

"She is most powerful." There was a reverential note in her voice that fascinated him. "The bringer of death and destruction across the land, but without her, there would be no life."

"A winter goddess?" It was surely verging on blasphemy to discuss such heathen beliefs, but he couldn't help himself.

"She is *the* Goddess of Winter and should not be spoken of lightly."

"The Scots have forgotten the old ways." Amusement threaded through Rohan's voice, and it took some doing to ignore him.

"Is she the goddess you worship?" he asked her.

She stiffened, as though his question had struck a nerve. "I worship her, as all true believers do. But I am a chosen one of the blessed Bride."

A great boom echoed around the hall and the dancing stalled as everyone shot startled glances at each other. Excited voices filled the air and nobles followed the Pict warriors who marched out of the hall.

Briana thrust her goblet at Rohan, who looked less than pleased by the gesture, before she turned to follow the others.

Before he could stop himself, he grasped her arm. God, that was a mistake, but he couldn't allow her to run into possible danger.

"My lady, you should remain here."

She glanced at his hand as if she couldn't believe he had touched her. With damning reluctance, he unhanded her and flexed his fingers. Her gaze met his. She didn't appear vexed, although her silent bodyguard glowered at him as though he'd like to commit murder.

"Come." Her voice was husky. "You may keep me safe, if that will appease your sense of honor."

He wasn't sure if she was mocking him, but it didn't matter since she was already making her way to the doors. He grasped the hilt of his sword and followed her.

The nobles and servants spilled from the great hall into the entrance, and Briana made her way through them. But it was plain enough what had happened.

The great wooden doors to the stronghold were flung open to the night sky. Biting wind whipped inside, bringing with it a furious snowstorm. Pict warriors slammed the doors shut but it seemed the force of the blizzard had shattered the massive bolt that had kept them closed.

Clearly, the wood was rotten, and anger licked through him at such carelessness. But at least the storm had exposed Fotla-eviot's potential vulnerability. How much worse it could have been if enemies had been attacking.

"The storm grows worse, I fear," he said to Briana, who appeared transfixed by the scene before them. "I hope you're right about the weather easing for tomorrow, but it's not looking good."

Slowly, she turned to him. There was a strange, haunted look in her eyes, but it vanished in an instant. Maybe it had been a trick of the flickering torches that some of the Picts held.

And then she spoke. "The storm will pass this night."

A HARSH GASP tore from Briana's throat and she sat bolt upright in her bed, heart pounding, clutching the furs to her chest. The fire had burned low, and shadows loomed from every corner, spreading branchlike across the walls and floors towards her.

A chill permeated to the core of her being, and she shivered. Phantom snowflakes drifted before her eyes and a flash of some-thing—silver? —glinted in the gloom before fading into the fog where dreams invariably died.

A dream?

Or something more?

Frantically, she tried to recapture the images in her mind, but all that remained was a lingering sense of unease.

Danger.

Blessed Bride, are you there?

Silence echoed. Surely, if the goddess had sent a vision, she would not allow it to float like gossamer, indecipherable, on the edges of her mind?

"My lady, is anything amiss?" Nairne whispered, as she sat up in the bed next to her.

Even though it was too dark for Nairne to see her face, Briana hastily composed her features. How different it would be if Mae was still here. As another chosen one of the goddess, they could have spoken of this. Tried to understand what Bride was showing her.

If, indeed, Bride was showing her anything at all. Maybe she was simply trying to see substance from nothing.

"Everything is well," she assured her friend. "It's still early. Go back to sleep."

Clearly relieved she didn't have to rise yet, Nairne rolled onto her side and Briana let out a long breath. Although guilt still twisted through her chest at the unknowing part she had played in allowing her dear cousin to be captured by the Scots, it didn't burn as fiercely as usual.

Because MacKinnon had told her he believed Mae was happy.

She hoped he had been sincere.

How she wished she could see Mae again, to ensure her cousin truly was content in her new life.

She lay down and closed her eyes. And saw once again the doors to the palace, wide open to the harsh winter skies.

A shudder raked through her, and she pulled the furs to her chin. It was of no significance. The security of the palace was not her province.

It was not a sign.

Are you certain of that?

She pushed the insidious question aside. There was nothing to gain from worrying about something that her father was sure to prioritize. The security of the palace was paramount. Another sturdy bolt would be in place by the following day.

The silence of her chamber, broken by the occasional sputter from the dying fire in the hearth, enveloped her. Only when sleep wrapped velvet arms around her, did sudden clarity pierce through her mind.

The glint she had seen in the darkness was an arrowhead.

It was a warning. One she could not afford to ignore.

CHAPTER 5

That night, the dark dream of Ewan's childhood gripped him once again. His heart hammered in his chest as Moreen, his father's new bride, entered the chamber and came over to his bed.

He sat up, mesmerized by how the candle she held lit up her beautiful face and long golden hair. He had never seen anything like her in his whole seven years. And his father had told him earlier this day that Moreen was to be his new mamma.

Would she hold him close and stroke his hair, the way his own mamma had, before she had been called to God?

Moreen sat on the edge of his bed and stared at him but did not say a word. Unlike earlier, when his father had brought her home, she didn't smile at him or say what a grand lad he was.

Her silence sent shivers along his arms and an unnamable fear scuttled through his bones.

This is not real...

But the dream held him in its unmerciful vise, and he was trapped in his seven-year-old self, unable to escape the unfurling nightmare that had haunted him for almost twenty years.

"How like your father you are." Her whisper echoed around

the chamber, and when she flicked his hair with one finger, it was not comfort that enveloped him at her touch. "He cares for you so deeply." She leaned forward until her face was so close to his he could feel her breath. "But that is because he doesn't know the truth, Ewan. What would he say, if he knew it's your fault your dear mamma died?"

Terror spiked through him and for a crippling eternity he remembered the water, the darkness, the agonizing horror as he had watched her tumble from the boat.

But it isn't my fault Mamma drowned in the loch.

His chest tightened and an unnamed fear clawed deep inside as Moreen smiled at his mounting distress. She stroked his hair, and it was not kindly or tender, or any of the things he recalled when his own mamma had done such things.

Moreen's touch sent slivers of ice through his heart.

"It's all right," she whispered. "It shall be our secret. You will tell your father how you adore me and how happy you are that I am your new mamma, and he will never hear the truth from me."

The chamber tumbled around him, and he was fourteen, holding the lifeless body of his half-brother in his arms, as Moreen's despairing screams ripped his soul. Then she fell to her knees and her wild gaze caught his.

"This is your fault. It should have been you, not him. Not my beloved son." Her voice broke before she drew in a sharp breath, hatred burning in her eyes. "Everyone who loves you, dies. Do you hear me, you wicked, cursed creature? I pray God will serve the justice upon you that you deserve."

Ewan's eyes snapped open. Sweat slicked his body and lingering condemnation echoed through his mind.

Everyone who loves you, dies.

Wicked, cursed creature...

He exhaled a long breath. It had been years since he'd been plagued by these nightly terrors, a penance he endured for his sins.

It had been a harsh lesson, but he had learned it well. The only way to prevent anyone else from perishing because of him, was to ensure no one became close to him.

It was the reason he only indulged in brief, inconsequential affairs with women who wanted nothing more from him. If they didn't care for him, they were not in danger from Moreen's curse.

Why the hell had it returned now?

But he knew why. Even if he tried to deny it. Because for the first time, a woman had snared his interest in a way he'd never imagined possible. And although he was not so arrogant as to think Briana might feel the same, he couldn't risk her safety simply because he enjoyed her company.

There was but one recourse. He would avoid her at all costs.

Ewan and his compatriots left the stronghold just before dawn, and as they met the Pict warriors who were to accompany them to the local villages, he conceded Briana had been right.

Although the snow lay heavy on the ground, the storm from the previous night had passed, leaving an eerie silence in the frost chilled air.

Ross rode to his side, accompanied by a surly Rourke who looked as though he hadn't slept last night. Maybe he hadn't. He had failed to return to the chamber once they'd all retired.

Ewan cast him a curious glance. "What vital mission did MacAllister send you on?"

Rourke's glare would have quelled any man who didn't know him, but Ewan was used to them. They were a frequent response, whenever his father was mentioned.

"To guard the horses." He enunciated each word as though they befouled his tongue.

"The horses?" Ewan glanced at Ross, who shrugged. He was

clearly in the dark as to MacAllister's motives. "Do we expect the Picts to slaughter them while we sleep?"

"Christ knows." Rourke slung a dark look at MacAllister, who rode ahead with the Prince of Fotla. Such an honor should have fallen to Ross, as the commanding officer, but no one argued with the king's man. "He likely didn't want me speaking to Lady Briana."

"Understandable." Ross transferred his mocking glance from Rourke to Ewan. "MacKinnon took your place easily enough. I doubt the princess even noticed you'd gone."

"How edifying," Rourke ground between his teeth.

"Unfortunately, you won't have a second chance to charm the princess," Ross continued, as they headed towards the nearest village, a smudge in the snowy distance. "Word reached us that we're not welcome at any more feasts. It's back to rations, unless we find time to hunt."

No more evenings in Briana's company, speaking of indelicate things that should never be uttered in the presence of a lady, never mind a princess. Ewan narrowed his eyes against the glare of the sun on the ice flecked landscape, but all he could see were her captivating green eyes, and the way the candlelight had caused her hair to glow like flames.

It was just as well there would be no further opportunities to spend time with her. It made his vow to avoid her much easier.

If only it was as easy to dislodge her from his mind.

AFTER THEY HAD BROKEN their fast, Briana was summoned to the queen's private chambers. Nairne and Gavina accompanied her and as they entered the great hall, she spied Rohan and beckoned him over.

He was sure to have the latest theories on how such a breach had occurred last night.

"What news do you have, my lord?"

He fell into step beside her. It was a minor infraction of etiquette that had begun the night he'd informed her of her husband's death, and when she had finally noticed it seemed churlish to rebuke him.

"Not good, my lady." His voice was low and unlike his normal countenance, his face was grim. "I have it on good authority that the bolt had been sabotaged."

"Sabotaged?" She came to a halt and gazed at him in horror. She had assumed the wood had rotted from within. "Surely not."

"I can only relay what I've heard."

She resumed walking, as the inevitable wormed into her head. "The Scots?"

Was that the order MacAllister had given Rourke during the feast? Yet it did not follow. Pict warriors were everywhere. And it would take more than a few furtive cuts from a dagger to destroy a hefty log.

"I cannot say." But his tone implied everything.

They reached the queen's chambers and she and her ladies entered, leaving Rohan to his business. Her mother stood and led her into the adjoining chamber, while their ladies remained behind.

The king was in there and turned as her mamma closed the door behind them. Her chest knotted with anxiety as he came to her and kissed her cheek. These chambers were her mother's domain, and it was most irregular for him to be here, especially when he needed to find out the cause for the disturbance last night.

"Daughter." He smiled at her before releasing her. "Doubtless you know why you have been summoned."

She thought it was because her mamma wanted to know everything she had learned from Ewan MacKinnon last night. But now, she was not so sure.

"The possible sabotage of our defenses?"

"Artair is leading the investigation into this as we speak. But I have another conjecture I must put to you."

She kept her expression serene, even though her heart thudded painfully in her chest. She knew what he was going to ask her. But she wouldn't jump to conclusions. "Which is?

"Might it be a sign of Bride's displeasure that we tolerate the Scots in our land?"

She wasn't surprised by her father's question. He had always been most attentive in acknowledging the rightful place of the old gods. Many times when she was a child he had told her how proud he was that the gods had blessed her so.

Yet the stark truth was, she didn't know how her beloved goddess felt about the intrusion of the Scots. For weeks, she'd feared her goddess had deserted her, but she had been wrong. The remnants of the dream—the vision—from last night haunted her.

What was Bride warning her of?

Not that she could share her uncertainty with her father, when he clearly needed clarity from the gods, not mortal anxieties from his daughter. "Bride does not wield power over the winter elements."

But the mighty Cailleach does.

It hovered on blasphemy to even think such a thing. Bride and Cailleach were the bitterest of enemies, constantly battling for supremacy. Ultimately, neither could win, just as neither could lose, for if one were to succumb, the entire fabric of existence would unravel.

She was a chosen one of Bride. She, and everyone around her, had known this since she was a small child. Bride had similarly blessed several of her royal cousins, and the annals of Pictland revered the names of all those in the past whom the goddess had touched with her benevolence.

There were no reverential inscriptions of anyone having been chosen by the fearsome Cailleach. Only whispered rumors, their origin lost in the mists of time, of those marked by the Goddess of Winter and the dark powers wielded in her name.

Witches.

"I fear," said the queen, "that the encroachment of the Scots across Pictland is forcing our gods to retreat."

"The Scots will not destroy the truth." Her voice was hushed, but fierce. "We *will* find a way to defeat MacAlpin."

Her mother's smile was sad. "I wish I had your faith, Briana."

"I do not trust the man." Her father's eyes were hard. "But regardless of our feelings in this matter, we need the alliance with the Scots to defend our land. And likewise, the Scots need us. Our spies in Dal Riada tell us the Vikings have set their sights on claiming Dunadd. I cannot fathom why they would sabotage our fortifications. What purpose would it serve?"

"As a distraction, while they pretend to hunt down this so-called assassin."

Briana glanced at her mother. "So-called assassin? You think the Scots themselves might have planned to kill their prince?"

Although she would put nothing past MacAlpin, if it helped him get his way, this seemed most extreme, even for him.

"You could be right about this merely being a distraction." The king inclined his head. "But whether the Scots were behind the outrage or not, we can be sure they'll find a culprit to make an example of. We need to ensure whoever is found doesn't undermine our own position."

A scapegoat, then. She had thought as much, although she'd hoped to be wrong.

"Briana," the queen said, bringing her attention back to her mamma. "Did Rourke MacConall let slip anything useful before MacAllister unpardonably ordered him from the hall?"

Goddess, she could scarcely recall a thing she and Rourke had discussed. But it had certainly not been anything useful. His scheming father had seen to that.

"Alas, he did not. But I shall attempt to converse with him once again today."

Ewan MacKinnon's rugged good looks settled into her mind. *No.* With a great effort, she attempted to erase his captivating features and replace them with Rourke's.

Unfortunately, she could not even remember the shade of Rourke's hair. But the intriguing blend of dark blond and light copper that graced Ewan's head appeared to be burned into her senses.

The queen sighed. "What of your ladies? Did they discover anything of interest?"

"I fear not. No illicit assignations were enjoyed last night."

"What of the other Scot? MacKinnon?" Her father's shrewd gaze bored into her and for a terrible moment she feared he could see right into her head, where she tried so desperately, and utterly failed, to suppress every errant thought of MacKinnon. "He appeared to have a lot to say."

Relief surged through her. Her father had no idea of how the Scot affected her. But at least he had given her information she could share.

"Indeed, he was most forthcoming. It seems the Scots were not privy to the plan MacAlpin devised for his bastard son, Finn, to wed Mae."

When this did not elicit any response other than blank looks from her parents, she added, "MacKinnon assures me that Finn wishes only for Mae's happiness, and I believe he speaks the truth."

Her mamma pressed her lips together and for a fleeting moment regret flickered across her face. But surely she was mistaken? Her mother never regretted anything she did.

Her father gave a grunt of displeasure. "It was a bad business, but Lady Mairi conducted herself as the Princess of Fortriu should and put the good of Pictland before all else. But what of current events, daughter? Does MacKinnon know anything worthwhile to us?"

It was not a rebuke, but heat seared her, nevertheless. She had been so relieved to learn of Mae's situation she'd confused it with vital information, but the truth was, Ewan had told her nothing politically useful.

To be sure, he had eased her worries over her cousin, but she couldn't lie to herself any longer. His enchanting accent beguiled her, the intensity of his blue gaze ensnared her, and the unexpected threads of their conversation had bedazzled her reason. And that was why she hadn't steered the discussion in the direction she should have.

Because she had inexcusably forgotten the very purpose for the feast.

"If he does, he did not share it." Thankfully, her voice was cool, belying how her pulse raced as she recalled their encounter last night. When he had grasped her arm, her blood had seared her veins and the breath evaporated from her lungs. It was quite disgraceful.

How she longed for him to touch her again.

Enough. He was a practiced charmer and seducer and even if she were inclined to dally with a foreign lover, it wouldn't be with any man who could so easily make her forget her duty.

"Perhaps there is no ulterior motive for why the Scots returned." Her father didn't sound convinced, though. "We shall remain vigilant, and ensure our warriors are on full alert at all times." He glanced at the queen, and she gave a brief nod.

"We will offer no more hospitality, save that of the palace roof over their heads. Which is more than they deserve. Inform your ladies accordingly, Briana."

"Yes, Mamma." She was *not* disappointed by the directive. On the contrary, it was relief flooding through her that she didn't need to seek out Ewan MacKinnon as a source of information.

It was clear the king had given orders to the warriors that this investigation should be concluded as swiftly as possible. She only hoped they found the truth in the process.

And then the Scots, and Ewan with them, would return to Dal Riada.

∼

THE SUN WAS low in the sky when they returned to Fotla-eviot, and Ewan remained behind in the stables, tending his horse, after the others left. Although the conditions were cramped, at least the animals had shelter from the bitter winter.

He rolled his shoulders and sighed as he left the stables. They had searched the local villages, but no one had reported any Northumbrians, and the villagers themselves had barely hidden their hostility towards the Scots. None of them admitted to seeing or being aware of a suspicious foreigner in their midst who might, or might not, have been responsible for the attempted assassination.

A commotion broke out and he swung around, frowning at a trio of full-grown menials who were making fine sport of a young lad by the side of the stable wall. They kicked him to the ground and stole whatever meagre meal the boy had clutched desperately in his hands.

Dull rage curdled in his gut. While he'd never been bullied by his contemporaries—his hard fists and fast wit had saved him from any such fate—he well knew how it felt to be helpless in the face of a seemingly inescapable power.

To hell with the fact he was in a foreign kingdom and should mind his own business. He strode back the way he had come, grasped one of the youths by the scruff of his neck and tossed him into the brown slush that covered the ground. The other two took one look at him and fled, leaving their companion behind.

Ewan glared down at him. "Get out of here," he growled, and

the Pict didn't need a second warning, scrambling to his feet and following the others without a backward glance.

He took a deep breath and turned to look at the cowering lad, who was using the wall to slowly push himself upright. "Are you hurt?" he said in Pictish.

The boy shook his head, despite how blood speckled his cheek.

"Hungry?" A redundant question, given what had just transpired, but life was full of such instances.

After a few moments the boy gave a wary nod. It was obvious he didn't trust Ewan an inch, and for that he could not blame him.

He retreated a step and dug into his pack. "Here." He handed the child a strip of dried meat from his rations. After another dubious look, the boy took it and crammed it into his mouth, before darting away.

Ewan watched him go and shook his head. What was he doing, interfering like that? Chances were, by humiliating the older lads, he'd just made the waif's life worse.

Too late now. It was done. He swung around and standing not a horse's length from him, was Briana.

CHAPTER 6

*S*wallowing a silent curse, Briana stepped forward, Lady Gavina following in her wake. It was too late to pretend she hadn't been watching. She only hoped the violet and pink hues of twilight that splashed the sky hid the annoying blush heating her cheeks. It was most unseemly that she had paused, enthralled by the sight of a warrior, and a Scot at that, showing such compassion to a beggar.

Even as she inclined her head in acknowledgement of Ewan's somewhat awkward bow, she knew the truth. It had nothing to do with the fact he was a Scot, and everything to do with the man himself.

"My lady." His tone was formal. The way it had been a month ago and unaccountably it jarred. Where had the charming companion gone from last night?

Stop. She didn't want the charmer back. He was entirely too hard to resist, and it was imperative for her peace of mind that she did. She took a calming breath while he acknowledged Gavina.

"MacKinnon." Thankfully, her voice was cool, despite the fire that raged through her blood. Her lack of control when it came to him was utterly vexing. She should simply walk on and see to her mare, as she had intended, but the words would not stay locked in her throat. "I see you are full of surprises."

Goddess, what had possessed her to say such a banal thing? First, she didn't wish him to imagine she found him surprising. And secondly…

No, that was it. She did not wish Ewan MacKinnon to think anything of her at *all*.

If only she meant it.

He grunted and shifted his weight from one foot to another. Like a flash of lightning, realization struck. He was disconcerted that she had witnessed his kindness.

Oddly, that made her feel better about her own rash words.

"The bairn was hungry." His voice was gruff, and he glowered at a spot over her shoulder. "I have enough provisions so I will not starve."

Indeed, but that was scarcely the point. "Nevertheless, it was good of you to send his tormentors on their way."

His agonized glance assured her he'd hoped she hadn't seen that. Why were men so averse for allowing anyone to glimpse that they possessed a streak of empathy hidden deep within their battle-scarred souls?

"I only hope my interference doesn't make things worse for him."

"Oh." That hadn't even occurred to her, but she could certainly see the truth of it. "I shall endeavor to discover who he is and ensure his protection."

There was certain to be something useful he could do, in the stables, perhaps, in return for food and lodging. And the protection of the equerry.

"Why would you do that?" He sounded mystified, and no longer gazed at her as though he wished she was anywhere but here. It shouldn't cause a little glow to flicker in her heart, and yet it did.

"It's impossible to help everyone. But when someone crosses one's path, perhaps it is a sign from the gods. That is what I have always believed."

"I like that." He smiled, and the breath stalled in her lungs at the sight. Men should not be blessed with such seductive dimples. "Although I should make it clear, that doesn't mean I believe in your gods."

It was hard not to laugh, which was absurd given that he had just denied her beloved gods' existence. But since it was a well-known fact that Scots had abandoned the true path three hundred years ago or more, his honesty could scarcely cause offense.

"That is quite all right. I won't hold your ignorance against you."

"I'm gratified. That would be a harsh burden to bear, I am sure."

A breathless laugh escaped before she could prevent it and he grinned back at her, as if this was the most natural conversation in the world. Although daylight was fading, she fancied she could still see the vivid blue of his eyes as he gazed at her so intensely.

They were so close, it would take no effort at all to simply reach out and—

She hitched in a sharp breath as the truth hit her. They *were* close. Inexcusably so. Which one of them had moved? She had no recollection. And the pounding of her heart filled her head, making it hard to think of anything other than this scandalous moment.

His hungry gaze roved over her face. Goddess, she should not imagine such things when it concerned Ewan, but she was helpless to banish the notion. As though in a dream, she was unable to move when he tenderly brushed an errant strand of hair from her cheek, his finger lingering as if he couldn't tear himself away.

Her skin tingled from the contact, sending tremors skittering through her body. Her breast tightened and nipples hardened, straining against her bodice and she gave a soft gasp before she could stop herself.

What was he doing? His touch was most inappropriate. She ought to reprimand him. Her tongue refused to say the words yet worst of all, her brain could not even conjure them. Not when dark desire swirled between her thighs, and her clitoris throbbed with unfulfilled need.

His arm dropped to his side and, for a mortifying second, she had the certainty he was about to apologize for his action. And while he had no right to touch her in such a manner, the notion of him expressing regret for doing so made her wither inside.

There was no reason for her to continue standing here, while they idly conversed. Perhaps it wouldn't matter, if he had been any other warrior than Ewan. Indeed, if it had been Rourke, she would encourage him to speak, despite her father's decree. A meeting like *that* would not have been merely fortuitous but surely engineered by Bride.

But he wasn't Rourke. He was Ewan MacKinnon and the more time she spent in his company, the harder it was to recall why he was the last man with whom she could let down her guard.

It wasn't because he made her feel things she had sworn never to feel again.

It was because, despite the alliance between Pict and Scot, his allegiance to MacAlpin—the man responsible for the betrayal in Dunadd and the imprisonment of her father and brother—could make him nothing but an enemy of her people.

Yes. She would leave. The decision was made. He stood before her, as though waiting for her to break this excruciating silence that had fallen between them. And instead of making good on her intentions, she said, "How was your day? Did you discover anything of worth?"

It was a reasonable question. It had nothing to do with wishing to hear his wonderfully seductive accent again.

"We did not." Frustration threaded through his voice. "I doubt we'll discover the truth, my lady. Whatever the outcome."

So he suspected a scapegoat would be held accountable, too. "What good will it do, to find some poor soul to blame just to put this matter to rest? The true culprit will still be out there. And if our suspicions are right, and it is a Viking conspiracy, who knows how many of those barbarians are hiding in Fotla?"

Consternation flashed over his face. "Do not worry about such matters, my lady. No harm will befall you within these walls. If the enemy are here, we will discover them."

She wasn't sure whether to be charmed by his concern over her safety, or impatient that he considered such political affairs to be beyond her scope of understanding. "It's to be hoped they are discovered, MacKinnon, and certainly I shall worry about such things, even if I don't ride into battle with sword and spear."

A frown creased his brow. It was most distracting, especially when she was trying so hard to be vexed at him.

"I confess I find your candor most illuminating."

"Illuminating?" That wasn't the word she had expected him to use. It was whispered that women in Dal Riada had little personal agency and were rarely consulted in matters of state. But if that was so, Ewan's reaction did not quite make sense. "I'm curious. Are the rumors true that Scotswomen are not involved in political matters in your homeland?"

"The king doesn't consult his queen, if that's what you're asking." He sounded reluctant to admit it. How intriguing. "I understand things are different in the royal courts of Pictland."

"Indeed." Although the kings of Pictland ruled their kingdoms, if not for their queens, they would rule nothing. And behind the throne, it was unthinkable that the queen would not be consulted, and her word given equal weight. "I pity the women of Dal Riada whose voices are not heard."

"I assure you, not all Scotswomen's voices are suppressed."

"I find that hard to believe." Although she dearly hoped it was true, for Mae's sake.

"You should meet my lady grandmother. I challenge you to find a more formidable woman in all the royal houses of Pictland."

The elusive glimpse into his personal life should not fascinate her so, yet the way he spoke of his relative with such casual affection, fairly took her breath away.

"And you should know that the royal houses of Pictland are blessed with a great many formidable women. Should I ever have the chance to meet this grandmother of yours, you may be sure I shall give you my opinion on your reckless challenge."

He grinned and before she could think better of it, she smiled back. Ah, goddess. How hard it was to resist his silken allure. What was she thinking to suggest, even in jest, that there was a chance she might one day encounter his family?

To be sure, it was merely flirtation. But when a man made her pulse race and flesh tingle, it became a dangerous pastime she needed to avoid.

A soft cough from behind her wrenched her sharply back to the present and guilt flashed through her as she glanced at Lady Gavina, and beyond her, caught sight of the glower on the face of Drest who had accompanied them. How had she forgotten her friend was even here?

It was merely one of the reasons why she should avoid MacKinnon. Because whenever he was near, everything else fled her mind.

The reality was stark, and distressing. She didn't want to end this encounter. Yet she had to. And not simply because it was unseemly to conduct a conversation with him in the bitter cold as dusk descended around them.

"I should not keep you," she said, inclining her head in farewell. He gave a swift bow and stepped back, and it took every shred of willpower she possessed not to glance over her shoulder as she continued onto the stables.

~

EWAN STILL LURKED in unwary corners of her mind when she returned to the palace and was summoned to the queen's private chambers. A fire burned brightly in the hearth, and candles chased the winter gloom into pockets of shadows.

Drest remained in the corridor. When she had confronted Artair earlier today, he'd been adamant she needed additional protection with the Scots' return. Frustratingly, her father agreed and so there was nothing to be done about it.

She wasn't certain why she minded so much. The taciturn warrior had been a part of her life since she was a child and they had always got along well enough. It wasn't as though she intended an illicit affair with Ewan, after all.

"We have been informed of some developments." Her mamma indicated she should sit next to her by the fireside, and their ladies followed suit.

"Developments?" Briana pulled her mind from Ewan. Surely even her former husband had not occupied her thoughts as fully as the Scot did. It was not a comforting notion.

"Lady Mairi has secured the release of ten hostages. They are already on their way back to their kingdoms."

"Goddess." Stunned, Briana stared at her mother. She had not imagined her cousin would be able to secure such a strategic victory against the upstart king—at least, not this quickly. But it boded well for her future, if MacAlpin was mindful of the need for diplomatic concessions. "That is excellent news, indeed."

"It is." The queen averted her gaze and smoothed her gown. "Lord Talargan was among them."

Briana knew that long ago her cousin had once dreamed of a

future with the Prince of Ce. But Mae had confessed last month that she no longer felt that way about Talargan. It was good he was among those released but she wasn't sure why her mother had mentioned only his name.

"The Queen of Ce will be happy to have her son returned to her." As too would Aila be relieved that her brother had been released.

Her mamma gave a brief nod as pain flashed over her face. With a stab of guilt, Briana acknowledged that her mother had spent most of the year hoping for the safe return of her own husband and son from MacAlpin's clutches. And certainly, *she* was grateful that her father and brother had returned unharmed.

But she still could not quite forgive her mamma for the betrayal of Mae.

"We must think of the future, Briana. It's clear MacAlpin has his sights set on infiltrating every kingdom of Pictland through political marriages. As a widowed princess, the king and I fear that sooner or later you will be ensnared in his web."

Unease knotted deep in her breast. She had returned home a little over a year ago, after the untimely death of her husband, and was grateful that she hadn't been immediately betrothed to another. To be sure, that was because she had asked her father for a respite from her duty, and he had readily agreed.

They had never spoken of it, but she feared her dear papa had guessed at the unhappy state of her marriage and blamed himself for it. Ecgfrith had been her choice, and although it had taken three years of persuasion, her father had finally given permission for them to wed.

But even at sixteen, she knew, deep down, he didn't approve of her choice. Yet because he loved her, he'd allowed his heart to rule his head.

Dynastic marriages strengthened alliances. She should have followed her two elder sisters' examples and wed for the strategic advantage it brought to Fotla. Not allowed her self-indulgent dream of love to eclipse the true nature of the man who had dazzled her.

The man who could not seem to help but charm every woman he met. Who craved feminine adoration as a necessity of life as much as the very air he breathed.

The man whose heedless inability to give her anything but superficial compliments and insincere promises had slowly withered her love until only the scarred husk remained.

Perhaps, if she had not been such a failure in the bedchamber, Ecgfrith would have loved her and not pursued his countless lovers. But she doubted it.

Yet despite her misgivings, she'd always known that one day she would need to remarry. It was her obligation as a princess of Fotla to follow in her sisters' footsteps and strengthen Pictish bloodlines with children of her own.

An old, familiar pain lanced through her heart, and she took a ragged breath, grateful her mamma was still focused on her hands clasped upon her lap. How dearly she had always longed for children of her own. No one knew of that bloodied night eighteen months ago when she had lost her most cherished dreams. Not her oblivious husband nor her ladies, and she had not even confided in Mae.

The miracle had been too new, too fragile to share, and the loss was hers to bear alone.

The crackle of the logs in the fire was the only sound filling the chamber. All the ladies, like her mamma, were focusing most intently on their laps.

And then it dawned on her.

"Oh." How unforgiveable of her not to have realized at once what her mamma had been saying. "You believe an alliance between the royal houses of Fotla and Ce should be sought?"

Finally, her mother caught her gaze. "Is this something you would consider?"

Talargan was only a few years older than her and from what she could recall from the last time they had seen each other, at her wedding, no less, he was certainly handsome, and his heritage was impeccable.

It was an excellent political alliance. And most importantly for her peace of mind, she was not in love with him. There were no reasons why she should not agree to the proposition.

Without warning, Ewan MacKinnon swirled into her mind, his dark blond and copper hair in wild disarray from the winter's wind, his beguiling smile as mesmerizing as though he stood before her.

She swallowed, her throat dry, and tried desperately to calm her erratic pulse. To wed a man like him would be a recipe for disaster.

Goddess, what was the matter with her? No one was asking her to do such a thing. And even if they were, MacKinnon was the last man in the world she would wed. Not just because he was a Scot. But because, just like Ecgfrith, he broke hearts without a second's thought, and she was not certain her heart was strong enough to recover from such a catastrophe for a second time.

"Briana?" There was a thread of anxiety in her mamma's voice. "If this is distasteful to you, we shall think again. But your father and I believe it's in your best interests to marry soon, as a tactical countermove against MacAlpin's possible machinations."

Brutally, she thrust MacKinnon's engaging smile from her thoughts. She should have kept him at arm's length, like she had last month. But all would be well. In time, she would forget about his entrancing accent, his summer-blue eyes, and the way his laugh caused delightful shivers to dance across her skin.

And perhaps time might even dull the memory of his compassion for a beggar child.

She forced a serene smile to her face. "This is not distasteful at all, Mamma. If Lord Talargan and the Queen of Ce agree to this alliance, I will enter it most willingly."

There were far worse things than a loveless marriage. She would do her duty for Fotla and for Pictland, and her heart would be safe.

CHAPTER 7

*E*wan hunched his shoulders against the icy wind that whipped through the trees as they left the forest and glanced at Ross who rode in stony silence by his side.

"I'd give a great deal to know what's really going on." He kept his voice low so the Picts that rode with them did not overhear. For five days they had been on this quest, and everyone's temper was frayed. "Why do we still keep the fact that the assassin is Northumbrian from the Picts?" Something else had been gnawing at him for the last week, also, and finally he voiced it "Why are the king and MacAllister so certain he's Northumbrian, anyway? For all we know, he could well be Norse."

Ross slung him a grim look. "I'm not privy to the king's man's schemes."

When, eventually, the stronghold of Fotla-eviot came into view, their party came to a halt. The horses snorted, plumes of white drifting into the air, as up ahead the prince, the warrior, Drest, and MacAllister conversed.

Ewan bit back a sigh and against his better judgement, Briana once more slid into his mind. They had barely spoken during the last five days, which, he reminded himself, was a good thing, but whenever their paths crossed, she always smiled at him and bade him good day, before continuing on her way.

He shifted on his horse, but it didn't help ease the discomfort thudding through his cock. Even out here, with the blood freezing in his veins, he only had to think of Briana and his damn body responded.

Frustration was his constant companion, and there was no end in sight. The careless dalliances he and his fellow warriors had enjoyed during the spring and summer in Ce were a distant memory. And although there had been a few clandestine encounters between Scots and Pictish ladies last month, to his knowledge, that also had ceased.

He'd not bedded a woman in weeks. No woman but the princess had damn well *enticed* him in weeks, but he wasn't going to dwell on that. When they finally left Fotla, that malady would pass. It had to.

Self-gratification was the only relief, but the sleeping arrangements in the stronghold precluded even that fleeting respite.

God, he was going mad.

"MacKinnon." Ross accompanied his word with a punch to his shoulder. "Wake up, man. Change of plan."

Ewan grunted, irked Ross had noticed his lapse in attention. The warriors were heading off the path that led to Fotla-eviot and back into the forest. He swore under his breath. Surely they had searched enough for one day?

Rourke turned back from where he'd been riding behind MacAllister and came to their side. "The prince recalls an ancient ruin somewhere close by and we are to examine it."

The hint of derision in his voice conveyed exactly what he thought of that plan.

Silence descended as they followed the prince through the forest. After a while the trees thinned, and they came into a small glade, dominated by a circular stone structure in the center.

Unaccountably, a shudder inched through him as they approached. He didn't believe in pagan things, but he could well believe this place had once welcomed heathen worship.

They dismounted, and with strange reluctance, he followed the others. The structure was large, but its roof was long gone, and one wall had fallen into disrepair with great chunks of snow covered stone scattered on the ground. Stone steps, set into another wall, led upstairs. It did not look especially stable.

MacAllister came over. He didn't appear pleased by the diversion. "The Picts' ancestors used this as a place of sacrifice to their gods. Leave no stone unturned."

Ewan frowned. So it had been used in the past for pagan rites. He wasn't certain how he felt at having been right.

The Fotla prince, with Drest by his side, directed Scots and Picts to designated areas. Ewan and Ross went through an arch that led to another chamber, where part of the wall had tumbled to the ground.

Ewan scanned the pristine snow outside. No, wait. He narrowed his eyes. Wolf prints marred the surface. Did the beasts use this place for shelter?

"The snow inside has been brushed over." Ross swept a glance across the chamber and Ewan followed his gaze. Beside the two sets of boot prints from him and Ross, was a trail of sullied snow. A hasty, and incompetent, attempt at camouflage.

They looked at each other, suspicion heavy in the air.

"It last snowed five days ago." Ewan didn't need to say any more. Ross understood only too well. Whoever had left that trail, had been here during the last few days. And if it was the one they were searching for, it meant the assassin hadn't left Fotla after attacking Constantine last month.

In a grim silence, they got to work, raking through the snow. Something glinted. He crouched and hooked something small from beneath a fallen chunk of stone.

It was a metal ferrule, used to strengthen the end of a spear and prevent it from splitting. He'd seen countless in his time, but this was not from a Scots' weapon. Frowning, he stood, and Ross came to his side. "That doesn't look Pict made."

It didn't look Northumbrian made, either.

Ross took the ferrule from him and examined it. Unlike the ones they used, this was closed and welded. "Could be Norse," Ross said. "Nothing else there?"

Stuart MacGregor appeared in the archway. "They've found something outside."

He and Ross followed Stuart outside. They trudged around the north side of the building and saw the rest of the party standing some distance away, just in front of a single, imposing standing stone, surrounding a dark mass splashed on the white snow.

It was a body.

There wasn't much left of the victim. Whatever the wolves had left behind, had been picked clean by eagles and crows, leaving only bleached bones, scattered over the spilled blood.

"Where are his clothes?" Stuart's voice was grim.

"Gone." MacAllister's voice was expressionless. "Nothing remains that might help identify the man's origin."

Ross stepped forward. "MacKinnon found this." He handed MacAllister the ferrule, and a swift frown marred the older man's brow before he once again assumed his normal impenetrable façade.

In silence, he handed it to Drest who passed it to his prince, who scrutinized it in silence for several long seconds. Finally, he spoke.

"Viking made." The prince returned it to Drest. "What say you?"

Drest examined the ferrule from every possible angle. "Viking," he confirmed, handing it back.

"It appears we have found not only the remains of the assassin, but proof of his origins."

"It does, my lord." Drest turned to MacAllister. "Are you in agreement, as the agent for your king?"

"This glade and the ruin must be thoroughly searched. Might I take possession of the ferrule, my lord?" MacAllister gave the prince a stiff bow.

"Certainly." The prince's voice was cold as he gave it to MacAllister before turning to Drest. "Have our men search every inch of ground. There will be no cause for the Dal Riadan king to doubt our integrity in this matter."

IT WAS dark by the time they arrived back at Fotla-eviot and Ewan and the others, both Scot and Pict, gathered before the fire in the great hall. News of the find had traveled fast, and excitement throbbed in the air as many of the Pictish court mingled with the search party.

So buoyant was the mood, they had been invited to join the feast again this eve.

Except what would MacAlpin say? The king had been certain the assassin was Northumbrian, yet the discovery of the ferrule pointed to the Norse. What were they missing?

"I understand congratulations are in order, MacKinnon."

He swung about and stared, stupidly, at the vision of Briana. The translucent veil that draped over her vibrant hair was the same shade of spring green as her gown, which sparkled in the candlelight with embroidered silver leaves.

Hastily, he offered her a bow, as he gathered his scattered wits.

"My lady." He straightened and although he knew he should walk away and not look back, he couldn't help but return her smile. "It would seem so."

She handed him a goblet of wine. A welcome upgrade to the

mead that had been supplied to them upon returning to the stronghold. It would be churlish to refuse.

"I heard the evidence was incontrovertible." She raised her eyebrows, as she took a sip from her own goblet.

"Aye." He should not voice his suspicions, least of all to the Princess of Fotla. Especially since he remained under oath not to disclose his king's conviction on the origin of the would-be assassin. "A Norse ferrule."

"And the remains of a body."

While such things would never be discussed with ladies in the Dal Riadan court, clearly, such topics did not distress Briana. He discarded the lingering sense of needing to censor his words and it wasn't hard. Hell, he enjoyed her uninhibited conversation. More than he should.

"Not enough remained to identify anything."

"I imagine not." She hesitated, pressing her lips together and he could not drag his fascinated gaze away. "Are you convinced he was a Viking?"

He exhaled a harsh breath. "We found no other weapons. Yet it was an arrow that injured Constantine."

"Indeed." She gazed into her wine. He tried not to notice the delicate profile of her jaw or the way a long curl had escaped her braid and brushed the curve of her cheek. His fingers itched to touch that curl and allow its silky length to slide across his palm.

He took a long swallow of wine, but it didn't help curb his unruly thoughts. Or cool the burn that had replaced the ice in his veins.

"It is just," once again she hesitated and although he didn't know her well, he knew enough that she didn't usually find it hard to say something.

"What?"

She sighed and shook her head. "You will find it foolish, I'm sure."

"Try me."

"It is said that place is haunted by the tortured souls of our ancestors."

He recalled the uncanny sensation that had crawled over him as they'd approached the structure. "I don't find that foolish."

She tilted her head. "Does your religion believe in shades, Ewan?"

He didn't wish to discuss his religion, "Do you believe it's haunted, my lady?"

"Perhaps." She cast a swift glance to her side, as though ensuring they could not be overheard. "It's not a place our people venture. Which would make it quite a convenient shelter for a spy, would it not? If only it was not open to the elements."

"Aye." It didn't add up. Although just because they'd found part of a weapon and a body didn't mean the assassin had stayed in the place. And then her words fully penetrated. "You've been there yourself?"

She blinked, as though he had caught her out, but that hadn't been his intention. After all, it was a ruin, and most ruins did not possess a roof.

"I have." There was a dignified note in her voice. Did she expect him to condemn her for it? But why would it matter? As far as he was aware it wasn't a forbidden place. "In the past."

"Then we are in agreement. I doubt the assassin used those ruins as his base. It's more likely he was on the run as we closed in on him and was attempting to hide evidence in case he was caught."

"Then where is his bow?"

"We didn't find it."

She was silent for a moment, her face averted as she frowned across the hall. He took advantage of her distraction to admire her regal profile once again. After tonight, he doubted there would be another chance.

And thank God for that. Because the more time he spent with her, the harder it was to remember his vow to keep his distance.

And he had to keep his distance from her. Not because he wanted to.

But because he had to.

For her.

CHAPTER 8

*I*nsubstantial glints of silvery light threaded through the forest, throwing the winter branches into sharp relief against the luminous full moon above. Briana stood in a small glade, her heartbeat echoing in her ears, yet she knew, at an instinctive level she couldn't explain, that this was nothing more than a dream.

A dream... or a vision?

An eerie howl rent the air, shivering through the snow shrouded trees as it was joined by numerous others. Wolves. But it was not the threat of the pack that caused the tightness in her throat or ethereal sense of alarm that whispered across her skin.

I've been here before. And every time she awoke, the details faded and died before she could fully grasp them.

A pair of glowing orange eyes watched her from the depths of the forest and her heart slammed against her chest as a wild hope engulfed her.

"Shadow," she whispered. It had been so long since she had last seen the magnificent alpha. And although this was not in the waking world, it had to mean something. But what reason could Bride have for sending him to her in this vision?

The forest vanished, and the full moon hung low in the sky, a magnificent shimmering disk that seemed to balance on the far horizon. She caught her breath at the stark silhouette of the giant wolf, as he raised his mighty head and answered his pack.

From nowhere, an arrow whipped by, so close she felt the breath of its passing across her cheek. She swung around as it thudded into the ancient, weathered, standing stone behind her, and its long swan fletchings quivered at the impact.

Alarm streaked through her. Goddess, that was close. Was this a sign that her life was in danger? Her hand shook as she reached out but before she could touch the shaft, the massive stone splintered in half with a soul wrenching roar and crashed to the ground.

Briana gasped awake, clutching her bed furs to her throat. The embers from the fire threw a flickering red glow around the chamber and for a heartbeat, her mind sank into the easy familiarity.

Fading. *Fading...*

A dark fog hovered around the edges of her vision, tempting her to once again taste oblivion. How easy it would be...

No. She would not forget again. How many times had this vision plagued her, only to retreat as soon as she opened her eyes? Carefully, so as not to wake Nairne, she sat up. *Focus.*

The forest. The moon.

Shadow. The wolf she had told no one of.

And the arrow that had so very nearly struck her.

A shiver trickled over her arms as the bone shaking crack that had awoken her once again reverberated through her. Now her mind had cleared, she saw the truth. The arrow had not been intended for her. It had struck the sacred stone with intent.

But why? What was Bride trying to show her?

Artair hailed the discovery of the Viking ferrule as conclusive proof as to the origin of the would-be assassin, and the king concurred, even though the Dal Riadan prince had been shot with an arrow. They both wanted the Scots to leave Fotla as swiftly as possible and now the quest was over, there was nothing to keep the Dal Riadans from their homeland.

Inevitably, Ewan's face materialized in the darkness before her. He had seemed reluctant to embrace the evidence as definitive, and it had fanned her own intangible concerns.

Last night she'd suspected it was simply because, deep inside, in a place she would never admit existed, she didn't want him to leave. But this vision from her goddess changed everything.

Stealthily, she slipped from the bed. For weeks she had feared Bride had turned her back on her, but it wasn't true. Bride had been sharing this vision since the day Mae had left. The question was, why had she been unable to remember it until now?

There had to be a reason, and surely the answer would be found in the haunted glade where her ancestors had once worshipped.

The same glade that had been in her vision.

Quickly, she dressed, before pulling on her sturdy boots and swinging a thick cloak around her shoulders. Her mamma would be furious if she ever discovered how many times Briana had escaped her ladies and guards over the years to enjoy a few stolen moments of solitude, away from the palace walls.

In the sacred glade, with its single standing stone.

But the queen would never discover her secret. It was her only fleeting glimpse of freedom here in Fotla-eviot, and she would never jeopardize it by being anything less than vigilant.

Nairne still blissfully slept as Briana closed the door to her bedchamber and made her way across the antechamber, where, thankfully, her servants had not yet awoken.

Heart pounding, she eased the door open a crack. The guard appointed to patrol this section of the palace was not in sight, so she slipped into the passage, just as a flickering light appeared.

He was returning. She hugged the shadows of the wall and

narrowed her eyes, but she wasn't mistaken. It was Drest, a great fur slung across his shoulders to ward off the chill.

Why had Artair chosen him to undertake such a task? Drest wasn't only one of their finest warriors. He was second in command, after Artair himself, and assuming such duties were scarcely within his purview.

Clearly, her brother and father were convinced only Drest could adequately guard her while the Scots remained in Fotlaeviot.

Stealthily, she made her way in the opposite direction. The door that led to a concealed passageway set between the palace's inner and outer walls was not far, and she soon reached the recess and opened the lock with the key that hung from her girdle.

Drest came perilously close to where she was hiding, and she held her breath until he swung about, and returned the way he had come. Carefully, she took the closest torch from its sconce and slipped into the stairwell, before closing and locking the door behind her.

The spiral staircase led downwards, a stone tunnel, much like any other staircase that graced every palace and stronghold in Pictland, and where a single false step could have one plunging to their death.

She pushed that terrifying possibility to the back of her mind as her fingers searched out every crevice and fissure in the wall as she descended the stairs. She wouldn't think of that now. Not ever. It did no good to fall into a vortex of fear, when there was nothing she could do about it.

When she reached the foot of the stairs, she quickly unlocked the gate of latticed iron bars which guarded the narrow passageway that led to the western wall of the palace. One more door, and she would breathe fresh air once again.

Outside, she secured the torch to a sconce before locking the door. Guards were scarce on this side of the palace and she pulled her hood over her head and hastened towards the forest edge. Dawn glimmered on the far horizon and there was enough light from the moon to guide her way through the hidden, but familiar, paths between the trees and it wasn't long before she reached the glade.

The snow was churned into a muddy slush by the previous day's activities, but it was no distraction from what remained of the victim lying before the sacred stone. She took a deep breath and walked across the glade until she stood by the side of the bloodied mess.

Goddess. She swallowed and willed her stomach to remain still. It was hard to tell it had ever been a man. Not only had the bones been picked clean, but there were signs of them having been gnawed. And more than one was missing.

Slowly, she went over to the standing stone and pressed her palm against its carved face. She closed her eyes and calmed her mind.

Great goddess, what do you wish me to see?

"Briana." The shocked voice pierced through the early morning air, and she gasped, spinning around. Ewan MacKinnon stood by the edge of the glade, gazing at her as though she were a fae apparition. "Why are you here?"

He glanced around, clearly searching for her guard. She tried not to notice how splendid he looked in his foreign plaid, with his glorious hair tousled in the fresh breeze, and snow laden trees framing him to perfection.

She also tried to banish how the sound of her name on his tongue caused a delightfully illicit caress across her skin.

Naturally, she failed. On both counts. She didn't know why she even tried anymore.

"I could ask the same of you, MacKinnon."

He stepped closer, a frown wreathing his face. It was surely not right that he looked so delectable no matter his countenance.

"I'm not a princess of Fotla."

A prickle of irritation pierced her rosy hue of him. "You mean you are not a woman."

He paused in front of her. So close, his scent of leather and pine tinged the frosty air. How annoying that it was so enticing.

"Aye. It's not safe for a woman to be out alone when enemies lurk all around."

"Scots, you mean?"

"Norse," he corrected. Had her barb irked him? She hoped so. "Scots and Picts are allies now."

More than one sharp retort hovered on her tongue, but she drew in a long breath, instead. Whatever his king had done, she preferred to imagine Ewan MacKinnon was not party to any of it.

A foolish wish, of course. But it did not matter. When the envoys her mamma had sent to the Queen of Ce returned, she would likely be betrothed to Talargan and a new path in her life would open.

She didn't want to spend what little time she had left with Ewan in reminding him of how despicable she found MacAlpin.

"I wanted to see the evidence for myself." Without quite meaning to, she glanced at the remains marring the snow. "Truly, that could have been anyone."

"This is not a sight for you, Briana." Once again, he glanced around, and once again she was inexcusably thrilled at how exotic he made her name sound. "Where is your guard?"

She should tell him they were beyond the tree line, poised to act at her slightest command. It was madness to let him know she was here, alone, and yet the thought of lying to him didn't appeal.

"It's not the first time I've been here alone. I am quite safe."

"I disagree. We don't know if the assassin worked alone. His compatriots might still be in Fotla."

Curse it. She hadn't thought of that. But she wasn't going to let MacKinnon know. "My goddess would not lead me here if it were unsafe."

His gaze sharpened, the frigid air causing his blue eyes to glitter with silver flecks. Why did she imagine such fanciful things, whenever he was near?

"Your goddess led you here?" He sounded mystified. "For what purpose?"

She sent me a vision. But she wouldn't tell him that. Although her status as a chosen one of Bride was well known among her people, there were only a few in whom she confided what the goddess shared with her.

Besides, Ewan didn't believe in her goddess. She didn't want to see the skepticism in his eyes.

But she could still tell him the truth, regardless.

"I'm not certain. I thought perhaps..." Her voice trailed away. In her bedchamber, it had seemed so logical that Bride wanted her to discover something that neither Pict nor Scot had found. Yet now she was here, how foolish that sounded. But Ewan was still waiting for her to continue. "Something does not sit right with me, that's all."

"It's a pity your goddess can't tell you who exactly we've been searching for." There was a faint smile on his face, but his tone was not unkind.

She sighed. "Alas, that is not how this works."

He was silent as he contemplated the ruin. She should take the opportunity to end this encounter but instead she could do nothing but gaze at his averted face. How she longed to trace her fingers along his strong jaw. Wind her arms around his broad shoulders and taste his lips upon hers...

"My lady?"

His questioning tone pulled her from her fantasy as readily as if iced snow had been thrown at her head. Goddess, what had he just asked her? Heat burned her cheeks and there was nothing she could do to prevent it.

"What?"

His gaze roved over her face as though fascinated. If he dared to mention her discomfiture she would leave *directly*.

"I merely asked why your people believe this place to be haunted."

Oh. Yes, of course he had. His thoughts hadn't traveled along the same path as her own. And thank all the gods for that.

She made much of brushing nonexistent snowflakes from her cloak, so she didn't have to look at him. "It is said that a thousand years ago our ancestors would offer blood sacrifice to the gods in this glade."

He cocked his head. "I grant you these ruins are old, but a thousand years?"

"The structure was built later, of course. But the sacred standing stone has always been here. That's why our ancestors chose this place. The power of the gods runs deep here."

Deeper even than within the circle of stones closer to the palace. Where, but a stone's throw away from the circle, the followers of the new religion had built their church more than one hundred years ago.

"And when the Picts stopped sacrificing their enemies on the altar of their gods, they abandoned this place?"

He was smiling, but again she didn't feel he was mocking her. Indeed, she got the distinct impression he found it quite intriguing.

Perhaps she was wrong. But there was something magical, being alone here with him, with only whispers from the past to act as intangible chaperones.

"For whatever reason, the chosen ones no longer came here. I cannot tell you why. Only that in living memory of the eldest of our people, tortured souls are said to haunt this glade." She paused and pressed her hand against the face of the stone. "But I've always drawn great comfort from being here."

He took another step closer, all but touching her as he looked over her shoulder at the stone. Her heart skittered and breath caught in her throat, and it took all her willpower not to turn around and fall into his arms.

Briefly, she squeezed her eyes shut. Madness. Yet she would not exchange this torturous moment for anything.

"We have standing stones carved with intricate symbols in Dal Riada, too." There was a note of awe in his voice, and she risked shooting him a glance. He was gazing at the stone, and not with the disdain of an unbeliever. "But their meaning has been long forgotten."

It was hard to maintain her composure, let alone clear her mind when tendrils of heat from his body coiled around her like ribbons of exotic velvet. It was nothing but her imagination, she knew that, but regardless, her flesh tingled with a seductive warmth she could not deny.

"This is the great cauldron of Cailleach." Her voice was husky as she traced a finger over the carved spirals on the stone. "When the mighty sea spins, it signifies the beginning of her reign."

"Cailleach. Your goddess of winter?"

"She is so much more than that." Her voice dropped to a reverential whisper. "She is the true Mother Goddess who created our land at the beginning of time. Everything we are and everything we have comes from her."

"A powerful goddess, indeed. Are you certain you're not a chosen one of Cailleach, and not Bride?"

She knew he was only jesting, but his words pierced through her like a sharpened blade, and she swung around to face him.

"Hush." Her tone was urgent and as she tipped her head back, her hood slipped onto her shoulders. "Do not say such things." Especially here, where the presence of the greatest goddess of them all was embedded into the frozen earth beneath their feet. "It is blasphemy."

He didn't answer, but his intense blue gaze roved over her face as though memorizing every feature. Lightning streaked through her, hot and white, and she couldn't have moved if her very life depended on it.

"Briana." His whisper was a molten caress against her skin and melted her paralysis. Before she could stop herself, she pressed her hand against the plaid slung across his chest. The wool was too thick for her to feel his heartbeat, yet it echoed in her ears and through her blood, just the same.

Or perhaps it was her own heart that hammered with such erratic disregard.

He gave a strangled groan, even though surely he could scarcely feel her gentle touch, and it was the most intoxicating sound she'd ever heard. Uncaring of the impropriety, she trailed her fingers over his jaw. His early morning stubble rasped across her fingertips sending shimmers of pleasure across her entire hand, and it was breathtaking.

He cupped her face, mirroring her action and she hitched in a shallow gasp. He lowered his head, and the rest of the world faded until all she could see was him.

For an unbearable eternity time stood still as he paused, and she had the terrible certainty he would pull back and shatter this moment forever. But before she could even unscramble her thoughts, his lips captured hers.

It was a featherlight touch, yet it ignited her senses with the power of a forest fire. She pressed closer, threading her fingers through his hair and his groan vibrated across her sensitized lips, sending ripples of need spinning through her.

He wound his arm around her, an implacable iron band that held her so tightly she could scarcely breathe. Her eyes fluttered shut and his tongue teased her parted lips before pushing inside.

A subtle hint of sage teased her senses and desire licked through her, hot and liquid, pooling between her thighs. She tangled her tongue with his and gasped inside his mouth when he wrapped her plait around his fist. It was barbaric and quite shocking, yet illicit prickles of pleasure raced over her head in delightful response.

He tore his mouth free and panted in her face. "I've thought of no one but you since the day we met." His voice was harsh, as though he confessed to a great sin. "What enchantment have you spun about me, my sweet Briana?"

His endearment should mean nothing, yet the evocative words took on a mystical significance when uttered in his beguiling accent. Here, in the sacred glade that had been so defiled, was the last place where she should allow such liberties. And yet somehow she could imagine no more perfect surroundings to whisper such scandalous confessions.

"I'm not the one weaving spells, Ewan. You have haunted my mind most grievously since you entered our kingdom."

He grinned, his dimple flashing, and her heart lurched. She shouldn't allow him to affect her so but was powerless to resist beneath his easy charm. But she was not blinded by his pretty words. She was aware of his reputation, and this was for only a few fleeting moments out of time. She could enjoy this, knowing it would never lead anywhere.

Her heart was safe because she willed it so.

"Why did we waste so much time avoiding each other, when we could have enjoyed moments like this?" He trailed a finger along her face, and she couldn't suppress a shiver of pleasure. Despite how she craved his touch she couldn't silence the tiny voice in the back of her mind that demanded she should stop this instantly. It was improper, not least because of her status. But the Scots would likely leave the following day, or perhaps even later today, now they had a culprit to blame, and she would never see Ewan again.

It was not as though she was yet betrothed to the Prince of Ce. This might well be the last time she experienced a fleeting taste of passion, and who better to share that with than a man she was not committed to spend the rest of her life with?

"At least we shall not part as enemies."

"You were never my enemy." He kissed her again, as though he couldn't help himself. "I shall—"

His body went rigid and his grip on her punishing. Confused, she gazed at him, but he was no longer looking at her. With a swift motion, he thrust her behind his back as he drew his sword.

Heat pounding, she followed his gaze. Scarcely a stone's throw from them, stood a giant wolf, his bared teeth sharp and gleaming in the early morning light, and a maelstrom of relief and alarm tumbled through her.

Shadow.

CHAPTER 9

*T*he wolf stared at them, unblinking, and silently Ewan cursed.

He'd been so focused on Briana that he hadn't seen the wolf's approach. But that was no excuse. Even if there was nothing left worth taking of the victim, the stench of spilled blood would linger far on the air, attracting predators.

He knew that. But the need for vigilance, hell, every sane thought in his head had vanished when he'd lost his mind and touched Briana, and now he'd placed her in danger.

He stepped forward and raised his sword. He'd hunted wolves before and there was usually a pack nearby. His muscles tensed and his grip on his sword tightened, but before he could let out a fearsome yell, in the hope that would be sufficient to send the wolf back into the forest, Briana darted around him.

Raw terror ripped through him. What in the name of God was she doing? He grabbed her arm and hauled her back, and from the corner of his eye saw the wolf pull back its lips and emit a low, rumbling growl that shook the ground beneath his feet.

It was preparing to attack. And Briana, who was far from a fool, appeared oblivious of the danger.

"Release me," she whispered urgently. "It's quite safe. Shadow will not harm us."

Stupefied, he stared at her. Had she just called the wolf *Shadow*?

She pulled her arm free and held out her hands towards the wolf, palms facing the sky. He tightened his grip on his sword, ready to attack at a second's notice, as she moved towards the creature.

The wolf no longer bared its teeth, but its orange eyes glowed with menace before it transferred its focus to Briana. But not only that. It prowled over to her, and not as if it were stalking prey.

Briana whispered something that he could not catch, and the wolf butted its great head against her. She wrapped an arm around its neck and briefly buried her face in its thick, dark gray fur before once again straightening.

For a seeming endless moment, she stared into the wolf's eyes. An eerie shudder inched along his spine. Were they communicating? Was this a pagan ritual?

He flexed his fingers around the hilt and the wolf shot him a piercing glance before returning its attention to Briana.

It was almost as though the creature had *warned him*.

Without a word, Briana stepped back, and the wolf retreated to the tree line where it proceeded to throw back its head and emit a blood-curdling howl before it vanished into the forest.

He exhaled a harsh breath, as he scanned the trees for any sign of more wolves. But the forest was quiet. Too quiet?

"Thank you." Briana's soft voice, and the touch of her hand upon his arm tore him from his jagged thoughts. He raked his gaze over her and despite what had just occurred, need once again blazed through his blood.

He battled it down. He should never have touched her, let alone kissed her, and he sucked in another calming breath. And finally noticed that her eyes glimmered with unshed tears.

"Christ." Guilt speared through him, and he cradled her face with one hand, tenderly caressing her cheek with his thumb. "Are you injured?"

"No." She gave a smile, but it seemed heartbreakingly sad. "I simply fear this is the last time I shall ever see Shadow again. He came to say goodbye."

A wolf came to say goodbye. He couldn't wrap his mind around such a concept. And yet it had just unfolded before his eyes.

There were too many questions thundering around his head to make sense of anything. "How?"

She didn't ask him what he meant, for which he was thankful. He had no answer for her.

"I was twelve when I found Shadow, here by the sacred stone. He was but a pup and had been injured by a golden eagle. Truly, it's a miracle he escaped the eagle's clutches at all."

"Aye." That was for sure. "You nursed him back to health?"

"I took him back to the palace to tend to his injuries. No one knew I kept him in my bedchamber overnight. It would have been considered most… unseemly."

He could imagine. And then something occurred to him. "Is Shadow the reason why you favor wolves in your embroidery?"

She gazed at him, clearly shocked he had noticed such a thing about her gowns. "Yes," she breathed. "I know it's foolish, but I feel as though it's a secret link between us. No one but you has ever seen Shadow before, or guessed why I love the image of the wolf so."

Barely aware of what he was doing, he grasped her plait before letting the silken rope slide across his palm. It was distractingly arousing, but that didn't stop him from wrapping it around his fist the way he had before the appearance of the wolf.

It was hard to concentrate when all he wanted to do was push her up against the standing stone and kiss her until she forgot about everything but him. Yet despite the hot lust that thudded through his blood, making a mockery of his pledge to keep her at a safe distance, her wolf story intrigued him.

"What happened to Shadow?" His gaze lingered on her lush lips and his cock stirred at the vision of her taking him into her mouth. God. He swallowed a groan and forced himself to focus on what she was saying, instead of fantasies that had no chance of coming true.

"I had no idea where his pack might be, so I brought him back here, and waited."

"You waited?" Had he misunderstood? "For the she-wolf?"

"I couldn't leave him, could I? He was vulnerable and unprotected. Thankfully, she had picked up his scent from the previous day and was already at the forest's edge."

"She could have killed you for touching her pup."

"But she didn't. She knew I had saved him."

He was about to disagree, before thinking better of it. "I've heard wolves are less threatening towards women." Not that he had any evidence of it. Until now.

"It was almost a year before I saw him again. He was hunting with his siblings, but he recognized me instantly."

Despite a thread of unease that such a connection with a wild wolf bordered on witchcraft, his fascination was too great to deny. "He approached you?"

"Yes. As the years passed, this became our meeting place." She gave a soft smile that caused a pain to twist deep in his chest. "He grew into a fine leader. On the day I wed, the forest echoed with the howls of the wolves. I thought Shadow and his pack were celebrating but I grew to believe he was simply wiser than a foolish sixteen-year-old girl."

Had her marriage been unhappy? He knew nothing of her past, save that she was a widow. So many marriages were nothing more than political alliances, yet knowing Briana had been caught in one grieved him, nevertheless.

"I'm sorry," he whispered, and he didn't know if he was

speaking of her marriage, or that she believed she would never see her wolf again, or the fact that this was all they could ever share.

"Alas." She tilted her head, so her cheek caressed his fist, still grasped around her hair. "I cannot blame the Scots for any of it. Rest assured I would if I could."

"I thought we had agreed we weren't enemies."

"Yet you are but one Scot, Ewan."

Regret pierced him that she thought so little of his people. Even though he couldn't blame her for it. "Not all Scots are untrustworthy, my lady."

"Perhaps…" she hesitated, then took a quick breath. "Perhaps it's just as well we only have this fleeting moment together. This way, our illusions will forever remain intact."

"Illusions?" Gently, he tugged on her hair. "I offer you no illusion, Briana. This is who I am."

A man who never offered more than a brief affair, with a woman who knew the rules of such illicit assignations. Aye, that was him. Always had been, always would be. Except when it came to her, he couldn't even offer her that.

"I know who you are."

Was it his imagination that a hint of sadness threaded through her voice? Hell, what was the matter with him? She didn't know anything about him, save for what he showed the world.

He knew what he was. And the last thing he wanted was for Briana to discover the sordid truth that permeated his blackened soul.

The bitter wind flayed his exposed skin and tendrils of Briana's hair whipped against her cheek. He should offer to escort her back to the stronghold, but that would mean ending this surreal encounter.

His lust for her burned as hot as ever, hotter, since she no longer looked upon him with eyes of ice. Would this obsession fade when he left Fotla, secure in the knowledge that this time he would never return?

He wanted to think so. But a dark place inside him doubted it.

"Do any of us truly know another?" He loosened his grip on her hair and cradled her jaw. Frustration that this was all there could be between them thudded through his veins, but it was infinitely better than the alternative.

Of doing the right thing and walking away.

"Perhaps not." Her whisper warmed his lips with forbidden promises that would never come to pass. "We all have secrets we keep from the world."

"I cannot imagine you possess a dark secret like that, Briana."

"What of you?" she countered. "Are there terrible things in your past that I would discover, if we had more time together?"

He couldn't help a grim smile. "Define what you would consider terrible."

"Perhaps you also are tainted by the blood of MacAlpin."

His smile froze, and it had nothing to do with the weather. His heritage was not a great secret, but it was never spoken of.

It had always been that way, since before he was born.

He couldn't break that silence, even for Briana. But at least he could tell her the truth in this.

"I'm not a son of MacAlpin."

"That is good to know." She smiled and involuntarily, his fingers tightened around her face. "I cannot imagine a worse sire for anyone."

"You need not imagine that on my account."

"What of your father, Ewan? Is he a great warrior like you?" Despite the faint hint of mockery in her voice, she was still smiling, but as much as her smile warmed him, he could not return it.

"He died in the battle of '39."

Her smile vanished and concern filled her eyes. "I'm sorry. I should not have jested about such things. We Picts also suffered heavily in that battle against the Vikings."

"You've nothing to be sorry for. But to answer your question, aye. He was a great warrior. I'm proud to be his son."

"I'm sure he was." Her voice was soft and her gaze unwavering. "Do you have any brothers or sisters?"

A dull ache gripped his heart as the memory of his younger brother filled his mind. He hadn't spoken of Gareth in years. It hurt too damn much. But there was no malice in Briana's question. Why would there be? She didn't know the truth.

She never would.

"A younger half-brother. He died when he was but seven years old."

"Goddess," she breathed. "Forgive me, Ewan. I hope I'm not usually so thoughtless."

He sighed heavily. The topic of their conversation was unconventional, but in an odd way that he couldn't explain, he was glad she knew that Gareth had once existed. Sometimes he had the crazed notion that his mischievous little half-brother had lived only inside his own head.

"You're not thoughtless. How could you know? There's nothing to forgive."

"You are most magnanimous. I believe it is your turn to ask me a question now, to help balance the scales."

Despite the lingering specter of his half-brother, and the fact his childhood nightmare had so recently returned, amusement flared. "I think my questions are best left unasked, my lady."

"Ah, I see. Perhaps you are right. Some things are best left to the imagination."

"If our mission was not completed here, rest assured I should do all in my power to convince you otherwise. There are some things that far exceed the limits of imagination."

"I have not found it so. Perhaps my secret dreams are too unrealistic to achieve for mere mortals."

"Yet I would still strive to prove you wrong."

She shook her head, but a smile lingered on her beautiful lips. "You are most persistent. Does your charm ever fail you?"

"If the lady is willing, never."

"And what if the lady loses her heart?"

"Hearts are never involved, Briana. That would lead only to disaster."

"Yet hearts are not always so easily commanded. Haven't you ever been in danger of losing yours, with one of your many conquests?"

Strangely, he wasn't certain he liked her casual assumption that he had a string of conquests in his past. Even though it was true.

At least the answer to her question was easy enough. "I have not."

Until now.

But Briana wasn't a conquest, and never would be. Why, then, could he not just shut his mouth and ensure her safe return to the stronghold?

"Not even when you were young and carefree?" There was a half-smile on her face, as though she expected him to confess to a great secret.

But he had no secret romances in his past. "Never."

"How fortunate for you. Tell me, does this extend to your wife, also?"

It wasn't the first time he'd been asked if he were wed. But it was the first time he sensed a hint of mild reproof in the words.

"I am not blessed with a bride, my lady." And with her barely disguised condemnation still ringing in his ears, he couldn't help himself. "If I were, I would not pursue such intrigues."

Her eyes widened in clear surprise. "Then you would be extraordinary, indeed."

"Not all warriors betray the trust of their wives."

She sighed. "I fear this is the third time I've unintentionally offended you this morn, Ewan. I cannot fathom why my tongue is so unruly in your presence."

His gut clenched as he recalled the sensual glide of her tongue inside his mouth, and his fingers tensed against her soft cheek as he struggled to recollect what they were talking about.

Why in the name of God was he still touching her? Yet he couldn't bring himself to break the contact.

"Like you, I'm not easily offended." His voice was hoarse with repressed need. He hoped she hadn't noticed. But it took everything he possessed not to press his mouth against hers and once again plunder her welcoming heat.

"For which I'm most gratified." She smiled at him and it all but unraveled his defenses. "I should be grieved if you remembered me only with distaste."

Despite the ravenous lust that burned his blood, he couldn't help but laugh. "Distaste is the last thing I shall feel whenever I think of you."

"How fortunate that within a week or so of leaving the Kingdom of Fotla our duties will ensure this interlude will fade until it's nothing more than a half-forgotten dream."

"Only a week?" There was a mocking note in his voice, as he tried to ignore the irrational sting her remark had caused. And the uncomfortable notion that he feared it would take him a great deal longer to banish *her* from his mind. "Is that how soon you'll forget me?"

"Marriage tends to occupy one's mind. Besides, it wouldn't be seemly for a bride to be thinking of another man, would it?"

Her words punched him hard in the chest, driving the air from his lungs. She was to be wed? Yet why was it such a shock?

She was young and to his knowledge had been widowed for a year or more. Two excellent reasons why any woman would be looking to remarry and on top of that, Briana was a princess and therefore of political significance.

And yet the possibility she was betrothed had never even

crossed his mind. Maybe that was the reason she'd been so aloof to him earlier. But it certainly hadn't stopped her from engaging with his compatriots.

He drew in a ragged breath. There was no reason why her revelation should affect him, let alone so keenly. Hell, he had no idea why the thought of her marrying another man had shaken him at all. And she was still waiting for his response.

"I wish you well, my lady." With more reluctance than he'd ever admit, he dropped his hand from her cheek. "Your groom is a fortunate man, indeed."

A delicate rose highlighted her cheekbones, and he couldn't tear his mesmerized gaze away.

"I thank you. The betrothal is not yet formalized, but I'm certain before Bride subdues the great Cailleach, I shall be wed to the Prince of Ce."

An icy wind whipped through the glade, bringing a smattering of snowflakes in its wake. Frowning, he glanced at the sky, but it was impossible to tell whether another snowstorm was imminent.

But that was inconsequential. The chill reminded him of where they were. Of whom he was with. And the possible consequences should they be discovered.

Reluctance clawed through him, but he could no longer deny that the sun had risen and if they were seen returning to the stronghold together, rumors would swirl.

He would not risk Briana's reputation any further. Or place her future marriage in jeopardy. Was it something she even wanted?

An irrelevant question. If her king had commanded it, she could do nothing but obey.

He managed to summon up a smile and offered her a half-bow. "Allow me to accompany you back to the palace, my lady."

With luck, later today he would leave Fotla forever. And with

Briana safely wed in Ce, at least there was no chance of him inadvertently destroying her with the curse that tainted his blood.

CHAPTER 10

*W*hen Ewan arrived back at Fotla-eviot, his countrymen were already in the courtyard. Were they leaving already? Relief thudded through him that Briana had declined his offer to accompany her back to the stronghold. Instead, he had stealthily followed her at a distance, to ensure her safety, as she had made her own way back along a different path. One that had been significantly shorter than the one he'd taken to the glade earlier.

Once he'd ensured she was back inside, he'd circled around, just in case there were any eyes spying from the Picts' stronghold and returned the way he had come.

Ross came to meet him. "Where the hell have you been?" He kept his voice low but there was no mistaking his irritation. "MacAllister wishes to speak with us alone."

He grunted. Trust MacAllister to notice he had been missing this morning. Thank God he hadn't insisted on delivering Briana to the stronghold walls himself. There was no doubt that the king's man would somehow have borne witness to it.

"What about?" he said, as they made their way to where the older man stood with Rourke by his side.

"How should I know?" Ross still sounded irked, and Ewan slung his arm around his friend's shoulders in a show of silent support. By virtue of his rank, Ross should have been leading this mission, but the king's man's status superseded all but MacAlpin himself.

When they halted by the side of Rourke, who had a familiar, disgruntled expression on his face, MacAllister gave Ewan an assessing glance. Unease flickered through him, and he dropped his arm from Ross' shoulder. He wasn't sure what it was, but there were times when he had the uncanny sensation that MacAllister could see straight into his head.

Without a word, MacAllister indicated the four of them should walk on and when there was a sufficient distance between themselves and the rest of their compatriots he paused and turned to face them.

Ewan bit back his impatience. This was dramatic, even for MacAllister. Why make such a show of telling them that their mission in Fotla was now completed?

"We have a situation," he said. "The Picts appear to believe the assassin was a Norse."

"The Norse ferrule we discovered by the pagan stone is the only evidence of a foreign presence we unearthed," Ross said.

"Aye, that was interesting," MacAllister said. "An unexpected development, indeed."

Maybe now Ewan's question would be answered. "Why is our liege so certain the assassin was Northumbrian?"

Instead of answering, MacAllister nodded at Rourke, whose glower intensified.

"The arrow pulled from Constantine is Northumbrian." He sounded surly. "The fletchings were swan feathers which is their specialty. The Picts use goose feathers while the Norse favor those of the white-tailed eagle."

Ewan glared at him. "You knew why we were searching for a Northumbrian all along?"

"I was not aware you'd been left in ignorance of this." Rourke's voice was harsh, and before Ewan could take issue with that, MacAllister raised his hand.

"It was the king's wish this information was not made public. We had hoped to discover more about the Northumbrian plot, but it seems our Pictish hosts may have their own agenda."

"You suspect the Picts left the Norse ferrule in the glade to put us off the scent?" Ross sounded skeptical. "Why would they put the alliance at risk?"

Ewan agreed. It did not add up, and he still had the disquieting notion that MacAllister was hiding something. "Are you suggesting the Picts have allied with the Northumbrians?"

"That's what I need to discover."

"Where does this leave us?" Ewan glanced at Ross before returning his attention to MacAllister. "I take it we're not leaving Fotla yet, after all."

"Not until our objectives have been achieved."

"Our objective being to find who attempted to assassinate the prince." Ross' voice was even, but Ewan knew him too well. His friend was seething.

"Of course," MacAllister said. But the air crackled with mistrust. What was the king's man holding back?

"We need to speak to the King of Fotla," Ross said.

"Indeed. I'm returning to the stronghold now to seek an audience with him and his advisors as quickly as possible."

"I'll accompany you." Ross took a step in MacAllister's direction, but the older man raised his hand.

"There is no need, MacIntosh." He glanced at Ewan. "When their king is ready to see us, you will join me."

With that, he strolled off. Ross expelled a harsh breath and swore roundly. "Have I been demoted without my knowledge?"

Ewan shrugged, equally confounded by MacAllister's parting comment. One thing was certain, though. "At least we know why

MacAllister headed this mission. He was in possession of a singular fact that we were not."

"When I saw the fletchings and told my father of their origin, I was sworn to silence. It didn't occur to me that you and Ross wouldn't be informed of the reason why MacAlpin suspected the Northumbrians."

"What new intrigues are our king and your father brewing now?" It was a rhetorical question from Ross, but Ewan shared the sentiment.

"Whatever it was in Dunadd, I'm sure MacAllister will use this twist to his advantage." Ewan expelled a harsh sigh. "The Fotla king won't be happy to learn the Scots held back vital information. I don't see why there was a need for any concealment."

"That's because you aren't our king." Ross growled the words and Ewan shot him a sharp glance. It was true that the three of them—and Connor MacKenzie, before he had wed his Pictish princess—had always confided in each other more than they would with anyone else. But Ross' comment bordered on outright condemnation of their king and what was more, skated uncomfortably close to his own recent opinion of MacAlpin.

"Aye." Rourke sounded grim. "They are up to something. I was banished from the king's inner sanctum as soon as they had my opinion on the arrow."

Ross grunted. "I'm going for a ride."

It was clear he didn't want company as he marched off towards the stables.

"It wouldn't surprise me," Rourke continued, "if they used this new information to trap Lady Briana in a political marriage."

Ewan's heart slammed against his ribs, and he rounded on Rourke. The very idea that she would be used in such a manner was abhorrent. "What?"

Rourke shrugged, but his expression was dour. "Tell me I'm wrong. You've been here this last year, Ewan. He's working his way through the Pictish kingdoms, capturing their princesses one by one. I'd wager Lady Briana is next."

He wanted to tell Rourke he was wrong but couldn't. From the moment he and his countrymen had been sent into the Kingdom of Ce nine months ago, MacAlpin's intentions had been clear.

Yet it hadn't once crossed his mind that Briana might be in MacAlpin's sights.

"That won't happen." His voice was harsh. "Lady Briana is betrothed to the Prince of Ce."

Or she would be, shortly. And he hoped to God that was enough to save her from MacAlpin's clutches. Who did the king have in mind for her? He was growing perilously short of nobles with the right connections that might snare a king's agreement to such a match for his daughter.

A possibility occurred to him. MacAlpin's half-brother, Donald, had been lately widowed. But he was close to forty if he was a day, and the thought of Briana being shackled to that bastard made his skin crawl.

Goddamn it, he had to warn her. Although how the hell he'd be able to find her to do that, he had no idea.

Frustration tore through him, and he swung around to face the Pict stronghold. And frowned, shielding his eyes against the glaring reflection of the sun against the snow.

Briana and her ladies were in the courtyard, conversing with his countrymen.

Rourke came to his side and followed his gaze. "Maybe the Fotla king needs to announce the betrothal."

Aye. Maybe he did. He ignored the oddly hollow sensation in the center of his chest and made his way to her, the glittering frost crunching beneath his boots.

She caught his gaze and her smile twisted something deep inside. Damn it, there was nothing that could induce him to stand silently while such an ugly future awaited her. If it came to it, he'd spirit her away from Fotla himself, and ensure her safe delivery to the Prince of Ce.

It was better than the alternative. A lifetime in thrall to Donald.

He blanked his mind to the consequences *he* would suffer for such treachery, should it ever be discovered.

"MacKinnon," she greeted him, holding out her hand for him to kiss. Something she had rarely done before and, until recently, only under duress. He swallowed a groan and brushed his lips across her knuckles. Even through her gloves he fancied he could taste her skin. "My ladies and I could not let you all depart Fotla-eviot without wishing you well."

Even the rest of the men were unaware of the change in plans, but since it would become common knowledge all too soon, it was scarcely a secret that needed to be kept.

Besides, he needed to warn her. And he couldn't do that without sharing his suspicions.

But first, he needed to get her alone.

DESPITE THE POSSIBILITY of one of her ladies noticing, Briana couldn't suppress her smile as Ewan clasped her hand, before he relinquished it with clear reluctance. Should she tell him she knew he had followed her through the forest earlier? Even though she knew she had been perfectly safe, his concern had been most charming.

Thank goddess he had returned from wherever he had been. Although she had agreed with her ladies' requests to bid the Scots farewell, there had been only one reason why she'd wanted to accompany them.

For one last encounter with her magnificent, foreign warrior.

His piercing blue eyes were surely mystically enhanced by the crisp morning air, and a delicate shiver chased over her as her errant gaze hovered on his mouth.

How she longed to feel his lips once again claim hers. Just one more scandalous kiss, that she could treasure for all time.

But it was a foolish dream. She was grateful for the stolen moments they'd shared in the sacred glade. Grateful, and relieved that there was no chance of them sharing anything deeper.

This way, his memories of her would be positive, even if they were shrouded with frustration. At least he would be forever in ignorance of her shameful shortcomings in the bedchamber.

"My lady." His bone-melting accent stirred embers of desire between her thighs and heat danced through her veins. "I don't believe we are departing Fotla-eviot just yet."

He isn't leaving this morn. She tried not to let her illicit pleasure show on her face. "Has more evidence come to light?"

Had Ewan discovered something at the glade? Surely he would have told her, if so? Unless he had returned there after ensuring her safe arrival at the palace, and had only just come back?

She didn't know why that thought disturbed her. Indeed, she didn't even know why he had been in the sacred glade earlier. The question had never even occurred to her until this moment.

He hesitated, a frown slashing his brow. Intrigued, she tilted her head, silently willing him to continue but before he could respond, Gavina came to her side and dropped a curtsey.

"My lady, the queen requests our immediate return."

She smothered the flash of irritation at the interruption. It wasn't Gavina's fault, or her mother's servant who had relayed the command to Gavina. Besides, Ewan was not leaving Fotla yet. There would be another opportunity for them to meet before he did.

She would make sure of it.

"We shall continue this discussion later." She kept her voice low, although her ladies gathered so close, she suspected they could hear every word she uttered.

"Lady Briana." The urgent note in his voice was unexpected and she clasped his outstretched hand, heedless of what anyone around them might think. "I must speak with you."

Goddess, what had happened in the short time since they had been together in the glade? She burned with curiosity, but she could not ignore her mother and take a walk with Ewan, no matter how dearly she wished to do so.

"I believe we shall go for a ride later. Perhaps you might join us?" Surely her mamma would not forbid it, now there had been a break in the weather. The last time she and her ladies had escaped the palace had been the day the Scots had returned.

For an endless moment his blue gaze captured hers. She had the uncanny certainty he meant to pull her into his arms, leap upon his horse, and gallop into the safety of the mountains.

When he instead gave a stiff bow, she released a soft gasp. What was she thinking? Ewan would never do such a thing. Her senses were still inexcusably addled from that kiss.

Besides, his horse was still in the stables.

Somehow, she managed not to wince at the inanity of that final defense.

"I should be honored," he said, and it took her an unforgive-able heartbeat to understand what he was talking about.

"Excellent." Heat washed through her as she realized she was still holding his hand. She released him with as much dignity as she could muster and inclined her head. "We shall doubtless see you later."

She fancied she could feel his hot gaze drilling into her as she made her way back to the palace. It took all her willpower, but she refused to glance over her shoulder to confirm it.

It did not matter how dearly she wished to. Despite the alliance between Pict and Scot, at their core, they would forever be enemies. She couldn't afford to forget it and she would not give the Scots any reason to start malicious rumors over a nonexistent connection between the Princess of Fotla and Ewan MacKinnon.

When Briana and her ladies entered the queen's private chambers, her mamma was pacing the floor, a sure sign of agitation. She paused before the fire and Briana dropped a curtsey before going to her side.

It was too soon to have heard back from the Queen of Ce, as it was doubtful their envoy had even arrived in the north-eastern kingdom yet. Which could only mean her mamma had news on the Scots.

"Doubtless you know the Scots are now not leaving Fotla this day." Her mamma drew in a deep breath, distaste clear upon her face. "MacAllister requests an audience with our king to discuss certain issues that have miraculously arisen." Derision dripped from each word. "Did MacKinnon give any indication on why this might be, Briana?"

Her heart slammed against her ribs and, for a terrible second, she thought her mamma knew of the early morning meeting by the sacred stone. She drew in a shallow breath and forced her jagged nerves to calm.

If the queen suspected any such thing, this conversation would not only be conducted without their ladies present, but it would have commenced along very different lines, indeed.

"We scarcely passed the time of day in the courtyard before I was summoned. He shared no reason as to why the Scots' plans had changed."

No—but he had wanted to speak with her, alone. Would he truly have confided in her? It was an agreeable fantasy, but she was not so naïve as to truly believe Ewan would betray MacAllister's confidences.

What, then, had he wanted to say to her that had been so important he couldn't share it within hearing of her ladies and his men?

Her mamma's lips thinned before she shook her head with impatience. "It's most unfortunate the goddess hasn't blessed you with any insight on this matter. If ever we needed her guidance, it is now."

Instantly, Briana was plunged back into her vision, and once again felt the ripple of air across her cheek as the arrow whipped by her face.

Unease shivered along her spine as the sense of impending doom that had shimmered around the edges of that vision assailed her. It was the reason she had returned to the glade this morning.

What had Bride wanted her to find there? Had she, yet again, displeased her goddess by ignoring a vital sign?

But her purpose had vanished when Ewan appeared. Even when Shadow had melted into the forest, she hadn't turned her focus onto why Bride had led her to the glade. Instead, she'd unforgivably pressed Ewan on his romantic attachments, hoping, for an obscure reason, he'd tell her of Moreen.

She had, after all, told him of Shadow, and had even shared a hint that her first marriage had not been as perfect as she had hoped. Indeed, she'd even confided in him of her forthcoming betrothal.

But it seemed he had no intention of discussing that elusive lady from his past.

"I am sorry," she whispered, and she didn't know if she apologized to her mamma, or to Bride.

Her mamma gave an impatient sigh. "It's not your fault. No one is blaming you. The gods' ways are not for us to understand. But your dear papa grew up overshadowed by the visions of his revered Aunt Brilicie and has always believed you easily rivaled her power."

Goddess, she wished her mamma would not speak so of Brilicie. Before the birth of her grand-aunt, the gods had not deigned to bestow their gifts for generations. Brilicie had always been greatly esteemed throughout the royal houses of Pictland, as the shining light that had subsequently given rise to a resurgence of those who were touched with the blessing of the great goddess, Bride.

It verged on blasphemy. But for all her mamma said about honoring the true gods of antiquity, Briana sometimes had the dark suspicion that, deep inside, she believed in the new religion that crept insidiously across the land.

She forced her mind back to the matter in hand. "When is our king granting the Scots request for an audience?"

"As swiftly as possible. Your papa and I have discussed this, Briana, and have decided you and Artair will attend. Whatever the odious MacAllister has to say will be heard by us all."

CHAPTER 11

*E*wan went to the stables after Briana left, mainly because he was in no mood for the bawdy banter that was sure to start among the men once the ladies had departed. He especially wasn't in the mood for any comments directed at him. And considering how Briana had held his hand in full view of the contingent, he knew damn well he'd be the target of their good-natured jibes.

When he'd spied her across the courtyard, he'd been certain it was a sign that he could warn her of MacAllister's possible plot to entrap her. Aye, it was only a suspicion, but the longer he thought on it, the more likely it seemed.

Hadn't he and Ross believed from the start there was something more going on here, aside from the hunt for the would-be assassin?

She would never know how close he had come to simply pulling her into his arms and urging her to *stay safe.*

It was fortunate she, at least, possessed a clear head and had released his hand before he'd likely signed his own death warrant for so mishandling a princess of Fotla.

As he entered the stables, he saw the young lad he and Briana had rescued the other day grooming his horse. True to her word, she'd ensured the lad received her protection and found him a job in the stables.

What a difference clean clothes and a few decent meals had made. The lad stepped back and bowed his head, eyes fixed on the straw covered ground and he appeared unable to answer Ewan's greeting. Although he did manage to help Ewan saddle his horse. He might be silent, but he was a fast learner.

Ewan led his horse outside. A brisk ride was what he needed before accompanying MacAllister to see the king. Not that there was any guarantee the king would see them this morning, anyway. It would likely be hours before he granted them an audience.

Stuart MacGregor hailed him, and Ewan stifled a sigh. What now?

"Glad I caught you," MacGregor said. "MacAllister wants you. The Fotla king will give you an audience at the fourth hour."

Damn it. There was no time to go for a ride now. He bit back his curse and gave a brusque nod before handing the reins to the lad who had followed him from the stable.

Stuart fell into step beside him as they went back to the courtyard. "Any idea what this is about?" Stuart's voice was low and for once didn't hold his usual note of laughter.

Ewan grunted. It was strange. He'd had little compunction in the idea of sharing his suspicions with Briana, yet he baulked at disclosing MacAllister's evidence without express permission to one of his own men.

"We'll find out soon enough," he compromised.

"Aye. God, I'm tired of this." Stuart exhaled a harsh sigh and Ewan agreed. He was tired too, of being an unwilling accessory to the systematic ensnarement of Pictish princesses and being subject to distrust and suspicion by everyone he encountered. Even if it was hidden by a superficial façade of flirtation from some quarters.

He just hoped his conjecture was wrong about Briana's fate.

~

AT A QUARTER to the fourth hour, MacAllister joined him in the great hall, where he had been lurking in the hope of seeing Briana. Unfortunately, that plan had failed. It appeared all the ladies of the court were elsewhere.

MacAllister cast a critical eye over him, which irked him greatly. If the older man didn't find his presence acceptable, then he should summon Ross, instead.

"There's no need to look so grim." There was a faint trace of amusement in MacAllister's voice, which did nothing to improve his mood. "We shall be back in Dal Riada soon enough."

"Won't we remain in Fotla until the Northumbrian link is uncovered?"

"I doubt there is anything left to uncover here, Ewan. The assassin is long gone. We always knew that."

Certainly, he had always suspected it. But this candid response from the king's man was unexpected. Had the last week been nothing more than a masquerade? To what end? "What of the victim in the glade?"

MacAllister shrugged, clearly unconcerned. "A diversion, nothing more."

"You think the assassin murdered his accomplice?"

"We may never know whether he was Northumbrian or merely an unfortunate Pict who strayed into his path. And it doesn't matter for our purposes."

"Our purpose was to bring the assassin to justice." But that was only an excuse to return to Fotla. He knew that now. Rourke's words haunted him, and he couldn't remain silent, despite MacAllister's status. "Or have we been misled, MacAllister?"

The older man smiled, but it didn't reach his eyes. "The king and I have long admired your loyalty, MacKinnon. Rest assured, you'll be rewarded for your endeavors in due course."

He didn't want a reward. He wanted an assurance that Briana wasn't to be sacrificed to the king's half-brother to appease MacAlpin's thirst for power.

"I'm not interested in—"

MacAllister cut him off by gripping his arm. "We have been summoned."

Ewan gritted his teeth and followed the messenger who had beckoned them, and then bid them to wait in what he presumed was the king's antechamber. Trammeled energy spiked in his chest and flashed through his blood, and it took a good deal of willpower to remain still and not pace the floor with frustration.

Ostensibly, this meeting was so that MacAllister could convey the information regarding the arrow. And that was bad enough, since the Fotla king could rightly have expected to have been told that from the start. But this audience was for so much more than that.

He was convinced of it.

This wasn't the first time he'd been involved in negotiating the fate of a Pictish princess. In the spring, he'd been party to the betrothal of the Princess of Ce to a prince of Dal Riada before she had subsequently wed Connor MacKenzie. Only now could he truly understand the depth of Connor's horror when he'd discovered the woman he wanted was promised to another.

His resolve strengthened. Somehow, he would find a way to deliver Briana into the safekeeping of the Prince of Ce. It was the least he could do.

It was all he could do.

The door to the inner sanctum opened, and they were ushered inside the small chamber. The king sat behind a heavy timber desk, the prince was present, and advisers flanked the back wall, as expected.

But sitting beside the king was his queen—and standing next to him was Briana.

She offered him a small smile. He hoped he didn't appear as staggered as he felt. In Dal Riada it was unheard of for the queen, never mind a daughter of MacAlpin, to attend such a political assembly. Yet he managed to return her smile, even while denial of the likely nature of this meeting's purpose thundered through his mind.

He only half listened as MacAllister launched into his speech. But as the smooth words flowed from his tongue, Ewan watched Briana's smile fade and an all too familiar ice glaze her eyes. It was glaringly obvious she saw the strategic withholding of information to be nothing less than calculated deception.

A fleeting glance at the king confirmed he shared her opinion.

The frustration bubbling in his blood was unbearable. Why was he here, anyway? MacAllister had confided nothing to him that made him a useful ally in this meeting, and his confidence was such that he didn't need another Scot to back up his claims.

But regardless, he was here. And witnessing firsthand any admiration Briana had reluctantly bestowed his way, irrevocably shatter.

"We find your reasons for failing to share this information with us upon your return to our kingdom disingenuous at best." The king's voice was cold. "However, it changes nothing. The culprit, whether Viking or Northumbrian, was dispatched by wolves and justice therefore served."

MacAllister bowed his head but there was nothing servile in his manner. "Indeed, my lord. Our concern is that the Northumbrians have established a network of spies in Fotla, a foothold into Pictland as a first step to sabotage the alliance between Scot and Pict."

Ewan didn't doubt for a moment there were Northumbrian spies in Fotla. Or in any of the other kingdoms of Pictland. Hell, there were likely some in Dal Riada itself. Spies were everywhere.

Generally, their purpose was to filter information back to their homelands, not try and kill a royal prince.

"When did this concern assail you, MacAllister?" Briana said, as if it were not an astounding phenomenon that she spoke for her king. "Back in Dal Riada, or when you discovered the Viking ferrule?"

Grim satisfaction wound through him at MacAllister's evident consternation that a woman, even if she were a princess, had questioned him on such a matter.

"My lady." He bowed his head, but Ewan knew the gesture was only to give the older man a moment to compose himself. Had the king asked the same thing, there was no doubt MacAllister would have responded instantly. "Naturally, the Northumbrian arrow concerned us greatly. But the Norse ferrule merely confirmed our suspicions that the Northumbrians wish to confound our efforts to seek the truth."

"Now you have the truth." The king rose from his chair and planted his fists on the desk. "Your business in Fotla is concluded."

"Aye, my lord. But the borderland chieftains grow bolder by the year. The threat of invasion for both Fotla and the Kingdom of Fib is strong."

"Which is why Pict and Scot have an alliance."

Briana glanced at him and caught his gaze but there was no trace of the warmth that had glowed from her eyes earlier. All he saw was condemnation. And worse, betrayal. She knew, as well as he, that MacAllister was tightening the threads of his noose. Had she also guessed she was the prize?

He could still be wrong about that. God, let him be wrong.

"Aye, my lord. And we Scots will honor it with our warriors to repel our mutual enemies. But there is also the threat of the Norse in the north of Pictland. They encroach ever closer to the Kingdom of Ce, where our lord Connor MacKenzie and his royal wife, the Princess of Ce, reside."

Silence echoed around the chamber as MacAllister's words thundered in his head. It wasn't a threat. It was a statement of intent.

If it came down to a choice, Scots' warriors would protect their own. And their own were in Ce, not Fotla.

Rourke had been right. God damn it. He clenched his fists and battled the urge to voice his disgust. His fury.

No. He had to keep his mouth shut. Let MacAllister think he was on board with these sickening machinations. The only way he'd have a chance of ensuring Briana could escape was if MacAllister didn't suspect him of subterfuge.

"The Northumbrians haven't attempted to invade since the spring." The king's voice was grim. "It's feasible they wish to fracture our alliance by other means before launching another attack."

"We have no wish to see our neighboring Kingdom of Fotla plundered, but aside from our obligation to protect the Kingdoms of Ce and Circinn, our warriors must prioritize the western seaboard of Dal Riada against the continuing onslaught from the Norse."

A thick, suspicion-soaked silence hung in the chamber as the king slowly straightened. His hard glare never left MacAllister.

"And what," said the king, "would induce the Scots' king to prioritize the borders of Fotla?"

Ewan exhaled a long breath. The jaws of the trap cast dark shadows across the chamber as MacAllister readied to slam it shut around the princess. He forced himself to focus on the brooch the king wore on his plaid, so he was not tempted to glance Briana's way.

But he couldn't help himself and looked at her, regardless. Seemingly unaware of his presence, her attention was fixed on MacAllister as though she'd like nothing more than to render him into dust.

Ewan knew what was coming. MacAllister would announce

under what conditions the Scots would prioritize the borders of Fotla. Briana would despise him, but he could live with that. All he needed was for her to trust him enough so he could ensure her safe transport to Ce. He'd fought alongside Talargan, the Prince of Ce, the last time they'd repelled the Northumbrians and he respected the man.

Talargan would protect Briana, in ways that Ewan never could.

Even if, in a broken place deep inside, he wanted to.

"If there is a royal blood connection between the House of Alpin and the royal house of Fotla, there's no question we would protect her sovereignty as fiercely as we protect our own."

Ewan's gut clenched. And there it was.

"A royal blood connection?" The queen's voice was ice. "State your intent plainly, MacAllister, so there can be no misunderstanding between us."

MacAllister inclined his head. "To unite our kingdoms and strengthen our defenses against the barbarous Northumbrians, the House of Alpin requests the hand of the Princess of Fotla in marriage with—"

The queen surged to her feet. "Be silent. How dare you enter our domain and utter such outrageous demands? We shall not consider sacrificing yet another princess of Pictland to the Dal Riadan king."

Silence descended, and the air crackled with hostility. He hadn't expected such a violent outburst from the queen. Was it possible the royal house of Fotla would turn down MacAlpin's offer?

He hoped, for Briana's sake, they did. But politically, he could not see any king doing such a thing. Even for a favored daughter.

Inevitably, despite how he tried to resist, his glance fell upon Briana. She was staring at him directly and he couldn't fathom the expression on her face. As though she could not decide whether she loathed him or simply despised everything he appeared to stand for.

"Tell me." Her voice did not betray any emotion and although she continued to hold his gaze, she spoke to MacAllister. "Who is this royal blood in the House of Alpin you wish me to consider?"

"A direct descendant of Lord Eochaid, the first king of the House of Alpin, my lady. A noble warrior, who also possesses royal Pictish blood from his grandmother."

MacAllister's words reverberated around the stone walls and pounded into Ewan's head. While Donald was certainly of the House of Alpin, he did not possess a Pict born grandmother.

But Ewan did.

Denial hammered in his chest. MacAllister could not be speaking of *him*.

From the time he was a small child, before he was even old enough to understand such things, it had been instilled into him that to acknowledge his royal link was tantamount to treason.

His father, Kinnon, had been a lifelong friend and close confidant of MacAlpin, but their status as first cousins was reduced to a whisper in the wind.

It was the only way his grandfather could ensure malicious rumors that Kinnon and his descendants coveted the throne might never gain traction.

He had to be wrong. He couldn't marry Briana. Even though, God help him, she was the only one he craved as his bride.

MacAllister gave him a calculating glance before returning his attention to the princess. And then he uttered the damning validation.

"Lord Ewan MacKinnon."

CHAPTER 12

*N*o. *No.* The denial screamed through Briana's head as she stared, transfixed, at the Scot she had so foolishly thought she knew.

But she hadn't known him at all.

Her heart thundered, squeezing the air from her lungs, and it was all she could do to remain statue still and not wrap her arms around her waist in a futile attempt to reclaim her composure.

The pronouncement that the Scots had returned to Fotla with a hidden agenda hadn't shocked her. Her suspicions on where the discussion was heading had solidified at the mention of royal blood. All her tender thoughts of MacKinnon had withered at the knowledge he had known of this clandestine plan of his king's all along. Why else had he accompanied MacAllister to this meeting?

But goddess help her, the revelation that MacKinnon was the secret prince on offer seared her heart like a white-hot branding iron.

She could accept a political marriage. One forged for the good of her land. But she could not bear to wed another man who consumed her good sense and made her feel things that could lead to nowhere but heartache.

The brief interlude she had shared with him, the moments she had treasured and folded into her heart, to remember with fond nostalgia in the years ahead, had been nothing more than a cynical plot to entrap her.

Shame burned deep at how easily that goal had been accomplished.

Her father spoke, but his commanding words flowed over her head. She remained ramrod straight, gazing straight ahead, avoiding eye contact with the man the Scots king had sent into Fotla to claim her hand.

Another Dal Riadan prince, masquerading as a commoner. Were all Scots blighted with the inability to speak the truth? How witless she had been to imagine, even for a few brief days, that MacKinnon was different.

The chamber emptied, leaving only the four of them, including Artair. Her mamma paced the chamber, before coming to a halt before the king. "We shall not contemplate this despicable offer from the Scots upstart."

"Agreed." Cold fury iced his word. "MacAlpin may think he has us cornered, but together with the Kingdom of Fib, our warriors can repel any attack from the Northumbrians."

Fib bordered both Fotla and Northumbria, but it was the smallest kingdom in Pictland. Just because her heart bled at MacKinnon's betrayal, did not mean she was blind to the political ramifications of refusing the Scots' king's demand. "And what if the Vikings gain a foothold in Dal Riada and invade Fotla?" She turned to her parents. "The Scots king has annexed Fortriu. He will fortify the Supreme Kingdom, and the kingdoms of Circinn and Ce, and leave us and Fib at the mercy of both Vikings and Northumbrians."

"He may have taken the Supreme Kingdom, but he won't abandon Dal Riada to the Vikings. It would be too dangerous," Artair said.

Her father took her hand. "MacAlpin does not wish for either the Vikings or Northumbrians to claim any measure of Pictland. If they invade, the Scots will uphold the alliance, if only to protect Fortriu."

"We shall inform them you are betrothed to the Prince of Ce," her mother said. "Your honor will not be tarnished by breaking your word."

The betrothal. She had told Ewan of it early this morning. Except she had told him the truth. It was not yet official. Nothing had been signed. But was it pure coincidence that MacAllister had laid out his king's plans now, or had it been expedited because Ewan had betrayed her confidence?

She didn't want to think he had repeated everything she'd said to him, but the time for wishful dreams had passed. Their meeting at the sacred stone had not been by fortuitous chance. However he had managed such a thing, it had been planned, with the precision of a military maneuver.

Even the kiss? Humiliation burned through her. She could still feel his lips upon hers and despaired at how her treacherous body had responded to his touch. But it had all been a lie, nothing more than a strategy to lower her defenses and have her look favorably upon this despicable proposal.

She had even shared her most closely guarded secret with him. Her beloved Shadow. Had he told MacAllister of her wolf, too?

"Yet I am not betrothed to Talargan." She turned to face her mamma. "What of my honor then, should that truth be discovered?"

"My cousin Devorgilla will have no objection to the marriage between you and her only son, Briana." Her father squeezed her fingers in a gesture meant to convey comfort, but strangely, it did not. "There's no need to concern yourself on that account. Your honor will never be questioned."

He was wrong. She would forever question her honor, at how she had been so dazzled by the false charm of a foreign warrior.

A prince.

How could she now believe Ewan's word that Mae was happy in her new life, when everything else he had said to her had been shrouded with deceit?

Something flickered in her mind, a jagged piece of the bloodied puzzle that made no sense at all. "Who is the Pictish princess that MacAllister spoke of?"

"There is no other Pictish princess besides the one who betrayed her homeland and gave birth to the upstart, MacAlpin." Her father's voice was harsh. "The Scots spew lies with every breath they take."

"Yet none of us knew of that princess until MacAlpin staked his claim on Fortriu." Artair's dark glare encompassed them all, even though Briana knew his anger was not directed at any of them. "How many other treasonable defections were buried, only to surface now and divide our land further?"

There was no answer to that. MacAlpin's mother had been erased from the annals of Pictland and her name forgotten.

Until the spring, when her son had invoked her heritage.

"We shall inform the Scots we decline their offer." The king released her hand, and his words released her from the mortifying prospect of another confrontation with the man she had so misjudged.

She could hide in her chamber until the Scots left Fotla. No one would despise her for it.

No one, but herself.

How much easier to pretend it was her pride that was injured, and not her heart. But although she would die before she ever admitted it aloud, she faced the truth.

Despite her best efforts, Ewan had managed to breach her defenses. It would be so less painful to remain silent, but she would forever be eaten up inside with things she had never said, and questions only he could answer.

Even if everything he uttered was false, at least by seeing him one last time would give her the chance to tell him what she thought of his dishonorable actions.

She took a deep breath, even though her entire body ached with the effort, and looked her father in the eyes. "I beg your indulgence to allow me a private audience with Ewan MacKinnon."

"Certainly not." Her mamma sounded outraged by the notion.

Her father's gaze was shrewd. "Does the goddess speak to you, daughter?"

If only. But now was not the time to show indecision. And for the first time in her life, she spoke an outright lie to her beloved papa. "I believe so."

EWAN MANAGED to keep his mouth shut until he and MacAllister reached the great hall, where he rounded on the older man. "Outside."

He didn't wait to see if MacAllister would follow, or have him disciplined for his insolence, and right now he'd like to see the king's man try. The image of smashing his fist into the other man's face was far too tempting.

Outside, he sucked in great lungfuls of freezing air and tried to clear his mind. But it didn't work. All he could see was the disdainful expression on Briana's face when she had learned of the fate the Scots demanded of her.

Christ, what a mess. He had made a silent vow to protect her from MacAlpin's plans, and now—God damn it. Now, it would kill him to deliver her to Talargan, knowing she could be *his*.

"My lord." MacAllister's even voice punched through his tortured thoughts, and he swung about. But it was still hard to keep his fists to himself.

"My lord my goddamn arse."

MacAllister's mouth twitched, and disbelief shot through him. Did MacAllister find this amusing?

"Your lineage has been recognized. Therefore, your title is appropriate."

His lineage. Distracted, he raked his fingers through his hair as he recalled Briana's words the other night. When she'd accused Finn of lying about his connection to the King of Dal Riada.

What must she think of Ewan now? Did she imagine he had lied to her, even though he'd told her the absolute truth?

"This is madness." Or he was mad. Aye, that was just as likely. He always knew that one day he would wed. But it would be an advantageous alliance, nothing more. He'd always believed he would be a just and faithful husband, but that was as far as he had allowed himself to speculate.

He'd been right about one thing. This was a marriage so politically advantageous the foundations of both Dal Riada and Pictland were at stake. But never, not once, had he envisaged caring for his bride-to-be to the point where he could contemplate committing treason to ensure her safety.

"We live in tumultuous times." MacAllister sounded so sanguine it scraped like thorns along his skin. "The princess will make an agreeable wife, I'm sure."

Agreeable? If his chest didn't feel as though it were being crushed by boulders, he would've laughed.

Briana would be anything but agreeable to this. MacAllister had just threatened the security of her kingdom. How could she be anything but enraged?

He needed to see her. To explain he hadn't deceived her from the moment he had entered Fotla. Somehow, that was of utmost importance.

He swung about and MacAllister grabbed his arm. "What are you doing?"

"I need to speak to the princess."

"The king will summon us when he is ready. And unless

they're in league with the Northumbrians, rest assured we *will* be summoned."

Ewan shook off MacAllister's hand. "To hell with that. I need to see her now."

Before the other man could argue further, he marched back into the stronghold. An eerie shudder snaked along his spine. In the spring, Connor MacKenzie had come close to violating another king's inner sanctum, because of the fate of a princess, and only Ewan had been able to hold him back from such insanity.

But this was different. He couldn't let Briana think he had been a party to this deception.

Guards crossed their spears as he approached the door to the outer sanctum, and from inside the chamber, the king's advisers eyed him as though he were a gangrenous wound.

He could scarcely blame them. But he wasn't about to let that stop him, and stifling the urge to fling the spears aside, and the warriors with them, he addressed the men in the chamber. "I request an audience with the Princess of Fotla."

Before they could answer, the inner door opened, and the prince emerged. His gaze was cold as it fell upon Ewan. "You," he said. "My royal sister would speak with you."

Relief pumped through him. Not only was she willing to see him, but she had also decided to before she knew he was here.

In silence, he marched past the advisers and entered the second chamber. Briana stood before the desk, looking so regal and elegant the breath caught in his throat. He only just managed to recover his wits enough to bow as the king and queen stalked by him as they left the chamber.

The door remained opened, but that was a small inconvenience when he had been granted this privilege without having to fight for it.

"My lady." He stepped closer to her, so they might not be overheard. How he longed to pull her into his arms but if he did that, he would never let her go. Regret pierced through him, sharp and hot, a burning reminder that he could never take her as his bride. Not if he wanted to protect her from the shadows that clung to him like a deathly shroud.

"My lord." Her voice was ice, and the honorific was a damning condemnation. "How well you concealed your true heritage from me."

Damn MacAlpin to hell. He sucked in a deep breath and shoved his king from his mind. The damage was done. "I didn't. My royal blood is not something we acknowledge. This is as much a shock to me as you, Briana."

Her lips thinned, as if the use of her personal name no longer pleased her. "You will forgive me if I do not believe you. It appears all Scots warriors are related by blood to the House of Alpin."

There was nothing for it but to tell her the truth. And even though it had never been hidden, he had never spoken of it before, either. He wasn't certain how to begin.

"My grandfather was King Eochaid's bastard son and never had a claim on the throne of Dal Riada. Aye, it is true I am of the blood of the House of Alpin, but until MacAllister declared it in this chamber, that lineage has never been formally acknowledged."

Did she believe him? The disdainful expression on her face suggested she did not.

"Indeed." Her voice expressed the same opinion, and he expelled a frustrated breath. This confrontation was even worse than he had feared. "And what of your royal Pictish ancestor? You are doubly blessed with your bloodlines, to be sure."

It wasn't meant as a compliment. But her scathing remark was a harsh reminder of the claim MacAllister had made so recently.

"My grandmother is a Pictish noblewoman." That was no secret. But a princess? Why would MacAllister say such a thing? If it were true, maybe it would carry weight with the Fotla king, but it was an absurd lie when, surely, the truth could be easily discovered.

"Indeed. From which kingdom?"

Ewan had the unsettling certainty that the truth would only cause her to further disbelieve him.

"Fortriu." Even he could hear the reluctance in his voice.

"How illuminating." Disdain dripped from each word. "Your heritage is almost as distinguished as that of your compatriot, Finn Braeson."

Nothing he said was going to change her mind about him. But he couldn't give up, not yet. Desperation made him take another step nearer to her, and his voice dropped lower, so there was no chance that their audience in the antechamber could overhear. "I'm still the same man I was yesterday, Briana. The same man who met you in the glade this morning."

"Yes, I know." Her whisper razed him with the sting of sorrow that edged each word. "It is only I who have had my eyes opened. You've always been my enemy, and I chose to forget that."

Frustration clawed through him, and it took every shred of willpower he possessed not to wrap his arms around her and kiss her until she believed in nothing but him. But if he so much as touched her, this meeting would be unceremoniously ended by her king.

He sucked in a jagged breath and forced his mind to clear. An impossible task. Yet he had to make her understand. "I'm not your enemy. I am not privy to the machinations of MacAlpin."

Beware...

Once again, he trod too close to the echoes of treason, but to hell with it. He spoke only the truth and she had to believe him.

"Perhaps not." She inclined her head and he allowed himself a sliver of hope. "But what of MacAllister? Did you betray my confidence, when I shared with you the news of my betrothal to the Prince of Ce?"

Her accusation was a smack in the face. Did she truly think he'd repeated anything they had spoken of to the king's man?

"I told no one, my lady." His voice was stiff, but he couldn't help it. And even though a despicable part of him wanted to claim her as his bride, he had already, in his heart, pledged to free her from MacAlpin's clutches. "But the bonds of betrothal are sacrosanct and both MacAllister and my king will honor them. I'll ensure you find safe passage to Ce, and Lord Talargan."

She gazed at him, clearly startled that he was willing to honor the betrothal above the wishes of MacAlpin, and he expelled a long breath. It was true the betrothal was a tenuous thread, easily broken if his king commanded it. But he couldn't live with himself if he didn't fight for her right to claim this slender chance of freedom.

"You..." she hesitated, as though unsure whether to believe him or not. "But I'm not formally betrothed to Lord Talargan. I told you this."

It was the last thing he'd expected her to say when he'd just admitted he would go against his king's wishes to ensure her liberty from MacAlpin. "That is a mere formality, surely. There's no reason why the marriage would not proceed." No man in his right mind would refuse the hand of Lady Briana. *Except me.*

Her smile did not reach her eyes. "Alas, I cannot fathom what you are saying. It seems you wish me to wed the Prince of Ce, despite your king's ambitions."

She was wrong. He didn't want her to marry Talargan. Or any man. The thought of her with someone else caused his guts to clench, and it was yet more proof that this Princess of Fotla had bewitched him in ways no mere mortal could withstand.

But at least with Talargan she would be beyond MacAlpin's grasp.

Beyond the reach of my curse.

There were some things that could never be shared. It was far better she believed this, than the truth. The words lodged in his throat, but he pushed them out, nonetheless.

"I do."

"I see." Ice froze the air between them, as if they had never shared that kiss in the glade, but her scorn was not enough to cool the anguished fire in his blood. "You would tarnish my honor by professing I am betrothed to another, rather than risk the indignity of wedding me yourself."

Even though she spoke in barely a whisper, every word slammed into his head with the force of a battle-ax. Stupefied, he stared at her, as her accusation echoed with thunderous condemnation around his mind.

He offered her an escape, and she was more concerned with her integrity?

But that was a secondary concern. How could she believe, for even a moment, that wedding her would be an indignity?

"That is untrue." He growled the denial, and heat assaulted him that had nothing to do with lust or desire. He hoped no one but her could hear his tortured confession. "I would wed you in a heartbeat if that was the only way to save you."

"How gratifying." Her voice was glacial. "Pray, allow me to consider your most gracious proposal." With that damning response, she turned her back on him.

CHAPTER 13

*B*riana flattened her hands upon her father's desk and drew in a shuddering breath. Why had she goaded MacKinnon about the nonexistent betrothal with Talargan? There had been no need for her to mention that at all, after she had confronted him with his heritage. She hoped he realized how deeply she despised him for his subterfuge but had the despairing notion he didn't care what she thought of him.

Yet how swiftly he'd used her unwary words against her. Perhaps he imagined she would be grateful for his promise to endorse the charade that her betrothal to Talargan was official. Did he think to charm her with this façade of solicitous care for her future? That by so doing, he would snare a wife who was thankful for his benevolent nature?

This entire deception was engineered by his king and like any loyal subject, MacKinnon would always obey his king.

But she was not beholden to MacAlpin. And her king, her beloved papa, would not sacrifice her on such a bloodstained altar.

"Briana." His whisper was husky but worse than that, his

warm breath caressed her cheek. How dare he move so close to her, when she had made it obvious she wanted nothing more to do with him by turning her back? "I want only what is best for you."

Even now, his silken tongue worked its magic. At least, it would, if she were foolish enough to believe him.

She would not play his games. MacAlpin would discover he could not ride roughshod through every Kingdom of Pictland.

Despair flickered through her. Even without all the falsehoods, Ewan was the last man she could marry. Nothing had changed in that regard. Yet still a tiny piece of her wished things —so many things—could be different.

With deliberation, she raised her hands from the desk and grasped her fingers together. The official response to the Dal Riadan proposition would come from her father. There was nothing left for her to say to MacKinnon. It was not her place. But nevertheless, she would tell him that nothing would induce her to accept the Scots' proposition.

Seeing his face when he realized he could no longer manipulate her to his king's will, would be a small recompense for how he had deceived her.

So small, it was negligible. But it was the most she could hope for.

And then her gaze fell upon a piece of parchment, where her brother had drawn the likeness of the Viking ferrule that Ewan had discovered.

Instantly, the chamber vanished, and she gasped, as once again she stood in the snow-clad glade. Fleeting wind whipped by her face and the thud of the arrow, as it embedded in the standing stone, reverberated around the chamber's walls.

Ice trickled along her spine as she turned and watched the mighty stone splinter before her. Thick blood oozed from the fearsome crack, and the acrid scent of fear and desperation billowed around the chamber like a smoke-fueled demon. Terror gripped her chest and her mind filled with the unmistakable howl of Shadow.

And woven into the howl, the familiar, haunting whisper of her goddess.

Protect Pictland above all else

The vision dissolved, but the echo remained like embers in her mind.

Bride's command could not be clearer. If Fotla did not entwine herself with Dal Riada through bonds of royal blood, Fotla would splinter like the sacred stone in her vision.

Fotla and Fib would fall to the Northumbrians, and there was no doubt that, alliance or not, the southern barbarians would not stop there.

Nerves collided in her stomach, and she had the distressing urge to vomit. But now was not the time for such weakness. She would die before she showed any pitiable shortcoming before Ewan MacKinnon.

She'd believed she had a choice. But Bride had brought her here, and to refuse MacAlpin's proposition would lead to the downfall of her beloved land.

There was no easy escape for her. The security of Pictland, and the preservation of the ancient ways, was paramount, and in the end, she was but a pawn in the hand of her goddess. Bride decreed she should wed MacKinnon to strengthen the alliance and it was not a request.

"Briana." His whisper, so intimate against her cheek, broke her paralysis. Her reprieve was over, but instead of an undemanding marital alliance with the Prince of Ce, her destiny lay with a man she feared could all too easily shatter what remained of her heart.

"MacKinnon." She turned to face him. Why did he have to be so close? Pride forbade her from stepping back so she might breathe more easily. Pride, after all, was all that she could rely on to get her through the rest of her life. "I have made my decision. We shall wed, to strengthen the Kingdom of Fotla and Pictland against our enemies."

For a fleeting moment a wild, fierce longing glowed in his eyes. But surely it was merely her own wretched imagination, attempting to shield her from the faint aura of dread that descended around him at her declaration.

"Are you certain this is what you want?" His voice was a low rumble that caused a distressing shiver of need across her flesh. Damn him for being able to shred her defenses so easily.

"Our wants have nothing to do with this." Thank the goddess she sounded as detached as Ewan. "I will not run and hide from my duty, when the alternative is watching my beloved land succumb to her enemies."

"This is not the future I want for you." He sounded agonized, and another tiny sliver of her soul withered and died. "You deserve a man who can love you, unreservedly." He sucked in a ragged breath that seemed to cause him untold torment. "And I can't do that, my lady."

At least, in this, he told her the truth. She gave a frosty smile and feared her face might shatter with the effort.

"My first marriage was a love match. I have no wish for a second. If you have no other objection to the alliance, I will inform my king of our decision."

Silence echoed around the chamber, but his gaze did not falter from hers. His blue eyes captured her, and she could not look away, no matter how dearly she wished to.

Except that was another lie. She wanted to stay here, forever, trapped in this false cocoon where she could pretend she saw tenderness in his gaze, and perhaps even a promise of something more.

Finally, he spoke, and shattered her witless charade. "I have no objections, my lady."

She inclined her head, but could not trust herself to speak, and left him standing in the chamber.

In the queen's private chambers, her mamma gripped her hands, while their ladies hovered in clear distress around them.

"You cannot do this, Briana. I forbid it."

"I have already given my word."

Her mamma squeezed her fingers but the pain barely registered when her entire chest ached for all that could never be. "This is outrageous. The king already told you he would not countenance this proposal from the upstart. I do not understand how you could fall so easily into this trap."

Briana pulled her hands free and paced to the narrow, arched window that looked out into a private courtyard. She closed her eyes and tried to clear her mind, but all she could see was Ewan's resigned expression as he acceded to her wishes.

"I did not fall, Mamma. I see the trap as clearly as you. But I also see how easily the Northumbrians could take advantage of what is happening. How can I stand by and see Fotla politically isolated, when this marriage ensures the Scots will stand shoulder to shoulder with our warriors if they are ever needed?"

The queen came to her side. "You will not sacrifice yourself on the altar of MacAlpin's ambitions."

Despite her predicament, memories flooded through her of when her dear cousin Mae had stood in this very chamber, when they had learned she was to wed a prince of Dal Riada. She herself had beseeched her mamma that they could not sacrifice Mae for such a thing.

And her mother's response had haunted her ever since.

She drew in a shuddering breath before catching the queen's gaze. "I'm not facing execution." There was a hollowness in her voice she could not repress. "But marriage into the House of Alpin."

A deadly silence fell. It seemed all the ladies held their collective breath, waiting for their queen's reaction.

"Briana." Her voice was hushed. "There's no comparison between this and Mairi's circumstances. She is the Princess of the Supreme Kingdom and her marriage ensured peace for Pictland. And besides, the great goddess herself approved the match. Can you tell me the same? Has the goddess shown you that you must tether your future with Ewan MacKinnon?"

An ethereal crack reverberated around the chamber, but only she heard it. Only she saw the sacred stone split and fragment, and scatter like ash into the void.

The goddess had not sent her a vision of Ewan MacKinnon, the way she had sent visions to Mae of Finn Braeson. But it made no difference. She knew what Bride demanded of her. Fotla had to align herself with Dal Riada, whatever the cost might be.

She bowed her head and tried to banish MacKinnon's image from her mind, but it was a futile task. Soon, they would be bound, and he would never fade from her memories, the way she had once so foolishly hoped.

Her mamma still waited for her answer and there was but one thing to say. "This is the will of the goddess. Or Fotla will fall."

EWAN SCARCELY HEARD the terse exchange between the King of Fotla and MacAllister. His head thudded, in eerie counterpoint to his heart, and if he did not get out of this chamber soon, he feared he would go mad.

He was to wed Briana. The woman he had hoped to save from a disastrous marriage into the House of Alpin had been chosen for him by his king, and he had walked into the trap as blindly as the princess herself.

As soon as the king and his advisers left the antechamber, he stalked out, MacAllister, curse the bastard, by his side. Once they were in the courtyard, the older man gave a satisfied grunt.

"Well played, my lord. Your diplomacy does your father credit."

Ewan expelled a long breath, but it did nothing to blunt the sharp edge of fear that lodged in his chest. Fear that Briana was in mortal danger and there was nothing he could do about it.

"I said nothing to the princess." He slung MacAllister a glare. "And it was not my intention to coerce her into this situation with pretty words. She decided to go through with this herself."

Sacrificing her future for the sake of her beloved Pictland. God help him. He didn't want that for her. But how despicably he wanted her for himself.

The outcome was the same. If he took her as his bride, a woman he cared for more than he had believed was possible, her very life would hang in the balance.

"Even better." MacAllister rolled his shoulders and glanced at the sky, as though assessing the possibility of more snowfall. "The princesses of Pictland are uncommonly shrewd. Didn't I tell you Lady Briana would make a most agreeable wife?"

He was not prepared to discuss Briana more than he had to with MacAllister. "I need to clear my head."

Moments later, he was in his saddle, navigating away from the Pict stronghold. His horse was well used to snow and galloped across the land but no amount of frigid wind in his face could dislodge Briana's face in his mind, or the scornful gleam in her eyes as she had agreed to proceed with MacAlpin's plans.

"MacKinnon, hold up, man." The shout came from behind him and with reluctance, he slowed, so Rourke could catch up. "Rumors are flying. Is it true?"

From the ridge ahead of them, Ross appeared. God damn it. He wanted time alone, not face an inquisition from two of his lifelong friends.

"What happened?" Ross said as he halted before them. It was obvious the ride hadn't improved his mood.

Ewan sucked in a harsh breath. There was no point in delaying the inevitable. "I am to wed the Princess of Fotla."

The grim expression on Ross' face transmuted into harsh sympathy. Which irrationally irked Ewan. "We should have seen this coming."

Aye, but they hadn't. And even if they had, what difference would it have made? Could he have saved Briana, if he'd been able to warn her the day they'd returned to Fotla?

An ugly truth seeped from the hidden darkness in his soul. Did he *really* want her to have the chance of escaping her fate, now he knew she was to be *his* bride?

"Huh." Rourke's voice shook him from the unwelcome depths of his thoughts. "So that's why my father ordered me from the feast that first night. He wanted you and the princess to become better acquainted."

"Manipulative bastard," Ross said.

Ewan narrowed his eyes at the nearby mountains, where heavy clouds obscured their lofty peaks. He wanted to refute Rourke's claim but how could he?

MacAllister's plan had worked.

"Do I offer congratulations or commiserations?" Rourke appeared unmoved by Ross' appraisal of his father. Likely because he agreed with it. It was an effort to dredge up the energy to respond, but it had to be done.

"You may congratulate our king on another advantageous alliance. The princess is aware as to why this marriage must proceed. She's willing to enter into it to protect the Kingdom of Fotla, and that's all that matters."

"Aye, but what of you?" Ross said. "She will be your bride, Ewan."

"And I will protect her with my life." The words reverberated around his head, hollow with mockery. How the hell could he protect her, when being with him was her greatest danger?

"But do you care for her?"

Savage fear gripped his chest. Aye, he cared for her. But a primitive conviction polluted his rational mind that if he admitted to it, he would unleash his curse upon her.

"I pray God will serve the justice upon you that you deserve." Moreen's voice echoed in his mind. He knew only too well what she would deem well deserved justice.

No. He refused to even contemplate it. They would wed and unite the House of Alpin and the Kingdom of Fotla as demanded by his king. But that was all. He would install her in his stronghold, Duncreag, leave her, and never return.

"That has nothing to do with it. This is a political alliance, Ross. Nothing more."

Ross contemplated him as though he didn't believe a word of it.

"Well," Rourke sounded resigned. "It's not the first political marriage and it sure as hell won't be the last. I offer my commiserations."

"Yet these Pictish princesses appear to have the gift of enticing their husbands to fall madly in love with them." Ross sounded deadly serious, and Ewan glared at him. "You may yet fall beneath her spell. Cameron MacNeil is scarcely recognizable as the same man since he wed Lady Elise."

"I am not Cameron MacNeil." He ground the words between his teeth and tried, without success, to banish the more than enticing sight of how Briana had gazed at him after they had kissed. Had it truly only been earlier this morn? It seemed like another life. "I've no intention of allowing any lady to spellbound me and cause me to lose my wits."

With that, he urged his horse into a gallop, but his cynical words echoed in his ears no matter how he tried to ignore them.

It barely mattered how hard he fought against the inevitable.

He couldn't forget how she had helped that young lad with a job in the stables, or her determination in investigating the sacred site because things did not sit right with her. Most of all, he couldn't overcome the despairing admiration that consumed him at how she was willing to sacrifice everything in a political marriage to save her beloved land.

There was no use denying it. He was already irrevocably under her spell.

CHAPTER 14

*B*riana wrapped her cloak more securely about her as she left the palace by the secret door. She had scarcely slept, yet had pretended to, so her faithful friend Nairne would not continue in her attempts to lighten the bleak future with promises that would never come to pass.

Neither of them believed that Ewan MacKinnon, with his reputation for breaking hearts, would ever fall in love with his bride. And she did not wish him to, either. This was a marriage for Pictland, and she was resigned to it.

Why, then, was she stealthily making her way to the sacred standing stones in the hope that Bride would deign to bestow more wisdom?

She didn't even try to answer it. But the sacred circle had always given her comfort, and all too soon she would be leaving for Dal Riada and would likely never see Fotla-eviot again.

Sorrow gripped her heart, but she refused to embrace it. She had made this decision without any illusions clouding reality. Her future lay in the land the Scots had claimed three hundred years ago.

The standing stones were not far from the palace, and

although the early morn was dark, the candles placed in the windows of the nearby Christian church gave enough light to guide her way.

As she approached the stones, awareness flashed through her and she stilled, senses on full alert. Yet it was not danger that hovered nor sent tremors racing across her skin. But surely Ewan MacKinnon was not following her? To what end? Unlike the previous day when he had undoubtedly tracked her to the glade, there was no further need to charm or flatter her.

Or steal an unwary kiss.

The searing memory of that kiss, which had been neither stolen nor unwary, was intolerable. She swung about but could discern no movement in the darkness. But that meant nothing. He was here, she was certain of it and stealthily, she continued along the icy path. A dark shadow standing before the church caught her eye and she gasped.

It could be anyone standing there, yet in her heart she knew it was he.

As though he heard her, although surely he had not, he swung around and for an endless moment they were frozen in time. Her heart thundered in her breast, and she was powerless to move until he took a step towards her.

"Briana?" He sounded as though he could not believe his eyes. Although why should he be so shocked, considering how they had met the previous morning? Perhaps, in Dal Riada, ladies did not go a-wandering before daybreak, and unaccompanied, at that.

They don't in Fotla, either. She ignored that irritating truth. And who was Ewan MacKinnon to show displeasure at anything she did? He was not her husband yet.

Would he forbid her any small measure of freedom, once they were wed? She could not believe it of him. And yet, she had never believed he was connected to the House of Alpin, either.

She tilted her head at a regal angle and turning her back on the sacred circle, she took a step closer to him.

"Ewan." Thankfully, she sounded calm, despite her sorely jagged senses. "It seems we are both of a mind to commune with our gods before the business of negotiation begins."

"I will tell you this here, my lady. Everything you bring into this marriage will remain yours. I give you my word."

Goddess. Although it was true her father would accept nothing less in the marriage contract, she certainly hadn't expected Ewan to be so fierce about granting that right before the talks had even started.

Not that she intended to let him know his remark had impressed her. It was, after all, most likely yet another tactic to win her approval. How less challenging life would be for him with a placated bride, rather than one who harbored resentment against him.

"I'm happy to hear it. But nevertheless, if these assurances are not formally approved and witnessed, they mean nothing."

"I shall ensure they are written in stone." His tone was oddly grim. How easy it would be to believe this betrothal had caught him as unawares as her, but for the sake of her heart it was vital she didn't fall into that trap.

"As will my father."

Silence fell between them, and it was not an amicable pause but prickled with tension and unrevealed secrets. It was as if the last few days had never occurred. And although the time they had spent together had been nothing more than a façade to win her trust, how dearly she longed for those carefree moments to return.

"My lady." His voice was low, a sensual caress that threaded through her wounded soul despite how she tried to resist. "We must talk. Are you permitted to enter the church?"

She gave a stiff smile although she doubted he could see it. "Certainly."

He opened the door for her, and she swept past him, ignoring the tantalizing sizzle of heat that invaded her blood as her arm inadvertently brushed his.

She stood by a window, where a candle glowed, and pushed back her hood. Ewan stood some distance from her, clearly not willing to repeat an accidental touch. Good. She certainly didn't want her Scots bred husband constantly wishing to take her hand or kiss her lips whenever they encountered each other.

Alas, the lie did not make her feel any better.

Since he appeared to have forgotten he was the one who had invited her inside so they could speak, she forced her regrets to the back of her mind and once again offered him a wintry smile. "What is on your mind, my lord?"

He visibly started at her use of his title. She could almost believe he wasn't used to being addressed so, but that, once again, was merely her pitiful determination to exonerate him from being a willing party to this tangled web.

Just because she wished it, did not make it so.

"I want to assure you that I'll do everything possible to make this marriage palatable for you."

Palatable? She had no idea what he meant by his comment but was certainly not going to give him the satisfaction of requesting clarification. "I'm sure the marriage will be as agreeable as are a thousand others in such circumstances."

"This isn't a thousand other marriages, Briana." He sounded irrationally frustrated, as though her chilly acceptance of their fate did not sit well with him. "This is us. You," he added, unnecessarily, his frown growing darker by the moment. "I'm determined this alliance between us will cause you as little inconvenience that is within my power to give."

"How generous of you. Yet I fear the inconvenience is inevitable since I am the one who must leave my homeland and beloved kin behind."

"You shall have my leave to visit your kin whenever you wish."

He was attempting to be reasonable, but his offer irked her, nonetheless. In Dal Riada, did women need their husband's permission merely to visit their own family?

She had a terrible certainty that they did. And if she displeased her lord, would he withhold that concession?

Ewan would never do that. Her instant defense of him was troubling. Why could she not believe the worst of him, when all the evidence pointed to his deceit?

"That is kind of you." She wanted to appear grateful, even though she wasn't, but the words sounded more like a curse. And by the way he cocked his head at her, he heard that undercurrent, too.

"I want you to be happy." He sounded vaguely irritated, which didn't improve her mood.

"I shall do my best." She only half hoped he didn't hear the mockery in her response but what did he expect? For her to pronounce she was delighted by this turn of events?

He expelled a harsh breath and for a fleeting moment looked defeated, which sent a sharp pain through her breast. Damn him for being able to manipulate her so. It took all her willpower to remain still and silent, and not offer him a comforting word.

It was all an illusion. She had to remember that.

"I know you would rather wed Talargan."

She certainly understood that Ewan would prefer her to wed the Prince of Ce. She would not deign to answer him. After a strained moment, he appeared to understand that.

"Briana." He took a step closer to her and she had the uncanny feeling he didn't even realize he had moved. "Whatever you may think, I have no wish to trap you in this marriage."

"By its very institution, marriage is little more than a trap for women." Goddess, had she said that aloud? She resisted the mortified urge to press her hands against her hot cheeks. He was, after all, going to be her husband, in a foreign land where, she had heard, wives were afforded little consideration. Why, then, did she continually bait him, when he appeared to be telling her she would not be treated like a mere chattel?

He gave an inpatient sigh. "You told me your first marriage was a love match, yet your views on wedlock appear to contradict this happy state."

Was he mocking her? "Love does not always ensure a happy union."

"You need have no fear of love entering our arrangement."

"So you keep telling me." Did he think his insistence that he would never find it in his heart to love her was a badge of honor, something to be proud of? But if this was the way he wanted their marriage to be, she would learn to play by those rules, too. "Your feelings in this matter are of no consequence to me."

He gave a brusque nod. "It will be better for us both."

Her chest tightened, crushing her, and she had the alarming urge to slap his face for his unfeeling coldness. Did he truly feel nothing for her at all? Even after that kiss in the glade?

Grow up. Why would it mean anything to him? And the way she had responded to his touch was irrelevant. After all, she had enjoyed such clandestine kisses with Ecgfrith before they had wed.

The kiss had meant nothing. Sex with Ewan would mean nothing. And how thankful of that she was. If the act was nothing more than a duty, he wouldn't expect anything more from her.

Ecgfrith had grown so tired of her inability to respond to his touch whenever they progressed beyond the preliminaries, that after the first year of marriage he had rarely shared her bed. Perhaps she could expect the same fate with Ewan.

She crushed the desolation that threatened to undo her. Unlike with Ecgfrith, this alliance with Ewan was not based on anything but politics, and she would be wise to approach it as such.

Now was the perfect time to set out her wishes on this alliance. Something she had failed to do with Ecgfrith, when she had been filled with girlish dreams and foolish fantasies of a wonderful life together. A life that had included children.

"Indeed. Although I am excluded from the negotiations that will determine the rest of my life, perhaps we could agree upon some details now, between the two of us."

"Name anything, and if it's within my power to give, it is yours."

She refused to be swayed by such lavish promises when they meant nothing. "I request nothing too onerous, and I trust you are able to deliver." Perhaps she should choose her words more wisely. Men were so outlandishly sensitive when it came to issues of their perceived virility. "Children."

"What?"

Goddess, why did he sound so shocked? It was not an outrageous request.

"Children." She hoped he hadn't heard the edge of desperation in her voice. "That is my wish for this alliance between us."

"That's—" He snapped his jaw shut and something akin to despair flashed over his face. "I didn't think you'd..." His voice trailed away, and he swallowed. It was clear her expectations did not match his and another tiny fragment of her heart crumbled to dust.

She gripped her hands together within the sanctuary of her cloak, but it was hard to cling onto her courage when all she wanted to do was run and hide from his obvious distaste at the prospect of fathering a child with her. Somehow, she found her voice.

"Yes. That is my wish. But pray do not presume I require a show of passion in the bedchamber." She caught herself and cursed her unwary tongue. "I mean, above the necessary level to, uh, perform the act."

Now would be the perfect time for a monk to appear and end this disastrous conversation before she died of shame. Alas, it seemed the church was empty besides Ewan and herself.

"Perform the act?" He repeated her words and there was no pretending that he sounded anything less than horrified. "My lady, more than a *show* of passion is required for what you request."

Did he think her ignorant of what was involved? She embraced the spark of affront. It was better than wilting with humiliation. She had, foolishly or not, begun this discourse and her pride demanded that she saw it through to the bitter end.

"Is it too much to expect?" Her voice was haughty. It was her only shield. "If the prospect repels you so profoundly, rest assured we need only copulate when my moon time is ripe."

She had never, in all her life, seen a man so dumbfounded as the way Ewan gazed at her now. She glared back at him. Nothing would induce her to turn and flee, despite every particle of her being that begged her to do just that. Indeed, she would show him she was not to be trifled with, and before she could think better of it, she added, "Answer me."

"Repels me?" He sounded incensed as he took another step closer, towering over her like a vanquishing warlord. The air evaporated, the rest of the church faded to shadows, and her mouth dried as Ewan immobilized her with the fierce glow from his eyes. "You mistake me, my lady. Nothing would give me greater pleasure than claiming you for my own."

Wait. What? This made no sense. Did Ewan want her or not? Denials floundered in her mind, but what was she denying?

It didn't help that he continued to take up all the space around her, or that his intoxicating scent of leather and pine caused her head to spin. Frantically, she attempted to pull her scattered senses together before he thought her entirely witless.

"So you agree to my request?" Her voice was husky, but she refused to clear her throat and show him just how under his corrupt spell she had fallen. And since she had come this far, she might as well press her advantage while she had his attention. "I do not require declarations of devotion, merely your word that we will undertake the necessary measures in order for me to conceive."

"Necessary measures meaning I take my rights as your husband."

Irrationally stung by his remark—after all, that was exactly what she meant—she retorted, "As I will take my rights as your wife."

Goddess, save her. Why had she answered him? He had just given her the perfect excuse for her shortcomings in the marital bed, and she had flung it back in his face.

"Beware, Briana." His voice dropped to a seductive growl and shivers raced over her skin. "If you welcome me into your bed, I won't be there merely to fulfil your request."

His promise—threat? —hung heavy in the air between them, a tantalizing glimpse of passion drenched nights filled with abandoned pleasure. Lust fluttered through her blood and pooled between her thighs, liquid heat that ignited scandalous fantasies she had no hope of attaining.

How could she think clearly when Ewan loomed over her, breathing her air, and befuddling her senses? Her gaze caught on his lips, but that was a mistake as heated memories of their kiss seared whatever remained of her sanity.

She had to *focus*. To ensure he understood the terms of this agreement, so she would not be subjected to his disappointment, or worse, on their wedding night. She hitched in a ragged breath, trying, and failing, to ignore his evocative scent that swirled like an invading aphrodisiac, but it was so hard to concentrate on what needed to be said.

"We must start as we mean to continue." If only she didn't sound so breathless. It made a mockery of her words, but what else could she do? "This alliance is for political reasons only. You have made it very clear you do not desire me, and I am—"

The words locked in her throat as Ewan grasped her shoulders, the strength and heat from his hands burning her even through her cloak and gown, and roughly he backed her up against the stone wall.

Trapping her.

But it wasn't alarm that flashed through her at the positively savage expression on his face as he glowered down at her. It was... exhilaration.

"When have I ever made it clear I don't desire you?"

His harsh demand sent illicit thrills through her. It was all wrong, yet she could do nothing to calm her erratic pulse. And even though she should remain mute, her incautious tongue would not be silenced.

"Your face gave you away when MacAllister declared his king's plans for us. And you cannot deny how you would rather I wed Lord Talargan than be shackled to me."

"What do either of those things have to do with whether I desire you or not?"

"I'm not condemning you for not wishing to marry me." *Yes, I am.* But that was a silly, girlish, emotion, and she refused to allow it to sway her. "I simply want to make it clear that while I desire children from our union, I most certainly do not require or expect *passion.*"

He swore under his breath, a savage eruption that caused the breath to catch in her throat with forbidden fascination. "God damn it, Briana. If you want children, I shall give them to you."

Her heart thundered in her breast. Surely he could hear it? If only he would pull back, so she could drag some air into her starved lungs. "Then it is settled. That's all I—"

"You speak of passion as though it's an easily discarded encumbrance." His hands tightened on her shoulders and his glance dropped to her mouth. "I burn for you. I cannot dislodge you from my mind. And I promise you, whatever else I can't give you, passion in the bedchamber is not one of them."

CHAPTER 15

*E*wan glared into Briana's startled eyes and attempted, futilely, to tame the beast that roared within his chest. She gazed at him as though he spoke of things she had no knowledge of, but she was not an untouched maid.

She had been wed. More, it had been a love match. Aye, she knew of passion. But only with a man she loved. Bizarrely, it was that fact that dug deep into the hidden shadows of his soul. That she had once loved another, even though it was his worst nightmare that she might one day fall in love with *him*.

"No," she whispered, as he wound her plait around his hand. A rope of fire, and before he could stop himself, he pressed the silken threads against his face and the delicate scent of lavender pushed him to the very edge of reason. "That's not what I want. Ewan..." Her voice trailed away as her gaze caught his, and he was lost.

All his noble pledges of a chaste marriage fled his mind. How had he imagined for even a moment he'd be able to keep his hands off his delectable bride?

"Then I'll make you want it." His mouth captured hers and her sharp intake of breath was a smoldering caress. He wrapped his arm around her, pulling her tight against his body, as his tongue took advantage of her parted lips.

A tortured groan razed his throat as she softened against him, her tongue stroking his in a sensual dance. She tasted of glens in spring, of sunlight in summer, and illuminated the dark corners of his wretched soul in ways he'd never imagined.

He released her plait and wrenched back her cloak. *More.* He needed her naked in his arms, but her gown was yet another cursed barrier. Roughly, he tugged on the ribbons at her bodice, before tearing his mouth from hers. It was still dark outside, but the glow from the nearby candle cast enough light to see her exposed breasts.

God help him. A groan ripped from the core of his being, and he cupped her luscious flesh, skimming his thumb over her erect nub. Her gasp rippled through him, an added torment, and he lowered his head and took her into his mouth.

He teased her with his tongue, swirling around her delectable nipple. Her muffled gasps stoked his blood and when she dug her fingers into his hair, pressing him closer, he sucked hard, eliciting a choked cry from her as a reward.

Blindly, he grasped her gown and dragged the material up her legs. Her fingernails raked across his head, lightning flashes of dark pleasure, silently urging him on.

Her thighs were silken and with each stroke he brushed higher. His knuckles grazed her damp slit and she bucked against his fist. God, he wanted her flat on her back, so he could spread her thighs and indulge his ravening lust.

Later. He would do all that, and more, when they were wed.

He teased her lips with his fingers, back and forth, dipping inside just enough so she writhed with need. Panting, he tore his mouth from her nipple and trailed kisses over the swell of her breast. Her head fell back, and he took advantage, using his teeth along the column of her throat, until all that filled his head were her seductive whimpers of desire.

His finger circled her swollen clit, and her erratic breath and the way she clutched at his shoulders caused the tension to coil ever tighter in his groin. A pleasurable torture he had never imagined existed.

She trembled and he pushed his advantage, lavishing her clit with delicate strokes and tempting pressure until she gave a soft cry as her release consumed her.

When he'd wrung every last convulsion from her, she sagged against the wall, and he pressed his forehead against hers. Fire scorched his blood, lust scalded his mind, and every ragged breath was a battle to retain his honor.

When he finally mastered a shred of control, he lifted his head and despite the frustration that throbbed along his cock and filled his balls, a flash of masculine satisfaction consumed him at the glazed expression in her eyes.

Slowly, he traced his finger along her parted lips, and she hitched in a shocked breath as she tasted herself on him. Without releasing her from his hot gaze, he slid his finger into his mouth, and her evocative scent all but incinerated his reason.

She swallowed and appeared transfixed by his action. Would she wrap her legs around him if he commanded it? Would she allow him to take her against a cold stone wall and empty his hot seed deep inside her writhing body?

The words locked in his throat. She was a princess, and they were all but betrothed. He would wait until their wedding night, but he had proved his point.

His lips brushed hers and he inhaled her breath as though it were his own. "This is the passion we'll share, Briana. Never doubt it for a moment."

For a heartbeat she didn't move. And then she stiffened, and pushed him back, and with a grim smile he complied because what the hell else could he do?

"I must go." Her whisper sounded strangely vulnerable as she straightened her disheveled bodice. Regret slashed through him that he needed to let her go at all when all he wanted was to return with her to her chamber, and finish what he'd so recklessly started.

But she, at least, was satisfied. And for now, that would have to suffice.

With damning reluctance, he released her, but she didn't instantly leave. Silence fell between them, condemning him for his actions, yet he could not regret them. Briana would not go into this marriage believing that he didn't want her or that their wedding bed would be a place of cold copulation.

Finally, she left the support of the wall and, wrapping her cloak tightly around her, turned from him without a word. As the heavy timber door swung shut behind them, he dragged in a deep breath, but the chilled air did nothing to cool his blood.

But it did send a jagged sliver of reason into his bewitched mind.

What the devil was wrong with him? He had all but ravished her within the sacred walls of a church. If he wasn't going to hell already, he certainly was now.

"I can find my own way back to the palace." There was a haughty note in her voice as she gave him a regal look. But her lips were bruised from his kisses and her hair unraveled from her plait, and his damn cock was so hard he could barely walk straight.

Never mind think.

Her scent ensnared him and the stifled gasps she'd made as he'd plundered her wet slit and made her come echoed like a cursed refrain in the early morning mist. Once again, the primitive urge to push her up against one of the ancient standing stones and sink into her welcoming heat pounded through his blood and all but fried his sanity.

But he had made a vow not to take her until they were wed.

It was an effort to locate his voice. Somehow, he prevailed. "You're not walking back there alone."

"So you would risk my reputation by accompanying me?"

"Your reputation is safe. We are all but betrothed." Strange how that notion no longer caused bleak despair to grip him. But he couldn't allow his lust to blind him to the truth. He'd given his word to Briana, and he would ensure to get her with child. Only then would he leave her.

How goddamn noble of him. He clenched his jaw. If he were truly honorable, he'd abandon her before their wedding night, as he had planned.

But that was before he'd tasted her. Before her sweet cries of completion had driven him out of his mind.

Before his rash promise to impregnate her had bound him to her side for who knew how long.

A bairn. God damn it, what had he been thinking to agree to such a thing?

"It is still not yet official." She pulled her hood over her head. "I should not be out without my ladies and a guard."

"I am guard enough for you." The retort was out before he could prevent it, not that he wished to retract it. She was, like it or not, his responsibility now, since there was no possibility that, having got this far, MacAllister would allow any aspect of the negotiations to deflect the king's plan.

But that wasn't the only reason. Yesterday morning he had followed her back to the stronghold to ensure she came to no harm. It was unthinkable he would allow her to wander unaccompanied.

When they entered the courtyard she halted and turned to him, although she didn't meet his eyes. "You may leave now."

Lust addled his mind, and he wasn't sure whether he was irked or amused by her haughty dismissal. "We have come this far. I shall see you safely into the great hall before I take my leave."

"I would rather not have the entire palace aware of our early morning... encounter."

"Then we shall say I met you upon your return from your walk. Will that appease you?" Exasperation threaded through his voice. Why was she being so stubborn? She'd already told him the day before that she often escaped the stronghold alone. Surely, she was often seen returning. The only difference today was he accompanied her, and that was easily explained.

No one would dare dispute his word or cast doubt on the princess' honor.

"My lady." The harsh voice from across the courtyard took him unawares and he swung around. Rohan was marching their way, and he appeared thunderous. He bit back a curse. He was in no mood for the other man's disparaging remarks. "Are you unharmed?"

Was she *unharmed*? Incredulity at the Pict's nerve rasped along every jagged sense, not helped by the untrammeled lust that still scalded his blood. Who the hell did Rohan think he was?

"Lady Briana is unharmed." He all but spat the words at the Pict. "I am escorting her back to the strong—the palace."

The poisonous glance Rohan arrowed his way suggested he didn't believe a word.

"I am quite well, my lord." Briana's voice held the merest tinge of ice, but she smiled at the other man and the sight of it did something ugly to the pit of his stomach. "I took the early morning air, and Lord Ewan was kind enough to accompany me home."

The honorific grated along his nerves, but he had no choice but to get used to it. Yet more than that, the presence of the other man irritated him beyond measure. He was always in the shadows, watching Briana. Or part of her entourage, whispering in her ear. As dawn broke, had he been peering from the stronghold's tower, watching for her return?

Rohan responded to Briana, his avid gaze fixed upon her face, but Ewan barely heard the words as finally—*finally*—the unpalatable truth hit him.

Rohan was in love with her.

~

BRIANA WALKED BACK to the palace, Ewan on one side and Rohan the other. While Rohan talked incessantly, she had no idea what he was saying and dearly wished he would be silent. She had intended to slip back into the palace through the hidden staircase, and avoid curious eyes and speculation, but Ewan's misplaced sense of honor had ruined that plan.

Ewan's honor, indeed. Her face burned as she recalled what he had done to her in the church, and quivers of residual lust assailed her.

Ecgfrith had never taken such liberties before they married. Would it have made a difference if he had? For three years she had dreamed of being with him, yet on their wedding night she had frozen with nerves. And over the following months, no matter how hard she concentrated on overcoming her failings whenever he shared her bedchamber, the knot of anxiety buried deep in her chest only became worse.

She expelled a shaky breath, grateful for her hood that hid her face from both men. It was true that, in unwary moments, she'd imagined how it might be with Ewan. But she had never expected those fantasies to spill into the real world. Their encounter in the church had been so unexpected, she hadn't even had time to think how scandalous it was, never mind anything else.

"This is the passion we'll share, Briana. Never doubt it for a moment."

Goddess, what had she done? She'd wanted to warn him their marriage bed would be one of duty, but now he would expect passion and think she was being deliberately cold when her body involuntarily froze and she failed to respond.

Her stomach churned with nerves, and she gripped her fingers together, concealed beneath her cloak. If only she hadn't gone to the sacred stones this morning, she would not have this additional worry to contend with.

But even though her plans were now awry, she could not regret her early morning visit. Although his reasons had been dishonorable, simply to prove he had no intention of embarking on a passionless marriage, Ewan had nevertheless shown her a glimpse of how glorious sex could be.

If only her body did not disgrace her once she was in the bedchamber.

"I shall see you later, my lady." Ewan held out his hand and for a moment she had the childish urge to ignore him. But of course she could not, for so many reasons, not least that they were all but betrothed.

Not that she intended seeing him again today.

With as much dignity as she could muster, she gave him her hand. He bent his head as he kissed her knuckles and desire speared through her, sharp and hot. The last time she had gazed upon him this way, his wicked mouth had been fastened upon her breast.

He lingered, his lips warming her even through her glove, but she could not pull away. The cursed man mesmerized her, even when she knew his touch meant nothing more to him than a way to bend her to his will.

She would not succumb. But a tiny part of her longed to, just the same.

He straightened, his blue gaze entrapping her as easily as the first time they had met, but she couldn't trust her voice not to give away how profoundly he affected her. So she merely inclined her head, instead, and saw the swift frown that marred his brow at her regal response.

He bowed and after a dark glare at Rohan, turned and marched away. Goddess, why did he cut such a magnificent figure, with his broad shoulders that put every other man to shame?

"Are you certain the Scot did not harm you, my lady?" There was a hard note in Rohan's voice and annoyance flashed through her. She didn't owe him any more of an explanation than had already been given. Yet he had been her loyal friend for so long. He asked only because he was concerned for her safety.

She forced a serene smile to her lips before she turned to face him. "I'm certain. You have no need to fear that Lord Ewan will cause me any such distress."

Just because she feared that very thing was all too possible, was no excuse to share it with anyone, least of all Rohan.

"This marriage is outrageous." His voice was low and for a moment she thought she had misheard. Certainly, it was not his place to make such judgements, when the king had now decreed it was to be.

"This marriage is for Pictland."

"Pictland would survive without this great sacrifice."

"Would she, though?" If Rohan wished to be blunt, then so could she. "We have both Northumbrians and Vikings eyeing our land, and if it's true the Northumbrians are working to discredit our alliance with the Scots, you know as well as I how easily Fotla could fall."

"We have only the Scots word that the assassin was Northumbrian."

To be sure, it was the Scots who had found the ferrule, and a Scot who had proclaimed the fletching on the arrow that had injured Constantine was Northumbrian made. Yet in her heart, she knew it was also the truth.

"It is done, my lord. I'm to wed Lord Ewan MacKinnon." Would MacAllister insist they return to Dal Riada for the ceremony? His king appeared to enjoy making princesses of Pictland tie the knot within his own jurisdiction.

A spark of rebellion stirred. She would have the marriage here, in Fotla, written into the contract.

"Then I offer my continued service to you, my lady." Rohan

sounded more as if he was going into battle rather than extending his protection, and she wasn't sure why his tone irked her. Surely his attitude had nothing to do with him believing she was betraying Ecgfrith's memory by remarrying?

Rohan and her late husband had been second cousins, but everyone knew a young widow of royal blood could not remain single indefinitely.

Yet she could not deny that she would welcome his familiar presence in her new home. She smothered her ire and offered him a smile. "I thank you for your offer and most gratefully accept."

He bowed his head, but it seemed to convey anger more than deference. Goddess, what was wrong with her, finding fault with everything Rohan did? Her rancor was misplaced. It was Ewan, MacAllister, and their despicable king who deserved her contempt, not faithful Rohan.

"It's the least I can do. And I shall protect you with my life, Lady Briana, of that you can be assured."

"I'm certain MacAlpin will allow no harm to befall me." Her voice was dry. The Dal Riadan king had gone to such lengths to secure his Pictish princesses, he surely did not wish anything to happen to them.

"Nevertheless, I am not bound to their barbarous king by warrior oaths. Your personal wellbeing will always be my utmost priority."

Why did Rohan's fierce assertion to protect her cause threads of unease? And why was she lying to herself?

It was not unease. It was resentment. Resentment that it was Rohan, and not Ewan MacKinnon, who offered her such unconditional loyalty.

"I am thankful you will accompany us." Even though she had now thanked him twice, he still appeared reluctant to allow her to continue on her way.

"My lady, it grieves me that you have been given no choice but to accept this proposition. It's always been my hope that, like your first marriage, you might find love a second time, but with a man worthy of your esteem."

She was used to Rohan's candidness, but this surpassed all bounds of propriety. How dare he remind her how little Ecgfrith had cared for her by the end of their marriage? Although her love had died long before her husband had drawn his last breath, the humiliation she had suffered through his countless infidelities still stung.

She couldn't trust herself to speak and so gave a brusque nod and swept past Rohan before he could continue.

Love, as she had discovered to her cost, was a poor foundation upon which to build a solid marital alliance. It had blinded her to signs that should have been obvious, had she not been dazzled by good looks, charm, and breathtaking horsemanship.

She had fallen in love with Ecgfrith when she was but thirteen and dreamed of him every night for three long years. Yet within a month of her widowhood, his features had faded from her mind and now, less than fifteen months later, she could scarcely recall his face at all.

But perhaps that was because she didn't want to remember him, or the heartache he had caused.

Yet although her second marriage was based on nothing more than political necessity, she had the resigned certainty that no matter how long she lived, she would never forget a single thing about Ewan MacKinnon.

CHAPTER 16

Today was his wedding day.

Ewan flattened his hands on the wall either side of the narrow window in the bedchamber and exhaled a long breath. It had been almost three weeks since he and Briana had become betrothed, and on the few occasions their paths had crossed, they had been surrounded by her ladies or warriors, and been unable to speak of anything but shallow pleasantries.

It was likely the queen was behind the princess' curtailed freedom, but sometimes he got the distinct impression it was Briana herself who was deliberately avoiding him.

She would not be able to avoid him after today.

He swallowed a frustrated groan and his hands fisted against the cold stone wall. He'd imagined his wedding night would be spent in his stronghold, Duncreag, but part of the negotiated contract had stipulated the wedding take place in Fotla-eviot. Which meant at least Briana would be surrounded by her kin as she pledged allegiance to him, unlike the other Pictish princesses who had all been married under MacAlpin's watchful eye.

The door opened and he glanced over his shoulder to see Ross and MacAllister enter the chamber.

"It's time," Ross said, and Ewan turned from the window.

Time for me to claim my bride. Since their kiss in the church, his nights had been tormented by visions of Briana, naked and passionate in his arms. Savage hunger scalded his blood, a constant throb that corroded his reason until all he could focus on was consummating this union with her.

And it had nothing to do with the promise he'd made to give her a child.

"The Picts are adamant the ceremony will take place within the stone circle." Exasperation, with a hint of affront, threaded through MacAllister's voice and Ewan silently cursed as he tore his mind from his lust filled fantasies. "A pagan rite we will have to suffer on this holy day to appease the princess. The marriage will be ratified once we return to Dal Riada."

He didn't care if the ritual was pagan or not. In the eyes of Briana, they would be legally wed and that was all that mattered.

She is only yours until you get her with child. For her safety, he needed to ensure that happy event occurred as swiftly as possible.

But a malignant shadow lurked in the corner of his mind, tempting him with a twisted future he could not quite crush.

For the longer he prevented such an outcome, the longer he could stay with her.

The three of them left the stronghold and trudged through the slush that covered the courtyard. It hadn't snowed since the night of the storm when the doors had crashed open, but the surrounding mountains and glens were still shrouded in white. Pict warriors encircled the standing stones, and it appeared all the court were gathered here to witness the ceremony.

He stood beneath an arbor that had been intricately woven with flowers and foliage, and the varying shades of green, russet, and gold were a splash of vibrant color against the wintery backdrop.

Outside the nearby church stood three men. Their long hair

and brightly colored tunics bore no resemblance to the monks of Dal Riada, but their hands were pressed together in prayer, and each wore a large cross hanging from a chain around their necks.

Maybe God would, indeed, be present at this ceremony after all.

A ripple chased through the crowd, and he turned to see Briana and the king approaching. She wore her winter's cloak, but a summer blue veil covered her hair and a circlet of jewels sparkled upon her head.

He could not take his besotted gaze from her.

She didn't glance at him, even when she stood by his side and the Fotla king took his place before them. The king spoke of ancient ways, invoking the names of gods Ewan had never heard of and myths that should have been long forgotten.

Ewan repeated the heathen vows in the foreign tongue, but their meaning was not so very different from the ones he knew in Dal Riada. And after Briana pledged herself to him for all time, the king took her hand and placed it on top of Ewan's, before winding silken bindings of green and gold, the colors of Fotla, around their wrists.

When the king stepped back, a single musician played a haunting melody on a flute, the notes echoing through the otherwise silent land. A shiver scuttled along his spine. In this earthy ceremony, so unlike any he had experienced before, how easy it was to believe that pagan gods existed just beyond the sight of mortal man.

The last ethereal note faded, and the king raised his hands, palms facing the skies. "May the great goddess bless your union, Briana, Princess Euphemia of Fotla and the Kingdom of Pictland, and Ewan, Lord of Duntorr and Duncreag, in the Kingdom of Dal Riada."

Briana turned to face him and finally, her gaze caught his. In the crisp winter light, her eyes glittered like the finest emeralds, more spellbinding than the green jewels that adorned her circlet or were threaded through her beautiful hair.

Without breaking their gaze, he raised their bound hands and pressed a kiss upon her bare fingers. He didn't know whether he broke ancient rules of etiquette and did not care.

Briana was his.

The lightest of breezes swirled around them, and as snowflakes drifted from the skies, a single wolf howled in the distance.

Briana gasped and for an endless moment he tensed, waiting for the other wolves to join the chorus, but only the lingering echo of that one solitary howl filled the air.

Not like her first marriage. It was pagan, but he couldn't help the stab of victory that burned through his chest.

Servants appeared and held a great canopy aloft to protect them from the weather as they made their way back to the stronghold. The great hall was festooned in the colors of Fotla, and the same winter flowers and foliage that had decorated the arbor were woven into garlands and draped around tables.

They sat at the high table, with the queen to his left and the king on Briana's right, and as the nobles and warriors filed into the hall, he leaned close to his wife and whispered in her ear.

"You look beautiful, Briana."

Her smile was restrained. "A bride should look beautiful on her wedding day."

"I misspoke, then. You're beautiful every day."

"It is kind of you to say so."

He wasn't sure why her response caused him unease. But this was their wedding day, after all, and maybe she was simply nervous which was why she didn't sound like herself.

He decided to change tack and raised their bound hands from the table. "How do we eat?"

"Most carefully."

"So we are not permitted to unwrap the bindings before the feast?"

She gave him the faintest trace of a smile. Good. His strategy was working. "Before the feast? I fear we are expected to remain bound together like this for a week at least."

He gave a disbelieving laugh. "You jest."

"As a sign of our commitment."

Hell, was she serious? It hadn't occurred to him to find out the details of the pagan rites, but he should have. He cleared his throat, suddenly unsure. "But what of... when we require privacy?"

Not that he cared when he was with his men. But damn it, he would not have Briana witness such base bodily functions.

There was no mistaking that she was now trying not to laugh. "Do not fear, my lord. We may loosen our bindings as soon as the festivities are over. You are not required to accompany me to the garderobe."

He exhaled a relieved breath. "These customs are unknown to me."

"I shouldn't have teased you so." Her eyes still danced with mischief. "And if it would not cause great distress to my dear papa, we could unbind ourselves now. But I trust you will not mind being tied to me for a few hours more?"

"I don't mind." He should, though. He was more deeply invested in this marriage than he had any right to be, and he couldn't afford to forget it. But could he not enjoy this for just one night, without the specter of his curse hanging over him?

The king stood, and everyone in the great hall fell silent as he gave a speech celebrating the joining of Fotla and Dal Riada. It was standard, political diplomacy, and only when he mentioned Briana did warmth enter his voice.

Ewan had expected nothing more. They had all been coerced into this alliance. Even if, now that it was done, he would have it no other way.

Remember your pledge.

He slammed the thought into a dark corner of his mind. He would never forget his pledge to keep her safe. But for now, he had to play his part in MacAlpin's game.

Aye, keep telling yourself that.

The king gave a toast, everyone drank to their health, but instead of taking his seat, the king once again raised his hands, palms facing up.

"Great Cailleach, Goddess of Winter and Life herself, we thank you for your wise benevolence and mercy as we emerge from the darkness to celebrate another turn of the wheel."

What the hell? It was one thing to wed his Pictish princess in a pagan ritual, but on today of all days, he couldn't shift the uneasy sense that this verged on blasphemy.

He looked at Briana, but her head was bowed, and eyes closed. Stealthily, he cast his glance across the hall, where every Pict appeared to be deep in prayer. His compatriots looked as uneasy by the turn of events as he felt.

And the king wasn't finished. He continued to extol the terrifying virtues of Cailleach, who sounded more like a vengeful warrior than benevolent feminine deity. When the king finally sat, Ewan expelled a relieved breath, grabbed his goblet, and downed the wine in a long swallow.

Briana regarded him over the brim of her goblet. "Is something amiss, my lord?"

He wished she wouldn't call him by that appellation. Every time she did, he couldn't help but wonder if, deep inside, she still believed he had deliberately misled her.

But he didn't want to ruin this day by dragging up that argument. There was something else he wished to know.

"Is Cailleach a goddess who also presides over matrimony?"

Briana replaced her goblet on the table, as servants brought platters of food into the hall.

"It's the winter solstice." Her voice was hushed. "After the

Cold Moon, we honor Cailleach, with the knowledge she holds all life in her hands. Her festival is celebrated on the shortest day of the year with much merriment, the light in the midst of the darkness which will see us through to the thawing of the ice. It seemed judicious to wed this day and take advantage of the great feast and rejoicing."

Now he understood why the Pict king had insisted on this day and refused to reconsider no matter how diplomatically MacAllister had objected. It also explained why a multitude of serfs had joined the feasting and were crammed into the hall by the great doors. "We, too, celebrate at this time of the year."

"Indeed." She inclined her head. "I am aware. Our monks here in Fotla-eviot share your beliefs."

Their bound wrists rested on the table between them. Her hand looked so delicate and fragile on top of his. Slowly he spread his fingers and with only a fleeting hesitation, she threaded her fingers between his.

Sparks flared through his blood at her gentle caress. How could her slightest touch cause such fierce lust to ignite? And there were hours to endure such sweet torture before he could sweep her away to her bedchamber.

Where, at last, he could strip her naked and worship her body the way he'd wanted to since the moment they had met.

A servant refilled his goblet, tearing him from his fevered fantasies. What had they been talking about? It was a struggle to recall, but the alternative was to sit here like a besotted mute. He took a mouthful of wine to clear his head, but all it did was enhance Briana's elegant beauty.

He would not admit defeat and somehow managed to pull coherent words from the bewitched fragments of his mind. "It is odd, don't you think, that our sacred festivals fall upon the same day."

"I do not find it odd." She gave him a soft smile and he tightened his fingers around hers, trapping her. "But I do find it interesting."

Her elusive scent of lavender should not affect him like a potent aphrodisiac from the mystic Eastern lands, but it stole his senses, nonetheless. He couldn't stop himself from leaning closer, so there was no chance of anyone overhearing his confession. "It may amuse you to know MacAllister is personally offended by this twist of fate."

"Alas, I cannot pretend to care for MacAllister's wounded feelings."

His own amusement faded at her reply. "Briana," he whispered, and waited until she turned to look at him, a serene smile on her face.

"Yes, my lord?" Her voice was perfectly agreeable. And that, he realized, was the problem. He didn't want her polite responses and although her remark about MacAllister could hardly be called diplomatic, there was so much more she wasn't saying.

He could feel it, simmering in the air between them.

Did he really want to go down this path, now of all times?

No. But he sure as hell didn't want to discuss it later, in the bedchamber. And before they were alone, he wanted the air cleared between them.

"I meant what I said. I'll do everything in my power to ensure this marriage meets your expectations."

"Ah." There was a note in her voice he couldn't place. "That is good to know. And since you are aware of my expectations, there's no need to overexert yourself while aiming to accomplish them."

Platters were placed on the table, but he scarcely noticed the enticing aromas as Briana's comment thundered around his head.

Did she mean what he thought she did?

Of course she did. For reasons he couldn't fathom, she was determined their marriage bed would be a passionless place, despite how he'd shown her otherwise. Was it because her first marriage had been cold? Or was it because she had shared such deep desire with her late husband, she couldn't bear to recreate it with another?

Whatever had happened in the past had nothing to do with him. Yet it seemed he couldn't get it out of his mind. The small hints she had shared of that previous life were confounding. She had married for love but had confessed her secret dreams were too unrealistic for mere mortals.

Some things are best left to the imagination.

He couldn't ask her. But he'd be damned if he'd allow her to labor under the delusion that he would need to *overexert* himself merely to fulfil her requirements.

He twisted his hand within the bindings, so they were palm to palm. A simple gesture that should not send bolts of heat plunging through his blood. He wrapped his fingers around her, and she let out a soft gasp but did not drop her gaze from his.

"Let me be clear, my beautiful bride, that what happened between us in the church the other week was merely a foretaste. Whatever else may be lacking in our marriage, rest assured I intend to satisfy every carnal desire you have ever imagined." He brushed his jaw against her warm cheek and whispered his promise in her ear. "I will have you writhing beneath me in mindless pleasure, Briana, make no mistake. And for as many nights as it takes to fulfil your *expectations*."

CHAPTER 17

*B*riana's heart pounded like a wild thing within her breast, stealing her breath and her wits, curse it. But it was so hard to remain cool and aloof when Ewan whispered such scandalous promises in her ear. And she couldn't even respond in the way she wanted to, since the hall was filled with an avid audience who would ensure everything that happened between the Princess of Fotla, and her Scots husband, was repeated with intoxicated delight.

No matter how she tried to prepare Ewan, he appeared determined to believe his male prowess would melt her frost with little more than a kiss.

She couldn't even blame him, after that encounter in the church. How many times had that interlude haunted her dreams and played on her mind since their betrothal? How many times had she wished he'd been driven by something other than a need to prove he could bring her to her knees so easily?

Slowly, he pulled back and his blue eyes ensnared her as surely as a spell cast from the fae folk themselves. But a mythical spell was not enough to heat her blood when it was most needed.

I cannot pretend any longer, Briana. Ecgfrith's regretful voice whispered through the shadowed corners of her mind. *You have ice in your veins that no man can thaw.*

No. She would not think of Ecgfrith now. But trepidation gripped her at the ordeal that lay ahead, when Ewan would blame her for her cold response. For unlike that encounter in the church, tonight was not unexpected, and her anxiety driven thoughts would not still.

There was only one slender thread she could summon, which might possibly stay his hand.

"I have already explained this." Her whisper was so soft, he had to lean in closer to hear, and his breath dusted her lips in a caress that sent erratic sparks dancing through her blood. *But it was not enough.* It never was. She drew in a shaky breath and focused her scattered senses. "Since we are both in agreement as to the outcome of this alliance, we need only copulate when my moon time is ripe. And that will not occur for another week."

He cocked his head, studying her so intently she had the alarming urge to fidget, to drop her gaze, to escape from the great hall entirely. But she did none of those things, for above all else she was a Princess of Fotla, and the honor of her land lay heavy on her shoulders.

Finally, when she could scarcely bear the tension that screamed between them any longer, he spoke. "How can you be so certain of these things?"

It was not the question she had expected from him, but at least it was easily answered. "It is wisdom from the goddess. All women know this." But perhaps she was wrong. Perhaps women in Dal Riada, who no longer followed the ancient ways, had no knowledge of such things.

After an eternity, he raised their bound hands and pressed a kiss to the back of her hand. She let out a ragged breath as his gaze finally released hers. But his lips against her flesh held her as securely captive in his thrall as ever.

~

As befit the solstice celebration, the platters were many and the variety of offerings vast. And once the feasting was done, the entertainment would continue until the rooster crowed.

Usually, Briana enjoyed the festivities. But tonight, she barely touched the food that the cooks had spent so many days preparing.

It was foolish to be so nervous of her wedding night, when she had been married for almost four years to her late husband. Yet the flutterings in her stomach were like those of an untouched maid, who knew nothing of men, but even when she had been a maid, she had never been ignorant of such fundamental knowledge.

She hadn't suffered so at her first wedding. But then, she hadn't been aware of her flaw. And despite their earlier conversation, she wasn't at all sure that Ewan agreed they should delay consummation for a week.

Ewan stroked the back of her hand with his thumb. He likely didn't even know he was doing it, but the featherlight touch was distractingly sensual. With an effort, she ignored it.

She couldn't ignore him when, once again, he leaned close, his magnificent biceps pressing against her arm. "Are you not hungry, my lady?"

How did he know? She had been most circumspect, pushing the food around her platter to create the illusion she was eating as much as anyone. Clearly, he was more observant than she had given him credit for.

There was no point demurring. "Alas, my appetite has fled."

"On my account?" There was a brooding note in his voice, and although the way their arms touched was most unseemly, she could not bring herself to pull back and break their connection. "I'll never hurt you, Briana. You must know that."

"I do." She managed to incline her head in a regal manner

although goddess only knew how. She had no doubt Ewan would never knowingly hurt her, but she feared he could do so, nevertheless, unless she could claw back control of her foolish feelings. "It's been a long week, that is all."

It had been a long, dark, year for Pictland. But she would not bring politics into this, now.

"Would we break etiquette beyond repair if we left the festivities early?"

Her stomach churned. But it had nothing to do with the lack of food she'd consumed this day, or even with trepidation of what might follow when she and Ewan were alone.

It was anticipation. Goddess help her. Despite her inability to perform when necessary, how desperately she wanted to be in Ewan's arms tonight.

"I cannot say. We have not had a handfasting during the winter solstice before. Royal weddings are generally undertaken during the spring and summer."

Which was one reason why none of the other Pictish Kingdoms had been represented at this alliance. That, and the fact this wedding had been so improperly hasty that envoys had not been dispatched.

Except one to the Kingdom of Ce. To revoke the question of betrothal with Lord Talargan.

The feast proceeded, and the bard sang a haunting song of the heroic sacrifice of her cousin Aila's first husband, who had given his life to protect her honor against the barbarous Vikings.

As a young girl she had been captivated by the romantic tragedy of Aila's loss. But as she had grown older, the underlying brutality of the gallant song gnawed into her soul.

Men went into battle and fought for their king and country. And women suffered their loss and were expected to weave together the frayed edges of the tapestry of life, so another generation could flourish.

Would certain peace ever bless her beloved land?

Briana could feel Ewan's probing gaze upon her, but she avoided his eyes and thankfully he didn't break their silence again. But they still held hands and his thumb occasionally caressed hers, and it was both astonishing and unnerving how such a casual touch could be so intimate.

Except there was nothing casual about his touch. He knew how he affected her. Doubtless, he was thinking of when they were alone in her chamber and how he would once again conquer her.

And how the illusion would all fall apart as soon as he attempted to claim his marital rights.

The great hall was too crowded to push back the tables so the nobles could dance, but in the narrow space in front of the high table musicians played, bards sang, and entertainers showed their elaborate skills. The babble of voices increased, and the stamping of feet and clapping of hands vibrated around the hall, creating a surreal maelstrom of strangely detached familiarity.

"My lady." Ewan's husky whisper in her ear caused shivers of need across her skin. "It is time."

Her mouth dried and a thousand flimsy excuses fluttered through her mind. But they remained locked in her throat, for what did it matter whether they left the hall now, or when dawn broke?

Either way, Ewan intended to make her his wife and all she was doing was prolonging the inevitable.

There was no discreet slipping from the great hall unnoticed when every eye turned their way as soon as they stood. The king stood also, and took her hand, sorrow gleaming in his eyes as he bade her goodnight.

The peasants at the end of the hall, fueled with considerable quantities of ale, let out great cheers that thudded against the walls and many drunken nobles joined in. Her ladies came to her side and Ewan wound his arm around her waist, clearly either unknowing or uncaring that he breached etiquette by doing so.

Not that she could fault him. His big body shielded her from the crowd, for which she was grateful. She could almost believe he had done it deliberately.

As they left the hall, she sent a silent prayer of thanks to Bride that this time, unlike her first marriage, there would be no public bedding of the bride. The archaic custom had been undertaken more in fun than anything else, with much laughter between herself and her ladies. And as soon as Ecgfrith had entered the bedchamber, everyone else had departed.

But she didn't feel like laughing this time, and it seemed Ewan had every intention of escorting her to her bedchamber himself. Away from the press of bodies, and dogs, and the multitude of aromatic dishes that permeated the great hall, his scent of pine and leather drifted around her like a gossamer caress, stealing her breath and intoxicating her mind.

At the foot of the stairs, he paused and breathed in her ear. "There is no need for your ladies to miss the rest of the night's festivities. Send them away, Briana. I shall attend to your every need this night."

Her every need...

His husky promise shimmered along her senses and for an endless moment the rest of his whispered command did not register.

She drew in a sharp breath. Her ladies were loyal, and would spend the night in her antechamber, in case she required anything, unless she gave them leave to remain in the great hall. The solstice was a time for merriment, and while she knew full well why Ewan had suggested it, and it had little to do with the comfort of her ladies, she wished she had thought of releasing them from their duties tonight before he'd said anything.

Well, she could rectify her oversight now, and she took Nairne's hand. "Return to the hall. I shall be quite all right."

Nairne shot Ewan a disapproving glance, but it was obvious she longed to return to the festivities. "Are you certain, my lady?"

"I am." There were still guards around the palace, including one that, inevitably, prowled the corridor outside her chambers. Not Drest tonight, though. He was at the feast, shooting dark glares at every Scot present. Besides, no harm would befall her while in Ewan's company.

Except for her pride, perhaps.

But it was hard to cling onto her pride when Ewan tugged her close as they made their way along the corridor. His presence took up all the space and all the air, and the flickering of the torches in their sconces added to the otherworldly sensation that had swirled around her during the feast.

If only she could remain in this silken cocoon, where nothing felt quite real, and Ewan's touch sparked such decadent pleasure. If only, when the moment of consummation was upon her, she did not *think* so very much—

"My lady." The brusque voice snatched her from her ruminations, and she pulled up with a start. Ewan's arm tightened around her, and tension spiked from him as they faced Rohan.

She hadn't even seen his approach.

"Lord Rohan." Flustered, and irrationally irked by the sensation, she straightened her spine. When had she all but melted against Ewan? How unseemly. "You are not enjoying the festivities?"

He gave a stiff bow. "Indeed, I am. However, I believed it prudent to ensure the palace is secure. Your safety is paramount."

Of course the palace was secure. Since the incident with the doors, security had been increased and even tonight extra guards were on duty. And Rohan most certainly knew that.

"Your conscientiousness is noted and appreciated." Ewan's tone suggested the exact opposite, and she shot him a confused glance. "The safety of the princess is all our concern."

Hostility thickened the air, and she drew in a deep breath. It was clear Ewan and Rohan would never see eye-to-eye, but she was not prepared to witness their antagonism on this night, of all nights.

"I bid you a goodnight, my lord," she said to Rohan, and when Ewan opened the door to her chambers, she swept inside.

He closed the door behind them a little too forcefully. "I confess I shall not miss that man when we return to Dal Riada."

They were leaving Fotla in a few days' time and although it was far too hasty for her liking, there was nothing to be done about it. They had, after all, scored a victory against MacAlpin by having the wedding here, among her own people.

But as he took her hands, she was compelled to respond. "Lord Rohan is accompanying me as part of my contingent."

Irritation flashed over his face. "Is that really necessary?"

Why was he discussing this now? Indeed, it was not even any of his concern. "It's part of the marriage contract that I bring my own men with me." And her ladies who, thankfully, had all agreed to travel into the Scots' savage land with her.

Somewhat to her surprise, Drest was also part of her contingent. It wasn't that she disliked the warrior. Quite the contrary, in fact. She had known him for many years, but he was a senior ranking warrior responsible for his own contingent here in Fotla, and she couldn't fathom why he had been assigned to her.

"I speak only of Rohan. Naturally you must bring your own contingent. I expect nothing less."

"I don't understand why you have a problem with Rohan."

"I don't have a problem with him. I merely find his attitude towards you... over familiar."

It was galling that she agreed with him. Rohan *had* become overly familiar during the last year, but she had left it too late to say anything to him now. And his small actions were not *that* great a breach of etiquette, after all.

Conversely, she didn't want Ewan thinking she was oblivious to what was so obvious to him.

"We are kin through my first husband." Hadn't she told him

that already? "He does, perhaps, breach protocol on occasion, but his loyalty is absolute."

Ewan gave her an oddly brooding look, as though he was searching for hidden answers. But she hadn't hidden anything—unless she counted how it had been Rohan who had disclosed to her how Ecgfrith had died. And although the nature of Ecgfrith's demise was scarcely a secret it was certainly something she did not wish to discuss with Ewan.

Finally, he sighed. "Why are we speaking of Rohan on our wedding night?"

"It is not I who started this conversation."

"That was my attempt at an apology, my lady."

There was an irresistible hint of laughter in his voice. How hard he made it for her to keep him at a distance.

"Alas, you clearly need more practice."

"It's true I'm not an expert in this art but I trust you'll allow me to make amends before this night is over."

Desire simmered through her blood, but nerves collided in the pit of her stomach, reminding her of her inadequacies. She had tried to warn him, to no avail. Should she tell him plainly, so there were no misunderstandings?

But her courage failed her. She would rather he think her dedicated only to duty when it came to the marriage bed, rather than the pitiable truth.

CHAPTER 18

*E*wan sucked in a deep breath. He would not rush this. They had all night. And although it should make no difference to him in this political marriage, he couldn't help the savage satisfaction in knowing that whatever feelings Rohan harbored about Briana, she didn't return them.

The bindings around their wrists were quaint, but they hindered his intentions. Without taking his gaze from her, he loosened the knots.

"Freedom." She raised her arm and gave him a sardonic smile. He threaded his fingers through hers and tugged her close.

"Not tonight." Lust thickened his words and her eyes darkened. It was all the encouragement he needed. He swept her into his arms and her gasp of shock, as she wound her arm around his neck, arrowed straight to his groin.

"I'm quite capable of walking." Her protest only fueled the fire in his blood, as he opened the door to her bedchamber and kicked it shut behind them. Candles flickered and flames burned high in the hearth, giving plenty of light to see Briana's face. "There's no need to try and charm me with your brute warrior strength."

He laughed and tightened his hold on her. "So you confess that I charm you?"

"I said *try*."

"Fear not. I shall continue until I succeed in this mission."

"You're very sure of yourself." But despite the note of condemnation in her voice, a smile curved her lips. God, her lips. He could not wait to taste them again. And why the hell was he waiting? She was his bride. He could kiss her whenever he desired.

Warning flickered in the back of his mind, but it was faint, and it was easy to ignore when Briana was in his arms, and her fingers were gently tangling in his hair. She tilted her head, a provocative invitation, and he didn't even try to resist.

Her lips parted beneath his, and their kiss was sweeter, and more potent, than even the one they had shared in the church. His groan vibrated in their mouths, throughout his whole body, until all he could hear was its frustrated echo in his mind.

She pulled back, breaking their kiss, and her uneven breath was a torturous caress. Primitive need throbbed, and it took all his considerable willpower not to lay her on the bed, lift her skirts, and take her like the brute warrior she had just accused him of being.

The image seared his brain, and the way she trailed her fingers along his jaw scrambled his senses. So damn tempting. But this was his wedding night, with the woman he had never dared believe could be his. And since she would be his for only a short time, he was going to make the most of it.

Even if it all but killed him.

He turned his back on the bed and strode over to the hearth, before slowly releasing her, and her luscious body slid along his in a sensuous whisper of immeasurable promise.

As he cupped her face, incomprehension glowed in her beautiful eyes. "You are not taking me to bed?"

He grinned, and feared he looked nothing less than feral, yet couldn't help himself. Luckily, there was a practical reason he could cite which was surely better than the truth. "I must strip you"—*naked*. Somehow, he managed to swallow the word before it could inadvertently escape— "Of your jewels first, my lady."

"Oh." Was she blushing, or was it a trick of the firelight? "But of course. Perhaps I should not have been so hasty in dismissing my ladies."

With great restraint, he plucked the gem encrusted circlet from her head and placed it on a small table beside the fire. "And deny me this unique pleasure?"

"It is certainly unconventional."

He slid his thumbs beneath the gossamer edges of her veil and slipped it from her head before letting it float to the floor in a cloud of summer blue. "I'm not adverse to breaking such customs."

"Nor I." Her whisper stoked the lust that flowed through his veins, but he would not succumb. Not yet.

He grasped the end of her plait and unwound the green ribbon. The silk of her hair caressed his palm but his plan of spearing his fingers through the rich auburn tresses stalled at the emeralds that were threaded through each lock.

"Ah." He glanced at her and her smile damn near sucked the breath from his chest.

"Should I assist you, my lord?" Her teasing question did nothing to help the deprived state of his lungs. "It is a delicate process, not a task a great warrior might easily undertake."

"Do you doubt my prowess?"

Her smile dimmed, but perhaps it was merely another illusion from the flickering light, for why would his words cause her any concern? He was seeing omens where there were none, because of his guilt at entrapping her in his world.

Not now. He shoved the darkness to the deepest recesses of his soul. His tarnished legacy would not cripple the few nights he could share with Briana.

"I do not doubt your prowess in the least." She soundly oddly prim and dropped her gaze. He cupped her jaw and raised her face, and once again there was a soft smile on her lips.

God, he was losing his mind. She was not a virgin bride who feared the marriage bed. So why did he keep imagining a sliver of reticence in her air?

"I shall strive to live up to your expectations." He couldn't help a wolfish grin, and he couldn't help stealing another kiss, either. With more restraint that he'd known he possessed, he straightened, his thumb gently stroking her warm cheek.

Aye, he'd do everything he could so she would remember this night forever. And although he wasn't conversant with her mystical talk of moon times, he believed her when she said she wouldn't conceive this week.

He had promised to get her with child, and he would not go back on his word. But the corrupt notion that had polluted his mind earlier this day gnawed at him, regardless.

The longer he prevented such an outcome, the longer he could stay with her.

Ewan's warrior hard fingers caressed her face, and it took every particle of strength Briana possessed to remain ramrod straight, and not wrap her arms around him and hold him close. But she couldn't do that. Because it would make the inevitable disappointment so much harder to bear.

"These emeralds are trickier than they first appear." He gave her another of his bone-melting smiles as he gently tugged on one of the jewels in her hair. "But I shall not allow them to defeat me."

"There are a great many pins involved," she conceded. If only he didn't smell so wonderful. Every breath filled her with his subtle scent, and although there was nothing unique about leather and pine, when combined with Ewan it was utterly exotic. She swallowed, her mouth dry, and tried to focus. "It's not too difficult, if you follow the golden chain."

He gave a grunt of satisfaction as he extracted a pin and carefully placed it next to the circlet. How could so simple a thing be so intoxicating?

"The workmanship is exquisite." He caught her gaze, and the back of his hand grazed her breast in a tantalizing caress as he held her plait. "I've never seen golden flecks enhance the beauty of emeralds before."

There were no golden flecks in the emeralds, and she smiled, unable to resist his outrageous compliment. "Workmanship?" There was a trace of laughter in her voice. "I confess, I'm confused. Do you pass judgement on my jewels, or my eyes?"

"Both?" He removed another pin from the chain and gathered the emerald in his palm. All without breaking their gaze. There was no reason in the world why that should feel so thrilling, and yet it did. "Your jewels are magnificent, but they fade to insignificance beside the allure of your eyes."

"Then I must return the compliment. Your eyes remind me of a summer sky, threaded with silver moonlight."

Goddess. What had possessed her to confess such a thing to him? Yet she didn't regret it. How could she, when his grin of delight warmed her deep inside, in places she scarcely even knew existed?

"Your kind words enchant me. No one has ever said anything like that about me before."

It was foolish to be charmed by the notion she was the only one who had admired his eyes so, and yet she was. She didn't even try to suppress the glow that flowed through her like the finest wine.

"I shall endeavor to find other words no one has ever said to you before, then."

"I've no doubt you will. You have since the day we met."

His knuckles stroked against her jaw and with a start she realized he had almost teased free the length of jewels from her hair. One more pin, and the final emerald fell onto his palm in a pool of gold and green. "You do not appear to mind my lack of discretion."

"I find your candor delightful." He dropped the emeralds and pins onto the table, and his hungry gaze roved over her face. Heat speared through her, sharp and exhilarating, warming her cheeks, and she couldn't tear her mesmerized eyes from him. "I trust you'll always speak your mind with me, Briana."

How she loved hearing her name on his tongue. He made each syllable sound so deliciously decadent, and tremors of need shimmered through her blood. "I fear it would be hard to stop me from doing so."

With infinite care, he removed her girdle and placed it on the table, before spearing his fingers through her hair, until her curls tumbled over her shoulders. He wound a lock around his fist and pressed his lips against it. The breath caught in her throat, and she couldn't drag her fascinated gaze from him.

"I've dreamed of seeing your hair loose like this and imagined how soft it would feel in my hands. Like silk from the east. Yet you surpass even my wildest fantasies."

He bent his head, and his kiss seared her lips. Instinctively, her mouth opened, and his tongue teased her mercilessly, until, goddess help her, her very knees trembled beneath his sensual onslaught.

When he tore his mouth from her, she gasped in protest, her fingers tangled in his hair. When had she grasped his head? She couldn't even recall. And it didn't matter, for all she wanted was for Ewan to never let her go.

He trailed kisses along her throat, and she tipped her head back, to give him access. His grip on her hair didn't lessen, and it was both barbaric and thrilling when he wound another length about his fist, his knuckles pressing against her cheek.

There was no fumbling or hurried tugging at her bodice. Instead, he leisurely loosened her ties as though they had all the time in the world. She shifted restlessly, her grip on his hair tightening, silently urging him on, but he seemed oblivious.

"Ewan," she breathed, as he stroked his thumb across her nipple. How she had craved for his touch again, ever since that morning in the church. She arched her back, pressing herself more securely into his palm, and a soft moan escaped when he captured her sensitive peak between his finger and thumb. "I cannot think..." Her words trailed into a vortex of pleasure, and she was scarcely aware she had spoken at all.

"Aye." His hot breath sent whirlpools of desire across her flesh. "I can barely think when you are near. You have tormented me since the day we met."

Such a confession deserved an answer, but it was hard to gather her senses when he inched her gown over her shoulders and pressed his hot mouth to her exposed breast. "It was never my intention to distract you."

Without answering, he wrapped his hands around her wrists and pinned her arms to her sides. Before she could protest, he continued to tug her gown from her, along her arms, and with growing impatience, she wriggled, until the material slipped from her and pooled at her feet. He grinned, his dimples causing the breath to catch in her throat, as he swiftly divested her of her long-sleeved under-gown.

Although clad only in her chemise, the heat from the fire dispelled any chill in the chamber. Indeed, she was fairly burning, not least because of the heat in Ewan's eyes.

He took her hand and kissed her palm. No one had ever kissed her there before and shivers raced through her. Who could imagine such a simple gesture could be so alluring?

"You distract me simply by being." There was a husky note in his voice and once again he bent his head and pressed a kiss to her inner wrist. She swallowed, transfixed, as he slowly kissed his way to the crook of her arm. "There is nothing that can be done about it."

She couldn't help herself and threaded her fingers through his luxuriant hair. His teeth grazed her skin, and she imagined his smile before he raised his head and caught her gaze. "You have bewitched me."

As you have bewitched me. But she kept that confession locked deep inside. "I did not think Scots held such ancient beliefs."

"When I'm with you, I can believe almost anything."

With the firelight glinting on the threads of gold that highlighted his copper hair, she could believe almost anything, too. But she had to clarify one thing, regardless. "I'm not a witch."

His hands traced along her arms, and shimmers of delight coursed through her. "I know that." Amusement hummed through the blatant desire that roughened his voice. "There are no such creatures as witches."

There were, but none had been glimpsed in generations and their existence was wreathed in shadows and never spoken of. But she was of no mind to explain that to Ewan. Not when he caressed her shoulders and breasts and teased her nipples until she could scarcely stand, never mind voice a coherent thought.

His mouth followed the seductive trail of his fingers, and she expelled a ragged sigh as he cupped her breast and teased her sensitive bud with his tongue. Her chemise followed her undergown and Ewan pressed burning kisses across her stomach and she clutched his hair, her only anchor in a swirling maelstrom of sensation.

When he dropped to his knees, she hitched in a sharp gasp, thoughts colliding in lust drenched disarray. He licked her, slow and sure, and damp heat flooded her, causing her legs to tremble. She tried to speak, but words were beyond her, and all she could hear was the harsh rasp of her breath and the thunder of her heart.

He pushed inside, kissing her slick sheath the way he had just kissed her mouth. The torches spun around the chamber, blurring everything into a golden, hazy glow except for the man kneeling before her.

Spellbound, she couldn't tear her eyes from him as he tasted her wet cleft and teased her swollen clitoris. Tension coiled low in her womb, fiery sparks ignited her blood, and when Ewan sucked her bud, a primitive scream of release whirled through her mind.

Not just my mind. The air was heavy with arousal and lust and the lingering echo of her rapture.

But she didn't care. Couldn't care. Only Ewan's hands on her hips kept her from collapsing; that, and the way she gripped his hair. She sagged, panting, but still couldn't release him, in case she punctured this intoxicating cocoon where tendrils of pleasure rippled through her like starlight.

He shifted, briefly releasing her as he placed his brooch on the table and unwound his plaid. Still wearing his saffron shirt, he stood, towering over her, his broad shoulders eclipsing the rest of the chamber before he tore his shirt over his head in one swift motion.

Taut muscles filled her vision, bronzed and glorious, and a silent sigh drifted through her dazed mind. She stroked her fingers along his magnificent biceps, and he wrapped his arms around her, pulling her close.

She gasped, sliding her hands to his back, and delicious ripples consumed her as he crushed her against his hard body. His thick cock pressed against her belly, hot and unyielding, and once more lust fluttered along her damp cleft.

"My bride." It was a low growl of possession, and she tightened her arms around him, delighting in the strength that emanated from him beneath her exploring fingers. With a feral grin, he lowered them to the precious Persian rug before the fire and lay on his back. "I will not subject you to the stone floor, but the bed is too far away for my comfort."

She laughed, and straddled his hips, her hair cascading over her shoulders and brushing his jaw. "You are very thoughtful, my lord."

Once again, he wrapped her hair around his fist. How could such a barbaric gesture thrill her so? "Kiss me."

It was a harsh command and she found it delightful. Slowly she lowered her head, drinking in every feature of his aristocratic face. His strong jaw, with a dusting of stubble, the way the flickering light played across his irresistible dimples as he smiled at her, and his compelling blue eyes that ensnared her and would not let her go.

Their lips met, and she teased him with the tip of her tongue before he gave a primal groan and tangled his tongue with hers. She clutched his shoulders, bracing her weight, as he glided his hands along her back and sensual waves of pleasure built deep inside.

He grasped her bottom, relentlessly pulling her back and forth along his erection. The pressure was unbearable, filling her, fogging her senses and she tore free, gasping down at him. She needed... she needed *more*.

"I must have you." His voice was raw with lust and her sensitized flesh quivered at his possessive command. "Christ, you're killing me."

"It's not intentional, I assure you," she gasped, as laughter threaded through the desire that burned within her. "Indeed, it would be most unfortunate if I did."

He laughed yet sounded as if he were in agony. "Aye, that it would." With a groan, he gripped his cock and nudged her wet entrance. She sucked in a sharp breath and involuntarily dug her nails into his shoulders. "I cannot hold on much longer, my love."

My love. It should not entrance her so, but did, regardless.

"Then don't," she whispered, barely aware she spoke, knowing only that she needed him as frantically as he needed her.

He pushed into her, so big, so thick, the air caught in her

throat and for an eternal moment she couldn't move, couldn't think. But sweet goddess, she could feel everything. He penetrated her, stretching her to accommodate his girth, the sensation so intense it consumed every particle of her being.

And his hands stroked her everywhere, along her thighs and over her hips, igniting flames that swept across her skin and swirled through her blood. She braced her hands against his shoulders, pushing herself up, and he cradled her breasts, tormenting her aching nipples with his thumbs.

Her heart thundered and pulse raced as he grasped her hips and thrust deep inside. The friction was exquisite, a heartbeat between ecstasy and agony, and she rode the wave, enraptured by the sight of Ewan's face as he brought them ever closer to the edge.

Harsh breaths filled the air. He swirled his finger around her clitoris, and it was too much. With a choked cry her release flooded through her, and she mindlessly convulsed around Ewan's shaft in a lover's embrace.

His body went rigid before he grasped her backside in a punishing grip and pumped his hot seed deep inside her.

Goddess.

She collapsed onto him, gasping for breath, her heart a wild thing that threatened to escape her breast. For endless moments neither moved, and all she could hear was the erratic thud of his heart beneath her hand.

And then he wrapped his plaid around her, a cocoon of warmth permeated with his evocative scent. His fingers idly played with her hair and slowly, so slowly, reality emerged through the lust drenched haze.

She hadn't frozen at the moment of penetration. She hadn't even *thought* about what was happening but had simply reveled in each glorious second.

Awe shivered through her, and Ewan's arm tightened around her as if he thought she might be cold.

But she wasn't cold. There wasn't ice in her veins, after all. With Ewan, she had not had time to worry and overthink, and tie herself up into nerve-wracking knots of insecurity.

And now it was done, he was not preparing to leave, either. Cautiously, she lifted her head. He gave her a lazy smile and her insides melted. She trailed a finger along his lips and passion flared in his eyes, reflecting the rising need spiraling through her.

Twice in one night? It was something she had never experienced or wished to endure during her previous marriage. But now...

Delicious thrills raced through her, and she wriggled up Ewan's body, delighting in how he drew in a harsh breath. And how fervently he held her close as she kissed him.

The earthy aromas of sex and woodsmoke perfumed the air, but it was the scent of leather and pine that filled her head as Ewan stood, with her in his arms, wrapped in his plaid, and carried her to their bed.

CHAPTER 19

*S*he had been married for ten days. It was no time at all, yet sometimes Briana felt as though she had been with Ewan forever. And soon, they would arrive at his stronghold. Not Duncreag, the home of his father, as he had originally told her, but his grandfather's estate, Duntorr.

Thankfully, it hadn't snowed since they'd left Fotla-eviot, and they had made good time. Her ladies and personal guard rode with her, with the Scots in front and bringing up the rear, behind the wagons that contained her personal possessions. Rohan, to her relief, had kept his distance since their last fraught exchange on her wedding night, although she was aware of his brooding presence on the fringes of her company.

Ewan broke away from the warriors who headed their blended contingent and cantered back to her, a smile lighting up his face as she caught his eye. Her foolish heart leaped in her breast, despite how she tried to deny her feelings, but it was no use.

Desire licked through her, an untamable hunger that now constantly lurked on the edge of her existence. It was doubtless scandalous how often during the day her mind replayed their bed sport in graphic, glorious detail, but she couldn't help it.

He had ignited a fire in her blood, and she did not regret it. But that didn't mean she would ever forget the reason they had wed was to strengthen the political alliance between Pict and Scot.

He drew up beside her. "Tonight, you shall sleep in your own bedchamber."

"I look forward to it." And not just because Ewan would be there. For the last week they had enjoyed the hospitality of nobles in Fotla, and then in Dal Riada, and it would be a relief to unpack the wagons and once again have her own possessions around her.

They followed the path to the edge of the forest, where the trees thinned. "Duntorr." Pride threaded through Ewan's voice, and she followed his gaze to where, on a mighty hill, stood a magnificent stronghold.

She wasn't sure what she had expected, but it exceeded anything she had imagined. Certainly, it looked grander than the other noble Scots' strongholds they had stayed in during the journey. The rumors she had grown up with of the Scots' primitive hillforts had been much mistaken. "It is grand, indeed."

He reached over and threaded his fingers through hers. "It's not a Pictish palace, but I trust you will find it to your liking. I had thought to take you to the stronghold where I grew up, but my lady grandmother sent word that you should be mistress of Duntorr. She would have it no other way."

She was curious to meet his grandmother, the mysterious Pictish princess who, according to Ewan, was not a princess. Yet she could not deny the trepidation that curled in the pit of her stomach at the prospect of her new life in this foreign land. But she had managed to keep her apprehension locked down since the betrothal and she wasn't going to let her fears overwhelm her now.

It was another two hours before they navigated the ramparts that surrounded Duntorr. As they passed through the village square there was a farrier's workshop, and beyond it lay a tavern. Somehow, she hadn't considered the Scots would be so civilized although that was positively foolish, considering all she had learned of them during the last year.

At last, they entered the stronghold's courtyard and Ewan helped her dismount, his hands lingering on her waist, and inevitable flutters of lust collided with the nerves that refused to die. He hadn't shared her bed the last two nights but surely tonight, in his own home, he would.

Beli, the young lad that Ewan had saved from a thrashing the other week, took their horses' bridles. He had begged Ewan to be allowed to accompany them to Dal Riada, and Briana had easily ensured the proper requirements were made.

The warriors dismounted and, she presumed, took their horses to the stables, while Ewan led her to the stronghold's entrance, her ladies, and Drest, following. Except MacAllister also joined them. But why? He had done his king's work. There was no need of him now.

An unpleasant possibility scraped through her mind. Unless the upstart, MacAlpin, awaited inside, to welcome her to Dal Riada? It scarcely seemed likely, but she would put nothing past the Scots' king if he believed it gave him an advantage.

The doors opened, and Ewan ushered her into the great hall. Tapestries hung upon the walls, a fire roared in the hearth, and a noblewoman and several ladies smiled in greeting. But surely this lady was not Ewan's grandmother? She looked of an age similar to her own mamma.

Ewan greeted her with warmth, before making the introductions. She was his aunt Sorcha, the daughter of his grandmother, whom, he had once informed her, was one of the most formidable women in Dal Riada.

"My lady." Sorcha curtseyed, a smile of welcome on her face, and the knots within Briana's stomach eased a little. "It is our great honor to welcome you to Duntorr. My lady mother is greatly looking forward to making your acquaintance."

She spoke perfect Pictish, without even a hint of an accent.

"I thank you for your kindness. I am most anxious to pay my respects to your lady mother."

"If you're not too tired from the journey, we've arranged for refreshments in my lady mother's private chamber. But it's no trouble to send refreshments to your own bedchamber, should you wish to rest."

Although the prospect of relaxing in her own chamber was tempting, she knew her duty. Here, at Duntorr, she represented the Kingdom of Fotla and Pictland herself, and she would give no one cause to level accusations of discourtesy against her.

"I should be delighted to take refreshments with your lady mother."

Sorcha smiled, before turning to Ewan. "My ladies and I shall follow you, Ewan."

As Ewan took her hand, she was distracted by MacAllister who strode over to Sorcha and gave a bow. "My lady."

"Ah, Conall." Sorcha sounded amused, and despite her best intentions, Briana couldn't help glancing over her shoulder, as Ewan led her past the foreign noblewomen. "It is good to see you again. It's been too long."

"A year, at least." MacAllister smiled, and it was not one of his cold smiles that never reached his eyes. Hastily, Briana tore her gaze away before anyone noticed her unseemly interest. "Yet you have not aged a day, Sorcha."

Good goddess. Was there something between them? Unforgivably, Briana stumbled as they left the great hall and entered a corridor and Ewan tightened his grip around her fingers. She shot him a glance and he gave her a wry grin, almost as though he guessed her thoughts.

She hoped he hadn't. Because no man would be amused to

know his bride suspected his own aunt of conducting an affair with the king's man.

Ewan bent his head and whispered in her ear. "I understand your shock at witnessing the unmasking of MacAllister. But he and my lady aunt grew up together. They care for each other like siblings."

"Indeed." She inclined her head, so he wouldn't see the conflicting thoughts in her eyes. To be sure, she was shocked MacAllister felt anything at all for anyone, given his heartless pursuit and ultimate entrapment of her cousin, Mae.

And herself, if it came to that.

But mostly, she was forcefully reminded that no matter how much she wished otherwise, Ewan was inextricably woven into the upper echelons of the House of Alpin through both blood and familial ties.

She would be wise to remember it, no matter how her body ached for his touch.

Guards opened a door that led into a richly furnished chamber, with tapestries on the walls and thick rugs on the floor to protect from the cold. Countless oil lamps were scattered across several decorative tables, a fire burned brightly in the hearth, and four noblewomen curtseyed as she entered.

Briana drew in a sharp breath as the noblewomen retreated, revealing another lady who was clearly Ewan's grandmother. But it wasn't her elegant beauty or the fact she, unlike her ladies, wore a gown in the Pictish style, that caused eerie shivers to race along her arms.

There was something... something uncannily familiar about her...

"Lady Briana." Ewan smiled at her, before giving his grandmother a charming bow. "May I introduce Lady Catriona Magaidh of Duntorr and the Kingdom of Fortriu, my esteemed grandmother?"

As Lady Catriona curtseyed, and Ewan continued with the

introduction, a discordant warning echoed inside her mind. Somehow, this was wrong. Lady Catriona's status was not inferior to her own. She was... she was...

Who is she?

Ewan completed the introduction and even though a princess of royal blood did not curtsey to a commoner, no matter how highly born they were, Briana nevertheless was compelled to do so.

"Lady Catriona, I am honored to meet you." She straightened and caught the older woman's steady gaze. Her faded auburn hair, in a long braid that trailed over her shoulder, was nevertheless still thick and glossy, but her emerald-green eyes were as clear and bright as Briana's own.

"The honor is mine." Her voice was soft but there was power seething beneath the words and another shiver skittered through Briana. She was in the presence of another chosen one of Bride.

But how? Even if Lady Catriona did, indeed, possess royal Pictish blood, she was of the generation where the goddess had blessed only one, Brilicie, the Dowager Queen of Ce.

She was pulled from her confusion by one of her ladies taking her cloak, and she accepted the chair opposite Lady Catriona. Ewan sat beside her, and the ladies sat on stools, while servants busied themselves by serving the refreshments.

MacAllister entered the chamber with Sorcha and Briana watched, fascinated despite herself, as he kissed Lady Catriona's hand in greeting. He appeared quite at home and certainly more relaxed than she'd ever seen him before.

It was most disconcerting.

"Do not fear," Ewan breathed against her ear, under pretext of refilling her cup with herbal tea. "MacAllister rarely visits Duntorr. You will not often have to suffer his presence."

She lifted the cup to her lips. "That is gratifying to know, indeed."

He gave a silent laugh, his arm brushing hers, sending sparks of heat racing through her blood. It took all her willpower not to glance at him, for if she did, she feared she would be lost. It was a dangerous game, to speak of such things when anyone might overhear.

When she constantly had to remind herself that her own husband could not entirely be trusted, due to his birthright.

How she wished he had no connection to the Dal Riadan king. Perhaps, then, they might have a chance of the kind of marriage she had always dreamed of. But if Ewan was a common rank and file warrior, they would never have wed, anyway.

After a few moments, MacAllister turned and gave her a bow, before taking his leave, and Lady Catriona smiled at her. "We hope you will be happy here, Lady Briana. I understand what it's like, starting a new life in a foreign land, and will do everything I can to ensure you feel at home."

Goddess, had Lady Catriona also been coerced into marriage, so long ago? It hadn't occurred to her. She'd imagined a scenario similar to how MacAlpin's mother had run away with her Scots prince, and the disgrace hidden by having her name erased from the annals of Pictland. Either way, she hadn't expected Lady Catriona to be so thoughtful and it touched her more than she could say. "It is very kind of you."

"Not at all. I'm delighted my beloved grandson had the good sense to find himself such a suitable bride. From Pictland, no less."

How intriguing Lady Catriona appeared more delighted by her Pictish heritage, rather than her royal blood. It was only her status, after all, which had caught MacAlpin's attention, and like it or not, that fact brought great prestige to Ewan's kin.

But perhaps it wasn't so surprising. From the hushed words she had overheard from the noblewomen, they were all Scots. Maybe Lady Catriona truly *was* happy simply to have another Pict born lady in the household.

"And I'm delighted Lady Briana was kind enough to accept

the proposal." Ewan grinned at her, and she smiled back, because it was expected, but inside, her foolish heart ached.

He hadn't said *my* proposal because he had never asked her to be his wife. It was *the* proposal, because it was a political maneuver by his king. One that Ewan had never wanted.

"Some things are destined," Lady Catriona said and when Briana glanced at her, the older woman had a sad smile on her face. "I only wish my dear lord, Tavish, was still with us to see this unfold."

Sorcha, sitting beside her mother, took her hand, and Briana hastily recalled her manners. Lady Catriona's odd choice of words most likely meant nothing. "I am sorry, my lady."

"We had forty-eight years together." There was a dreamlike quality in Lady Catriona's voice, as though she had slipped back into her past. "Far longer than many. It has always been my hope that Ewan would find a love such as the one I found with Tavish."

Ewan shifted by Briana's side, clearly uncomfortable by his grandmother's candidness. Goddess, she was somewhat unnerved herself. It didn't matter how dearly she had once wished for a love match. This alliance with Ewan was based on nothing but political advantage.

Even if she couldn't stop thinking about him at the most inopportune moments, that did not equate to love. It was lust. That was all.

She was, at least, wise enough to understand the difference. And remind herself of it, whenever she might be in danger of forgetting.

"My beloved father passed in the early summer." Sorcha drew in a deep breath. It was clear she had loved her father dearly, and Briana's thoughts flew to her own beloved papa. When he had been held hostage by MacAlpin, she had lived in dread of one day receiving the news that he had died. Truly, she couldn't imagine a time when he would not be a vital presence in her life.

Even if the likelihood of ever seeing him again was remote.

"And in keeping with the Dal Riadan laws of inheritance, Duntorr now belongs to Ewan." Lady Catriona gave her grandson a fond smile, obviously not concerned by the strange ways of the Scots, who didn't honor their matrilineal heritage the way Picts did.

Unless it suited them. It was, after all, the Picts' inheritance laws that had enabled MacAlpin to claim Fortriu, the kingdom of his mother's birth.

"I had no thoughts to claim Duntorr." Tension radiated from him, and it was hard not to take his hand and offer what comfort she could, but she wasn't sure he would appreciate the gesture. Besides, it was not seemly to show such affection in public. "I intended to take my bride to Duncreag."

"The shadows in Duncreag will fade in time, driven out by the new memories you make together," Lady Catriona said. "It is far better to begin on your new path here, in Duntorr, where sunshine bathes every cornerstone."

Awe trickled along Briana's spine, and she couldn't tear her gaze from the older woman's serene face. Lady Catriona's words were cryptic, but she spoke with the conviction that came only from those chosen by the gods.

As though she could read her thoughts, Ewan's grandmother looked at her and Briana remained transfixed. Several of her cousins were blessed by the goddess, but none of them caused the very air around her to prickle like lightning when they were near.

"Lady Briana." Lady Catriona stood, and Ewan leaped to his feet. "I should very much like to show you my courtyard garden, if you would do me the honor?"

Hastily, she placed her cup on the table, and took Ewan's hand as she rose to her feet. "I should like that very much."

Nairne brought her cloak, but as her ladies made to follow her, Lady Catriona raised her hand. "May I speak with you alone, Lady Briana?"

Briana glanced at Ewan, who still held her hand. He caught

her gaze, and she wasn't sure whether concern glowed in his eyes or whether it was merely a trick of the light.

"It is quite all right, Ewan." A thread of amusement heated his grandmother's voice. "I merely wish to get to know my grand-daughter-by-marriage a little better. I promise I shall not allow the princess to freeze out there."

Briana smiled at him, and his grip tightened around her fingers before he released her hand, and she followed Lady Catriona across the chamber. One of the Scots ladies opened a door that led directly outside. How intriguing. She had not come across such a thing before.

She drew up her hood as she stepped outside, Lady Catriona following her. It was midafternoon and there was still enough light to see the graceful courtyard garden with its stone seats, troughs that would, undoubtedly, overflow with vibrant blooms in the warmer months, and a sundial in the center.

"Come." Lady Catriona beckoned her and together they went across the courtyard to the chest-high stone wall that surrounded the garden.

Briana gasped as she gazed at the breathtaking view of a snow-covered glen. "This is quite magnificent."

"Indeed. I'm pleased you like it. When I first came to Duntorr, I spent many happy hours in this courtyard, with its beautiful view. In the spring, it reminds me of the glens in Fortriu."

It was an opening and any other time she would have taken advantage of it. She was, after all, a princess of Pictland and enti-tled to question anyone should she wish. But Lady Catriona was her grandmother-by marriage, which gave her certain rights, yet that wasn't the real reason why she hesitated.

It was the sense of otherworldliness that spun around the other woman, and it was unsettling. The gods chose only those who possessed royal blood, which meant Ewan was wrong about his grandmother's heritage. But in truth, that was a secondary matter. Lady Catriona was a chosen one, and for that alone outranked Briana.

The older woman remained silent, and Briana understood the unspoken permission to say what was on her mind. "My lady is from Fortriu?"

"I grew up in the palace of Forteviot. I have never regretted my decision to follow my beloved Tavish to his homeland, but I confess sometimes I've missed this… familiarity."

Nerves twisted through Briana although she could not understand why. If she recognized another child of Bride, it was only to be expected Lady Catriona did, too. Except Briana had an unfathomable fear that Lady Catriona saw so much more.

What am I so afraid of?

It was not her place to broach the sacred subject and so she ignored it and took the easier path. "I cannot fathom how it must be, to be in a foreign land without any of one's kin."

Except that was now her life, and she would have to get used to it.

Lady Catriona smiled. "Fotla-eviot is not far from Duntorr. And although you are in a foreign land, you are blessed with a husband who will do anything for your happiness."

With difficulty, she returned her smile. "Lord Ewan is an honorable man, indeed. But this marriage is at the bidding of the King of Dal Riada."

Lady Catriona took a step closer, and a sliver of alarm chased through her. She should have simply agreed with Lady Catriona, not reminded her this was a political alliance to further MacAlpin's ambitions, and she and Ewan had been given little choice in the matter. In this new life she needed to make friends, not powerful enemies. Yet she couldn't shift the conviction that this matriarch would far prefer to hear the truth, rather than pretty lies.

"You are correct." Lady Catriona's voice was soft, but Briana wasn't fooled into thinking the other woman had changed her mind about her grandson's reasons for this marriage. It didn't matter how she wished it were true. "But there is more to this than King Kenneth's desire to unite our land, Lady Briana."

She had never heard MacAlpin referred to by his first name before, and it put her on edge. Just how close was Lady Catriona with the upstart? But it forcefully reminded her that just because this lady was a Pict, she could not be trusted.

"It's a good political strategy," she said, even if how it was being attained sickened her. "Of that, there is no doubt."

Lady Catriona waved her glove-clad hand in obvious dismissal of the political advantages. "We are in agreement, my lady. But I do not speak of politics. When I was a young woman, newly married, my beloved goddess showed me elusive glimpses of what would be. How my grandson would find his light in the darkness, his Pictish princess to help heal the wounds of the past and find their path together. Lady Briana, I have been expecting you since Bride told me of you on the night of the Wolf Moon, twenty-two winters ago."

CHAPTER 20

*L*ady Catriona's words still haunted Briana as Ewan led them to her bedchamber.

For so long, she had been uncertain she had chosen the right path. Fearful she'd offended her goddess by misinterpreting the signs. But ever since the night of the sacred Blood Moon, when she'd brought Mae to Fotla, she had been following Bride's wishes all along. Every step had brought her closer to this marriage with Ewan. An event that been destined since the night of her birth, when the great goddess had shared it with Lady Catriona.

Ewan opened the door, and she entered the antechamber, her ladies following. Like Lady Catriona's private chamber downstairs, vibrant tapestries hung upon the walls and rugs covered the floor. The tales of her childhood, where Scots' nobles lived in hillforts little better than stables, could not be further from the truth.

Her parents had insisted she take the valuable Persian rug from her chamber, so she might have some luxury in her new life, but it seemed Duntorr was far wealthier than Fotla-eviot when it came to material comforts.

Her ladies went over to the chests that had been brought into the chamber while they had been with Lady Catriona, and began to sort through them. Ewan led her to where a fire blazed in the hearth and took her hands. "Does Duntorr not please you, Briana?"

"It pleases me well." She tightened her fingers around his and wished he would pull her into his arms. "How could it not?"

There was a brooding look on his face. "This is the master's chambers. My lady grandmother was willing to give you her bedchambers, but I insisted she kept them. I realize this is unconventional. But she has lived here so many years—"

A delightful heat suffused her and sent ripples of desire flowing through her blood. To be sure it was unconventional for a royal wife to share chambers with her husband, but the thought of doing so with Ewan was exhilarating. "It was the right thing to do. I have no wish to disrupt your lady grandmother's life, Ewan."

He smiled in evident relief. "You're very gracious." He kissed her hand but alas his lips didn't linger long enough for her liking. "And speaking of my grandmother, what did she say to you in the courtyard? You looked stunned when I joined you. Maybe I should have come outside sooner?"

She certainly hoped she *hadn't* looked stunned. But she didn't want to talk about that, when there was something far more important she wished to discuss. Once, she had teasingly told Ewan that should she ever meet his grandmother she would be sure to give him her opinion on the lady. She had never imagined quite how formidable his grandmother would turn out to be. "Why didn't you tell me Lady Catriona is a chosen one?"

He cocked his head. "What?" He sounded baffled and consternation washed through her. Did he truly not know? Hastily, she tried to mitigate her unwary words.

"Forgive me. I was unsure if Lady Catriona followed the new religion or... or not."

"No. She's a very proud pagan." Affection threaded through

his words. "The local monks despair of her but would never raise their voices against her. She is both a generous benefactor to the church and a favorite of the king."

Her head thundered. Ewan didn't know his grandmother was a chosen one of the goddess. And he had just confirmed she was a close confidante of the king.

But how could she be both? It went against everything Briana believed in. If Lady Catriona was a Scotswoman, her evident closeness to the king might be palatable.

But she was a Pict. With unknown royal blood. How could she not loathe MacAlpin with every fiber of her being?

EWAN SAT at the high table, in the seat which, until recently, had been his grandfather's, Briana by his side. The feast, to celebrate his marriage and officially welcome him as the lord of Duntorr, had been suitably grand, and the great hall was filled with his kin, the Scots warriors who had accompanied him from Fotla, and many nobles from the surrounding area.

His father's younger brother gave a hearty speech that was greeted with much applause and stamping of feet. When the noise died down, Ewan stood and gave the requisite responses. Neither his uncle nor he made mention of how the king had recognized their blood ties. Rumor might abound, but no confirmation would come from him.

Then he turned to Briana, and his chest constricted when she bestowed a dignified smile his way. God, how he had missed her these last two nights. But he hadn't dared to share her bed. He knew his limits. And although he didn't fully understand her talk of moon times and nothing was certain in these matters, if he wanted to ensure at least an extra month with her, he could not afford to get her with child this week.

Just one month. That was all he asked. And then he would do everything to fulfil the promise he had made her.

"To my beautiful bride," he said, and raised his goblet. "Briana, Princess Euphemia of Fotla, may you find all the happiness you deserve in your new life here, at Duntorr."

A great cheer erupted and echoed around the hall and when he sat, Briana took his hand. He kissed her fingers, uncaring that everyone could see, because the only one who mattered was his wife.

The tables were pushed back, and the musicians tuned their instruments, readying for the entertainment that would last late into the night. He led Briana to the floor and as others joined them, something occurred to him.

"This is the first time we've danced together."

"How remiss of us."

"I pledge to make amends on that oversight."

She smiled, and he gazed, transfixed, and ignored the insidious warning in the back of his mind that reminded him he couldn't afford to make such carefree plans with Briana.

He refused to spoil this treasured moment by recalling the bleak future that lay ahead.

She spun in his arms, then they were parted, and he faced one of his cousins, Sorcha's daughter, Keita.

"The princess is delightful," she said. "You are fortunate, indeed, Ewan."

"Aye." He grinned at her, before casting his gaze to where Briana danced with his uncle. "That I am."

Beware... But the effort was too great to pretend indifference towards his bride. Besides, Keita would see through him. She always had.

He returned his attention to his cousin, a question burning in his mind. Did she know about their grandmother? But why would she, if he didn't? Although all the family had been aware of Lady Catriona's eccentric preference for worshipping ancient ways that were generally no longer tolerated, it was never spoken about.

Just like his grandfather's royal blood was never spoken about.

Christ, it hadn't occurred to him before just how many secrets his family kept.

"Do not let the darkness of the past cloud your future," Keita whispered, and an eerie shudder inched along his spine. But before he could question her on it, the music ended, and she was gone.

He and Briana danced again, and her elusive scent of lavender spun through his mind, clouding his thoughts to all but her. Primitive need thudded in his head and through his veins, an intoxicating counterpoint to the heavy beat of his heart. He pulled her close, a breach of etiquette, but no one would call him out on it tonight.

She melted against him as though she had no care for what others thought, her soft curves a tantalizing reminder of the nights they had shared. The insane urge to clasp her head and plunder her sweet mouth assailed him, the notion so visceral white-hot daggers clawed his vitals.

It physically hurt to pull back from her. But his honor hung by a thread, and he feared if it snapped, he would sweep her into his arms and march from the hall, and God help him, he doubted they would make it to her bedchamber before he took her.

Against a stone-cold wall.

The image seared the very core of his being. Christ, he had to damn well *focus*.

"May I tempt you with some refreshment, my lady?" He sounded hoarse. He could only hope she didn't notice.

"You may indeed." Her voice was breathless. From the dance, or from the way he held her? Did the memories of their bed sport haunt her, too? "I am quite parched."

They threaded their way through the throng to where

servants stood by one of the tables with jugs of wine. When their goblets were filled, Keita and her sisters, along with two young noblewomen, flocked around Briana, admiring her gown, her jewels, and elegance on the dance floor.

She smiled and responded, and although he couldn't hear what she said, the other ladies laughed in delight. An unfamiliar warmth spread through his chest. No one here, observing her regal charm, would imagine she had been coerced into this marriage. She was the perfect mistress of a stronghold as renowned as Duntorr.

His perfect bride…

"It's good to see you so happy, Ewan." His grandmother's voice splintered his unforgiveable reverie, and he took a hasty swig of wine to cover his lapse before turning to her. He hadn't even been aware of her approach.

"Thank you for this night," he said. "I didn't expect such a grand affair, given the short notice."

His grandmother patted his arm. "I've waited a long time for this, but it has been worth it. Lady Briana is more than I had even dared to hope."

For a moment, he merely smiled, basking in the knowledge that she approved of Briana, although who could not? His bride was everything he might have dreamed of, had he ever allowed himself to cherish such dreams.

And then discordance stirred, and his gaze sharpened on her. How many times in the past had his grandmother uttered enigmatic observations that almost, but not quite, made sense? He was so used to it, he barely noticed it. And if he ever had, he'd brushed it away as a consequence of her foreign heritage.

But now, Briana's words echoed in his ears.

"Why didn't you tell me Lady Catriona is a chosen one?"

Her casual question had staggered him, but she hadn't pursued it for which he'd been thankful. But how had she, after mere moments in Lady Catriona's company, discovered such a thing, when he'd been oblivious for his entire life?

Because Briana is a chosen one, too.

"My lady grandmother," he said, and she looked at him, and he had the uncanny notion she knew exactly what he was about to ask her. "It was always my belief you worshipped the gods of old because of your heritage. But there's more to it than that, isn't there?"

She was silent and had she been any other lady, he might have feared he'd offended her. But Lady Catriona was not easily offended and when she sighed and took his hand, he knew he'd been right to question her. Hell, he had the strangest feeling she'd been waiting for him to.

"There is." Her voice was quiet. "I've often questioned the wisdom of keeping my beloved family ignorant of the fact I am a chosen one of the great goddess Bride, but please understand. Your grandfather and I made this decision many years ago. It is not the way of Dal Riada, and for Duntorr to continue to flourish, we had to make certain... sacrifices. Yet Bride blesses me still."

"I see." Except he didn't, not really. He had no idea what being a chosen one of a pagan goddess entailed. And except for the fact that Briana had befriended a wolf, and his own self-mocking notion that she had bewitched him, she had done nothing to enlighten him on the ancient ways that were forbidden by the church.

"I regret not telling your dear father." His grandmother tightened her grip on his fingers. "Your uncle doesn't know, either. But I told Sorcha, for I was so certain..." Her voice trailed away, and she sighed. "It was not to be. Yet Bride, in her wisdom, blessed Keita and goddess willing, one of her daughters will inherit the gift too."

Speechless, he stared at her. He had grown up with Keita, four months his junior, and not once had he guessed she hid such a secret. And yet, she'd always possessed an uncanny ability to know things she had no business knowing.

Was that part of it? Did Briana possess that gift, also?

~

IT WAS LATE when the merriment finally ceased, and Ewan accompanied Briana upstairs, her fingers trailing along the wall in a way that was becoming familiar to him. Her ladies followed, busying themselves in the antechamber as Briana led him into the bedchamber.

He left the door open, and she tilted her head, a questioning smile on her face, but he found he could not return it. Every beat of his heart, every tortured breath he dragged into his lungs, urged him to sweep her into his arms and carry her to their bed.

His cock thickened and his mouth dried. The image of her naked, her glorious hair spread across the pillows, scalded his mind and primal lust throbbed through his blood.

She is my bride. Sleeping alone was a torture he could easily avoid by withdrawing before completion. It was something he'd done many times in the past. But he feared that, with Briana, his resolve would not be strong enough. Not when she wrapped her arms around him, when her soft sighs of pleasure filled the air, or when her lush body entranced him in a silken cocoon of unimaginable rapture.

He could not risk making her pregnant tonight. Because once she was with child, his promise to her was fulfilled.

And he would have to leave her.

A groan razed his throat, and he hastily disguised it with a cough.

"Are you well?" Concern laced her voice. Somehow, he managed to smile.

"Aye." His voice was raw with need. He had to leave her, now, before he did something he might regret. With more reluctance than he cared to admit, he stepped back from her, but her entrancing scent wove around him, regardless, tempting him to forget everything but the molten lust that threatened to consume his reason.

"Are you certain?" She glanced at the bed and his conviction wavered. "I have wondered—"

He could guess what she had wondered, and he was in no fit state to discuss it now. Or ever. He gripped his wavering resolution before it deserted him completely.

"It's been a tiring day, my lady. I will leave you with your ladies to rest and look forward to seeing you in the morning."

"Leave?" There was a brittle note in her voice. "But this is the master chamber, my lord. I thought—" She drew in a sharp breath, obviously reconsidering whatever it was she had been about to say. "We are not sharing this chamber, then."

If only. He forced a light note in his voice although it nearly damn well killed him. "I would not burden you in such a manner. I've claimed a bedchamber along the corridor."

She inclined her head in a regal manner and it seemed the air around them chilled. "Then I shall bid you good night."

He kissed her hand and marched from the chamber, ignoring the sideway glances from her ladies. One more night. That was all. And tomorrow he would make it up to Briana, worshipping her body until she begged for respite.

The enticing image scorched his brain, imprinting on his eyes. God alone knew how he made it to the bedchamber he had claimed for himself, for he had no recollection of it. And when he flung himself down on the bed, he shoved his hands behind his head before he could grip his engorged cock and find relief.

Tonight, he would suffer. It would make tomorrow all the sweeter.

If I manage to survive this night...

CHAPTER 21

The following morning, after Briana had dressed and she and her ladies had broken their fast, she received a message that Lady Catriona wished to show her Duntorr, if it pleased her.

"We shall be down directly," she said, and the servant bobbed a curtsey and left.

She turned to her ladies, thankful none of them had passed comment on the fact that, for the third night in a row, her husband had not shared her bed. But then, they would never bring up such a sensitive subject unless she did first. And that would never happen. "Are we ready? It will be fascinating to learn more of our new home."

Although she should be grateful Lady Catriona had offered, she couldn't help the sting of rejection that burned through her at the knowledge her own husband could not find the time to show her Duntorr instead.

The stronghold was magnificent, indeed, and Lady Catriona was the perfect dowager, both gracious and informative. They inspected the kitchens, an impressive construction attached to the stronghold by a corridor, and the cook proudly showed them the well-stocked pantries and shelves of preserved goods that would see the household through the winter months.

"Our kitchen gardens are abundant," Lady Catriona said as she led them back through the corridor and into the great hall, with Drest bringing up the rear. It appeared his orders to shadow her superseded anything she might request of him. "Do you care to inspect them? I shall send for our cloaks, if so."

"Perhaps later. I should not wish to inconvenience you any further."

Lady Catriona smiled. "This is no inconvenience, I assure you. I adore Duntorr, and hope you will grow to love it too, Lady Briana."

"I'm sure I shall." It was the correct response, although that didn't mean it wasn't true. Duntorr was to be her home, after all, and it was far better she liked it than not.

Lady Catriona gave her an odd glance, but thankfully didn't question her further as they walked through the great hall.

"Duntorr had been empty for a generation before my lord Tavish's lady mother inherited it. Tavish's father spared no expense to ensure the stronghold was the epitome of luxury."

"It is a grand household, indeed."

The tour continued. She had been taught how to run a royal palace, and had been mistress of Ecgfrith's stronghold, and the responsibilities entailed did not daunt her.

It was Lady Catriona. A favorite of MacAlpin. Had she insisted Ewan bring his bride to Duntorr not because it was the jewel in her grandson's inheritance, but so she could keep Briana in her sights?

To report back to the upstart king?

Finally, they returned to the chamber where Lady Catriona had received them yesterday, and refreshments were brought for them.

"We will arrange for you and your ladies to have your own withdrawing chamber," Lady Catriona said. "Although I should be delighted if you wish to use this chamber for your own use, also."

The chamber was certainly delightful, and its access to the courtyard garden was something she would love. But she and her ladies needed a place where they would not feel as though they were constantly being watched.

Besides, with a private withdrawing chamber she might find a use for the Persian rug she had brought with her.

"I should not dream of imposing upon your kindness by sharing your personal chamber," she said.

"Of course." Lady Catriona inclined her head before summoning one of her ladies, who unclasped something from the dowager's girdle and handed it to her. The older woman faced her once again. "Allow me to present you with the keys to Duntorr, Lady Briana."

"Thank you, Lady Catriona." It was more than a symbolic gesture. It was the handing over of power over the household, but despite her royal lineage, Briana had the feeling she would never be the true mistress of Duntorr, the way Lady Catriona was.

It seemed the very walls of Duntorr were infused by the older woman's connection to Bride. And while that should be a comfort—after all, there couldn't be many places in Dal Riada where the true gods were still worshipped—for a reason she couldn't quite fathom, the notion made her uneasy.

With due reverence, she attached the keys on their silver chain to her girdle and for the rest of the afternoon, as their ladies embroidered and got to know each other, Lady Catriona enlightened her on the finer points of the inner workings of Duntorr.

Ewan's lady grandmother was kind and gracious, and no

matter how hard she tried Briana could not detect any malice in her manner. How dearly she would love to trust this lady, another native of Pictland, in her new life. But, just like Ewan, her loyalty was with MacAlpin.

It didn't matter what she wished. She would never have the deep connection with either her grandmother-by-marriage or her husband that she secretly craved. It would all be superficial, a façade of acceptance and pleasantries, and truly, what more could she expect from this political alliance?

It was enough. It had to be. For what other choice did she have?

THE SKY WAS DARKENING when Briana and her ladies escaped the stronghold to check on their horses. How wonderful it was, once again, to not have to ask permission to do such an ordinary thing. Her mamma had not believed it was the place for a princess or noblewomen to undertake such duties as grooming one's own horse, never mind venturing outside if the weather was inclement.

"Tomorrow, we shall go riding," she told her ladies as they approached the stables.

"We should seek out the glen that Lady Catriona's garden looks upon," Nairne said.

"Surely, we would need a guide." Gavina opened the stable door. "None of us know this land."

"We would likely need guards, too." Nairne sighed, and Briana knew she was right. They were the foreigners in this land, and their safety outside the stronghold could not be guaranteed.

"I'll hand pick the warriors myself." Drest scanned the landscape as though he expected Vikings to appear at any moment. "From our own Pict contingent."

"Thank you," she said, although deep inside unease stirred.

How could this alliance truly work if they didn't even try to include the Scots?

"My lady."

She swung about and Rohan gave a half bow as she greeted him. Curses. She didn't feel like talking to him. She just wanted a few quiet moments alone with her beloved mare.

"A word, if I may?"

It was obvious he wanted to speak to her alone. She turned to her ladies. "Please, continue. I will join you shortly."

Her ladies went into the stable and Briana swallowed her impatience before she returned her attention to Rohan. "Is something amiss?"

"It is a delicate matter and I have wrestled my conscience all day as to whether I should bring this to your attention."

The pit of her stomach churned. The last time Rohan had brought a *delicate matter* to her attention, it had involved the reason for Ecgfrith's untimely death. But that didn't mean anything had happened to Ewan. What a foolish thought. Whatever had happened, it had taken hours for Rohan to decide to tell her, which meant it was scarcely urgent.

She took a long breath, and the chilled air helped steady her galloping nerves. "You had best tell me, before we both freeze out here."

"I understand this marriage is nothing but a political alliance, but you are a Princess of Fotla and deserve more respect from MacKinnon. Forgive me, that had to be said."

Dull dread tightened deep in her chest at what Rohan insinuated. But she could be wrong. He might not be suggesting what she feared at all.

"Speak plainly, my lord. I am at a loss as to what you are telling me."

His dark eyes flashed, as though he doubted her word, but surely she was mistaken, and it was merely a trick of the wintery light.

"I regret to be the one to advise my lady that early this morning I observed MacKinnon leaving the bedchamber of one of the visiting noblewomen."

Her heart slammed against her chest. No. *No*, she would not believe it. Somehow, goddess only knew how, she managed to keep her face serene. Rohan was only looking out for her, but in this, he was wrong.

"Doubtless there is a satisfactory reason for this." Did she sound calm? Her mind whirled so, it was hard to gauge. The words stuck in her throat, but she forced them out, regardless. "I thank you for your concern."

"I shall look out for you always." There was a thread of anger in his voice, and she stared, shaken, as he once again bowed and took his leave.

Briana didn't see Ewan again until she and her ladies were preparing to go to the great hall for the evening meal. He arrived in her antechamber, looking more captivating than any man had a right to, and strode over to her with a smile that very nearly turned her bones to liquid.

"Briana." He kissed her proffered hand and did not release her afterwards. "Forgive me. I've been with the steward and much as I wanted to escape earlier so I could be with you, it does mean I'm now free to spend all day tomorrow with my delectable bride."

He has not been unfaithful.

She returned his smile and smothered the urge to demand to know where he had been last night. In the hours since Rohan had spoken to her, she had been plagued with images of Ewan with another. Which noblewoman was it?

Pride had kept her from confiding in her ladies, for there was nothing they could say to ease her mind. His reputation was well known. She had been fairly warned by Nairne, even if she had seen no evidence of it with her own eyes while he had been stationed in Fotla. What made her think marriage would change his ways?

"I look forward to it." Her voice was cool but if he noticed, he chose to ignore it as they made their way to the great hall.

It was not a great feast, like the previous evening, but the food was plentiful, and she forced herself to eat while Ewan regaled her with amusing tales of his day. He was the epitome of an attentive husband, offering her the finest choice from the serving platters and ensuring her goblet was never empty, while appearing fascinated by the anecdotes she shared of her own day.

She took a sip of wine and could not help glancing around the hall at the young noblewomen. It shouldn't hurt, and she despised herself that it did. In Pictland, there was an ancient, unspoken understanding that fidelity was not a requirement when it came to political marriages.

Love was a luxury that some found outside of the marriage alliance and was not restricted only to men. Once a legitimate heir or two had been produced, the woman's duty was done.

She didn't know if the same view applied in Dal Riada. And she didn't care. It was foolish to wish Ewan, who had wanted this marriage even less than her, would remain faithful and yet the fact he had warmed another's bed, so soon after they had wed, wounded her soul.

"My lady, what ails you?" Ewan's concerned whisper sent a needy ripple through her blood, no matter how she tried to suppress it.

"I'm quite well. Simply a little fatigued."

"Then perhaps we should retire."

She caught the wicked gleam in his eye and his dimples flashed. Clearly, he intended to spend this night with *her*. It shouldn't thrill her, not when he had ignored her for three nights, but the despairing truth was, she couldn't control her feelings when it came to him.

"Very well." Thankfully, her need didn't reflect in her voice. She had some pride, after all. She bid her ladies to remain, so they could continue the delightful pastime of flirtation with the Scots' warriors, and Ewan took her hand as they left the great hall.

He brushed his lips against her ear. "I missed you." His voice was thick with lust, and she exhaled an unsteady breath. They had wed for political stability. The only other thing she wanted from this marriage was children, and Ewan didn't need to be faithful to her for that outcome.

There was no earthly reason why she should confront him. This was not a love match. Yet even her much dreamed of love match hadn't prevented her first husband from straying. And whenever she'd confronted him, their arguments had battered her self-worth into the mud.

But Ewan, surely, could not level the same accusations against her as Ecgfrith had.

At the foot of the stairs, she came to a halt and turned to face him. He stood by a wall sconce, and the torchlight flickered in the draft, creating intriguing shadows across his aristocratic features.

Rohan was right about one thing. She did deserve more respect from Ewan. If he was going to bed noblewomen in his own stronghold, he could at least be more circumspect about it.

That's not what I want at all.

She gave him a perfunctory smile. "Yet it was your choice not to share our bed, my lord."

Consternation flashed across his face. Had he not expected her to question him on it?

"Forgive me. I did not want to overtire you on your first night in Duntorr."

Goddess, did he think her a half-wit? Guilt dripped from every word he uttered.

"Pray do me the honor of telling me the truth, Ewan. I assure you I can stomach it far better than insipid falsehoods."

"What?" He sounded staggered and a sharp pain speared through her breast. Even if he said nothing more, she had her answer. And it was not the one she wanted from him.

"We both came into this with our eyes open. I don't expect protestations of undying devotion, but you owe me the truth, at least. I will not be made a fool of."

He swallowed. "Briana, this is not the time nor place to discuss such things."

She had to concede he was right. It was most improper, but they were alone, and her chest ached, and she had to clear the air now before they reached her bedchamber, and she was lost. He had to know she was not blind to his affairs.

"I must hear it from you."

He cast a furtive glance around, as though assuring himself no one could eavesdrop, and she braced herself for the unpalatable confession.

"I promised to get you with child, Briana." His voice was so low, she had to lean close to hear him, although why he should bring up that promise when she was waiting to hear he had been with another woman, she could not fathom. "I will not break that pledge. But God forgive me, I wanted just a little longer to have you all to myself."

She stared at him as tangled thoughts tumbled through her mind. "A little longer?" she echoed, stupidly, but he spoke in riddles, and she wasn't certain what he was talking about.

"Aye." He raked his fingers through his hair, and it was far more enchanting than it should be. "It was wrong, when I gave you my word. But I thought if I didn't share your bed during your..." he cleared his throat and hunched his shoulders. "Moon time..." clearly, it pained him deeply to utter the phrase, and she was too stunned by the turn in the conversation to correct his misunderstanding, when surely, he meant when her moon time was *ripe*. "We would have another month, at least, together."

His confession, so unlike anything she had imagined, pounded through her head. "That is the reason you left me alone these last three nights?"

A tortured expression flashed over his face. "It damn near killed me to stay away, if that makes my sin any less in your eyes."

Her senses were still reeling to give this so-called sin of his much thought. "This is a most unexpected disclosure, indeed."

A frown slashed his brow. "But I thought you knew. I thought that was why you asked."

"How should I know that was the reason you didn't share my bed? It never even entered my mind."

"God." The word sounded more like a groan. "So there was no need for me to confess this to you? I thought your goddess had whispered in your ear."

"She did not. And I thought you didn't believe in the ancient ones."

"I don't." He sucked in a harsh breath. "But you do. And I have no idea what being a chosen one of your goddess means."

A spark of warmth heated her at his tortured words, at the knowledge he respected her beliefs even if he didn't follow them himself. "It is not Bride's way to be so..." she hesitated, picking her words carefully. One never could be certain if the gods were listening, and it would never do to inadvertently anger them. "Specific when she graces mere mortals with her wisdom. But Ewan, I am not certain I understand your reasoning. We are wed, and likely to spend many years together." A bizarre possibility occurred to her, and she gasped. "Is it a tenet of your religion that a man must avoid his wife when she is with child?"

There was no mistaking the guilt that throbbed in the air around him and she gripped his fingers, willing him to share what was causing him so much anguish. Then he dragged in a harsh breath that expanded his magnificent chest, and she all but lost her thread of thought.

"No. It was—" He cut himself off and briefly closed his eyes, before looking at her once again. "We're at cross purposes. What was it you wanted to speak with me about?"

Goddess, yes. She had almost forgotten in the light of his extraordinary confession, and a knot of anxiety tightened in her chest. "Where did you spend last night?"

He cocked his head. "In my chamber. And I discovered a most extraordinary thing. Tomorrow, we shall—"

He was doing it again. Distracting her from her purpose, and her accusation burst from her. "Whose chamber did you emerge from this morning?"

For a moment he stared at her blankly, and then comprehension glowed in his eyes, and he gave what she could only describe as a rueful smile. "Ah, you mean Lady Eilidh. I had hoped no one would witness that."

Lady Eilidh? But she was a noblewoman as old as Lady Catriona. "I'm trying to understand, my lord."

He sighed. "It's a sorry state of affairs and my lady grandmother would be mortified if she finds out. It was fortunate I was up early, on my way to meet the steward, when Lady Eilidh's companion ran into my path. My help was required to rid the bedchamber of a rat."

"A rat?" she repeated, having the absurd desire to laugh.

"Aye. The stronghold's cats aren't doing their jobs. I shall have to reprimand them in the strongest possible terms."

"I wish you well with that." This time, she couldn't help giving a muffled snort of laughter. "Cats can be most contrary creatures."

"I've always found them so." His smile faded as he trailed a finger along her face. "I'd never dishonor you by spending the night with another woman, Briana. I'm grieved you felt the need to ask. Who put this idea in your mind?"

She took a step closer to him, breathing in his wonderful scent of leather and pine. "It is of no consequence." Feeling less burdened than she had for three days, she cupped his jaw, delighting in how his whiskers abraded her palm. "We have three nights of abstinence to make up for and I confess a cruel desire to punish you for such a transgression."

He bowed his head, his lips brushing hers in a caress so featherlight she should not feel it at all. Yet intoxicating prickles of pleasure scattered across her flesh with erotic promise.

"I shall relish whatever punishment you devise." He turned her around, so she faced the stairs, before wrapping his arm around her waist. His hot breath grazed her ear. "But God help me, if we don't reach our bedchamber soon, I'll take you here on the stairs and to hell with propriety."

"That is most barbarous," she gasped, even though the shocking image burned into her mind and hot spirals of need collided low in her belly. "I trust you jest."

His rumble of laughter vibrated against her back, enhancing the desire that licked through her blood and caused her breath to catch in her throat. "Should we wait to find out?"

This conversation was entirely improper, and utterly compelling. She could not help but respond.

"The cold stone stairs would be most uncomfortable." Instinctively, she trailed her fingertips along the wall, even though Ewan still held her securely around her waist and there was not the slightest chance of tumbling down the stairs.

"I would not have you so inconvenienced. You would sit astride me, my lady."

"You have a scandalous tongue, to be sure." She glanced over her shoulder, but her mocking frown dissolved into a besotted smile as their gazes meshed. "Your punishment increases with every transgression."

"In that case, I shall endeavor to transgress at every opportunity."

They reached the top of the stairs, and before she could catch her breath, he scooped her into his powerful arms and marched along the corridor to her bedchamber. How she had missed him holding her like this, even though it had only been a few days. It was a foolish fantasy, and in the cold light of day she knew better, but here in his arms he made her feel so cherished and safe.

She wound her arms around his shoulders and tangled her fingers in his hair. "Your dedication is admirable. I shall be sure to punish you most thoroughly."

CHAPTER 22

*E*wan gave a silent laugh and opened the door to the antechamber, before kicking it shut behind them. "I'm gratified my diligence pleases you."

Her smile was enchanting. "Pray do not imagine I'm so easily swayed by your pretty words."

"I wouldn't dream of it." He entered the bedchamber and strode to the bed. In the back of his mind the troubling notion of who had whispered in her ear about his early morning departure from Lady Eilidh's chamber wouldn't be still. It had been a malicious action, intended to disturb Briana's peace of mind.

To drive a wedge between them.

Damn Rohan to hell. It could be no one else but him. Somehow, he had to find a way to send the man far from Duntorr, without causing Briana any distress.

"Wait. Take me to the hearth."

He paused and gave her a quizzical look. "Are you giving me orders, my lady?"

"Indeed I am. You are to be punished this night, are you not?"

He groaned as he obeyed, and with reluctance set her on her

feet. "Tell me this punishment doesn't involve denying me your exquisite body tonight."

"I believe that would be a just punishment. But alas, that is one I would have to suffer, too."

He laughed and grasped her hand. "I'm thankful to hear it," he said and pulled her close for a kiss. They had been wed for such a short time, and he had denied himself this pleasure for only three days, and yet it seemed like forever since he'd held her in his arms.

His tongue teased the seam of her lips, and she gave a delicate shiver that rippled through him, stoking his lust.

She sighed into his mouth but then pulled back. "I see you don't take orders well."

"You have yet to issue one, my lady."

"I command you stand there." She pointed to the rug beneath his feet. "And not move until I give you leave."

He grunted when she stepped back, out of his arms. "I'll not go back on my word. I only hope I won't live to regret it."

"I should be most grieved if you do." She tilted her head and ran a leisurely gaze over him, from head to boots. It was astoundingly arousing, and he already regretted his rash promise not to move until she allowed it. "Oh, and by not moving, that means you must keep your hands to yourself."

"I'm not certain I shall survive this night."

She stepped closer and unclasped his brooch. Her veil slipped from her head and her hair brushed against his jaw in a tantalizing caress as she focused on her task. He swallowed and breathed in deep but that was a mistake, as her elusive scent invaded his senses with delectable intent.

Carefully, she placed his brooch on a table before proceeding to unwrap his plaid. He itched to assist her, since she appeared to be taking great delight in taking her time, but somehow, he managed to resist. When the last of the plaid dropped to the floor, he expelled a relieved sigh. "This is a rare form of torture you've devised."

"I'm glad you approve."

"Approve isn't the word I would use."

She cast him a seductive glance as she untied the laces of his shirt. "Good. I shouldn't wish your punishment to be without any form of discomfort for you."

He gave a choked groan as she grasped handfuls of his shirt and slowly eased the material up his body. "I burn for you. I'm in agony. How much more discomfort do you wish to put me through?"

"Raise your arms so I might pull your shirt free."

He did as she bid, lowering his head so she could complete her task. "I'm at your mercy, my lady."

She dropped his shirt to the floor and her gaze fixed upon his throbbing cock. He fisted his hands in a futile attempt to cool his blood and grasp his unraveling control, but the endeavor was beyond him. To stand before her, naked save for his damn boots, while she remained clad in her exotic gown, stretched his willpower to its limits.

"This is quite a sight, to be sure." Her voice was husky and despite his discomfort, a raw laugh seared this throat.

"This punishment is most cruel. I beg for salvation."

Her gaze meshed with his and his breath stalled in his chest at the dark desire glowing in her eyes. "I am not finished yet."

She trailed her fingertips across his shoulders and along his biceps. Instinctively, his muscles flexed beneath her touch, and he tried, in vain, to regulate his harsh breaths. An impossible charge when he needed all his concentration to obey her command to keep his hands to himself.

With gentle fingers she clasped his wrists and pressed her lips against his chest. He shuddered, his mesmerized gaze fixed on her as she dusted light kisses across his flesh, before swirling her tongue around his nipple. He expelled a ragged hiss, as white-hot darts of pleasure ignited beneath his skin and arrowed straight to his groin.

"You're fair killing me." The words burst from him, unintended, and he dug his fingers into his thighs before he plunged them into Briana's hair, instead.

She didn't reply although he felt her smile against his chest. Her fingernails raked over his ribs and hips, as she explored him with her lips and teeth, and damn if this wasn't the most erotic encounter he could ever recall.

Her hot sigh grazed the head of his erection and he hitched in a shocked breath.

Was she...?

Her fingers skimmed over his rigid shaft leaving embers of fire burning his flesh and his entire body tensed. This punishment was one he would gladly endure as many times as she commanded. And when she wrapped her fingers around him and flicked her tongue across his slit, his growl of frustrated pleasure echoed around the chamber.

"I trust this is giving you a great deal of time to contemplate your sins." Her teasing words were accompanied by a sultry smile that gripped his vitals in a merciless, lust-fueled vise.

"Aye." It was a tortured confession and God help him, he would have agreed with anything she said, for his mind could process nothing but the knowledge his princess was on her knees before him.

"Good." She increased her grip around him and cupped his heavy balls. Christ, help him. *I won't disgrace myself.*

But his self-control was a tattered thing, unraveling with every agonized beat of his heart.

Her mouth was warm and wet, and he sank into her. The vision of her lips around his cock scorched his mind and the graze of her teeth pushed him perilously close to the edge. Her nails scraped the underside of his balls and tension coiled, tightened, *unbearable.*

A primitive groan, dredged from the pit of his soul, reverberated through his chest and her name was guttural on his tongue. *"Briana."*

She released him, panting, her head tipped back as she gazed up at him. His fingers flexed, but he managed to keep his hands from grasping her head, although God alone knew how. Except she had asked him not to move, and he wouldn't break his word to her. "Release me from your command."

For an endless moment she didn't answer and then she smiled. "I release you."

His control shattered and he hauled her to her feet. Spearing his fingers through her hair he held the back of her head while he plundered her sweet mouth. She wound her arms around him, her nails raking his back, and he reared into her, his cock throbbing for release.

Feverishly, he tore at the ties of her bodice, pulling her gown over her shoulder but the sight of her naked flesh was his undoing.

The bed was too far away and so was the floor. He backed her up against a tapestry that hung on the wall, and she gasped into his face as he seized her gown and roughly hauled the material up her legs.

"This is quite outrageous." She sounded thrilled and he offered her a feral grin in response. "Do you mean to ravish me against the wall?"

"Aye." It was a growl that vibrated in the very marrow of his bones. He grasped her backside, her skin delectably smooth against his calloused palm and her ragged sigh echoed around his mind like a siren's song.

He nibbled kisses along the column of her throat, delighting in her delicate shivers at his touch and the way her nails dug into his shoulders.

Urging him on.

Her gown was a cursed hindrance, but conversely provocative, as the soft layers tangled about his arm as he stroked her thighs and teased her wet cleft. Her husky moans and breathy sighs mingled with the frenzied hammer of his heart until nothing else existed beyond Briana.

With a harsh curse he hiked up her skirts and she wrapped her legs around him, her heels digging into his lower back. Her hair, no longer in a neat plait, had escaped its bindings and errant curls tumbled across her cheeks in alluring disarray.

Her gown was disheveled, revealing her tempting cleavage and the heady scent of arousal and need infused his senses. His elegant bride, so regally aloof in public, undone in his arms.

It was too much. With a choked groan he thrust inside her tight sheath and her legs clamped fast around him, pinning him in place. Her wet heat wrapped him in a sensual cocoon and her fingers tangled in his hair as his gaze meshed with hers.

He rocked into her, and she contracted around him, squeezing him tight until stars exploded behind his eyes. Her soft gasps were as potent as the sharp spirals of lust that consumed his balls and commanded his cock and he rammed her against the wall, claiming her, just as she claimed him.

She arched, eyes closed, sucking in elusive air, and clutching him as though she might drown without him. Shudders claimed her, clenching him in a glorious surge around his shaft and his last restraint fell. As her cries of completion claimed his sanity, he let go, pumping his seed deep inside her, his bride, his princess.

His woman.

CHAPTER 23

The following morning, Ewan took Briana by the hand and led her along the corridor to the chamber he'd used the other night. He'd wanted them to be alone when he shared his discovery with her, but it seemed a Pict princess, unlike Pictish noblewomen, did not go anywhere without her ladies.

Not that he really minded. They were Briana's friends from home and made her happy. It was no great hardship including them, even if he doubted he'd ever get used to not having his wife to himself during the day. But although he acknowledged her rank required a bodyguard, he couldn't deny he'd much rather not have the dour Drest shadowing every move Briana made when she was with him.

He, after all, was her husband and would never allow anything—or anyone—to harm her.

In the back of his mind, so faint he could scarcely make it out, danger whispered. *Do not fall...*

He shoved the notion into the deepest chasms in his mind. He would not dwell on it. He would not fall. And he most assuredly would never put Briana in danger by staying with her longer than he had silently pledged.

"This is most intriguing." Briana smiled up at him, before glancing at her ladies. "We cannot imagine what the great surprise is. Or why you urged us to bring our cloaks."

"I doubt I would have found it had a tapestry not fallen from the wall." He took a lighted torch from the wall sconce before opening the door to the chamber and led her and her ladies inside. "My father and uncle slept in here when they were boys but kept its secret to themselves."

He had repaired the broken fixing and the tapestry covered a great section of the wall, but before he could pull it back and disclose its secret, Briana was by his side, admiring the fine work.

"This is beautiful, Ewan. What does it portray?"

He knew its history. He'd learned it years ago, and he ran his finger across the group of tall, lavishly attired people with their distinctive blonde and red hair. "It shows the Tuatha Dé Danann, the mythical folk from Eire, our homeland across the sea."

"Mythical folk?" She sounded enthralled and he grinned, knowing full well where her thoughts had traveled. "Do you speak of ancient gods?"

"They are fantastical stories, nothing more. This tapestry was brought from Eire two hundred years ago, when my great-grand-mother's family came to Dal Riada."

"It is precious, indeed. I wonder why it's kept here, out of sight, when it should surely grace the great hall."

He gave it a considering look. For as long as he could recall, the tapestry had been in this chamber, and he had thought nothing of it. But now, his grandmother's words whispered through his mind.

It is not the way of Dal Riada, and for Duntorr to continue to flourish, we had to make certain... sacrifices.

To be sure, this tapestry was from his grandfather's lineage, not his lady grandmother's, and the beliefs were different. But still, the principle remained the same. The tapestry, with its heretical imagery, had been hidden from public view.

As had Lady Catriona's gifts from a pagan goddess.

"It's likely safer here."

Briana didn't answer, but when he glanced at her she gave him a small smile and he knew she understood.

Carefully, he lifted the tapestry to show the door it had concealed for so many years.

"Goddess." Briana pressed her hand against the wood. "Where does this lead?"

"Open it and see." He drew back the bolts, and she twisted the large iron ring and pushed it open. He raised the torch so light spilled into the darkness beyond.

"A secret passageway." She laughed and turned to him. "How thrilling! And you did not know about it before?"

"No. And you will soon see that whoever designed this didn't understand the reasoning behind secret passageways. It would be useless during a siege."

"There's always a reason for a secret passageway. Otherwise, what is the use of them?"

"Then I await with bated breath for you to enlighten me."

She laughed, and a strange warmth filled his chest. Yet not so strange. Not since meeting her. From the first time he had seen her in Fotla, she'd affected him in ways he could not grasp.

Stop.

The longer he and Briana were together, the harder it was to remember this was nothing but a moment out of time. He had no future with her, and he would be wise not to forget it.

But he wouldn't dwell on that today.

"You had best don your cloaks." He included her ladies in his comment, before he led them through the passageway.

"Does Duntorr have many secret passageways?" Briana asked from behind him.

"I know of only one other, although Lady Catriona is the one to ask." In fact, now he was the lord of Duntorr, he should ask her himself. It was his duty to know all the secrets of the stronghold, now.

They reached another door and he unbolted it before leading them into the small, round tower chamber. As he lighted a few small oil lamps that he'd brought here yesterday, in readiness for today, Briana glanced around, a questioning smile on her face, and he laughed.

"Aye, it is intriguing, is it not? And before you ask, there are no hidden ways that lead elsewhere. I explored the walls thoroughly yesterday."

"And what of... that?" She gave the wooden ladder in the center of the chamber, that led up into darkness, a doubtful look.

"See the roof?" He pointed upwards and she appeared oddly reluctant to follow his finger. "It's nothing but a lid, easily removed. It opens onto a watchtower—at least, that's what it resembles, but there's no other way to reach it but from here."

"How extraordinary." For some reason, she no longer appeared amused by his surprise. "Perhaps this was once a strangely positioned goal."

"Let me show you the view. It looks out upon the same glen you can see from my lady grandmother's courtyard garden."

BRIANA'S HEART slammed against her chest, and it took a great effort not to shudder. The ladder loomed at her from the gloom, broken echoes of long-ago screams rattled through her mind, and her courage quailed.

"Forgive me, but I am happy to remain in the chamber. My ladies, I am sure, would love to take in the view."

Her ladies' excited responses confirmed her words, but she was unable to tear her gaze from Ewan. A shadow fell over his face as though he took her demurral personally. But she wasn't trying to be difficult. The very thought of ascending such a flimsy structure caused her stomach to churn, but of course she couldn't tell him *that*.

"It's quite safe." He gripped a lower rung and gave it a good tug. "And the top of the ladder is secured into the stone ledge. I shall allow no harm to come to you or your ladies."

Her mouth dried and panic clawed at her breast. Before she could think better of it, she gave a dismissive wave of her hand. "I have no wish to take in the view. But thank you for the offer."

She swung about to face her ladies, so she didn't have to keep up a false smile for Ewan, and within moments they ascended the ladder with him.

She exhaled a ragged breath, and when daylight flooded into the chamber, she looked up, to see her husband and her ladies disappear through the opening. She wrapped her cloak more securely about her and tried not to think. But it was impossible. Why had Ewan brought them here today?

Last night had been so wonderful. And not just the blissful bed sport they had enjoyed. He had eased her mind about his possible infidelity, but more than that, he had confessed the real reason why he hadn't shared her bed.

She believed him. No man would fabricate such a tale to spare his wife's feelings. Indeed, Ewan had appeared to believe she would be angered by his revelation, and she supposed, in truth, she should be.

Except how could she be angry with him when his reason was so gratifying? To be sure, she still didn't understand why he imagined having a child would make any difference to the time they spent together, but then, he was a Scot, and their ways were different to Picts.

When she had awoken this morning, his arms around her, her cheek pressed against his naked chest, she had dared to dream that, perhaps, their marriage could be so much more than one of pure political convenience.

Had she shattered that hope by appearing to slight him just now?

Agitated, she paced the small chamber as her heart thundered in her ears. She had hidden her fear so well over the years that no one knew of it. She doubted her parents even realized that she still remembered the incident, since she had been so young, but the terror had never left her.

Shadows fell across the chamber as her ladies and Ewan descended the ladder and she forced a smile to her lips as Lady Nairne described the breathtaking views. Ewan remained by the foot of the ladder, not engaging in the conversation, and when she risked glancing his way, there was a brooding expression on his face.

Until he caught her eye, when his face shuttered and he bowed his head in acknowledgement.

No. She could not allow this to continue. Not when there could be the chance of having—if not love, then surely affection —between them?

She took a deep breath and addressed Lady Nairne. "Please return to the bedchamber. My lord Ewan and I will return shortly. Drest, please accompany my ladies."

Nairne curtseyed and her ladies left, taking the torch with them. Drest cast a grim glance around the tower before, with obvious reluctance, following the others. The small oil lamps cast a dull glow across the stone walls and Briana turned to face Ewan.

"I must explain," she said.

"There's no need." He smiled, but it didn't reach his eyes. "There was no reason for me to imagine you'd wish to climb up a ladder simply to look at something you can see far more easily from the courtyard garden."

"I'm afraid of heights." The confession tumbled inelegantly

from her, and she gripped her fingers together under cover of her cloak. "That is the reason I could not climb the ladder."

Concern etched his features, and he came to her, his hand a gentle presence upon her shoulder. "Briana, I'm sorry I caused you such distress. It was not my intention."

She sucked in a ragged breath. "To be truthful, it's not merely heights. It is any kind of stair. When I was a child, my mother's companion fell down the palace stairs while holding me. She—she hit her head, and the blood..." she swallowed, as the vivid images shivered through her mind. "Goddess only knows how I escaped any injury, but the lady's cries of pain haunt me still. She did not survive the night."

"So that's why you always trail your hand along the wall when you're on the stairs."

She blinked, shaken from those bloodied memories. "What?"

"It's subtle," he said, as though he sought to reassure her. "I thought it might have something to do with your goddess."

Heat flooded her face. She thought she had managed to hide her nervous habit admirably. No one had ever mentioned it to her before. But then, why would they?

"You have strange ideas indeed about the great goddess." But since that was a most foolish response, she sighed and shook her head. "It's a fear I've had to overcome, for it's impossible not to use stairs, of course. But I find my courage wavers when faced with a ladder."

"I understand. Rest assured I shall never bring you to this tower again. And for causing you such upset, I intend to spend the rest of this day at the mercy of your every whim."

She gave a soft laugh and took his hand. "That sounds most delightful."

The light flickered and a footfall behind them had her spinning about. Rohan stood at the doorway, and she felt Ewan stiffen with displeasure by her side.

"Forgive the intrusion." Rohan gave a half bow. "I've been

searching for you, my lady, and Lady Nairne explained where you were when I knocked on Lord Ewan's door."

"What is it?" Ewan sounded brusque and Rohan's face tightened with affront. After a swift glare in Ewan's direction, Rohan once again addressed her.

"The Scots king has arrived, and Lady Catriona requests the pleasure of your company. And that of Lord Ewan."

CHAPTER 24

*B*riana held her head high as she and Ewan entered Lady Catriona's private chamber. The lady herself sat on her chair by the fireside, her ladies standing behind her, but her focus arrowed onto the Scot who stood with such arrogant confidence in the center of the chamber, with MacAllister by his side.

"My liege." Ewan bowed, and from the rustle of skirts behind her, she knew her ladies dipped curtsies, but she remained ramrod straight, and corrosive rage pumped through her blood.

Upstart. *Bastard.* The man not only responsible for taking her father hostage last year, but for ordering the slaughter of so many Picts with royal blood last spring. Simply so that his own claim to the Supreme Kingdom, Fortriu, was unchallenged.

She scarcely heard Ewan as he made the introductions. A high-pitched buzzing filled her head and her chest tightened, and she had the alarming compunction to grab MacAlpin's sword and run him through with his own blade.

But through it all, a faint thread of sanity prevailed. She would never do such a thing. Not here, not ever. MacAlpin held all their lives in his hands and to openly attack him would court nothing but disaster.

It was not just the safety of herself or her ladies, or the men and servants she had brought with her. It was the future of Fotla. Of Pictland.

And perhaps even of Ewan.

"Lady Briana, welcome to Dal Riada." MacAlpin gave a half bow and extended his arm. Self-preservation left an acid taste in her mouth as she inclined her head in recognition of his status and offered him her hand.

He kissed her knuckles and somehow she managed not to shudder at the contact. "I thank you, my lord." He was not *her* king, and she would not address him as such.

MacAlpin smiled, clearly disposed to overlook her breach in protocol, and still holding her hand, led her to a stool beside Lady Catriona, before taking his place on the other chair that flanked the fireplace. Gripping her fingers together on her lap she pasted a smile upon her face. No matter what her thoughts, MacAlpin would not have cause to criticize her demeanor.

Ewan stood by her side, his hands clasped behind his back. Was it her imagination that tension radiated from him?

She caught sight of Drest, standing by the door, arms folded, and untrammeled loathing distorted his features as he glared at MacAlpin. Thankfully, it vanished in a heartbeat, but she resolved to speak to him as soon as possible. To be sure, he had ample reason to despise MacAlpin. They all did. But he couldn't let his personal feelings show so freely when they were in the upstart's own land.

"This is but a brief visit," MacAlpin said. "We are on our way to Dunadd, but we could not travel so close to Duntorr without paying our respects to the princess." Once again, he bestowed a smile in her direction. As if she should be honored that he had made a diversion to see her. If she had to smile any longer, her face would crack. "Naturally," he added, turning to Lady Catriona, "We wished to see our gracious lady, also."

"You are always welcome." There was a warm note in Lady Catriona's voice, and the knot within Briana's chest burned in outrage.

"I trust your esteemed father and brother are well," MacAlpin said, once more looking at her. She clenched her fists, digging her fingernails into her palms. He had no right to enquire after her beloved father, after the way he had so foully imprisoned him last year.

But the honor of Fotla lay upon her shoulders and she would not disgrace her homeland by telling MacAlpin what she really thought of him. "They are both well."

"Good." He nodded, then appeared to dismiss them from his mind. "We must make haste in sanctifying your marriage in the Christian church, Lady Briana. We should not wish anyone to cast aspersions upon Ewan's future heirs."

Stung by the implication that her own faith was worthless, she could no longer hold her tongue. "Lord Ewan and I are wed in the eyes of the ancient ones and by the laws of Pictland. There will be no aspersions cast upon any of my children."

"Perhaps a simple blessing in Duntorr's church will appease the monks." Lady Catriona smiled at her before turning to MacAlpin. "It's always wise to be prepared for any eventuality and Lady Briana's status may never be questioned."

"Indeed," MacAlpin agreed. "That is our paramount concern."

How dare they speak of her as though she wasn't even present? She drew in a deep breath, but before she could share her opinion there was a commotion behind her. She glanced over her shoulder, just as Ewan caught Lady Eara in his arms before she collapsed onto the floor.

"Goddess." She jumped up from the stood and took Eara's hand. "What ails you?"

"Forgive me, my lady." Eara straightened, her face ashen, and with a troubled glance at Briana, Ewan released her. "Deepest apologies for causing such a spectacle. I am not quite myself."

It was clear Lady Eara was on the verge of tears, and Briana could not bear for her friend to be so mortified in front of MacAlpin. Still holding Eara's hand, she returned her attention to the others. Lady Catriona was standing, a concerned expression on her face, and MacAlpin leaned back in his chair, a faint air of amusement emanating from him.

She reined in her ire, since it would get her nowhere, and spoke to the older woman. "Lady Catriona, I request your indulgence for my ladies and I to take our leave."

"Of course." Lady Catriona didn't even glance at MacAlpin for permission which, truth be told, surprised her. "Let me know if there's anything you or your lady needs. I will send for my healer, if you wish."

"You are very kind." But she had a good idea what ailed Eara. Two months ago, she had spent much time with her husband, and two mornings ago she had been distressingly ill.

She inclined her head at MacAlpin, even though a childish part of her wanted to sweep from the chamber without acknowledging his odious presence. He pushed himself to his feet and offered her another of his half-bows which she found excessively irritating.

"It was a pleasure to meet you, Lady Briana," he said. "Doubtless, we shall meet again soon."

Unfortunately, he was likely right, if Lady Catriona was such a favorite of his. "No doubt," she said, as graciously as she could, before she turned her attention to Ewan, who looked set to accompany her from the chamber. "There is no need, my lord," she said quietly. If she was correct, this was women's business and Eara would not wish Ewan to be present. "I shall see you later."

～

EWAN WATCHED Briana and her ladies leave the chamber and attempted to quell the resentment burning through him at his king's unexpected arrival. He'd planned on spending the day with Briana, but more than that, he wanted to make up for inadvertently upsetting her. He was under no illusion that having to greet MacAlpin had likely spoiled the day for her beyond repair.

He was pulled sharply back to the present by the sound of MacAlpin's laugh. "The princesses of Pictland are a spirited breed, are they not, Conall?"

"Aye." MacAllister sounded satisfied and Ewan shot him a dark glare. "They are perfectly suited for our noble born warriors."

Ewan clasped his hands behind his back so no one would see how they fisted in frustration. Each princess had been coerced into marriage, including Briana. At least his king and MacAllister had retained the decency not to make such comments while she was still present.

"It is fortunate," his grandmother said, "that our noble born warriors please the princesses."

"You speak wisely, as always." MacAlpin inclined his head at her, clearly not irked by her remark.

Only rarely had he been present when MacAlpin visited his grandmother but now a memory stirred. She was the only woman, including MacAlpin's own wife, the queen, whose opinion he appeared to consider worthy.

"The four greatest kingdoms of Pictland are now protected under the banner of the House of Alpin," MacAllister said. "A good year's work, sire."

Anger smoldered through Ewan's veins as his suspicions on what had really occurred during the meeting with the royal Pictish lords last spring thundered through his head, and he could remain silent no longer. "Dal Riada benefits greatly, also, from the alliance with the Picts. Especially if we need to shore up our borders with Northumbria after the attempt on Lord Constantine's life."

"Aye." MacAlpin's voice turned hard. "They will come to regret that error in judgement. We will have vengeance upon them, just as we avenge ourselves against the Picts for the brutal slaying of my royal father, Alpin, after the battle of '34."

He wasn't used to MacAlpin speaking so frankly in front of him. He wasn't one of the king's trusted advisers, like his own father had been, after all. And while Alpin's death had certainly been brutal—after the battle, the Picts had captured and beheaded him—surely that wasn't the driving force behind MacAlpin's determination to bring the kingdoms of Pictland under the Dal Riadan banner?

"Vengeance is a cruel master." Lady Catriona's voice was filled with sorrow, and Ewan shifted, uncomfortable. To disagree with a king, even obliquely, was tantamount to treason.

"Aye." MacAlpin sounded grim but didn't appear affronted by Lady Catriona's candor. "But I pledged to unite Pictland and will not rest until it is done."

Silence echoed around the chamber, before MacAlpin once again leaned back in his chair. "But let us speak of happier things. We have decided our coronation will take place in the spring, in Fortriu. The princesses will be our guests of honor."

Ewan doubted Briana would take kindly to that.

"However, there is time enough to plan for that. Alas, my lady aunt, we must leave for Dunadd. We shall take with us the warriors who were lately in Fotla."

God damn it. Did MacAlpin want him to join the contingent, too? He attempted, without great success, to bury his distrust of his king, but it was hard to keep his voice neutral.

"Does my liege require my presence?"

MacAlpin stood and gave him a considering look. "No, MacKinnon. Your duty now is to strengthen your strongholds of

Duntorr and Duncreag, and sire healthy sons for Dal Riada. We shall only prevail when the blood of Scot and Pict becomes one."

~

WHEN MACALPIN TOOK HIS LEAVE, along with MacAllister and the contingent of warriors who had accompanied him to Fotla—including Ross and Rourke—Ewan walked with his grandmother through the great hall, intending to see her back to her private chamber before going to Briana.

"Ewan, I need to see the princess."

"Now?" He wasn't sure that was a good idea. Even though Briana had hidden her feelings well, he'd seen her face tighten as his grandmother had spoken with MacAlpin. It did not bode well for the future harmony of Duntorr, but he was at a loss as to how to resolve things. Maybe the answer was for them to follow his original plan, and make their home in Duncreag, instead.

"Yes." His grandmother sighed and shook her head. "I believe the princess has questions for me."

Ewan was sure she had, but he doubted his grandmother wanted to hear them. And while he was certain Lady Catriona would never knowingly distress Briana, he didn't want to risk any confrontation where his bride might feel even the slightest hint of reproach.

"I will speak with her. She has understandable issues with our king, but she is knowledgeable of politics and this alliance is precious to her. She'll not allow her personal feelings to jeopardize the safety of Pictland."

"Naturally." His grandmother gave his arm an affectionate pat. "But it's not politics she needs to hear from me."

Briana and her ladies were in the antechamber although Drest, surprisingly, was absent. His grandmother enquired after Lady Eara, and for several minutes the talk was of womanly matters. Unease stirred and he edged further away from the fire, in the hope their conversation would become inaudible. Should he leave? Everyone appeared to be getting along well. But his grandmother had wanted to see Briana for a specific reason, and he was damn sure it had nothing to do with Lady Eara.

"Lady Briana," his grandmother said, at last, "may we speak privately?"

"Certainly." Briana led the way to her bedchamber and the three of them entered, leaving the noblewomen in the antechamber. The air was chilled, and he built up the fire, while his bride and his grandmother eyed each other over his head.

He stood, and brought chairs for them, reluctant to leave even though he was certain that was what Lady Catriona wanted. But what of Briana?

"Please stay, Ewan." His grandmother's voice was soft, as though she had heard his thought. "I do not want any secrets between the three of us."

Briana sat, his grandmother followed suit, and he stood with his hands clasped behind his back as wariness roiled through his gut. Even at the risk of upsetting his beloved grandmother, he could not let her say a word against his wife.

"My lady grandmother, you have my undying devotion, but Lady Briana is the mistress of Duntorr and is under no obligation to defend her position."

From the corner of his eye, he was aware Briana shot him a startled glance, but he kept his gaze on Lady Catriona, willing her to understand. He didn't want to hurt her, but she had to know he would protect his wife with the last breath in his body.

He should have known she would not be affronted. She merely smiled, as though his statement was not in the least unexpected.

"That is only right, Ewan. I would have it no other way. I'm here only so Lady Briana can ask me what she wishes to know."

"I'm sure I do not know what you mean, Lady Catriona." There was an uncharacteristically reserved note in Briana's voice.

"If I need to know anything concerning Duntorr, I shall certainly ask you."

"Indeed. But we are not speaking of Duntorr, are we?" Lady Catriona said.

Something sparked in the air, something pagan, like unseeable lightning, and an eerie shudder crawled along his spine as he cast his glance between the two ladies.

Aye, God help him. Just because he did not believe in the ancient ones, didn't stop him from imagining blasphemous scenarios.

Briana drew in a deep breath. "We are not. And I respect your offer for bluntness, but I will not risk offending Lady Catriona of Duntorr and Fortriu."

Those were her words, but even that wasn't what she meant. The hair prickled on the back of his neck as understanding seeped through him.

Briana would not risk offending another who had been chosen by her goddess.

"You won't offend me." Lady Catriona's voice was serene. "Nothing we say shall go beyond these walls."

Briana gripped her fingers together and Ewan had the wild compunction to yell, *say nothing*, but he could not move, could not speak, as though a spell had been cast upon him and wouldn't break until he'd witnessed this outcome.

"Very well. I accept one must always make the best of one's situation, but I cannot fathom how you, a noblewoman of Fortriu, can look so kindly upon the Dal Riadan king."

And there it was. If his throat wasn't paralyzed, he would've groaned aloud.

"You fear I betray the heritage of my birth and my noble bloodline?"

"I do not presume to say such a thing. Merely that I find it incomprehensible, given the Dal Riadan king's actions last year."

The air stilled around him. She did not speak of the marriages

MacAlpin had engineered. She spoke of last year. Of the meeting of the Pictish nobles in Dunadd.

The massacre. The *betrayal*.

"Yes." Lady Catriona's voice was soft and filled with sorrow as if she, too, knew exactly of what Briana spoke. "It's hard to reconcile, to be sure. And..." she hesitated before taking a deep breath. "Whatever you may believe, I do not condone. But I cannot turn my back on him, and it has nothing to do with him being the king of Dal Riada."

"What, then?" The words burst from him, unintended, but he could not remain silent. Even though they spoke of his king, to whom he owed fealty, the dark suspicions that had plagued him since the spring were an ugly chasm in his soul. "All these years, we could never speak of the blood that linked my grandfather and Alpin, yet now the king uses that very heritage to bind Lady Briana in a royal marriage."

"Everything you say is true. But there's more to it, Ewan. The king's father, Alpin, was my beloved Tavish's half-brother, but his mother, the Princess of Fortriu—she was my half-sister, Clodrah. Kenneth MacAlpin is of my blood, too."

Briana drew in a sharp breath, as his grandmother's words thundered around his head. "The king is your nephew." His voice was hoarse.

"You are of the royal line of Fortriu," Briana said.

Lady Catriona gave a sad smile. "Clodrah was a princess of Fortriu. I was never acknowledged by my father, the king, until it was too late to matter to me. My dear friend, Brilicie, Princess of Circinn, and I tried to protect Clodrah from herself, but she was determined to be with her handsome Scots prince."

"Brilicie?" There was a wondering note in Briana's voice. "The Dowager Queen of Ce?"

"Ah, yes. When I knew her, she was still a princess of the kingdom of her birth."

"She is my grand-aunt," Briana whispered.

"I see her in you." His grandmother drew in a shaking breath. "You have her eyes and hair."

Ewan had met the dowager last year in the Kingdom of Ce, but her relationship to Briana, while doubtless of note, was not the reason his head reeled at his grandmother's revelations.

"My father was cousin twice over to MacAlpin."

"A half cousin twice over," she corrected him. "But yes. Clodrah wanted a babe so dearly, but when it became clear she would not survive the birth, she made me promise." Lady Catriona swallowed, and her lip trembled. "She begged me to love her son as I loved my own. To give him the mother's love she would now never be able to give him herself. I swore on the name of my beloved Bride I would do all she asked, and more."

Silence echoed around the chamber, and then Briana held out her hand. "Lady Catriona." Her voice was scarcely above a whisper. "I understand."

His grandmother took her hand. "I know."

CHAPTER 25

"*A*re you ready, my lady?"

Briana smiled at Ewan, as he sat astride his fine black stallion outside the stables. His hair was tied back with a black, velvet ribbon, and his padded deerskin jacket merely enhanced his broad shoulders and muscular biceps. A delicious thrill raced through her. Would she ever tire of simply looking at him? "I am, my lord."

He grinned, and the elusive aura of melancholy that she could sometimes feel drifting around him, vanished.

As they left the courtyard, he glanced at her. "It's quite a novelty, having my bride to myself during the day. I feared there was no way to ever sweep you away from the attentive presence of your ladies."

"It's most unconventional, to be sure. My lady mother would be most disapproving." And when Drest discovered that, with the help of her ladies, she had escaped his watchful eye, he would be most disapproving, too. She pushed him from her mind and focused on Ewan, which wasn't hard to do at all. "But who better to accompany me on a ride in the countryside than my own noble husband?"

He possessed royal blood, but after MacAlpin's visit just over a week ago, and the confidences Lady Catriona had shared, she had come to understand Ewan a little better. He hadn't lied to her about his heritage when he had come to Fotla. In his heart, he was not a part of the House of Alpin, whatever his king might now command. His royal blood was not his defining attribute, and she wouldn't insult him by alluding to it.

"I'm taking you at your word that you don't mind a trek through the snow." He shot her another of his irresistible smiles, and despite the winter chill, warmth flooded through her.

"I do not. Duntorr is magnificent, but I confess that after days of being confined within its walls, I long for this freedom."

"Aye, it was a fearsome snowstorm, but we should be safe enough today."

Once they had passed through the village, they cantered through the soft snow. The wind chilled her face and whipped at her cloak, and her heart thundered in her ears as she urged her mare on. They kept to open land, skirting a great forest, and finally, Ewan drew to a halt. "Here it is. The glen you can see from Lady Catriona's garden."

She gave an appreciative sigh, her breath a white plume in the air. Surrounded by mountains and forest, the glen lay before them, a mantle of untouched white, with ancient yews, their drooping branches blanketed in snow, and a frozen loch that disappeared from view around a copse of great, gray fissured alders.

"It's beautiful," she confirmed. "My ladies will be most jealous. They long to visit this glen."

"I shall escort you and your ladies here another day. But for now, I'm glad to have you to myself." He dismounted, before helping her from her mare. Even though she was entirely able to manage by herself, the temptation to have him hold her proved too great to resist and she wound her arms around his neck as he lowered her to the ground.

"I cannot argue with that." She smiled up at him. Since she had confronted him about their sleeping arrangements, he had spent every night in her bed. Indeed, he had all but moved into her bedchamber and she certainly wasn't complaining. To wake up each morning with Ewan's big body by her side, his arm slung across her, holding her close, made her heart sing. And that was before the inevitable pre-dawn lovemaking…

"If you continue to gaze at me in such a manner, I shall not be responsible for my actions." There was a note of laughter in his voice, and she threaded her fingers through his hair and pulled his head down so she could kiss him. He groaned into her mouth, and she pulled back, gasping.

"I could say the same to you."

"We are well matched, and that's a fact." He grasped the reins of their horses in one hand, and she hooked her arm through his. "Rest assured, when the weather is fine, I shall bring you back here and ravish you against that pleasingly situated tree." He nodded at a nearby two-trunked alder, and she laughed at the scandalous image he painted in her mind.

"Beware, my lord. I might hold you to that promise."

"I expect you to," he told her, as they looped the reins around a branch. "Let me find that mulled wine. It will keep the chill at bay."

Briana gave him another lingering kiss before she strolled along the bank, beside the alders.

"Don't go too far," Ewan said from behind her. "I must keep you in my sights."

She shook her head and turned back to him, a mocking response upon her lips.

And then she stilled, as a faint whisper rustled in the breeze.

What was that?

Frowning, she spun about and continued along the bank, scanning the snowy landscape although she could not think what she was searching for.

And then she saw it. A dark smudge against the glaring white of the loch, and her heart kicked against her ribs.

It was a wolf, almost full grown. But where was its pack? A young one should not be hunting alone yet. She scanned the edge of the forest on the far side of the loch but could see no stealthy movement nor the glint of orange eyes.

That didn't mean the wolves weren't there. There was no need to concern herself about the wolf pup. It would find its way home. She smiled as the creature play pounced on the ice. For all its size, it was still a pup, and reminded her of Shadow. Her dearest boy. Sorrow squeezed her heart. Would she ever see him again?

An ominous crack reverberated around the glen and the wolf disappeared. She gasped and ran forward, just as the wolf's head bobbed back into view.

Goddess, no. It had fallen into the water and appeared unable to climb out. Wildly, she glanced around, but there was still no sign of its pack. If the pup didn't climb out soon, the icy water would freeze over, and the poor thing would drown.

She was halfway across the frozen loch when Ewan's horrorstruck voice hit her.

"What the hell are you doing, Briana? Get back here."

She hesitated only long enough to glance over her shoulder. "I'll be careful. I cannot leave the pup."

"The *hell* you can't." He sounded furious but she didn't have time to argue with him. The pup was within touching distance, struggling desperately for purchase on the slick surface, and for an eternal second, its terrified orange eyes met hers.

She sank to her knees. She wasn't oblivious to the danger. The wolf could easily injure her, but she trusted in her goddess, and this was the reason why Ewan had brought her to the glen this day.

"It's all right. I am here." She spoke soothingly as she inched closer, but as she wound her cloak clad arms around the drenched animal, a dreadful vibration shuddered through the ice as Ewan followed her across the loch.

A menacing crackle vibrated beneath her, and desperately she hauled the wolf from the water and set it—her—on solid ice. As the pup skidded away, she caught sight of a she-wolf by the edge of the forest, but as she slowly stood, the ice gave way and she crashed into the frigid water.

EWAN WAS BARELY two strides from Briana, when the ice split, and she vanished into the bitter depths. His heart slowed to one thunderous thud, that echoed through his head, and blocked out the sound of everything but a high-pitched keening that paralyzed his very soul.

Black memories of another time flashed through his mind. His mother, disappearing under the water. The terror that had gripped him. The *helplessness*.

"*No.*" He roared the denial but maybe the endless refrain was locked inside his head, as Briana surfaced, gasping.

He wasn't a helpless child anymore. He wasn't too far away from her to do anything. This was Briana, his bride, his... the words froze in his brain, and he flattened himself on the ice, spreading his weight, before he grasped her arms and pulled her out.

There was no time to lose, and he brutally stamped down on the memories that threatened to drag him over the edge. He stood and lifted her in his arms and her teeth chattered, as she shivered uncontrollably. Her sodden cloak was useless against the cold, but he couldn't do anything about that yet as he raced across the rapidly cracking ice to the safety of the bank.

Without releasing her, he grabbed the jug from where he'd dropped it, before continuing to the horses. Gently, he lowered her to the ground before ripping off her cloak and wrapping her in his thick jacket. Christ, was it the light or were her lips blue?

He tore out the stopper and handed her the jug of mulled wine. "Drink." His voice was hoarse as he untied the reins without taking his gaze from her. The wind bit through him and he wasn't even that wet. Panic clawed his vitals. He needed to get her to Duntorr, fast. Before—

He slammed down the thoughts before they could manifest. He would not think on it. Couldn't.

Moments later, he set off, his arms wrapped around Briana as she hugged the warm jug against her. Her hair was turning into strands of ice and her shivering was so severe his own bones rattled with the force of it.

Had it ever taken this long to return to the stronghold before? He should have brought a servant with them. God's blood, where was Drest when he was needed? He could have ridden ahead to ensure Briana's bedchamber fire was fully stoked and water heated for her.

And she hadn't said a word. Not that he'd said anything, either. What could he say? That she was a damn fool for having run onto a frozen loch just to save a wolf?

His grip around her tightened as the image of her vanishing beneath the ice stabbed through his mind once again. The way his lady mother had vanished, so many years ago. But his mother hadn't survived.

A vise squeezed his chest, making it hard to draw breath. Grimly, he urged his horse on, Briana's mare following in their wake. Briana would not succumb. He would not allow it. He refused to even *consider* it.

The villagers stared as he cantered towards the stronghold and when he entered the courtyard the boy, Beli, ran to take charge of the horses. With Briana in his arms, Ewan strode into the stronghold, and she clutched his shirt, her fingers so cold they chilled his blood. He wanted to comfort her, to say all would be well, but the words locked in his throat, unsayable, as primitive fear relentlessly pounded through him.

He knew the dangers of extreme cold. How one could fall into a sleep and never awaken. That couldn't happen to Briana.

She could not die.

In the great hall, he came face to face with his grandmother, Drest looming beside her. Without a word, and before he could say anything, two of Lady Catriona's ladies tucked a great blanket around Briana. His grandmother came close and spoke directly to her.

"Lady Briana, can you hear me?"

Briana slowly pulled her head from his chest to look at his grandmother.

"Yes." Her voice was hushed, but relief streaked through him that, thank God, she hadn't lost the power of speech.

"And do you know where you are?"

Another great shiver wracked her, and he sucked in a harsh breath. "My lady grandmother, I must see to Briana's comfort."

"Indeed," Lady Catriona said. "But we must be certain. Lady Briana, where are you?"

"Duntorr. The ice cracked, and I fell into the loch."

Lady Catriona gave a strained smile, and briefly squeezed Briana's shoulder. "You will recover," she said, with such certainty that awe flickered through the fear that still permeated every tortured breath he took. "Ewan, wrap Lady Briana in warm blankets. When she has had some soup, she may take a lukewarm bath. Please let me know when you are recovered enough to see me," she added to Briana, who gave a tired nod.

As he strode past Drest, the warrior looked shaken. "I failed to keep you safe, my lady."

Aye, and so had he. He went up the stairs and when he entered her antechamber, Rohan turned from the fire and glared at him.

"Is this how you care for my lady?" Loathing rolled from him, and any other time Ewan would have called out his insolence. But what did the Pict's words matter, when Briana lay all but lifeless in his arms?

He flung open the door to her bedchamber and came to a halt. There was no need to command that the fire be stoked, or hot water brought. The fire burned brightly, a wooden tub filled with steaming water sat before it, and the area had been enclosed by blankets attached to poles, to keep the heat from escaping into the rest of the chamber.

How had they known?

Gavina shut the door behind him, and Nairne came to his side. "Lord Ewan, we will care for our lady, now."

It didn't matter how they already had blankets warming before the fire, or that a bowl of soup sat upon the table. All that mattered was that Briana was well.

He went over to the hearth and tenderly sat her upon a stool, before dropping to his knees and relieving her of his jacket. "There's no need. I shall tend to Lady Briana."

Her ladies surrounded her, appearing flummoxed.

"But my lord, Lady Catriona was most insistent in her instructions," Nairne said.

"The great goddess must have whispered in her ear." Gavina pressed her hand to her throat as she gave Briana an anxious glance.

"Leave us," he said, trying, and failing, to vanquish the apprehension that curdled his blood. "I'll call if you're needed."

Still they remained, until Briana looked at Nairne and gave a small nod. With a flurry of skirts, her ladies left the chamber and he continued to undress Briana. But his fingers were clumsy, and he couldn't slow the erratic thunder of his heart. He gritted his teeth and ripped the wet material from her, and she shuddered as he wrapped the warm blankets around her naked shoulders and over her hair.

She sighed and closed her eyes, and he knelt before her,

fisting his hands until his knuckles ached. Slowly, a pink tinge returned to her cheeks and her lips lost the terrifying hint of blue and only then did his fingers relax their death grip.

After an eternity, she looked at him and because he couldn't trust himself to speak, he handed her the bowl of soup. Without a word, she began to eat, and the knot inside his chest eased enough that he could take a deep breath.

And that simple action unlocked the dam.

"How could you put yourself in such danger?" Accusation pulsed through every word and his head throbbed with a combination of relief that she would recover, and *fury* that she had been so careless. "To run across broken ice is sheer folly in the extreme."

Her eyes flashed with affront, and he battled the urge to gather her into his arms, to hold her close, to never let her go, to assure himself that *she was safe* because she had to know he could never allow her to do anything so reckless again.

"The ice was not cracked when I *ran across it* to the wolf pup. There was only one small hole that she had fallen into."

His mind blazed with the image of watching her disappear into the frigid water and the words burst from him, unthinking. "I forbid you to do anything so foolhardy again, do you hear me? I'll have you confined to the stronghold, rather than allow you to put your life in danger again."

"I apologize for this inconvenience." Her voice was icy as she swept her glance from the tub to the soup bowl. "But I was not foolhardy, and I reject the accusation. You will not keep me tethered like a disobedient dog when it was not I who caused the ice to crack behind me."

Her scathing words echoed in his ears. But she was wrong. When he'd seen her crouch down to rescue the wolf, the ice was already cracking. God damn it, if he hadn't been there, she would have *drowned*.

His heart hammered, his chest tightened, and it was hard to

breathe. The lamps flickered, and shadows gathered, creeping from the corners of the chamber and across the floor, until he could see nothing but Briana's face.

It was not I who caused the ice to crack.

The words reverberated around his skull, becoming louder and louder, until the ceaseless echo even blocked out the harsh rasp of his breath.

The ice had not cracked until he had stepped upon it. Briana had been in danger, but not as much as he'd feared. If he had remained on the bank, would the ice have shattered? Would she have plunged into the loch?

Condemnation roared through him, remorseless, as nightmarish images flashed through his mind. His mother, drowning. His little half-brother, who had died of the fever while he had survived. And his stepmother's bitter cry.

You wicked, cursed creature.

Aye, he was cursed. It was his fault Briana had fallen into the water.

His fault she had almost drowned.

CHAPTER 26

The hot burst of indignation that had swept through Briana at Ewan's accusation dissolved as the color leached from his face and his eyes glazed over. Dear goddess, what was wrong? Alarm sparked through her as he staggered to his feet and took a step back from her.

"Ewan?" Her voice was hushed. All she had done was defend herself against his accusation, and yet her words had affected him in a way she could never have imagined.

He exhaled a harsh breath. "You might have died."

Gingerly, she stood, clutching the blankets around her. Thank the goddess she was once again in possession of her senses. "But I didn't die," she said softly. "I'm here, and I am perfectly well."

Their gazes clashed and she hitched in a sharp breath at the wild gleam in his eyes. "I almost killed you, Briana."

"What? No." The blanket slipped over her shoulder as she reached out and gripped his hand. "How can you even say that? It is madness. You pulled me from the loch. You saved me."

"You wouldn't have needed saving if my rash actions hadn't resulted in the ice cracking."

She couldn't dispute the truth of his claim, but she had no

intention of agreeing with him. Something more than the fact he had feared she might drown was happening here.

"I'm sorry I worried you." Her voice was soft, but still he gazed at her as though he could not quite believe she was uninjured. "I did not mean to."

"When the ice broke, and the water sucked you under, I..." He dragged in a harsh breath and a shudder ripped through him. "I feared you would perish, the same as she did."

A shiver prickled over her arms and her fingers tightened around his fist. "She?"

He swallowed and for a moment she thought he wasn't going to answer her. "My lady mother drowned when I was five. I couldn't save her."

"Oh, my love." Now she understood his flash of anger. It had not been anger at all. She pressed her lips against his knuckles, wishing there was something she could do to let him know she grieved for his loss. "What a terrible thing for a child to witness."

"It was my fault." His voice was flat. "I did not heed her warnings. She paid the price for my folly."

Surely he could not believe such a thing? "It wasn't your fault, Ewan. You were a child. There was nothing you could have done."

Uncertainty clouded his eyes. "When you vanished beneath the ice, I was thrust back in time, to that moment when I saw my mother fall into the water. I wasn't by her side in the boat, as I've always thought. I was on the bank, with the other children. It was summer, and all the cousins had come to Duncreag."

"Yes," she whispered. The air crackled with tension and although these memories were causing him great pain, she knew he had to speak of them, if he ever wanted to be free of them.

"My father and the other men had gone hunting. My lady mother was in a boat with some of her relatives, but I wasn't with her. I was with my cousins."

She bit her lip. He had already told her he was on the bank, but it was clear this was important to him. "There was an accident?"

"The weather turned." A frown creased his brow as though he searched for more details of that long ago day. "Black clouds blotted out the sun. Keita—my cousin—suddenly grabbed my hand and we ran into the water, I don't remember why. Except we were afraid? The wind whipped through the glen, and I saw my mother fall into the loch."

"I'm so sorry." What else could she say? Her heart ached for a woman she had never known, and her small son, who had been haunted by this memory all his life.

"The guards pulled her out, but it was too late. Her face…" He gave a great shudder and when his blue eyes meshed with hers, she had the absurd wish that she could wrap him in her arms and soothe all his pain away. "I've been in battles. I've seen death, God help me. But she was the first. And when I saw you fall into the water—"

She pressed against him, holding him close as well as she could with the restriction of the blankets. "I grieve for the loss of your lady mother. And I grieve that I reminded you of that sad day."

His arms came around her, and he crushed her in a brutal embrace, his face buried in her hair. "I thought I was in the boat with her. That it was my fault she fell. Until the water sucked you under, and it was too terrifyingly familiar. I realize now I couldn't have been beside her that day."

"Memories are strange things. And you were very young."

He didn't answer. Merely held her close and it seemed she could feel the coiled tension seeping from his body. Finally, he sighed and eased back, although he didn't fully release her.

"It wasn't my intention to burden you with my dark history." There was a thread of self-mockery in his voice as though he truly believed he should not have shared such a thing with her. "Especially not now." He pulled the blankets more securely around her, covering her shoulders and neck. "My lady grand-mother would skin me for such dereliction of duty."

She gave a soft laugh, relieved to see the gleam of humor in his eyes. "Lady Catriona would do no such thing. I believe you could do no wrong in her eyes."

"I don't know where you got that idea from." He smiled, and a silent sigh rippled through her breast. "But I'm happy that you enjoy her company."

"I'm very fond of her." It was strange how she could say that, and mean it, when a little over a week ago she'd harbored such distrust of Lady Catriona. But it was true. Since the disclosure of her relationship to MacAlpin, so many things had become clear to Briana.

Lady Catriona was bound to the Scots king by blood and an oath made to their goddess. Neither could be denied and to break either bond would be grievous indeed. Yet she had not forsaken all the ways of her heritage to blend into her new life. She did not dress in the fashion of a Scots noblewoman and while she supported the local church, she didn't pretend to follow the new religion that prevailed in Dal Riada.

"Good. In that case, you will not protest her command that you take a bath." He backed her up to the tub, before peeling the blanket from her, scooping her into his arms, and tenderly lowering her into the warm, scented, water.

AFTER NAIRNE and Gavina had helped her dress and tidied her hair, Ewan brought Lady Catriona to see her. They sat before the fire in her bedchamber, and their ladies brought hot herbal tea for them before retiring to the antechamber. Ewan stood beside her, his hand on the back of her chair and Lady Catriona leaned forward and gave her blanket covered knee a gentle pat.

"We are so relieved you are well, Lady Briana."

"Please forgive me for causing such a fright. It was not my intention." She reached up and gave Ewan's hand a small squeeze, and didn't miss his grandmother's smile at her action. "I might have perished but for Ewan's quick actions."

"I'm certain you would not have." There was a hint of grimness in his tone, as though he didn't want her to pretend. But she had made her decision. The truth of the matter would remain between the two of them.

"The ways of the gods are at times unfathomable." Lady Catriona smiled benignly but Briana had the uncanny notion the older woman had a shrewd idea of what had truly happened.

"With respect, your gods had nothing to do with it."

Lady Catriona sighed. "Perhaps I was remiss in not teaching you more of the old ways, Ewan. But perhaps we can agree there are things in this world that are beyond our understanding."

"Aye, I'll give you that." Warmth threaded through his words, and a corresponding wave of comfort flowed through Briana's blood. "For I don't understand how you knew of Briana's accident before we arrived home."

"I didn't know exactly what had happened. I merely knew we needed to be prepared. It's hard to explain the *knowing* that can descend. The imperative to do what one must."

A shiver of awe trickled over Briana's arms. And even though Lady Catriona hadn't been speaking to her, she was compelled to respond. "Yes. The compunction, even when the reason is clouded with doubt."

Ewan grunted. "This talk is not for my ears. Should I leave?"

"There's no need to leave," Lady Catriona said. "But I confess, there are things I wish to say to Lady Briana that might be considered blasphemous in Dal Riada."

He gave a great sigh. "Then I shall leave you in peace so that my eternal soul is not in peril." His accompanying grin reassured her that he wasn't completely serious. But she would beseech

Bride, nevertheless, to embrace Ewan despite his unfortunate views.

Once he had closed the door behind him, Lady Catriona placed her cup upon the table and took a deep breath. "You recall that I told you, the day you arrived, that Bride told me of your birth on the night of the Wolf Moon."

"I do."

"She didn't share anything more with me, until the night Ewan was sent back to Fotla, after the attempted assassination of Lord Constantine. It was," she hesitated, as though unsure of how to explain. "Somewhat disconcerting."

Briana clasped her fingers together on her lap as a frisson of trepidation assailed her. "What did our goddess share, my lady?"

"A vision of a glade, with an ancient standing stone. A place I've never been. The full moon hung in the night sky, and the orange eyes of wolves watched me from the forest."

Eerie shivers scuttled along her arms at the familiarity of this vision. "What happened?" she whispered even though, in her heart, she knew.

"The forest vanished, and only a single wolf remained, silhouetted against the moon. And then an arrow was let loose and embedded into the stone and split it asunder."

Mouth dry, Briana nodded. "I too have had this vision."

"It assailed me every night, until the day you arrived in Duntorr." Lady Catriona leaned forward and placed her hand on Briana's. "The wolf is you, Lady Briana."

Shocked, Briana snatched her hands free. "Indeed, that is not so. The wolf is Shadow."

"Shadow?"

She licked her lips, trying without success to calm her racing heart. "I rescued him as a pup. Afterwards, over the years, I would often see him. But that is the wolf in our vision, my lady."

Lady Catriona was silent for a moment, and Briana flexed her fingers. There was no need to be so distressed over a simple mistake. Because this was all it was. How could the other woman possibly imagine that the wolf represented *her*?

"Today you rescued another wolf pup."

The unease that churned her stomach magnified. "I couldn't let her drown."

"Perhaps not. But what compelled you, Lady Briana? Not everyone who possesses a kind heart would risk their life on the ice to save a wild creature."

She wanted to retort *they would*; but knew that wasn't true. If she said it was Bride herself who had compelled her, surely that would satisfy Lady Catriona. Except, deep inside, a kernel of doubt would not be still. Because she didn't believe Bride had been involved at all.

"I was not compelled," she said with as much dignity as she could, considering how apprehension swarmed in her chest like trapped wasps. "I have... an affinity with wolves."

Lady Catriona gave a small smile. "Indeed, it would seem so. And why would you not, as a chosen one of the great goddess, Cailleach?"

Briana sucked in a harsh breath as her heart hammered painfully against her ribs. How could Lady Catriona suggest such a scandalous thing? "You are wrong. The Goddess of Winter hasn't whispered in mortals' ears for countless generations. I'm a chosen one of Bride."

Her own grand-aunt Brilicie had told Briana she was so attuned to the winter elements because Cailleach had reigned supreme on the night of her birth, but had her grand-aunt meant more than that? Had she, also, seen what Briana refused to?

"Lady Briana, I didn't mean to upset you."

"I'm not upset." She brushed nonexistent fluff from the blanket across her lap, but her hands shook and so she gripped her fingers together, instead. "I am merely taken aback by such speculation."

Lies.

She wasn't taken aback. It was so much worse than that. All the deeply buried suspicions she'd had since she was a child burst from their constraints and flooded through her blood with malicious intent.

Stop. It wasn't true. Lady Catriona was wrong.

I am not a child of Cailleach.

"You were not aware of your true calling?" There was a note of awe in Lady Catriona's voice which didn't help settle her dismay in the slightest. "Did you not know it is the great Cailleach who sent this vision to us both?"

She pounced on the only thing she could. Even though she knew, in her heart, what the answer would be. "Are you a chosen one of the Goddess of Winter?"

"I am a child of Bride." Lady Catriona's voice was soft. "I had to hide my gift from the time I was a child, as my royal blood could not be spoken of. And as we know, the gods only choose those with a royal lineage."

It was true. But it was also true that, for the female line at least, it was Bride, the great goddess of spring and new life, who bestowed her gifts.

The mighty Cailleach, who needed to be worshipped and appeased so she would yield her snowy cape of winter to Bride in the spring, possessed powers that were only whispered of, and only then if one was reckless. It was said that once, long ago, she had taken mortals for her own, but not many believed the fantastical tales that had filtered through the ages.

Not many believed. But Briana always had. Was it because, even from her earliest years, she had somehow *known*?

No. It wasn't true. Fear churned her stomach, but she managed to push out the words. "When Cailleach took a mortal in the old days, she was born a witch."

Concern etched Lady Catriona's face. "Such tales cannot be taken seriously, Lady Briana. The great Cailleach has not embraced any in the royal lineages of Pictland for generations and nothing is certain. But of one thing, I am sure. The Goddess of Winter has marked you as her own and until you can accept that, your path will be forever clouded."

How could she accept it? For as long as she could remember, she had been comforted by the knowledge the goddess Bride had blessed her. The way Bride had blessed so many of her cousins. Their generation was truly a golden one, after so many years when the goddess had seemingly turned her back on her faithful believers.

None of her cousins had been touched by Cailleach. And when her grand-aunt Brilicie had spoken of her own great-grandmother's generation, and of all the many cousins who had been so blessed, not one had been called to the Goddess of Winter.

It was a terrifying, unknown legacy. But just because Lady Catriona said it was so, did not make it true. Except…

Unbidden, half-forgotten memories stirred. Of times when she had called upon Bride and felt a chill pass through her, even in the height of summer. Always, she had ignored it, for it meant nothing. Yet despite her denials, disquiet had lingered in the shadowed corners of her mind.

And from those corners, a recent memory flooded her. The night Ewan had returned to Fotla, and he had asked her if she worshipped the great Cailleach.

And her instant response.

"I am a chosen one of the blessed Bride."

A shiver crawled along her spine as a great boom echoed around her head, but it was another memory, when the doors to the palace had burst open, bringing a fierce gale and drifts of snow inside.

She'd told herself it was not a sign. But even then, she hadn't managed to convince herself.

Another recollection pushed to the surface, of when she had met Ewan in the sacred grove, and he had met Shadow. Heat seared her as her words burned her mind.

"I'm certain before Bride subdues the great Cailleach, I shall be wed to the Prince of Ce."

A freezing wind had bit through her, chilling the very marrow in her bones. Yet still she hadn't connected the sharp change in the weather to her arrogant dismissal of Cailleach.

But she could no longer hide from the truth. Cailleach had shown her displeasure at how Briana refused to acknowledge her rightful status. Because to accept she was a chosen one of Cailleach was to venture into the unknown where, whatever Lady Catriona might say, the wraiths of witches lingered.

"Lady Briana." Although Lady Catriona's voice was soft, it was enough to shock her back to the present. "There's a reason why we've shared this vision. Do you have any insights?"

"I thought it was a sign that the goddess approved my marriage to Ewan. For the safety of Pictland."

"Yes." Lady Catriona sounded troubled. "And I do not disagree. Yet I feel there is something more to it. Otherwise, this vision would be yours alone."

Briana knew there was something more to it. And had the dread certainty that it was somehow connected to Ewan.

CHAPTER 27

*B*riana woke with a start, heart thudding. Dawn had not yet broken, and the only light came from the faint embers from the dying fire. Next to her Ewan stirred, his movements fitful. His skin was damp, and she realized he was having a bad dream. Concerned, she cradled his jaw, and it seemed her touch soothed him. She settled once more in his arms, her head nestled against his shoulder. But his body was still tense, and he twisted, before letting out a low groan.

"No more, Moreen."

She drew in a deep breath. His words pierced her like shards of ice.

Perhaps her ladies had been right, when they'd speculated Ewan had, indeed, once loved the mysterious lady, Moreen. She could not blame him for that. After all, she had once loved Ecgfrith. Yet now, despite her best intentions, she cared for Ewan.

And he cared for her. She was sure of it.

But while she had told him of her former husband, he had told her nothing of Moreen.

All she wanted to know was if he had placed the lady firmly in his past. If he was committed to making their marriage the best it could be.

He had trusted her enough to share the horror of losing his mother. Tomorrow, she would ask him to trust her again in the matter of Moreen.

It was a daunting prospect, for if he told her the other woman had captured his heart, where did that leave her?

～

THE FOLLOWING morning Ewan left early to speak with his steward, and although her ladies were with her, the chamber felt empty without him. Distracted, she went to the narrow window and gazed onto the snowscape below. How magnificent would the view be, from the top of the tower Ewan had wanted to show her?

If only there was a safer way to reach it. She glanced at her ladies. They had all been most impressed by the vista. And if they could navigate a ladder, then surely she should put aside her terror and do so, too?

All it took was one foot in front of the other. She did not need to overthink it.

But that wasn't the reason why she wanted to go to the tower. It was because Ewan had taken her there as a special surprise, and she had ruined it. Did he believe she didn't trust him enough to look after her and ensure her safety at all costs? Was that why he hadn't confided in her about Moreen?

He had instinctively reacted when he'd seen her on the ice. He'd risked his own safety to pull her from the water. She had to show him that she did trust him.

She took a deep breath for courage. "Ladies, I need your assistance."

～

AFTER HIS DAILY discussion with the steward, Ewan strolled to the stables. He hadn't checked on the horses since bringing Briana back from the loch yesterday and although he knew they would be well looked after, it wasn't the same as making sure for himself.

Beli, the lad they had brought with them from Fotla, was grooming Briana's mare and by the look of it, had just finished tending to Ewan's own horse. He should have known there was nothing to worry about. The boy was dedicated to his tasks.

He scratched his horse behind his ear and tossed Beli a grin. "Are they treating you well here?"

"Very well, milord." Beli returned his grin. It was hard to believe he was the same scrawny creature he and Briana had rescued back in Fotla. "Are you going riding?"

With a final scratch along his horse's neck, Ewan drew back. The day was fine, the air crisp, and for once the wind did not bite like ice. Much as he'd enjoy a ride, he'd rather go and find his bride and persuade her to join him. "Maybe later."

He caught sight of Drest, grooming his own horse, and for a heartbeat their gazes clashed. As always, there was nothing but suspicion in the warrior's glare, but he had taken Briana's accident hard and appeared to blame himself.

Ewan had no personal quarrel with the man, although it was blatantly obvious Drest resented the Scots. But they both had Briana's best interests at heart, and it would serve him well to reach out to the Pict and attempt to forge a bridge between them.

Tomorrow.

He left the stables and drew in a deep breath. Damn, but the cold winter air felt good. He filled his lungs, and there was no intangible band crushing his chest, slowly suffocating him from the inside out. For the first time in as long as he could recall, he felt free, and it was astounding.

Talking with Briana about that dark day had helped him see the truth. He hadn't been in the boat with his beloved mother. He hadn't inadvertently caused her to fall into the water. It wasn't his fault she had drowned.

Last night he had dreamed once more of his stepmother, the first time since his marriage. But it been different from the other times he recalled. He hadn't been a child and the dream had splintered before the fear had encompassed him.

Moreen was wrong. He wasn't cursed.

There was no reason to leave Briana.

He laughed out loud, and servants gave him wary glances as he entered Duntorr. Maybe he did grin like a drunken fool, but he couldn't help himself. For the first time in forever, a new future stretched ahead. A future he could share with his bride, his Briana, a future where he could stay and watch his own bairns grow.

The prospect was enthralling. As was the delightful notion of conceiving those bairns. His cock thickened and lust thundered through his veins. Despite the night of lovemaking that still lingered in his thoughts, he needed her again.

Now.

If only he could find her.

Not even the sullen glower of Rohan, as he strode across the great hall towards the stairs, could dull his mood. Although by God, he would soon need to speak to Briana about sending the man back to his own stronghold in Pictland.

He flung open the door to the antechamber, anticipation sizzling through his brain. Briana spun around, and the welcoming smile on her face caused a strange ache to grip his chest.

"I have a wonderful surprise," she said, before he could command her ladies leave the chamber so he might thoroughly ravish his wife. "You and I shall share a romantic repast at the top of your secret tower."

"The tower?" Had he heard right? He glanced at her ladies. He had no idea if they knew of her fear, and he didn't want to break her confidence if they did not. "Are you certain, Briana?"

"Quite certain." She smiled again, as though she guessed his thoughts, and took his hand. "I have decided it's quite unacceptable that my ladies have enjoyed the breathtaking views, and yet I have not. And since the day is so fair, we have put together some delicacies to take with us on this grand adventure."

It was only fair to warn her. "Alas, there are no stools or table up there."

"We have thick blankets to sit upon." She indicated a neat bundle by her feet. "I confess I'm quite excited by the prospect."

"In that case, we should make haste." He picked up the bundle, and a basket that was filled to the brim with wrapped goods. "You've picked a good day. The sky is clear of clouds and the view will be outstanding."

"A good omen," she said, as they made their way along the corridor to the bedchamber that was, ostensibly, his, but which he had scarcely used. "I do not want clouds in my eyes."

He gave her a curious glance, but she appeared oblivious to his silent question. It likely meant nothing, anyway. Despite his ungodly obsession with her pagan faith, not every strange utterance had to be linked to her goddess.

When they entered the secret chamber, he lit the lamps with the torch he'd brought with them, before placing it in a wall sconce and turning to face her. "I'll go up first with these," he indicated the blankets and basket, "then come back for you, so I have my hands free should you need assistance."

"That's very thoughtful of you, but there is no need. I've thought about this, Ewan, and it's time to face my fear. The way you faced yours, yesterday."

He frowned. "I fail to see the connection."

"Please don't think I'm trying to diminish what you've been through." There was a note of anxiety in her voice now, and she pressed her hand against his heart. "But you were so brave, facing what had happened to your lady mother. Facing that fear, you see? That I thought it only right I face mine, especially when it pales by comparison to yours."

She thought he was brave, because he had told her what had happened when he was five years old? He, a warrior, who had faced down both the Norse and Northumbrians in battle?

He sucked in a great breath and then slowly exhaled as a strange sense of recognition flickered through him. In a way, she was right. It had taken a lot for him to confess to her. More than he'd ever admit. But Christ, the relief it had given him could never be measured.

He covered her hand with his own, pressing her close. "Don't belittle what happened to you either, Briana. It's a valid fear and," he gave a rueful grin. "I think you're brave to face this, too."

"Well." She patted her fingers against his chest and with reluctance he released her. "I confess, it pleases me to hear that. For if I'm truthful, I'm still quaking inside at the thought of it."

"I'll be right behind you," he promised. And if she so much as stumbled, to hell with their romantic repast. He'd drop the lot and catch her in his arms.

She pushed back her cloak, gripped the rungs, and began to climb. He followed; the blankets tucked under his arm, so he had one hand free to steady his ascent. Darkness wrapped around them as the light faded beneath them, and he cursed his lack of foresight. He should have come up here first, to light a torch at the top, so Briana could see her way. When he'd shown her ladies the view the other week, he'd held a torch aloft to light their path, but hadn't today, as he needed a hand to grip the ladder.

He hadn't noticed, the few times he'd made this trek before, just how high the tower was. Briana hadn't said a word, but he could hear her jagged breath and although he wanted to ask her if she was all right, he didn't want to distract her.

"Goddess," she gasped, and not for the first time he had the uneasy sense that she could somehow read his thoughts. "It's very dark up here."

"Aye, I apologize. But it's not much further. At the top of the ladder, you'll feel a wide stone ledge. Wait there, and I'll open the covering."

In the gloom, he could see the dark shadow of the ledge. Just a few more steps.

It happened so fast he didn't even have time to think. One moment, Briana was six rungs above him. And then an ominous crack filled the air and she swung off to one side, before losing her footing and falling.

He dropped the basket and blankets and caught her, inelegantly, roughly, but before he could set her to rights, the whole damn ladder shuddered, and he had the surreal sensation of swaying in midair.

With one arm clamped around her, he descended the ladder, heart hammering in his ears. Before he reached the ground, the ladder unhinged from its moorings and with a curse, he leaped to the floor, skidding across the stone on his arse, clasping Briana in a death grip.

Silence thudded all around. Beneath his arm, Briana's heart thundered and as the roar in his ears faded, he heard her staggered breath.

She could have died.

He screwed his eyes shut, but it didn't stop the graphic images of what might have been from lighting up his mind. Her broken body, lying on the stones.

My fault.

"Ewan?" Her hushed voice tore him back to the present, but did nothing to banish the bloodied visions from his eyes. "Are you hurt?"

Was *he* hurt? He deserved to be hurt, hell, he deserved far worse, and that was God's own truth. But for her to ask him when she was the one... when she had almost...

"No." The word was harsh, torn from his throat, as burning acid ate through his chest. Fear crawled through his gut, melding with the acid, magnifying it, twisting it, consuming his very soul, but he had to ask. "Are you?"

"Only a little winded. Thanks to you breaking my fall."

It was due to him she had fallen in the first place. If only he had never found this cursed tower. If only he had never thought it a good idea to share its existence with her.

If only.

It hurt to drag air into his lungs, but not because he was injured. The guilt that had bound him since he was a child reared up once again, reclaiming what had so recently tasted freedom, and the shackles bit deeper than they ever had before.

He was not free of the curse. Its shadow held him in its grip, and it always would.

"Ewan?" There was a note of anxiety in her voice now, and she shifted in his arms, turning to face him. Christ, how could he ever face her again? But there was nowhere to hide and grimly he met her gaze. "Are you certain you're not hurt?"

His backside burned with the impact and his back would likely ache for days but that was a small inconvenience for his arrogance. For his willful determination to ignore the price those close to him paid.

That Briana would pay, if he remained by her side.

"I must return you to your ladies." He pushed free from her and stood, before helping her to her feet, and she dropped the broken rung she'd been clutching when she fell. In the dull illumination from the lamps, he saw a graze mar her temple, and his gut clenched in self-disgust. "You're injured."

"What?" Her hand shook as she touched her face and she winced. She might as well have plunged a sword through his heart. "Oh, goddess. So I am. It is but a scratch, I think. Are you certain you're not harmed?"

Why did she keep asking him that? Of course he wasn't

injured. That wasn't the nature of the curse that blighted his existence.

"We must leave." His voice was hoarse as he took the torch from its sconce and without pressing the matter again, Briana left the tower. He followed her along the secret passageway, but it was not the echo of their footsteps that reverberated around his brain.

It was his stepmother's anguished cry as she clutched Gareth's lifeless body in her arms.

"I pray God will serve the justice upon you that you deserve."

A shudder inched along his spine, and he hunched his shoulders, but the spectral imprecation would not die.

He had wed Briana and sworn to himself he would never put her in danger. That he'd protect her from his curse, but instead he'd put his own selfish desire to remain by her side first.

After she had nearly drowned in the loch, he'd allowed her to coax him from what he knew was the right course of action. And the very next day she had narrowly avoided breaking her neck.

Because he had chosen to ignore the first warning. He couldn't afford to ignore this one. The final one.

There would be no lucky third escape.

If he didn't leave her, she would pay the price, and he could not—*would not*—stand by and let that happen.

Far better she thought him a cold-hearted bastard than the inevitable alternative should he stay at Duntorr.

They reached the bedchamber, and he took his time bolting and locking the door, for once he turned around and faced her, it was the beginning of the end.

"That adventure did not quite go as I planned."

With reluctance, he slowly turned, to find Briana sitting on the edge of the bed. The graze showed livid on her ashen face and guilt seared his heart. "Your ladies must see to your wound."

"Indeed. But first let me sit for a while. I fear my legs are quite shaky after our tumble."

She was trying to make light of the situation and that made him feel worse than if she had flung accusations of negligence at his head. "I shall find your ladies and bring them to you."

"You could simply carry me back to our chamber." A faint smile lit her face.

He released a pained breath and flexed his fingers. If he took her into his arms, he doubted he could ever let her go. And he wouldn't do that to her.

There was a knock on the door and Nairne and Gavina entered.

"Forgive the intrusion, my lady, my lord," Nairne said. "But—" She gave a gasp as she caught sight of Briana's face. "My lady, what has happened?"

Briana shook her head. "A small accident with the ladder. Nothing to trouble yourselves with. Is there a problem?"

"Lord Rohan is most agitated, my lady," Gavina said. "He came to speak with you a short while ago and was insistent that we find you. He—"

Rohan marched into the chamber and appeared momentarily lost for words as he stared at Briana. Then he shot Ewan a poisonous glare, but Ewan could not fault him for that. He deserved it, after all.

"Apologies." Rohan gave a stiff bow. "I have received urgent word from my steward and must return to my stronghold in Fib without delay."

"I hope all is well." Concern laced Briana's voice, but he couldn't find it within himself to echo her good wishes. How many times had he wanted Rohan gone from Duntorr? And now the Pict was leaving.

But so was he.

CHAPTER 28

*B*riana went back to her bedchamber, Nairne and Gavina flanking her, supporting her arms as though they feared she might collapse. To be sure, her head ached from where the rough wood from the ladder had knocked her, and she felt somewhat nauseous from the terrifying fall, but the panic had ebbed when Ewan had clasped her in his arms.

But when they emerged from the secret passageway, a different kind of panic had swirled in her stomach. Ewan scarcely glanced at her when she'd tried to reassure him she was unhurt, and she supposed she couldn't blame him for not believing her, when blood trickled from her temple.

Yet it was more than that. She could feel it, even though she couldn't understand it. She had the uncanny certainty he was distancing himself from her. But why would he do that?

Surely it wasn't because he blamed himself for this accident?

They entered her antechamber, and she sat on a chair by the fire. She clasped her fingers together and clung grimly to her patience while her ladies fussed around her, cleaning the graze, and applying astringents to ensure no poisons manifested.

Ewan and Rohan had followed them and stood either side of

the chamber with identical glares on their faces. A flicker of irritation stirred. Why had Rohan followed them in here, anyway? It was not his place. Truly, she needed to overcome her reluctance and speak with him.

Except he was leaving on an urgent matter. She didn't even try and quell the relief that flowed through her at that knowledge, which was strange, since he had been such a comfort to her when she had been married to Ecgfrith.

Finally, her ladies finished. Before she could request privacy so she might have Ewan to herself, he stepped forward. His face was grim, and the intangible sense of lightness that had emanated from him since he'd confided about his lady mother had vanished.

Instead, a dark cloud surrounded him, and she shivered in the sudden chill that assailed her.

"Lady Briana, a word if I may?"

"Certainly." She'd already raised her hand when she realized Ewan had not offered his and she hastily pretended to smooth her hair, instead. He opened the door to the bedchamber and waited for her to enter, before shutting it behind them. Trepidation slithered through her. Was he not touching her deliberately, or was she imagining things?

He brought a chair and set it beside the hearth, and she had the irrational urge to ignore it. Somehow, it boded ill, to sit while he towered over her.

Goddess, what was she thinking? Ewan was her husband. He was more than entitled to sit in her presence and what was more, she would insist upon it.

"What of the other chair, my lord?" It was irrationally difficult, but she managed to smile at him as she sat down.

"I prefer to stand, my lady." His tone was formal and even though she had used his title to address him, she certainly hadn't sounded so... remote. Had she?

She attempted to quash her unease and injected a coaxing

note in her voice. "Come, Ewan. Tell me what is wrong. Are you injured and your manly pride forbids you to acknowledge it?"

Not even a ghost of a smile touched his face, and her unease deepened.

"There's no easy way to say this." His gaze shifted to somewhere over her shoulder and apprehension constricted her chest. Nothing good could follow that ominous assertion. She had the debasing urge to leap to her feet and press her hand against his mouth, as though stifling his words might somehow prevent him from continuing.

But she remained mute, frozen on her chair, as he dragged in a deep breath, as though this confrontation was the last thing he wanted.

Why was he confronting her, then? What had changed?

Great Goddess, please let me be wrong.

"I told you, before we wed, you deserved a man who could love you unreservedly and I wasn't that man. Nothing's changed. I can never love you as you deserve."

Mouth dry, she fixed her gaze on his shoulder as her heart pummeled in her chest, so fiercely, she feared it might crack her ribs.

Yet surely, even a cracked rib couldn't hurt as savagely as her foolish heart. He told her nothing new. Why did his words rip her to shreds?

Because I thought something precious had grown between us.

"It doesn't matter how hard I try to put the past behind me, it's with me still. It always will be." He rolled his shoulders, as though a great weight bore down upon him, but he still didn't deign to look at her. "I won't pretend any longer. I'm leaving Duntorr in the morning."

He wouldn't *pretend* any longer? Mortification burned through her, and her pride demanded she regally dismiss him, without so much as a disdainful glance, but it was so much worse than merely her pride he had trampled upon.

And she could not remain silent.

She stood, so she didn't have the disadvantage of him looming over her like a barbarous warlord. The enemy of her people.

A Scot.

"And why, pray, should you pretend anything?" Thank the goddess, her voice was as icy as the loch she'd so recently fallen into. Had it truly only been yesterday? It felt like another life. "Have I ever given any indication in wanting more from you than we mutually agreed upon before we were formally betrothed?"

She was certain she hadn't. But how could she be completely sure, when in her heart she desperately wanted so much more from this marriage?

From him?

Did I give myself away?

Yet what did it matter, either way, if Ewan felt nothing more for her now than he had that day in her father's inner sanctum?

He spared her a fleeting glance and she fancied she saw desolation glowing in his incomparable blue eyes. But it was nothing more than her imagination. How could she continue to delude herself, even now, that there was something deeper lurking beneath his callous words?

"No." His voice was expressionless. Did he not care at *all*? How had she been so careless, so witless, as to allow the painstakingly constructed walls around her heart to crumble?

Yet when had they fallen? She couldn't even recall. It seemed from the first moment she had met Ewan MacKinnon her fate was sealed.

If she retained any fragment of pride, she should dismiss him and let him go on his way. But it was pride that kept her upright. Pride that forbade her to clasp his hands and beg him to stay. Her pride was all she had left, and it was ripping her apart.

It would be so much easier to turn her back on him. Did she really want to give him the chance to slay whatever remained of her battered heart?

Yet she could not let him go so easily. She deserved the truth, even if he didn't wish to share it.

Even if that truth proved that Ewan, as his reputation had attested, was nothing more than a faithless charmer?

Just like her first husband had been.

"Then what has changed?"

"There's nothing to discuss."

Did he think he could dismiss her so lightly? Anger flared, and she thanked the goddess, for anger gave her a shred of power to fight against the suffocating mantle of despair that threatened to crush her.

"You're wrong. We made a pledge, and it's not a thing that can be discarded so lightly, whatever your personal reservations."

"I do not make this decision lightly." He ground the words between his teeth, as though she was in the wrong for pressing him on this matter. Perhaps a Scotswoman would never speak to her husband in such a manner, but she was a Pict and Ewan had always known that. "You haven't the first idea—"

He snapped his jaw shut and swung away from her, and something tiny and precious broke deep inside her breast.

"Do not turn your back on me, Ewan." She sounded so calm. Regal, even. He would never guess how much it cost her.

With clear reluctance, he turned to face her, but she scarcely recognized him as the man she had wed. It seemed in the blink of an eye he had aged ten years and an aura of wretched inevitability tainted the air around him; an intangible, noxious cloud that caused dark dread to unfurl in her soul.

"It was wrong of me to marry you. I should have insisted you wed Lord Talargan."

Each word thrust directly into her heart, with the deadly force of poisoned daggers. Her chest tightened, crushing her lungs, yet somehow she managed a scornful laugh. "Yes, for my honor is meaningless to you, is it not? But perhaps you are right. At least Talargan possesses the integrity of a prince."

Her barb hit home, and Ewan flinched, as if she had struck him. But it was only a fleeting scratch, nothing more, for she meant nothing to him, and her words were mere irritants, if that.

If only she could so easily brush aside Ewan's cruel words.

"Don't make this any harder than it has to be."

How dare he stand there and say that to her? As though her feelings were of no account. Yet he had never asked her to care for him. Had she not told him she didn't need love in this marriage? It wasn't his fault she cared more than she should. She knew that, even if it didn't help ease the raw pain in her heart.

But that did not mean he shouldn't be held accountable, now he wished to break the bonds of their arrangement. Surely, there were only two reasons why he would leave like this. Either the shackles of matrimony had proved too great, and he wished to return to bedding every woman who caught his eye, as he had in the Kingdom of Ce, or there was a specific lady, one he had loved before MacAlpin had forced him into a political marriage.

Infidelity was bad enough. She had lived through that once. And a man didn't need to leave his wife to follow such pursuits.

Distress squeezed her heart. Was this, then, the answer? Did Ewan truly love another? No wonder he had been so willing to risk the wrath of his king, by encouraging her to admit to a betrothment with Talargan.

And yet, even though the specter of Moreen haunted the shadowed corners of her mind, she couldn't bear to face that possibility. After all, there was another reason why he would leave. A reason that would negate any promise he had made to her.

If his king commanded him to.

She clung onto that possibility, even though she despised his king, for it was far more palatable than the alternatives. Yet if that was the reason, why would Ewan not simply tell her?

Was it because MacAlpin had another brutal betrayal of the alliance between Pict and Scot in mind? Were his warriors under oath not to speak of it, the way none of them would speak of the bloodied massacre that had occurred in Dunadd last spring?

Surely, that was worse than anything. But in her heart, where she dared not probe too deeply, she still hoped it was his king who had summoned him, and he wasn't leaving because he loved another.

"So, you leave because your king commands it." She didn't frame it as a question, and ignored the swift frown that marred his brow, as though he wondered at her sudden shift in focus. "You are the king's man, as your father was before you."

This time there was no ignoring the spasm of pain that flashed over his face, and she almost—but not quite—regretted her sharp accusation. He *was* the king's man. It was only her own foolish hopes she had harbored for this marriage that had prevented her from seeing it before.

"I'll not deny my father held that title, and proudly so. But it was a different time, and now only MacAllister remains of the men who once had the king's ear. But I have never held that privileged position." He paused, and for a wretched heartbeat, their gazes meshed. And then he spoke. "Nor should I wish to."

"Nevertheless, he is still your king, and you answer to him in all things."

His jaw tensed. "Aye."

Her throat ached with tears she could never shed before him. Why was she torturing herself so? But she knew why. No matter how much it hurt to hear him confirm he would always put his loyalty to his king before her —which had never been in doubt, anyway—at least this way she could comfort herself he was abandoning her because MacAlpin commanded it.

Not because Ewan wanted to.

She had the proof she needed, to console herself on why Ewan was doing this, and yet she couldn't help goading him further. "What a strange strategy MacAlpin employs. To ensnare the princesses of Pictland in political marriages, and then command their husbands to abandon them."

"This has nothing to do with—" he cut himself off and expelled a harsh breath. "You are not abandoned." He ground out each word as though they personally offended him.

"So, you will return to Duntorr when your mission is completed?" But what mission was it? And if it was as terrible as the massacre last spring, how could she even contemplate welcoming him back?

"Enough." His tone was savage, and instinctively she recoiled. He took a step towards her and for a moment she imagined he was about to grasp her arms, but he appeared to think better of it and flexed his fingers into fists, instead. "I will not be returning. But you shall want for nothing, I give you my word."

She would want for nothing but her husband.

And the unborn children she had so craved yet were now forever out of her reach.

Mortification burned through her, and she straightened her already rigid spine and flung him the most derisive glance she could muster. "Then go. I surely do not want you here. Our marriage was to protect the alliance between Pictland and Dal Riada, and I only hope the sacrifice was not in vain. Or does your king plan another betrayal of my beloved land under the guise of a treaty?"

Tension crackled in the air, and she braced herself for his response. Would he deny all knowledge of the treachery?

"Briana, I—" He sucked in a harsh breath, and she waited for him to confirm, or deny. Please, great goddess, let him deny. As much as she hoped he left to do the bidding of his king, she couldn't face the ugly possibility that Ewan was involved in another treacherous betrayal of her countrymen.

Had he been involved in the one last spring, when her father had been captured and held hostage? She couldn't bear to think he had, but perhaps she should.

"Yes?" Her voice was cold. He would never guess her true thoughts. She'd had much practice in hiding them, during her marriage to Ecgfrith.

He shook his head, but it seemed in response to an internal battle, rather than her question. "I never wanted to hurt you. I have no choice." Despair threaded through his words, and then he swung about and marched to the door. She just caught his tortured whisper as he gripped the door ring. "I shouldn't have ignored her warning."

He pulled open the door and closed it behind him and she remained frozen by the hearth, as his parting shot thundered around her head.

Her.

His last words to her were of another woman. A woman whose warning he should have heeded. What was the warning? That he should have stood firm against his king and married the woman he loved?

Briana's stomach churned and she pressed her fingers against her lips.

I can never love you as you deserve.

Because he had already given his heart to Moreen.

CHAPTER 29

*E*wan marched through the antechamber, ignoring the curious glances from Briana's ladies and the glare from Rohan. All he could see was the shock on Briana's face when he'd told her he was leaving.

He escaped the antechamber, and the chilled air of the passageway wrapped around him as he leaned against the cold stone wall and squeezed his eyes shut. It didn't help. He still saw her eyes, gazing at him, as her shock gave way to barely concealed contempt.

Her accusation flayed his mind.

Does your king plan another betrayal of my beloved land under the guise of a treaty?

She believed her countrymen had been betrayed at Dunadd in the spring. Of course she did. Did anyone still believe the official word, that it was the Picts who had turned on their hosts, the Scots, and had been slain in self-defense?

The truth of that night had haunted him for months, but it wasn't spoken of. Yet to think Briana believed he had been a part of that treachery, curdled his guts.

And MacAlpin had all but confirmed it last week when he'd

spoken to Lady Catriona. The king had thirsted for vengeance against the Picts for years, because of the way his father had died at their hands.

Yet even suspecting Ewan had been a part of it, Briana had wed him—for the sake of her beloved Pictland.

His curse clawed deeper than even Moreen could have imagined. It was bad enough Briana deplored his actions by forsaking her. He'd braced himself for that. But to know how deeply she despised him—how she must always have despised him—because she believed he stood with his king in all matters, constricted his chest as though a great rock was lodged between his ribs.

He battled the treasonous urge to storm back into her bedchamber and tell her he wasn't guilty of that crime, at least. And God help him, if the only deadly thing between Briana and him were the actions of his king, he'd risk his damn head and tell her, regardless. Just to see her scorn for him die.

But there was so much more at stake than merely his own wretched life. It didn't matter that she filled a dark void within him. A void he hadn't even been aware of until he had met her. Even as he slumped against the wall he could feel the darkness snaking through him, sucking all the light that Briana had infused by the simple fact of her existence.

He'd learn to live with the emptiness inside. There wasn't any other option. He had to leave Duntorr, before he dragged her into the infernal abyss where his mother and half-brother lay broken.

Because of him.

AFTER EWAN LEFT, her ladies brought refreshments and she didn't have the energy to protest when Nairne insisted on examining the scratch on her temple.

"Is anything amiss, my lady?" Nairne whispered, as she bent close so no one else could hear.

How she longed to confide in someone. But her pride was a tenacious thing, and she couldn't forget Nairne had warned her of Ewan's nature, but she had chosen to ignore it. And even though this marriage had been a political alliance, and not one made through the transient follies of love, she had, nevertheless, been dazzled by her Scot's silken charm.

Yet there was no point in hiding the truth. Soon, the whole of Duntorr would know Ewan had abandoned his bride. But she still couldn't bring herself to tell Nairne the real, sordid reason why he had left. It was too raw, too humiliating, and she feared the tears that clogged her throat might find a way to spill from her eyes if she confided that her husband could no longer bear to live with her.

"Lord Ewan must obey the command of his king." It wasn't a lie. It was simply not the whole truth.

But Nairne was a noblewoman; and had served in royal courts since she was a young girl. She knew the subtleties of nuances, of how a simple phrase might mean something else entirely. She inclined her head, hiding her expression, although Briana could well guess her dear friend's dismay.

"Perhaps we should send word to Lady Catriona that you need uninterrupted rest after the alarming event in the tower?"

A dull sense of relief at such a respite crawled through her at Nairne's suggestion and she gave a nod of agreement, but disquiet stirred and would not be stilled.

It was the coward's way out, and she had always prided herself on facing her difficulties and not hiding away. But the thought of spending time with Lady Catriona, who was sure to see far more than Briana was willing to share, was too much.

Tonight, she would allow herself to mourn for something she had never had, and tomorrow...

Tomorrow she would start her new life.

TONIGHT, she wanted to be alone, but it had taken her an age to fall asleep. She wasn't used to sleeping without one of her ladies in her chamber. Such a thing was unthinkable for a princess unless her husband stayed the night. And although Ewan had shared her bed for such a short time, she had become used to him lying beside her. Holding her in his arms, caressing her. The feel of his heart beneath her fingers, and the sound of his breathing a comforting buffer against reality.

She tossed and turned, unable to get comfortable, and her head ached miserably. Ewan's face tormented her, and his uncaring words before he had left haunted her mind in an incessant refrain.

But in the end, exhaustion overtook her.

Once again, she was in the sacred glade, gazing into the dark forest, where a pair of unblinking orange eyes observed her. It was her vision, she knew that in the core of her being, but trepidation echoed through every beat of her heart because something was different this time. Something she couldn't place, only feel.

Transfixed, she watched the huge wolf prowl from the shadows, and flecks of red in its jet fur glinted in the moonlight.

He wasn't Shadow.

Goddess help her. Shivers skittered over her arms. The great predator was a she-wolf.

Terror coiled through her as the Goddess of Winter—for surely the she-wolf could be none other than the manifestation of Cailleach herself—tipped back her mighty head and howled to the starlit sky. The grasses rustled and the trees swayed, before the landscape faded, and only the luminous full moon filled the horizon.

This time, she saw the arrow as it streaked from an unknown source towards her. As if time had slowed, she reached out her hand to clasp the arrow, and the shaft burned her palm as it continued upon its trajectory. Her fingers clenched around the fletchings, and the shaft vibrated in midair for a heartbeat before stilling.

Slowly, she brought the arrow closer and ran her gaze over the fletchings. The feathers were long, elegant, and white. Swan feathers. The same feathers that had been in her last vision.

From a great distance, MacAllister's voice swirled in the shadows, from when he had confronted her father in Fotla.

Northumbrian made.

She swung about, and the massive standing stone loomed in the darkness, but unlike in her previous visions it remained unbroken. Because she had stopped the arrow before it had struck its target.

What does it mean?

There was no reply. She had, instinctively, beseeched Bride, and there was no point trying to delude herself any further. This vision was not sent by Bride. It never had been. All the times she'd heard whispers in the howl of wolves, it had been Cailleach.

And the Goddess of Winter confronted her now, in her own domain of snow and ice, the incorporeal plane where no mortal could enter unless the gods allowed it.

But her mind froze. She wasn't used to communing with Cailleach and her courage failed. Except hadn't she been communing with Cailleach all along, even though she believed she had been praying to Bride?

The knowledge made no difference. For the terror was real. And the great she-wolf bared her teeth in a savage snarl at the insult.

"Briana."

The feminine voice pierced her paralysis and she spun about. Incomprehension tangled her senses. "Lady Catriona?"

"How can I be here?" The older lady raised her hands, and blood dripped, thick and damning, to the icy ground. "This is your vision to unravel."

How could she unravel it, when she was too afraid to even ask her goddess for guidance? Reluctance crawled through her, but she forced herself to look back at the majestic manifestation of Cailleach.

The breath caught in her throat at the visage that dominated the far horizon. Cailleach, in perfect silhouette against the moon. An image she had seen before but hadn't connected to the rest of her vision, the warning that Pictland was in danger. A danger she had once thought she had averted by wedding Ewan.

But the goddess, in her wisdom, had not merely warned her Pictland was in danger. She had shown her, over and over, when this great catastrophe would occur. Yet she had been blind to it.

Awe prickled along her nape as she finally understood.

The Wolf Moon.

That was the night when Pictland would be at her most vulnerable.

Gasping, she awoke, clutching the furs as her heart hammered against her breast. How had she not realized that before?

And the Wolf Moon was due to fall the following night.

NERVES ASSAILED her stomach as she and her ladies made their way to Lady Catriona's private chamber. Earlier, she had sent Gavina to ask for an audience, only for her friend to return within moments with one of Lady Catriona's ladies, with the same request.

It was proof enough for her that Lady Catriona had, indeed, shared her vision last night.

As she descended the stairs, trailing her hand along the stone wall, her defenses crumbled, and Ewan's face intruded. How she had tried to keep him from her thoughts this morning. But why was she trying to fool herself? He never left her mind, and even when she focused on trying to decipher Cailleach's message, his presence lingered. She feared he always would.

She only hoped Lady Catriona would not remark upon his absence. Was he still in Duntorr? Or had he departed as soon as he had left her bedchamber, and spent last night with the woman he loved—Moreen?

Her heart twisted with distress at the prospect. Should she have begged him to stay? Reminded him of his promise to get her with child? But how could she live with herself—never mind with Ewan—if the only reason he didn't leave was because he pitied her?

Stop thinking about it. There was nothing she could do to change what had happened. She had been so sure her vision told her to wed Ewan, to save Pictland. But perhaps, instead, this marriage was her punishment from Cailleach for failing to acknowledge the truth of her calling for so long.

She lifted her head and straightened her shoulders as they entered Lady Catriona's chamber, but her smile felt brittle, and she was sure the other lady would see straight through her charade.

Lady Catriona came over to her and took her hands in greeting. It was unexpected and for a terrible moment she thought Lady Catriona was going to say she was sorry Ewan had left, that he had broken her heart, that he had always loved another. She wasn't sure she could bear it.

"I have never shared another chosen one's vision before." Lady Catriona's voice was hushed, and relief flooded Briana that she wouldn't need to pretend Ewan meant nothing more than a political alliance to her. "Lady Briana, I'm greatly troubled."

Her relief spiked into fear. She hadn't expected this confession and didn't know what to do with it. Truly, she had hoped the older lady held answers, not more uncertainty. They stood before the hearth, and their ladies retreated to the other side of the chamber to give them privacy, and Briana drew a steadying breath.

"Was it the great goddess Bride who invited you into my vision?"

The flames leaped high, as though a sudden gust of wind had escaped into the hearth and Briana shot the fire a startled glance. No, it was not an unexpected breeze that disturbed the flames. It was Cailleach, showing her displeasure.

A shiver rippled over her arms and gripped her heart. She had meant no disrespect to the Goddess of Winter, but it seemed Cailleach's patience had finally died when it came to Briana's unwillingness to acknowledge her.

Her disastrous marriage to Ewan was living proof of that. No, not simply the marriage. The way she had given him her heart, against all her better instincts. A divine retribution indeed, for refusing to see the truth for too long and she would endure Cailleach's vengeance for the rest of her life.

"It was not Bride who parted the veil between the worlds." Awe threaded through Lady Catriona's voice. "But I'm not privy to the Goddess of Winter's insights. She took me there for a reason. But a reason only you can unlock."

What wasn't she seeing? Only one thing was certain.

"Pictland will fall this night if I cannot untangle the warning."

"Does Ewan go to Duncreag because of this warning?"

Briana' heart squeezed with pain. Not only did Lady Catriona know Ewan had left Duntorr, but he must also have seen her before he left, to tell her where he was going.

"I do not think so," she whispered.

"I can't help thinking there is a connection. I know he must see to Duncreag, but so soon after your marriage... I fear something is amiss, Lady Briana."

A memory stirred of something Lady Catriona had said the first time they had met. She had been struck by it at the time but hadn't known the older lady well enough to question her on it.

She knew her well enough now.

"My lady, what did you mean when you said the shadows in Duncreag will fade in time? What shadows?" Yet even as she spoke, the answer came to her.

Ewan's beloved mother had died at Duncreag. Of course that was it. Why hadn't she realized that before?

Lady Catriona gave a shuddering sigh. "Perhaps it's not my place to tell you, but I feel I must. My son, Kinnon, dearly loved his first wife, Ewan's mother. He never truly recovered from her death. But within two years, he wed another." Lady Catriona bit her lip and appeared reluctant to continue, but then she drew in a deep breath as though she had already committed herself. "She was from a minor noble family and set her sights on Kinnon, determined to have him at any cost. Three months after the marriage, she gave birth to Gareth."

"Ewan told me his half-brother died when he was but a child of seven."

Lady Catriona's bottom lip trembled. "He was such a sweet boy." Her voice was husky. "He and Ewan were devoted to each other. Ewan never said anything, and I saw no proof that anything was amiss, but from the moment Moreen entered Duncreag, shadows fell around the stronghold and, to my grief, around Ewan."

Shock spiraled through her and before she could think better of it, she clasped Lady Catriona's hand. "Moreen is Ewan's stepmother?"

"Yes. After my son died in the battle of '39, I ensured Moreen remarried as swiftly as possible. She needed to leave Duncreag. I knew this in my soul, even though I could not explain it. I know in time, whatever darkness she brought with her to the stronghold will fade when you and Ewan make your own memories there."

"I shouldn't have ignored her warning."

He hadn't been speaking about the woman he loved. He had been talking about his stepmother.

But why had Moreen been on his mind in that moment? It made no sense. Ewan had walked out on her, on their marriage, and the last thing he'd spoken of was his stepmother's warning. What nature was the warning, for it to have such importance to him?

A thread of possibility glowed in the darkness. If he hadn't abandoned her because of another woman, there was hope for them yet.

Stop.

The cold voice of reason froze her fragile dreams. Regardless of whether Ewan loved another or not, the truth was, he had still walked out on her. And she didn't know why. Even if he'd obeyed the command to leave her from his king, there had been no need for him to say the things to her that he had.

She simply had to face the truth. He had never wanted to wed her, and at the first opportunity he had left her.

"Lady Briana." Lady Catriona's voice was gentle, and Briana wrenched her scattered thoughts back into line, but she feared her face gave away too much to fool the other woman that all was well. "I don't presume to think you will ever look upon me as your kin, but I want you to know I'm here for you, should you ever need me. Not because my grandson is your husband, or even that we are blessed with the gifts from our goddesses, but because, in the end, we are women."

She swallowed, and the knot that had filled her chest since Ewan had flung his uncaring words at her yesterday, expanded, unbearably, the ache filling every particle of her being. How strange that this touch of kindness could so undo her.

"I thank you." Her voice was husky. How easy it would be to embrace Lady Catriona as her kin but how could she, if Ewan no longer wanted anything to do with this marriage?

She couldn't—*wouldn't*—remain in this foreign land if he considered her nothing more than a burden.

Once again, he flooded her mind, pushing out all other thoughts. She didn't want to admit that her own husband had told her nothing, but the need to know something—anything—was too great. "Ewan was not forthcoming on his reasons for going to Duncreag. I wondered if, perhaps, his king sent him away?"

"Not to my knowledge. Indeed, when the king was here the other week, he was most insistent that Ewan's priority was now you, and tending to his estates. I confess I was startled when he informed me he was traveling to Duncreag without you."

Her last tiny hope that there was, after all, an outside reason as to why Ewan had deserted her, died a pitiable death. There were no other reasons save the one he had given her.

"I won't pretend any longer."

Then neither would she. If Ewan expected her to be a dutiful wife and remain hidden in Duntorr, while he did goddess only knew what, he could think again. She would forge her own future, beyond the shadow of his indifference.

Drest was loyal and would make the necessary arrangements with her men. Although now she thought of it, where was he? She hadn't seen him since her tumble into the loch.

But as she left Lady Catriona's chamber, Ewan once again flooded her mind, banishing all other concerns, and apprehension crawled along her spine. Was that truly what he expected of her? Doubt gnawed at the corners of her mind, but was it of any significance or merely her inability to accept the inevitable?

CHAPTER 30

*R*ohan was pacing her antechamber when Briana returned, and it was an effort to conceal her irritation at his presumption. After he had spoken to her yesterday, she'd expected him to leave to deal with his urgent matter, yet here he still was.

This time, she didn't even try to temper her thoughts. She was too weary, and her marriage to Ecgfrith was in the past and not something she wanted reminding of every time Rohan gave her a knowing, sideways glance.

In the past...

Foreboding rasped along her senses, just out of reach. What was she trying to recall?

"My lady, I could not leave Duntorr without bidding you farewell." Rohan took her hand, even though she hadn't offered it, and kissed her fingers. It was an effort not to snatch her hand back, but she owed him this courtesy, at least.

"I trust all will be well, my lord. You have been a good friend to me, but I understand it's time for you to return to your own stronghold."

Something dark flashed across his face, as though her good

wishes affronted him. "I shall return once my business is completed."

How much plainer could she be? "It's not fair of me to expect you to remain by my side forever. I know you have your own life to live."

His smile did not reach his eyes, and disquiet shivered through her.

"Your health and happiness are my life's duty, my lady. I leave only because this matter cannot be entrusted to anyone else."

With that, he gave a smart bow and marched from the chamber but as the door shut behind him, the fog concealing her memory lifted and Ewan's voice echoed in her mind.

"It doesn't matter how hard I try to put the past behind me, it's with me still. It always will be."

She spun about, wrapping her shawl tightly across her breasts but it didn't help check the chill that assailed her. What had Ewan been trying to tell her?

It was a strange thing to say, when he was deserting her and their marriage.

Just as mentioning his stepmother was.

The past. His stepmother. The darkness that Lady Catriona confided had descended upon Duncreag when Moreen had become its mistress. It was all connected, and yet it was the guilt over his lady mother's death that had haunted him all these years.

The guilt she foolishly believed he had overcome, when they'd spoken after her own tumble into the loch.

Frowning, she gazed into the fire that blazed in the hearth, but it was Ewan's face she saw, and his tortured words that filled her head.

"I never wanted to hurt you. I have no choice."

What had made him change his mind? Yesterday morning, he had been lighthearted and carefree.

And then, without warning, everything changed.

After I fell in the tower.

She exhaled a long breath. The tower. That was when his mood had darkened. When he saw she was injured.

Surely, that wasn't why he had left. It was too bizarre.

Why did the ladder collapse?

She had been too distracted by Ewan's announcement to consider it before. She glanced at her ladies. Poor Eara looked very wan after another morning of sickness, despite the infusion Gavina had given her to help settle her stomach. Whatever happened, arrangements would soon need to be made to reunite her with her husband.

She turned to Nairne. "We must return to the tower."

They both held oil lamps as they made their way along the corridor. "Lady Nairne, when you ventured up the ladder, was it unsteady?"

"Not at all, my lady. It was as unyielding as stone."

"I thought as much." Panic hammered through her as she recalled the sensation of falling, of gripping onto a rung, only to have it come away in her hand and she drew in a shaky breath. "I fear the great goddess," *Cailleach*, but she couldn't find the courage to say her name aloud, "tried to share something with me, and I failed to see."

The way she had failed to see so many things when it came to the Goddess of Winter.

Nairne dipped her head but didn't answer. Not that Briana expected her to. Nairne was not a chosen one and couldn't understand, no matter how she tried.

If only Mae was here. Yet Briana had the uneasy certainty that even her dear cousin would not be able to help her. Mae, after all, was a child of Bride.

They went through the secret passageway, but no great revelation revealed itself when they entered the tower. She held her lamp aloft and gazed at the ladder, that fell drunkenly against the wall. In the glow from the flickering light, she could see several broken rungs hanging from the side rails and renewed terror spiked through her.

How easily she could have broken her back, or her neck, if Ewan hadn't been there to catch her fall.

Nairne stood by her side and gazed up at the ladder. "It is most extraordinary, my lady. How could so many rungs break at once, when only last week they all seemed most sturdy?"

"It is strange, to be sure. Lord Ewan would never have invited any of us here if he had the slightest suspicion it might be dangerous." She peered into the darkness beyond the pool of light as Nairne's comment swirled around her mind. It was true. *How* had so many rungs crumbled at her touch?

She swept her gaze over the floor and saw the rung she'd been clutching when she fell. Frowning, she picked it up. One end was jagged. The other appeared cleanly cut.

Great goddess, save her. This was no accident through the passage of time eroding the robustness of the wood. This was an act of sabotage. Her shocked gaze met Nairne's. There was no need to say anything. Her friend understood.

"How can this be?" Nairne whispered. "Who could possibly wish to harm you, my lady?"

"I don't know." But she was a foreign princess in a strange land. Who could say how many might want her dead?

Except this was Duntorr. A stronghold that had been under the influence of a Pict born noblewoman with royal blood for nearly fifty years. Lady Catriona was not the kind of woman who would allow an intolerant household to flourish.

They examined the tower but found nothing, save for a coating of sawdust strewn over the floor. Whoever had sabotaged the ladder had neglected to sweep away the evidence. Briana picked up the discarded basket she'd left there the previous day, and Nairne collected the blankets, before they made their way back through the secret passage.

"Should Lady Catriona be informed?" Nairne asked.

"I shall think on it." But with every step, her disquiet grew. If someone wanted to harm her, why would they damage the ladder? It was too obscure and how could anyone be sure she would even go there?

They entered the bedchamber and locked the door, before straightening the tapestry once again. She cast her glance around, but there was nothing of Ewan's to see. Besides, he had scarcely used this chamber, and the vital sense of his presence didn't linger the way it did in her own chambers.

But officially, this *was* his chamber.

She hitched in a sharp breath. Had the saboteur been targeting *Ewan*?

The more she thought of it, the likelier it seemed. Although who would do such a thing, when he was the master of Duntorr? Who stood to gain if Ewan was killed?

Distress squeezed her heart, but grimly, she pushed it aside. Now was not the time to allow her foolish emotions free reign. She had met his relatives the night she'd arrived in Duntorr. Surely, if Ewan was in danger from any of them, she would have sensed it?

Would I, though?

Why would Cailleach warn her, when Briana had been so blind to the goddess who had bestowed her gifts upon her?

An ethereal chill, as insubstantial as a snowflake, dusted along her spine and she gasped. Cailleach *had* warned her. Time and again.

Her vision had shown her of the destruction of Pictland if the great goddess' warning was not heeded, and that was terrible enough. Surely, it was *everything*.

But it meant more. So much more. And only when time had almost run out, had Cailleach revealed the final harbinger. The blood that dripped from Lady Catriona's hands hadn't signified a great battle between Pict and Scot, or Viking, or Northumbrian.

The connection was more visceral than that. It was Ewan's

lifeblood she saw draining away, and if she didn't reach him in time—before the Wolf Moon descended upon the far horizon at dawn—*he would die.*

Did she truly have a traitor in her midst? One she had always trusted with her life, yet one who hated Scots with such intensity they would go to any lengths to kill Ewan, because of his blood connection to MacAlpin?

"My lady," Nairne breathed. "Has the great goddess shared her wisdom?"

Briana clutched Nairne's hand. Her heart hammered and fear spiked her blood as the visions Cailleach had sent her over the last few weeks shattered her mind in a horrifying surge of understanding.

"I must go to Duncreag." It no longer mattered that Ewan had turned his back on her. He was in danger, and she needed to warn him.

It didn't take long to muster the men she had brought with her from Fotla, and the fact Drest was not among them grieved her more than she could say. It seemed her suspicions were right. But Drest was a noble born warrior and his loyalty to the royal house of Fotla was absolute.

Distress churned her stomach. Anything that Drest had done —or planned on undertaking—would have come as a direct order from her brother.

Or, goddess help her, her beloved father.

Thankfully, Lady Catriona, far from asking questions Briana could not answer, merely offered her the use of a small contingent to bolster her safety on the journey.

Despite their protests, she instructed her ladies to remain at Duntorr. She would not put them in knowing danger for anything.

In the stables, Beli readied her mare but even as distracted as she was, she couldn't help noticing his anxious, sideway glances.

"Is something amiss, Beli?"

"Beg pardon, milady." His head bobbed and color stained his cheeks. "Not for me to question."

And yet clearly he had something on his mind. She would be wise not to dismiss it. For all she knew, Beli had crossed her—and Ewan's—path as a direct result of Cailleach.

"You have my leave to speak freely." It was hard to smile when agitation ate through her like a canker, but somehow, she managed it.

He licked his lips and glanced around, as if checking no one could eavesdrop. "'Twas said Lord Rohan was headed to his stronghold in Fib. But I overheard him asking the equerry directions to Duncreag."

Her smile froze and ice bit through her head, forcing every other thought to flee her mind. "Are you certain?"

"Just thought you should know, milady."

"Indeed. You were right to tell me."

Her head pounded and alarm spiked through her blood. Why had Rohan lied to her about where he was going? She could think of only one reason. He was following Ewan because he wanted him dead.

Rohan was not beholden to obeying such orders from her brother, or even her father. He had taken an instant dislike to Ewan from the start, but would that dislike be enough for him to harm Ewan?

He'd overheard the conversation between Ewan and herself when they were in the tower. When she'd confessed her fear of heights. Had Rohan sabotaged the ladder, believing only Ewan would ever use it again?

Was that why he had concocted a tale that he'd received an urgent message from his steward yesterday morning? As an excuse to see if she'd been injured?

From the depths of her memory, Rohan's voice echoed in her mind, from the night when the doors to the palace had burst open. *I have it on good authority that the bolt had been sabotaged.*

But on whose authority? She had never thought to question him on it. Rohan had always been a source of information, and until now, when she feared Ewan was in danger, she had never had cause to disbelieve him.

He hadn't placed the blame on the Scots, but his silence on that matter had spoken volumes and the inference was clear.

Lightning streaked through her mind and once again she saw the doors to the palace, wide open to the harsh winter skies and dread understanding gripped her heart.

Her father had been concerned it was a sign of Bride's displeasure that they tolerated the Scots in their land. But the sign hadn't been from Bride. It had been from Cailleach, for her, warning her of betrayal. And yet again, she had not seen it.

She spun about and gasped as Drest entered the stables and marched her way. "The men are outside," he said. "Are you returning to Fotla-eviot, my lady?"

"No." Guilt ate through her at how she had misjudged him, but there was no time to agonize over that now. "Where have you been, Drest? We're riding to Duncreag without delay."

He frowned. "Duncreag? No, you're in danger in Dal Riada. I shall ride to Duncreag and deal with the traitor."

Unthinking, she grasped him arm. "What do you know? Tell me."

"It will not please you, Lady Briana. I know you think highly of Rohan. But I grew suspicious of his actions shortly before the body was found in the sacred glade."

"What?" That was weeks ago. Why had she been so in the dark?

Unease flashed across his face. Or perhaps she merely imagined it. "It was decided I would accompany you here, to ensure your safety and keep watch on Rohan. I fear we were right to suspect him. I just found the equerry, left for dead. Alas for Rohan, there was enough life left in the man to tell me the name of his assailant."

Why is Rohan doing this? It was true that many Picts had reason to despise or hate the Scots. Their peoples had been enemies for generations. Even she hated MacAlpin but for all that, she knew this alliance between them was their best chance at holding back the encroaching Vikings and opportunistic Northumbrians.

But for now, Rohan's reasons were of no consequence. Only one thing mattered.

Urgency thrummed through her veins. She had to reach Duncreag and find Ewan before the Wolf Moon dominated the night sky and her visions became a bloodied reality.

She left the stables with Drest, and Beli followed with her mare. Her men, and Lady Catriona's warriors, were outside waiting for her. Rohan had a good head start, but it was time she put her trust in Cailleach. She could only pray the goddess would give her this one last chance.

She took a deep breath. "We must make haste."

CHAPTER 31

*E*wan well knew the forest that grew to the east of Duncreag and with the full moon high in the sky, throwing light across the land, he scarcely needed the lantern to show the way.

It was madness, trudging through the snow at night, when he didn't need to. But the walls of Duncreag had pressed in on him, when he'd arrived earlier this day, and every chamber he entered, he half-expected to see Briana waiting to greet him.

But she was not here. She would never be here. And the sooner he accepted the fact he'd never see her again, the easier it would be.

Who the hell am I trying to fool?

He might not have a choice, but he would never accept it.

The loch glinted in the glen as he left the shadows of the trees. Although he had not deliberately set out to come here, it was no great surprise. This loch, where his lady mother had drowned, was the reason why Briana could never truly be his.

He hitched in a sharp breath. *The water, the darkness, the agonizing horror as he had watched her tumble from the boat.*

A lone wolf howled in the distance. He would always think of

Briana whenever he heard that haunting sound. Would forever see, in his mind, how she had wrapped her arm around the mighty predator beside the standing stone in the glade.

How she had rescued the wolf pup, before disappearing beneath the ice.

The way he had seen his mother disappear beneath the water.

The howl faded, yet its echo vibrated through him like a fog shrouded portent. He had recently recalled this experience with Briana, and a blazing truth roared through him, this time gripping him with an irrevocable certainty that shook the foundations of his soul.

I wasn't in the boat.

He'd been standing on this very bank with his cousin, Keita. He hadn't been misbehaving in the boat with his mother. It hadn't been his fault the boat had capsized.

Why had he ever thought it was?

Moreen's malicious whisper seeped from the depths of his mind, where only nightmares and the monsters of small boys lurked.

Your father doesn't know the truth, Ewan. What would he say, if he knew it's your fault your dear mamma died?

He sucked in a harsh breath, and the icy air splintered the lingering tendrils of guilt and grief, and embers of a long-denied rage sparked in his gut.

She'd lied to him. She had *goddamn lied.*

And her venom had permeated his blood and bones, becoming such a part of him he'd no longer been able to distinguish what was real—and what was not.

For too long he'd been trapped in a web of corrosive guilt and false memories but now the lies were over, and he saw the truth.

He wasn't cursed. He never had been. Briana had told him he'd been a child and not responsible, and he'd wanted to believe. Sharing the past with her had unlocked that hidden memory and he'd tried to cling onto it. But deep inside, an ugly knot of doubt had still refused to die.

And when she'd fallen from the ladder, when the bloodied scenarios had pounded through his mind of all the ways she might have perished, the doubt had roared through him like a pestilence. Devouring every shred of sanity in its path as his step-mother's anguished cry reverberated around his head.

"It should have been you, not him. Not my beloved son."

But the fever that had taken Gareth yet left him alive wasn't because he was cursed. Fevers could rip through families and entire communities, and there was no telling who would succumb and who would survive.

The ladder, though. He should never have taken Briana there and exposed her to the risk.

A harsh rebuttal thundered in his head.

What risk?

The ladder had been stable only days earlier when her ladies had ascended it to take in the view. His senses sharpened and in the back of his mind he registered the eerie silence that blanketed the land. Not even a faint rustle of nocturnal creatures in the forest disturbed the frosty night.

But in that singular silence a stark truth blinded him.

If the wood had decayed through age, what were the chances that so many rungs had collapsed at the exact same moment?

"Christ. *No.*" Horror crawled through him, more potent than any residual nightmare from his childhood. Someone in Duntorr had sabotaged the ladder. And he had left Briana there with a killer on the loose.

His cousin, Keita's, enigmatic words, the night he'd brought his bride home, whispered in his mind.

"Do not let the darkness of the past cloud your future."

He hadn't understood what she meant. But he did now.

For years, he'd let Moreen's spite rule his life. But now he'd seen the truth, was it too late to claim the future he most wanted in the world?

A future with Briana?

A wild hope flared, for things he had never dared to dream of before, but it was tempered by the harsh reality that she wasn't safe.

He had to leave Duncreag this night. He'd be home by morning, and he'd rip every last stone from the walls of Duntorr until he found the one who would dare try and harm Briana.

And when he'd delivered justice, he'd ask her for a second chance.

Shit, would she forgive him for walking out on her? How could he convince her he had only done it in a mistaken belief that it would protect her?

Yet even that wasn't the real reason why the thought of facing her caused his courage to rebel. There was more, so much more, he wanted to tell her. But to lay bare his heart and risk her turning from him, regardless, filled him with a bleakness he could not name.

He had been brought up in the sight of God. He'd lived all his life with peripheral understanding that his grandmother's pagan beliefs were accepted but should not be spoken of. In his experience, God did not answer prayers.

Yet his grandmother and, as he had lately learned, Briana, not only believed with every fiber of their souls in their heathen deities, they were quietly confident their goddess not only listened but responded.

What did he have to lose? No one was here to witness it. And if, by some miracle, his God heard his heartfelt wish and allowed Briana to look favorably upon her husband once again, he'd banish all the doubts he'd ever harbored. Hell, he would even confess his sins to the local monks.

Before he could think himself out of it, he dropped to his knees in the snow. Instantly, a rush of air disturbed the silence, a *goddamn arrow*, aimed at the spot where, a heartbeat before, his neck had been exposed.

Instinct kicked in and he rolled across the ground to the protection of a tree. Panting, he unsheathed his sword and scanned the area. The lantern, that he'd left on the bank, threw out a dull glow and the arrow that had so narrowly missed him was embedded into a tree, its goose fletchings still quivering from the impact.

Goose fletchings. Favored by the Picts.

He exhaled a measured breath and despite the danger, relief streaked through him. Briana wasn't in peril. The treasonous Pict was after his blood, not hers.

In the tree line opposite him, a dark shadow shifted. Ewan narrowed his eyes, focusing, and stealthily crept through the undergrowth. He could scarcely see his quarry but that went both ways. At least now, sheltered by the edge of the forest, his location wasn't easily found.

As he drew nearer to the shadow, which remained unmoving as though waiting for Ewan to inadvertently reveal himself, he slowly straightened.

Closer…

Just as he was within striking distance, the shadow whirled around, and moonlight glinted on his drawn sword. Ewan bared his teeth and their blades clashed before they both stumbled into the clearing by the bank of the loch.

As he parried the other man's attack, Ewan saw his face and shock slashed through him.

"Rohan. What the hell?"

"Filthy Scot barbarian," Rohan snarled. "Polluting the land."

Ewan kept his distance, deflecting the other man's blade, learning his style before going in for the kill. "It was you who sabotaged the ladder."

"And you who put my lady Briana in harm's way."

Rage surged in his blood for everything that Rohan did not say but clearly meant. "She will never be yours."

"Rest assured that I'll dispatch any number of her husbands until she is."

Ewan slid on ice but clung grimly onto his balance, even as Rohan's careless confession rang in his ears. Had the man murdered Briana's first husband? How did she imagine he had died?

Rohan lunged, but skidded on the same patch of ice, bringing him too close for Ewan to use his sword. Instead, he shouldered the other man back, and Rohan landed on his arse, his sword falling to the ground.

Ewan backed up, swinging his sword in a deadly arc, but Rohan dived headfirst at his groin and Ewan doubled over, the air gushing from his lungs as his sword tumbled from his hand.

God damn it. His vision blurred but white-hot fear of what this madman might do to Briana propelled him forward. He grasped Rohan's wrist and wrenched his arm behind his back, before grabbing his dagger.

A soft gasp distracted him. Incomprehension slammed into his chest as the vision of Briana materialized from the depths of the forest. What the *hell*? She couldn't be here. His mind was playing tricks.

He hoped to God his mind was playing tricks.

But before he could draw in more than one staggered breath, Rohan twisted in his lax grip, smashed his fist into his face, and pressed his own damn dagger to his throat.

CHAPTER 32

*E*wan was not at Duncreag when Briana and her men arrived, but she wasn't surprised. He wouldn't be inside his stronghold. He was by the loch where his lady mother had drowned so long ago.

She did not question her knowledge. It was as clear as the Wolf Moon that glowed in the cloudless night sky.

Ewan's steward, rumpled from sleep, offered to show them the way to the loch. "If it pleases my lady to retire to the master chamber, we shall bring back Lord Ewan without delay," he assured her.

"I shall accompany you."

It was clear her response flummoxed him, but she was in no mood to be dissuaded. And the longer they lingered, the greater danger Ewan was in.

"Aye, my lady," he said at last, when it was obvious none of the warriors who had accompanied her were willing to dispute her command. Not even Drest. Several of the men carried lanterns and they rode to the edge of the forest where they dismounted and left the horses with a stable lad.

Her men flanked her as they entered the forest, following the steward through barely visible pathways. Briana hugged her cloak tighter around her, but the insidious feeling of unseen eyes watching her would not diminish.

Great goddess, please let us be in time.

It was the same desperate prayer she had sent to the goddess throughout the ride to Duncreag, and although she hadn't called on Bride by name, she couldn't help the uneasy certainty that Cailleach was affronted by all the times Briana had not acknowledged her.

The sound of boots on the forest floor became muffled and the flickering beacons of light faded. Silver fog swirled through the snow coated trees, its damp fingers tracing across her cheeks before sinking to the ground.

There was no sound save the thunder of her heart in her ears and the rasp of her breath in the cold air. The gleam of the lanterns had vanished, swallowed up by the billowing fog, and the steward no longer led the way.

Only shafts of moonlight through the stark silhouettes of winter branches kept the black of night at bay. And again, the conviction gripped her that the eyes that watched her were not of this realm.

A breeze eddied around her, and a single feather flapped against her cloak. Instinctively, she grasped it and stared at it, uncomprehending.

This could be nothing less than a sign from the goddess. But why show her a goose feather, when in her visions the fletchings of the arrow had been swan?

Did it mean she was too late?

Terror flooded her, and she picked up her skirts and hastened along the forest path. She would not believe it. Ewan was here and he *could not die.*

The forest ended abruptly, and she faced a small clearing that banked an ice-covered loch. But they were meaningless details when her gasp of shock caused Ewan to lose focus and Rohan pressed his dagger against her husband's throat.

"Rohan, release my lord Ewan instantly." It was perhaps a foolish command, but she had to try.

"God no." Agony threaded through Rohan's words as though he regretted she had witnessed his treachery. "What are you doing here, Briana? Why did you have to follow?"

"Get back to Duncreag." Ewan's urgent demand pierced her heart. "Christ, get back to Duntorr. You'll be safe there."

"I will not leave without you." But dear goddess, how was she to manage that? "Rohan, I beg you, release my lord Ewan."

"You've ruined everything, Briana."

He still held Ewan in a punishing grip, but his attention was now on her. Perhaps, in the end, that was the only advantage she could give Ewan.

She took a step closer. "Why are you doing this, Lord Rohan?"

He gave a savage laugh, but only the sound of madness echoed in the still air. "You bewitched me from the moment I saw you. Nothing else mattered. I did this for you, Briana. It's all been for you."

She froze, his deranged protestations thrumming through her mind. No, this could not be right. What of her visions? She hadn't misunderstood them so badly. Had she?

"How can any of this be for me?" Her voice was hoarse as, once again, she saw the arrow plunge into the ancient standing stone before it split asunder. "What of Pictland?"

"I care nothing for that heathen land." Derision dripped from his words. "My mission to bring down the pagan Picts has always been clear. But you—*you* are my reward."

His *reward*?

"You're no Pict." Ewan's voice was calm, as though they conversed in a great hall and not by the edge of a forest while a dagger was held to his throat. Wait, Rohan was not a Pict? But how could that be so? He was Ecgfrith's cousin. "I'd wager you're Northumbrian."

Goddess preserve her. Rohan was *Northumbrian*? She clenched her fingers around the feather she still held. She had always seen swan fletchings in her visions because the unseen archer had been Northumbrian. All the time, Cailleach had been showing her Rohan's true heritage.

Yet here, when he had attempted to kill Ewan, he used goose fletchings, favored by Picts. What was she missing?

But before she could pull her jagged thoughts to order and question him, Ewan spoke again.

"It was you who attempted to assassinate Constantine."

Rohan sucked in air between his teeth. "I would not have failed so despicably. Not only did the fool miss his target, but he also neglected to use a Pict made arrow. Instead of destabilizing the cursed alliance with the Scots, it had the potential to merely strengthen it."

"The body in the sacred glade," Briana whispered. "You killed him for his error." And had stripped any identifying item from him to conceal the truth.

"You left the Norse ferrule there for us to find." Ewan's voice was grim, and Rohan gave a harsh laugh.

"The hell I did. The ferrule was left by your precious Drest, Lady Briana, on the orders, no doubt, of your honorable royal brother." Mockery dripped from the last words. "I witnessed the act myself. Fortunately for Drest, he left before the fool arrived."

No. She would not believe her brother capable of such a betrayal. But even as outrage at Rohan's lie burned her pride, the brutal truth seeped through.

Her father and brother had both wanted the problem of Constantine's assassin to be resolved without delay. And without antagonizing the Scots. Who better to lay the blame upon than their mutual enemy, the Vikings? And it explained the flash of guilt on Drest's face when he had told her of his misgivings. He must have seen Rohan that night in the glade, while he was carrying out his dishonorable orders to hide the ferrule, and Rohan's doubtless stealthy behavior had roused his suspicion.

She ignored his taunt. The deed was done, and her brother had to live with it. She would not waste precious time trying to avenge her brother's honor, when Ewan's life hung in the balance. Her stomach churned and despite her best intentions, the terrible vision of his lifeblood seeping into the snow pounded in her mind. How could she bear to survive, if he did not?

Do not think of that. But how could she focus on anything else, when the blade glinted, and its wicked tip dug into his flesh? Desperately, she trawled her scattered thoughts, to find something, anything, to distract Rohan. To give Ewan a chance.

"How can you be Northumbrian? Ecgfrith knew you all his life. You're a Pict, Rohan, even if you do not wish to be."

"Rohan spent three years at sea before he was taken prisoner. I learned a good deal about his life before he… succumbed to his injuries. We were not unalike in looks. It was a relatively simple matter to inveigle myself into his family after his long absence."

"Briana." Ewan's voice was low, almost comforting, and managed to stem the panic rising in her breast. The man before her, whom she had trusted so implicitly, was a stranger. A spy. He shared no bloodline with Ecgfrith and there was no shred of empathy in his soulless visage now his mask had been ripped away. She tore her eyes from Rohan and met her husband's steady gaze. He drew in a long breath. *"Run."*

"Do not move." Rohan's menacing growl caused the hair to rise on her nape, but that was nothing to how he wrenched Ewan's head back, exposing his throat. Terror clawed through her heart. She couldn't lose Ewan now, not when there were so many things she had to tell him. Not when he would never know how much he meant to her. How she couldn't imagine enduring the rest of her life without him by her side. "You will witness how I dispatch those who get in my way."

Between one breath and the next her fear vaporized, and instead of despair filling her, an ice-cold resolve chilled her veins. How dare this traitor attempt to take everything she cared about from her? The Goddess of Winter had claimed her long ago. It was time to embrace her destiny, whatever the cost.

She took a step forward which clearly astonished both men and raised her arms to the starry sky.

"Great Cailleach, bringer of death and destruction across the land, your humble servant beseeches your forgiveness. My blood is yours to heal the breach."

I beg you with all that I am to spare Ewan MacKinnon.

Wind rustled through the trees, a primal whisper from the depths of creation. Had Cailleach heard? Did she understand the sacrifice Briana offered in exchange for Ewan's life?

The wind dropped and a silence so profound it hurt her ears fell across the clearing. The eerie sensation of unearthly eyes watching her magnified unbearably, an intangible sigh across her soul. And then, from the forest, two mighty wolves prowled to flank her. Shadow on her right, and to her left the she-wolf, whose pup had almost drowned just days ago.

Awe shivered through her. The powerful Cailleach had answered her, indeed.

"Witchcraft." Rohan's voice was hushed, but repulsion throbbed in the word. "When we returned to Northumbria, I would have given you everything as my wife. But you are a *witch.*"

It happened so fast. Her tactic of distraction clearly worked, and Rohan loosened his hold on Ewan, as her husband escaped his grip and flung him to the ground. Rohan kicked out, felling Ewan, before scrambling to his feet and lunging her way, his dagger gripped in his hand.

"I'll never have you now, Briana. But neither will anyone else."

Before she had time to flee, Ewan's blade glinted in the moon-light as it flew through the night to embed in the back of Rohan's neck. And the wolves leaped as one, and Rohan's strangled scream was silenced as they tore out his throat.

CHAPTER 33

*E*wan charged to Briana's side and swung her around from the bloodied scene unfolding scarcely a sword's length from where she stood. The sound of the wolves as they devoured their prey was sickening, yet he couldn't find it within himself to feel any regret.

Although his blade would have taken Rohan's life as surely as the wolves, it would have been a cleaner death. But the man had been intent on murdering Briana. And for that, he deserved this ignoble end.

"Are you harmed?" His voice was harsh, but he couldn't help it. He cradled her face and tried to drive the image of Rohan brandishing his dagger at her from his mind. And failed.

He'd never banish that terrifying memory, or the stark possibility of how easily she might have died.

"No. But you are." Her finger traced his throat and for the first time he felt the sting where Rohan's blade had pierced his skin.

"It's nothing." He pressed his forehead against hers as relief throbbed through him like a living entity. "Christ," he ground between his teeth. "What were you thinking, to enter the forest on your own?"

Not just the forest, though. She had left Duntorr and traveled to Duncreag at *night*. A thousand dangers she might have encountered shredded his reason and a shudder wracked his body.

"I wasn't alone. Cailleach keeps my men in the forest."

He risked glancing at the mutilated body, and the wolves, and thought twice about disputing her claim. For all he knew, the pagan goddess *was* in the forest this night.

"Don't look," he said, when Briana followed his glance, but she merely sighed and shook her head.

"It is justice, Ewan. The wolves must sustain themselves through the harsh winter months. And the flesh of a treacherous man will not poison them, after all. It is the will of Cailleach."

It was the third time she'd named Cailleach. Yet she had told him she was a chosen one of Bride. He didn't believe in any of her gods, yet in his heart he recognized a primal truth. Briana was, indeed, protected by her powerful Goddess of Winter.

The wolves wouldn't turn on her after they'd gorged themselves and he suspected through Briana he, too, was not in danger.

There was so much he wanted—*needed*—to say to her. Yet he didn't know how to begin. Wasn't it enough she was here with him now? Surely that meant she was willing to give him another chance to prove he was worthy of her?

Cautiously, he took her hand and led her from the wolves to the bank of the loch, where the lantern still stood. Fog curled across the loch and around his ankles, dampening the sound of the wolves' ferocity and the surrounding forest took on a surreal, dreamlike prospect.

Tell her you cannot live without her.

But it was too big. And even though she stood before him, holding his hand, and gazing at him as though he was the only one in her world, he couldn't quell the fear that once he told her what she meant to him, she would walk away.

He might not be able to tell her what lurked in his heart, but he wanted no more secrets between them. And the confession Rohan had flung at him would forever stand between him and Briana if he didn't share it with her.

"Forgive me. I know this is hard, but Rohan spoke of your first husband's death. What do you know of it, Briana?"

She shivered, and he hated himself for asking, but he'd hate himself more if he kept the truth from her.

"It is shameful." Her voice was hushed, and he fought the urge to pull her into his arms and tell her to forget he'd ever asked. "Ecgfrith was not faithful and took many lovers. In the end, after I lost our babe, I didn't even care anymore."

He'd no idea she'd lost a bairn. "I'm sorry."

How inadequate. Yet he could find no other words to say, and instead squeezed her fingers and hoped she understood how deeply he wished he could soothe away her pain.

Her tremulous smile hurt his chest.

"You're the only one who knows, Ewan. It was very early but the dreams of what might have been never leave."

A child was all she had asked for in this political marriage. And he had failed her. He hoped to God—or even her heathen goddess, if that was what it took—that she would grace him with the chance to grant her the one thing she most wanted.

"Briana." His voice cracked, but she pressed her fingers against his lips, and he was grateful, for he wasn't certain what else he could say.

"Ecgfrith's luck ran out and the husband of his last conquest challenged him. Rohan was Ecgfrith's witness and held him in his arms as he died. He was the one who told me, and goddess forgive my blindness, but I believed him when he pledged his undying loyalty to me."

He had the savage, illogical, urge to run that dead bastard Ecgfrith through with his sword for the way he'd treated her. What man in his right mind would dishonor her so? Ecgfrith had

CHRISTINA PHILLIPS

deserved that ignoble death and truth be told, he didn't much care whether the cuckolded husband or Rohan had committed the deed.

"Rohan intimated he was the one who dispatched your husband. Maybe he simply took advantage of the situation and finished what the challenger started."

She sighed, and briefly closed her eyes, before looking at him once again. "It is possible. We shall never know for sure."

He didn't want to talk about her dead husband, or Rohan, anymore. He wanted to wipe those bad memories from her mind and banish the sadness in her eyes.

God help him. He had to say something, and soon, before the men she mentioned she had brought with her found their way to this clearing.

Where the devil were they?

But it was a distant query because he didn't want this moment shattered. Not yet. *Give me just a few more moments with her before the outside world intrudes.*

He took a deep breath, but it didn't clear his mind or ignite words of wisdom in his brain. Instead, Briana gasped and clutched his arm.

"Rohan tried to assassinate you, like they tried to assassinate Constantine."

He followed her shocked gaze and glanced over his shoulder. There was just enough light from the moon and the lantern to see the arrow embedded in the tree.

"Aye," he agreed reluctantly. "It was a close call."

"The great goddess herself must have been with you. Rohan is —was—a skilled archer."

He recalled the rush of wind as the arrow had sped through the air. It should have hit him.

It *would* have hit him—if he hadn't dropped to his knees to send an urgent prayer to God.

Eerie shudders ran along his arms. Who had compelled him

in that moment? The God of his forefathers, or the goddess who protected Briana?

Without releasing his hand, she went over to the tree and traced a finger along the fletchings. "Goose feathers. He wanted to lay the blame for your murder on the Picts."

"Which would have reignited suspicion over who was really responsible for the attack on Constantine." Ewan's voice was grim. "The Northumbrians would have succeeded in their aim to destabilize the alliance."

"And that would have split Pictland asunder." Awe threaded through her voice, but it was the hint of fear that pulled on his heart, and he wrapped his arm around her before he could think better of it.

"Pictland isn't in danger." Not from this attempt to shatter the alliance, at least. "Don't be concerned. MacAlpin will honor the alliance. More so, now we have evidence of the Northumbrians involvement in the attack on Constantine."

"I love my land, Ewan, and will do much to ensure her continued safety. But it's the thought of you—how close you came to—I cannot even bear to say it."

"Then don't. I'm here, and so are you." Once again, the image of Rohan lunging at her blazed through his mind and cold terror gripped his heart at what might have been. "That's all that matters."

"Rohan sabotaged the ladder in the tower. I'm sure of it. And when I discovered he hadn't returned to his stronghold in Fib, but instead had asked the way to Duncreag—I finally understood what Cailleach had been trying to warn me of for so long. Rohan was the hidden archer in my visions."

Guilt gnawed through him at how the curse of Moreen had blinded him to what had been as clear as day. If only he'd opened his eyes. "I should have connected the broken ladder to the sabotaged door bolt in Fotla-eviot as soon as it happened."

Not that he could see the sense in why Rohan had spent God

knew how long hacking away at that massive log. Unless it was a long-term plan by the Northumbrians to weaken the defenses of the Fotla stronghold for such time in the future when an attack was launched.

Even though that plan had failed, the prospect was chilling.

"I knew the great Cailleach was showing me a sign when the doors burst open that night." Briana clutched his arm, distress clear upon her face. "The bolt was not damaged enough to break without her will behind it. But still I refused to acknowledge her. I cannot help but believe this is my fault, Ewan."

"None of this is your fault." He gripped her shoulders, willing her to understand. "I should never have left you in Duntorr. If I'd stayed, Rohan would've shown his hand and we could have settled this without putting you in danger. I'll never forgive myself for that."

"Why did you leave?" Her whisper was filled with confusion. "I feared it was because you loved another and could no longer bear to share your life by my side. But I think I was wrong."

God Almighty, how could she ever have thought that? Yet why wouldn't she? Her first husband had been unfaithful. Why wouldn't she think the same of him?

That she thought so little of him stung. But he could not blame her for thinking it.

"You were wrong." His voice was hoarse and unwelcomed energy surged in his blood, akin to the sensation when he was about to ride into battle. But he had to put Briana's unwarranted fears to rest, even if it meant sharing things he didn't even know how to put into words. "There's no one but you, Briana. There never has been. Never will be."

Her bottom lip trembled, and it all but undid him. "When you spoke of Moreen, I feared the worst. I didn't know she was your stepmother."

Moreen? Surely he had never mentioned her name to Briana.

"Aye. She was. But she means nothing to me. Why would you think I'd left you for her?"

"You whispered her name in your sleep yesterday. And the last thing you said to me before you left our chamber was that you should have heeded her warning. I'm grieved I came to the wrong conclusion."

Damn it. He didn't remember saying that when he had left Briana yesterday, but he'd been half mad with guilt and grief and the truth was, he could scarcely recall much about that last tortured conversation he'd had with her.

What the hell else had he said?

"Ewan." Her voice was soft, irresistible. "Tell me why you left Duntorr."

He had never repeated the things Moreen had whispered to him in those nights when she'd pretended to care. The prospect of dredging up those nightmares now curdled his gut.

But Briana had followed him to Duncreag, when he'd given her no reason to seek him out again. The possibility of reuniting with her glinted on the horizon, almost within reach, and if he wanted the chance to make this marriage more than merely a political alliance, she deserved to hear the truth.

He would trust her with the truth.

His chest burned as he dragged in a deep breath, and when the wolves left their prey and stood behind her, gazing at him, unblinking, with their orange eyes, the words all but lodged in his throat.

"Moreen was scarcely sixteen when she wed my father. I see now she was jealous of the bond between my father and me, and the love he cherished until the end for my lady mother. Yet I was a child of seven and all I saw when I looked at her was a beautiful, golden-haired creature who promised to love me. But at night," he swallowed as the memories crowded close, yet for the first time, they didn't threaten to drag him into the mire and smother him.

"I'm sorry." Briana sounded grieved, and that was the last thing he wanted her to feel. "I do not mean to pry when it brings back such sadness."

"I need to tell you. So you understand." And so that, finally, he could bury Moreen's callous assertions forever. Tenderly, he wound one of Briana's curls, that had escaped her hood, around his finger, and found the words to continue. "At night, she whispered how it was my fault my mother had died. She painted pictures in my mind that I know now were never true. And when Gareth perished from the fever, she cursed me to suffer as I had made her suffer."

"To suffer the loss of your loved ones?" Briana's voice was hushed. "That was cruel, indeed."

He expelled a ragged breath and just like when Briana had almost drowned, and they had spoken in their chamber, the rock that was permanently lodged in his chest eased.

No. It was more than that. Madness, he knew, but it felt as though the imaginary rock crumbled to dust.

"It stayed with me. I've never allowed anyone to get close. A wife who cared for me was out of the question. I couldn't risk her life." *Your life.*

"Yet you love your grandmother, and your aunt, and all your cousins. Your fellow warriors, too."

He sighed. "I don't deny it. I never said my fear was rational."

"No, but," she hesitated before offering a small smile. "It is understandable."

One of the wolves prowled closer and recognition shuddered through him. It was Shadow, her wolf from Fotla. It had traveled miles from its territory to protect her.

Briana turned from him and faced her wolf.

"Thank you." She bowed her head and pressed her forehead against the wolf's muzzle. Alarm hammered through him even though, in his heart, he knew she was in no danger. "I shall love and honor you always, my beloved Shadow."

She straightened, and although she didn't touch the she-wolf, he had the uncanny certainty that an unspoken understanding flowed between them, nonetheless.

And then, as one, they bounded into the forest behind them and vanished, just as lights appeared through the trees and Briana's men stumbled into the clearing before them.

The silvery fog, that had swirled about them, sank into the ground. It was a coincidence, nothing more, yet an insistent, heathen, voice in the back of his mind whispered *Cailleach is gone.*

"My lord." His steward approached, clearly shaken by the sight of what was left of Rohan. "I can't explain it. We were accompanying Lady Briana and then the forest seemed to…" His voice trailed away in confusion.

"Lady Briana is unharmed," Ewan said. "You have nothing to explain."

Visibly relieved, the man bowed his head. "Should we take the body back to Duncreag?"

He glanced at Briana before replying to his steward. "Leave the body for the carrion to feast upon." A bloodied sacrifice to the ancient ways, perhaps, but it was fitting. "I shall return to the stronghold with Lady Briana shortly."

"Aye, my lord." His steward bowed his head, and after Briana nodded to Drest, they were once again alone in the clearing.

There was one thing he had to know. "Why did you leave the safety of Duntorr and come here?"

Her sigh was a fragile whisper in the wind. "Surely, you know why. I have no wish to survive in this world if you are not in it."

"Ah, God." He squeezed his eyes shut for a brief moment, trying, without success, to temper the way his heart hammered against his ribs. But his blood pounded in his ears, a tormented tangle of hope and fear that the promises she offered were nothing but a figment of his imagination.

He grasped her hands and pressed them against his chest. Over his heart. "I left you because I feared if I stayed, my curse would kill you. The image of your death haunted me, and I could see nothing else. Nothing but how, in that moment, Moreen's wish would come to pass."

"What happened at the loch was an accident. And the ladder was an attempt on your life by Rohan. You understand that, don't you?" There was an urgency in her voice that pierced straight through his heart.

"Aye. I see that now. I saw it before Rohan challenged me this night. I'm only grieved it took me so long, and that my actions caused you any distress."

"It's in the past. We must look to the future and ensure the treaty remains strong and unbreakable."

The glint of hope that she had followed him to Duncreag because, God help him, she cared for him the way he so desperately craved, darkened. Was their marriage still nothing more than a political alliance to her?

Her choice of word burned inside his mind. *Treaty.* And once again he recalled the scathing accusation she'd leveled at him, the accusation that had gnawed at the core of his being since he'd left their chamber the previous day.

"Does your king plan another betrayal of my beloved land under the guise of a treaty?"

Briana was willing to give him a second chance. But it wasn't enough. It wasn't nearly enough. Because he didn't want a wife who stayed with him out of duty for her beloved land. And he sure as hell couldn't face the possibility that Briana, of all people, suspected he had anything to do with that massacre at Dunadd last spring.

"The treaty is important for Dal Riada and Pictland, Briana. I'll not deny it. But our future together should be based on more than a promise to our kings."

"It will be. We will forge our own future, Ewan."

But how strong could that future be, if the foundations were cracked with suspicions from the past?

It was treason to even think his king was wrong, never mind share it with another. But Briana was his wife. He would not keep the truth, as he saw it, from her.

Her good opinion was worth more to him than the threat of MacAlpin's wrath.

"MacAlpin will have no one speak of that night when the Pict nobles were killed at Dunadd. We were told the Scots reacted in self-defense, but it is all shrouded in secrecy."

"You... you were not at Dunadd that night?"

The uncertainty in her voice tore through him like a broken blade, confirming his darkest fears. "I was fighting the Northumbrians, alongside many of my compatriots—and Lord Talargan."

"We Picts would not have betrayed the Scots in the way we were accused." For such a strong assertion, her voice was gentle, and he understood. She didn't blame him for the betrayal of her people.

"There's no proof to be had. But I want you to know that I'm of the same mind as you."

"I'm glad you trusted me enough to tell me. I know a warrior must always obey his king, but I confess, in my heart, I hoped you hadn't been party to that."

It was true. A warrior had to obey his king. And yet...

"If MacAlpin's orders ever put you in danger, you should know this. I will always ensure your safety above all else."

She gave a soft gasp. "Lady Catriona told me MacAlpin ordered you to stay by my side. She couldn't fathom why you had left me in Duntorr. You ignored his command because you thought being with me put me in danger."

He sighed. "I know. My judgement was foolish. I should not have left you."

"No, Ewan. That's not what I meant." There was a breathless quality to her voice he couldn't place, but her smile radiated happiness. Bemused, he smiled back. "You put me before your king."

"Aye." Of course he had. And only then did he realize the magnitude of his confession. It made no difference. And he had come this far, he might as well tell her the rest. "You will always be first, Briana."

"The day of our betrothal, you were so reluctant. I feared we might never find true happiness together."

He groaned and tugged her close, and she wrapped her arms around him as though she never wanted to let him go. Dare he hope that was true?

"I was never reluctant. From the moment I met you, I couldn't banish your face from my mind. You captured my heart, and I knew it, but I fought against my fate. Not because I didn't want you. But because I wanted you so damn much."

"You hid your feelings so well." Her voice was muffled but he heard the lingering trace of pain and cursed himself for being the cause of it.

"I had to. I couldn't risk you thinking kindly of me in case Moreen's curse found you. Yet no matter how hard I tried, I couldn't push you away. When I said you deserved a man who could love you as you deserve, I meant a man who wasn't tarnished by his past like I was. That's why I tried to make you wed Talargan. A noble prince. One whose presence would never be a threat to your life."

She sniffed. God, was she crying?

"You have quite the way with words when you try."

Gently, he pulled back so he could see her face. Shadows fell around them, but the moon bathed her in a mystical glow. Or maybe that was just the way he saw her.

The way he would always see her.

Many times in the past women had laughingly told him he had a silken tongue. That he was an incorrigible flirt, and always knew the right things to say. But he had never uttered pretty, meaningless phrases to Briana and he didn't want her thinking he was now.

Not when he'd never been more serious in his life.

"It's the truth, Briana." He didn't know what else to say. How could he make her understand?

"I know." She gave him a sweet smile and his worry faded. It was true. She did know.

But there was still something he hadn't told her, although surely she had guessed how he felt about her. How could she not?

I love you.

He had never said it before. It had never even crossed his mind. But the need for her to understand just how much she meant to him thundered through him, filling every thought with a terrible foreboding.

What if, despite everything that had occurred this night, she could never love him back?

Far better to take what they had found, and forge their future together, as she had already suggested. Yet the ache inside his chest demanded more.

Whatever the outcome.

He gripped her hand with both of his and she gave him a mystified smile as he attempted to find the right words. But they eluded him, and the longer he stood here, like a mute fool, the harder it was to recall any damn words at all.

"What is it?" she said softly, and the sound of her voice broke his paralysis.

"I had never given much thought to marriage." His statement was blunt. Her smile wavered and silently he cursed. Why couldn't he conjure up sweet utterances when he was with her? But he knew why. It was because those pretty phrases meant nothing.

He sucked in a deep breath and the cold air, thank God, helped clear his wool stuffed brain. "Until I met you. To make you my bride became my impossible dream, until MacAlpin commanded it. Yet by doing so, he took away your choice."

Before she could answer, he dropped to his knee. "Briana,

Princess Euphemia of Fotla, I fell in love with you the first time we entered your kingdom. You fill my heart with light and make sense of this world when all I would otherwise see is darkness. I love you above my king and above my country, and pledge my life to keeping you safe for all time. I offer you the choice, my lady. Will you grant me the greatest honor and consent to be my wife?"

She sank to her knees and pressed their clasped hands to her breast. "My beloved Ewan." There was a catch in her voice, and he exhaled a ragged breath filled with hope. "I told myself I would never love again, but when I met you, my heart saw what I refused to. I love you more than I believed it possible to love anyone. I am most delighted to accept your proposal and be your wife."

He gave a laugh before claiming her lips, and even though damp seeped into his knee from the slush on the ground, a great heat warmed his blood and flowed through his body. Without breaking their kiss, he helped her to her feet before wrapping his arms around her.

She melted against him, her glove-clad fingers raking through his hair and a groan razed his throat. It felt like forever since he had held her like this, and her elusive scent of lavender was both enticingly familiar and intoxicatingly exotic.

Finally, they parted, and her erratic breath dusted his jaw. "This is the perfect gift for the anniversary of the day of my birth."

He cast a glance at the luminous full moon that was slowly slipping beyond the horizon. A fitting, majestic, backdrop for his exquisite bride.

"The Wolf Moon," she whispered.

Awe and recognition rippled through his soul as he gazed into the beautiful eyes of the woman who held his heart. "You truly are the chosen one of Cailleach and protector of wolves."

His wife. His love.
Briana.

HER OUTCAST SCOT

THE HIGHLAND WARRIOR CHRONICLES
BOOK 5

A warrior haunted by his cursed past...

Pledged to protect dark secrets that could destroy his family's honor, Ross MacIntosh cannot afford to lose his heart. Sent by his king into Pictland, he knows his duty. To report back on any signs of treachery. He might not trust his king but as a warrior his fealty is absolute, and his path is clear. But when he's attacked and left for dead, he awakes to discover his healer is the intriguing Pictish princess, Orabel, and his carefully planned future unravels.

A healer princess forbidden to love by her goddess...

After enduring an arranged marriage to a brutal Northumbrian warlord, Orabel wants nothing more to do with politics. Now, she will follow her true destiny and pledge her life to her beloved goddess. But when fate thrusts Scots warrior Ross MacIntosh into her life, her conviction falters. How can she feel anything but contempt for a man whose king is responsible for the death of her royal father?

A political marriage that could shatter everything they cherish...

Compelled to wed to prevent bloodshed blighting their land, trust is a fragile illusion. But with a vengeful goddess demanding restitution, Ross will need more than Orabel's healing skills to mend the rift that threatens to tear her from his arms forever.

HER REBEL SCOT

THE HIGHLAND WARRIOR CHRONICLES
PREQUEL

When the prince falls for the wallflower...

Tavish O'Eochaid, favored son of the King of Dal Riada, has no plans to settle down until forced to by duty. But when he enters Pictland on a diplomatic mission, he's captivated by an enigmatic noblewoman, who hides secrets in her eyes.

Bound by blood to the shadow of the royal court, Catriona cannot afford to fall for the charms of a visiting Scots warrior. As a chosen one of her goddess, she knows where her duty lies. Yet as her visions of a splintered future grow ever darker, she risks everything for a few stolen hours in his arms.

But when betrayal rocks the foundations of Pictland herself, Tavish must choose between sacrificing his honor – or surrendering to his enemy, for the woman he has grown to love.

ABOUT THE AUTHOR

Christina Phillips is an ex-pat Brit who now lives in sunny Western Australia with her high school sweetheart and their family. She enjoys writing historical romance with a touch of fantasy, paranormal romance and contemporary romance, where the stories sizzle and the heroine brings her hero to his knees. She is addicted to good coffee, expensive chocolate, and bad boy heroes. She is also owned by three gorgeous cats who are convinced the universe revolves around their needs. They are not wrong.

Discover all of Christina's books on her website
ChristinaPhillips.com

ACKNOWLEDGMENTS

A big thank you to all the usual suspects who keep me on track while I'm in the writing cave! Special snuggles to Ava and Theo, my floofy office companions, and sweet Miri who visits me in dreams. Thanks to my awesome family, who barely bat an eyelid whenever I regale them with absolutely fascinating tidbits from the 9th century(!!!). Clearly, they know better than to question me since it only sends me further down the rabbit hole.

To Cathleen Ross and Ann Daniel for proofreading, thank you for your eagle eyes!

Finally, I must give special thanks to Amanda Ashby for her frankly scary ability to take my book and dig down deep until she finds its heart. Thank you from the bottom of mine!

AUTHOR'S NOTE

Although Kenneth MacAlpin, King of the Scots of Dal Riada, became King of Pictland in 843 AD or thereabouts, this is a work of fiction based on myths, legends, and my own imagination.

Timekeeping in the 9th century was a variable thing. They used sundials and water clocks to tell the time and the rich used hour candles. The three observable parts of the day were sunrise, noon (when the sun is at the highest point in the sky) and sunset. Dawn was the first hour, noon was the sixth hour, and 3pm was the ninth hour.